Forbidden

The Raptor Castle Series

Forbidden
Seduced
Ruthless
Surrender

SOPHIA JOHNSON

Forbidden

In loving memory of my Dad, Albert Edward Johnson, Sr.,
who introduced me to Alexandre Dumas.
Reading *The Man in the Iron Mask*,
The Count of Monte Cristo and *The Three Musketeers*
primed my imagination for historical romance.

If he was with me today, he would argue they
weren't romances, and rightly so.
But to me, they were historical
romances in a grand way.

Acknowledgements

Many thanks to Lori Devoti and the rest of the Debitudes (the original Kensington debut authors) for their encouragement and help in showing me how to break into epublishing, and to the Nuts of the Round Table, my critique partners.

Thank you Delle Jacobs for your patience in designing a cover that will carry through with the Raptor Castle Series.

I very much appreciate and thank Jessica Trapp for her review and edit of *Forbidden*. Her time away from her own writing was a gift of kindness

CHAPTER 1

Raptor Castle, Scotland's Border, 1128

"MAKE HASTE, RANALD, AFORE someone discovers us."
Moridac staggered and near dropped the reins of his
father's destrier when the great horse stamped and huffed.
Blinking rapidly, he wrapped the leather around his fist and
held fast.

"All are sleeping off the feast, Moridac. 'Tis a wonder they
didna drown in the wine vats while celebrating yer betrothal
to Catalin."

The massive double doors to the stables near reached the
ceiling, allowing room for a knight to ride through and dismount inside. Only one door stood open. This morn's sun was
still hiding behind the mountains to the east. The young men
had barely enough light to see the courtyard remained empty.

"Aye, but dinna tarry."

Moridac, the elder of the twins by twenty heartbeats, gave
an explosive belch, staggered and near fell. The startled horse
jerked its head so high it lifted the young man off his feet.
Clutching its mane, he tried to steady himself.

"Do ye ken I canna fly through the air, brother? Dinna let
him move. I'll make it next time."

Moridac snorted in disbelief.

Ranald's head was as heavy as if he wore a helmet forged
for a giant. He blinked, clearing his wavering vision. Mayhap
standing atop an upended barrel was not so wise? Huh, mayhap
it was. He couldn't mount using stirrups, for his unsteady legs

refused to stop wobbling. The steed sidestepped close. Seizing his chance, he leapt. His ballocks hit the saddle, shooting pain clean up to his chest.

Humph! "Satan's spawn!"

With one hand clutching his throbbing sex, he fumbled for the reins his twin tossed at him. Triumphant laughter burst from his throat.

He had achieved the forbidden: he would ride Goliath, their father's prized warhorse.

A loud groan signaled the second door opening. Two dreaded shapes framed by the dim light outside, appeared in the doorway. Blessed saints! Ranald had no need to see who stood there. Angry shouting near shook the rafters.

"What means this? Ye drunken fool!" Chief Broccin of Raptor Castle charged toward his sons, his right hand uplifted clutching a whip.

Goliath snorted and threw his head about, jerking the reins from Ranald's hand. The horse's angry stamp bounced him around in the saddle near unseating him. He grabbed the heavy black mane and clamped his long legs around the heaving sides.

The horse had a mind of its own. Chief Broccin barely jumped aside before Goliath made a leap through the doorway. Angus, the stable master, slammed against the doorframe then righted himself and ran after the beast.

He had no need, for Broccin's whistle split the air. Goliath skidded to a halt. Ranald flew over the horse's head to land in deep, wet mud left from last eve's downpour.

The thud took his breath. The surprise near sobered him.

His nose wrinkled with the rancid odor. The mud tasted as rank as it smelled. He gagged and spat it from his mouth. Had every bone in his body cracked like last morn's eggs? He giggled, picturing himself as a huge yellow-yoked egg, floating atop the mud. Trying to get up on his knees, he slipped. Feeling his father's presence, his gaze traveled from naked toes planted firmly in the mud, and up hairy, muscled calves' sturdy as a block of wood. He got no farther.

The whip whistled. Pain streaked Ranald's back.

"Ye drunken fool. Ye dared defy me and sat my mount?"

Ranald gasped and tried to stand. His father's foot slammed him back into the mud. The whip whistled again then struck. He barely had time to draw the next breath before more blows landed. Chief Broccin cursed and ranted like a brainsick man.

How many times had the whip struck? He clamped his teeth tight and struggled to get a firm grip on the land to fight his way out of the mud. A foot crashed into his hips, knocking him to his left side, his back to his father.

"Nay, Father!"

From the sounds of it, Moridac's shouted protest earned him a forceful backhand.

The next lash caught Ranald's right shoulder, his forehead and cheek. To his shame, he screamed. Blows continued to rain down on him. The agony in his face was worse than his back, for the cold mud soothed it. Desperate, he tried to catch the whip, to cover his face. His sire was too swift for him.

"My lord, ye'll kill him," Angus shouted.

"Broccin. Enough!"

'Twas Domnall's bellow. Footsteps thudded across the ground. Sounds of scuffling followed and the beating stopped.

Had he passed out for a short time? The next thing he knew, he heard others talking.

"Dunk him in the horse trough afore ye carry him to his room. I canna tend the poor lad's wounds if they be hidden by filth," a woman's shaky voice demanded.

Ranald could not bite back cries as brawny arms grasped his legs and under his arms then lifted him. Each step jarred his torn flesh. Soon icy water surrounded him.

"Hold yer breath, lad," Domnall muttered.

It was enough warning before his head slid beneath the water. He near drowned when unbelievable pain tore at his face. He screamed again.

"Dinna lie to me, Domnall. He is near death and burns with

fever. It has been days, yet he hasna spoken."

Why was Moridac's voice strange? Like he choked on a sob? His twin was too much a man to cry. He hadn't since the fevers took their sweet mother five years before.

Ranald strained to hear Domnall's answer but couldn't. Longing to be free of the pain and heat ravaging him, he hoped his father's commander said aye. Death would be a blessing.

Heavy boots striking the floor announced his sire's baleful presence approaching the bed.

"He doesna even resemble a man. Turns my stomach to look at him."

"Through no fault of his own! 'Tis your handiwork." Domnall's footsteps came closer, as if to force Broccin to move back from the bed.

"The fool deserved it. He should have protected his face."

"How? When you kicked him over? Gave him no chance?"

His father snorted. Uncaring. His voice sharpened.

"He fares no better. Joneta canna always stay at his side. I grow tired of foul meals since my sister hasna had time to instruct the cook. Put him in a cart and take him to Kelso Abbey."

"To move him now may well kill him!"

A muffled sound followed Domnall's words. Like his fisted hand striking his thigh in anger.

"'Tis close enough. Monks from Selkirk have settled there. I have heard talk of a healer skilled at treating wounds. He is far more learned than Joneta."

Did his father seek to rid himself of an unwanted burden? Ranald sensed he leaned close again, perusing him.

"Hmpf. He is of no use to me now. I know no man desperate enough he would wed his daughter to such a horror. Leave him at Kelso and return."

Chief Broccin's footsteps faded. The door banged shut.

Ranald tried to find voice, but his body would not respond. For all the power he had over it, he may as well have been stone.

Ranald thought his suffering couldn't be worse.

He couldn't be more wrong.

CHAPTER 2

Kelso Abbey, 1143

"HO, THERE, BROTHER RANALD. 'Tis good the sun is hiding else yer pate would rival a lush apple. Why did yer sword not greet me when the bell rang?"

Smiling, Raik of Castle Douglas strode toward the monk kneeling in the dirt amongst medicinal herbs in the Infirmary's garden.

"What need have I of a sword, cousin? Ye know full well I can lay ye flat without its use." Ranald kept his head bowed as he grasped the edge of his black cowl and pulled it to shield his head. He leapt to his feet. "Besides, all know yer pretty face and remember ye couldn't knock over a wee kitten."

"Aye, mayhap when last ye saw me. Take a look, my friend."

Raik wore naught but a kilt gathered around his slender waist. Leather boots covered his feet. He stretched strong arms out to the sides, his muscles bunching at his shoulders, and turned slowly. The sun highlighted shining hair so deep a brown it looked near black. Startling blue eyes that could hold a person in a trance when they stared into them, laughed back at Ranald when he completed his turn. His skin, browned from the sun, was taut over a broad, muscled chest that tapered to a flat, hard belly.

Ranald studied him, glad to find he looked strong and healthy, though he didn't like the dark circles under troubled eyes that watched him in turn.

"Ye dinna look to need my care. Have ye been plagued with

the fevers again?"

"Nay." Something flashed in Raik's dark eyes as he answered. Uneasiness? Hesitation?

Raik huffed and reached out a big hand to grasp the monk's hood and toss it backward, revealing Ranald's ravaged face.

"What need have ye to hide from me?"

Ranald shrugged for answer. "Come, I must check on Brother Mathias. He fell down the dormitory stairs when coming to Matins this last night." He strode through the garden outside the Infirmary cloister. His long legs ate up the distance, but Raik was not outpaced.

"Ah. So that is why pain lingers on yer face. 'Tis *that* ye tried to hide." Raik clasped him on the shoulder and gave it a little shake. "How do ye stand it, Ranald? All the anguish ye see when ye aid their healing? How do ye control yer feelings?"

"Hsst. There are those here who know not of my "problem." I wouldna have them affrighted for naught."

"I was not affrighted when ye tended me."

"Hmpf. Ye say that now. Do ye not remember? Ye didn't know me. Ye seized my throat and held yer knife to it whilst asking if I was the Angel of Death?"

Ranald had been careless that night they had brought Raik to him so badly injured. In the struggle to save his life, and needing light to see to the man's wounds, he had merely crooked his finger at the brace of candles, and they appeared at his side. One hard look from his eyes and the unlit candles flamed. He had not noticed his cowl had slipped, revealing the scarred face of a man Raik believed dead years ago. 'Twas no wonder he thought Death had come for him.

Not wanting his cousin to know how very tired he was, he squared his shoulders. He had not slept well of late. Anguish had filled his soul for the past three sennights. He knew not the cause of it, but he couldn't shake it off.

"I dislike remembering what a fool I was." Raik sighed and looked away, ashamed.

"Come, I must wash before I go in." Ranald shrugged and led him to the lavatorium across the courtyard. They stepped inside the long, vaulted room. Water fed by a nearby stream ran in a raised smooth wooden trough down the length of the room; a wide groove in the floor led outside to release water sloshed from rinsing.

He threw off his black robe and bent over to splash water on himself, before taking a gob of soap from a wooden bowl. After scrubbing his hands and nails, he lathered his face and torso then took a wooden bucket and upended the water over his head.

Raik scrutinized the man before him. Naked, no one would have believed him a monk. He viewed a man in his prime at thirty years. His undamaged left profile was toward Raik and showed the same beauty as Moridac's face. Not so the right side.

Broccin's whip had done much damage there, for thick scars streaked it. One rose from his hairline down across his right temple to his ear. Another from temple to jaw. A third crossed them, slanting from his forehead, across his eye to the side of his nostril. His brow forever looked as if he arched it in question. The last mark was between his brows, across the bridge of his nose, ending at the right corner of his lips.

Thick, black hair cut short in the monks' way, rimmed his tonsure. A bold forehead with black brows rode above eyes as dark as damson plums, that fruit that holds a hint of some deep color other than true black. The pain in his soul reflected in his eyes was made more startling by a proud nose jutting above full, sensual lips and a dominating jaw.

Ranald was about Raik's own height of eighteen hands, and weighed mayhap thirteen stone. The man was naught but hard muscle.

Nay, no monk's body but one of a hardened warrior. Raik shook his head. When would he get the courage to speak on why he had sought Ranald out?

"How do ye do it, man? The water is cold as melted snow. Even in the dead of summer, 'tis icy in here." Raik handed

Ranald a large drying cloth from those folded on a nearby table.

"We dinna have the comforts of a heated bath. Ye grow used to the cold." Ranald reached for a clean robe hanging nearby. The abbey Chamberlain had placed it there earlier, knowing Ranald would have need of it. He rolled his soiled clothing and drying cloth together and tossed it in a large bin.

"We are Tyronesian monks, not soft by any means. We rotate hours of devotions and manual labor. Many are skillful farmers, expert carpenters and smiths." He nodded to Raik. "Ye were too ill on yer last visit to observe anything but the Infirmatorium. Several brothers are skillful in architecture and drawing. Tis they who planned the beautiful lines of the buildings, the openness of the Infirmary. Other than a few sturdy laborers, we had no need of outside help to build the Abbey."

He halted then corrected himself, "And King David's gold for supplies."

He lengthened his stride, heading for the Infirmary kitchen to order food prepared for his patients. Once done, they entered the Infirmary Hall.

Windows aplenty brought in fresh air and sunshine on cloudless days. Beds lined the walls, each standing beside a window. At one end, men hale enough to take their meals did so at a long table with chairs. A chapel at the east end allowed them to have their devotions.

The sick and aged lived in comfort here. All but one sat in the cloister outside to enjoy the sun and flowers. His patient from last eve slept peacefully in the third bed, his color normal, his breathing calm. Ranald's palm cupped the aged forehead, his fingers stroked over the lined cheeks, feeling for heat. Finding none, tension eased in his neck.

Breaking the serenity of the quiet Infirmary, a bell clanged in the distance, warning that someone sought entrance. He listened for the pattern. Two rings spaced apart meant a known and trusted visitor. Two bells with but an interval before the next two indicated an unknown. The steady striking without pause he heard now signaled urgency.

Ranald broke into a run, heading toward the main gate.

Raik's boots striking the cobblestones behind him was a welcome sound. He could use his cousin's strong sword arm, should he need it, for the knights who had lodged at the abbey last eve had resumed their journey once they broke their fast at sunrise.

He dodged the steady stream of workers and monks, wood for scaffolding, barrows of stone, all needed in the steady building of Kelso Abbey. Men dropped what they were doing to look toward the iron gate.

Prior Godric stood framed in the arched stone doorway of the newly finished Abbot House. Worry creased his forehead, his hands stole inside the flowing sleeves of his robe.

Brother Octavius, in charge of all weapons brought within the abbey walls, waited with Ranald's broadsword. The young novice beside him grasped the reins of a prancing horse. Ranald nodded, strapped on his weapon then vaulted onto the horse's back. A stout man, who had sought sanctuary at the abbey, ran across the crowded courtyard to bring Raik's mount and weapons. He sported a flaming red beard that accented his frightened face. Once he handed the weapons and reins to Raik, he scurried to hide himself from sight.

As he watched Ranald, Raik raised his brows and smiled.

"So, 'tis true then? I should have known yer muscle and brawn didn't come from pulling weeds or working as a carpenter. Ye are the Protector as well as the Infirmarian, as I have heard?"

"Who else could? As ye saw from yer lengthy stay before, we dinna lack for visiting warriors. They kept up my knightly training after Father discarded me. Someone must protect the meek and godly."

"Brother Ranald! An army rides from the forests beyond the village," a portly monk shouted as he ran from the bell tower.

"Could ye spy their crest?"

Ranald frowned. Who would approach the abbey with so many men? Did they seek lodging? Nay, it was too early in the day. And if they brought an injured man, they had no need of such a force.

The monk's eyes bulged, and he gulped before speaking.

"A black banner with a centered yellow eagle. Its talons are spread for the kill."

Ranald stiffened. His father's standard.

"Another standard bearer rides aside it." The monk glanced uneasily at Raik.

"Shite! The fools." Raik growled the words through tense jaws.

"Well?" Ranald's eyes narrowed to mere slits. Cold dread swept through him as he studied Raik's face.

"A yellow gryphon upon a field of red, its beak stretched wide in a screech," the monk continued.

Ranald's saddle creaked as he shifted to contemplate Raik with hot speculation while waves of rage crashed through him and threatened his tight control.

"Why has my father come with an army when he has never set foot in this valley since sending me here? And why do yer own men ride with him?"

"I am sorry, Ranald. Much has happened that ye do not know of. They were to wait until I had time to apprise ye of it. King David requested I bring my men. To assure no harm comes to ye." Raik's fist struck his thigh, his lips tightened afore he spoke again.

"Come. Ye must allow yer father entrance. He will explain all."

CHAPTER 3

Raptor Castle, three sennights earlier.

"Is not Moridac the most comely man in all of Scotland?" Catalin wore a bright smile as she paced the carpeted floor of her sleeping chamber. She glanced at her friend Letia, but she could not keep the worry from her voice.

"Without doubt. Women on both sides of the borders would sigh for a word from him," Letia responded. She looked hesitant to say more.

Catalin stopped to arrange items on her dressing table, things already neatly placed there. She sighed and chewed at her lower lip.

"Ye need not bide your tongue. Before I came here, I heard the servants whispering of Moridac's, uh, hunt parties."

She glanced at Letia before walking over to smooth the bright green bed covers and pat the plump pillow. Turning, she rubbed her arms and looked down at the tips of her shoes peeping from beneath her blue kirtle. Thinking, she rocked back and forth on her feet. They were no parties but a place where young men gathered to drink in excess while tupping women carted from nearby villages.

Letia, sitting beside the small hearth, wrinkled her nose. "Aye. 'Tis shameful, though it is hard to tell how much truth there are to the tales."

"I fear they are too true." She cleared her throat. "Two morns past, I was below in the orchard. An angry villager was in the bailey yelling, claiming Moridac had ruined his daughter."

She stopped, near fearful of repeating what she had heard. "Chief Broccin laughed and threw him some coins. While the man picked them up, Moridac's father said something strange."

"What was it?" Letia's brows rose.

Catalin knotted her fingers together. Her voice was so low Letia leaned forward. "He said the girl served as a lusty filling between his son and him."

Letia's eyes widened. "I spoke to Warin of these loathsome, um, excesses. He believes they will cease once you are wed." She looked down at her lap then up, her eyes filled with sympathy. "If they do not, mayhap you can prevail on Raik to put an end to them?"

"Aye. Moridac is always different around him. Calm, even. And he does not drink overmuch when he's here."

"Good. Seek him out if there is a need." She rolled her brown eyes at Catalin. "Has Old Hannah spoken of the marriage bed?"

Catalin blushed and tugged her right earlobe.

"Uh-huh." She darted a look at Letia then buried her nose in pink gillyflowers amongst the floral arrangement on the bedside table. Her voice floated out, muffled from the petals. "At first, I didn't believe what she told me. Until I arrived here."

"Why here? What changed your mind?"

Catalin plunked down in a chair next to Letia.

"Moridac thrust me into a dark alcove last eve." Her face burned as if she sat too close to a flame. "When he pressed me against the wall, I felt a hard bulge beneath his kilt." She squirmed in her seat. "He drew my hand to cover it."

She cleared her throat, remembering how her heart had thumped. "He whispered what he wanted to do. 'Twas the same as Old Hannah told me."

Letia chuckled. "I am surprised a woman so ancient would remember."

Catalin giggled. "Her eyes near popped from her head. Later that day, I saw her watching the castle steward's fine arse as he passed by her."

Letia laughed aloud. "One is never too old to enjoy thinking of bed sport."

"Uh, Letia? Your Warin is a lordly man. He is still comely even in his advanced years. But are you happy in your marriage?"

"He is a gentle, loving man. I shudder to think of living with some cruel man who would not hesitate to beat me."

"I love Moridac. Though, when I was but seven years of age, 'twas Ranald I pined for. Never will I forget hearing a tumult in the bailey. It was the day after my betrothal to Moridac. I stood on a chair to peer out the window opening." She shook in a violent shudder. "I saw Chief Broccin beating what I believed was a dog on the muddy ground. Not until two men pulled him away did I see it was a young man."

"That was a terrible thing for a child to witness." Letia's lips thinned. Eyes the color of dark earth wet from a summer's rain, frowned with displeasure.

"Worse yet was learning Ranald was that bloody body they picked up and sloshed in the horse trough. When I asked about him, no one would speak of it. Soon after, Chief Broccin said he had died."

"I have heard the same." Letia watched Catalin's face. "Are you afeared of your new father-by-law?"

Catalin nodded. Her pulse pounded, remembering how a year past he had glared at her and fisted his hands in anger. He looked about to snap her head from her neck. All because she had asked for a delay of her wedding vows as her father lay dying.

"I would not care to cross him. I think his fingers yearn to add my father's riches to his coffers."

They had no more chance to talk, for a heavy fist rapped on the door.

"Come out, come out, sweet bride to be," Moridac's deep, rich voice called, "else I must break down the door and steal ye away."

Her betrothed's speech, usually crisp and clear, was slurred. She glanced at Letia and noted a slight crease between her brows.

"I am coming." Catalin's teeth worried her lower lip. She ran her hand over her light blue kirtle, smoothing any wrinkles from it. She had chosen the color to please Moridac, because he oft claimed her eyes were the color of a clear summer sky.

Before she could reach it, the door burst open and Moridac swept her into his arms. His lips were about to take hers when Letia cleared her throat. He took his time letting Catalin free.

"Ah, not one but two lovely lasses." Moridac swept low in a dramatic bow. His rich, black hair brushed his cheeks. "Such sweetness to the eye is like honey to the tongue."

Catalin rolled her eyes at him.

"Ye dinna believe me?" He grasped her hand and brought it to his lips. His hot, wet tongue licked over the palm. She yelped and snatched her hand back.

"Aye. Warm, sweet honey."

Her body heated when his gaze probed the cloth over her breasts. His eyes flashed with hunger and he wet his lips when her nipples hardened and thrust shamefully against her gown.

"Time enough for tasting after you say your vows, Moridac." Warin de Burgh stepped through the doorway and smiled gently at his wife. "You must be hungered, love. You have not eaten since last eve."

"That I am. Come. Let us go below before Cook sends someone to hunt us down."

The baron smiled at his wife and motioned Moridac to precede them with Catalin.

Guests had started arriving for the wedding. After her father's death, Chief Broccin had insisted they hold the ceremony at Raptor Castle. As they descended the stairs, the din of people milling about increased in volume.

Bright banners hung from every rafter above the great hall. As each guest arrived, servants placed the man's standard on wall brackets, adding to the cheerful colors. In between, picturesque tapestries done in vivid threads described the family history. They gave the room a warm effect. Huge iron candle branches stood every twenty paces, chasing the shadows into the corners.

Servants had set up long trestle tables and benches below the high table. Pewter plates, drinking horns and pitchers of wine waited on white linen cloths. Clay vases of red roses, lilies and rare white heather decorated the tables. Everywhere Catalin looked, flowers appeared. She knew it was Moridac's doing.

He bent to murmur in her ear, "My lovely Catalin, mine own sweet flower. The finest rose cannot rival the beauty of yer lush, red lips. Mmm, or cheeks like the softest of petals," he added as his teeth nipped her ear. His tongue lapped over it before he drew back.

Shivers shot to her core. Saints! Was it wicked to feel such excitement? Far from being uneasy about her marriage bed, she looked forward to it. Moridac had found frequent opportunities to kiss and caress her. To her shame, she had responded with eagerness.

Catalin felt anxious with everyone watching her. Did they expect her to act differently because she was from Northumbria? As they made their way to the high table, she saw no familiar faces other than Baron de Burgh, Letia, and Moridac's family. She was thankful when Elyne, his young sister who had just turned her seventeenth year, came over to hug her.

"Soon I will have a sister to aid me. These lumps of clay that call themselves men are more fit for the stable." Elyne made a face and dodged Moridac, who reached to pinch her arm. "None of that, brother. Ye wouldn't like a horn of wine to soil yer green tunic, now would ye?"

"Hm. Ye wouldn't like to be dunked in the wine vat yerself, would ye?"

Catalin waited uneasily, watching Chief Broccin stalk over to them. His face wore its usual scowl. He seemed to dislike laughter or light feelings whenever he was about, for he never ceased to quell it.

"Take yer seats so we may begin the meal." He scraped back his chair and sat.

Moridac placed Catalin to his father's left then took the space beside her. She wished Letia was closer, but she and the baron were to sit on the other side of Catalin's new father-by-law.

Her mouth watered when servants placed steaming platters of roasted lamb basted with a mint sauce, roast pork, honeyed poultry, roasted filets of whitefish and goose covered with a sauce made from grapes on the table.

Moridac knew her preferences and grinned when he placed the choicest morsels of pork in front of her. She couldn't help licking her lips. With just a slight motion of her head toward the carrots flavored with honey, he filled the spaces between her meats.

He waved a fistful of hot bread beneath her nose and waggled his brows. She laughed aloud at his silly expression. Broccin's cold regard stifled her outburst.

Throughout the meal, her husband-to-be was ever courtly, seeing she had the best of each serving and keeping the chalice they shared filled with wine. By the time the sugared fruits and pastries appeared, Catalin feared her stomach would burst.

She jerked in surprise when Chief Broccin blasted a belch worthy of a giant and rubbed his taught belly. As if it were a signal, servants cleared the tables and the entertainments began. A succession of performers took over the center of the room.

Moridac twirled the wine chalice, making Catalin fear it would upend at any time. He insisted she sip each time he drank. Had she not eaten like a veritable pig, she feared she would have been unable to steady herself when she stood to retire.

As it was, her knees were none too firm when she started up the stairs with the other women.

Old Hannah awaited Catalin within her bedchamber.

"You should be snug abed, not biding your time in these big, drafty rooms, Hannah." Catalin spoke slowly, for her words did not sound right to her. She threw her arms around the old woman and hugged her.

Hannah clucked her tongue and sniffed. "Too much wine, lovey."

She expected a scolding, but instead Hannah shooed the servant away and helped Catalin prepare for bed. When she stretched and found they had heated the bed with a warming pan, she sighed with comfort.

"Thank you, Hannah. You have been like a mother to me."

"Then heed me, girl. Strong wine is for men. It causes them enough trouble. You do not want to find what it could cause a young lady. Sleep now."

Hannah tucked the covers around Catalin's shoulders then, as she had done so many times before, gently stroked her hand over the warm, curly hair spilling over the pillow. She pinched out the candles before leaving to find her own pallet in the room provided for personal servants.

"Mmm," Catalin sighed and snuggled deeper against the glorious warmth. Had Hannah returned to warm her bed again with heated stones?

Something tickled her cheek. She wriggled her head. It stopped. For a moment. Then a warm tongue stroked her ear; a cheek rubbed against her own. 'Twas Sport? Had she not left her father's dog at Hunter Castle?

"What …?" It was far as she got, for a hand clamped over her mouth.

"Shhh, love," Moridac whispered in her ear.

Of a sudden, she realized what caused the splendid warmth. She stiffened. Stretched tight against her side from head to toe was not a down filled coverlet, but hot, solid man.

Not just a man. A very *naked* man.

"My lord, you should not be here. You will bring me shame."

He tapped a finger on her lips and whispered, "No one will ever know."

"You have slept overlong, sweetness. 'Tis time to rise." Old Hannah bustled around the room, selecting Catalin's clothing for the day.

Catalin's lids flew wide. Overlong? What did she mean.

She hadn't slept late, had she? She sat up, winced, then hoped Hannah had not seen. Sun glinted through the window. She blinked, not believing it.

A servant scratched on the door before entering with a pitcher of warmed water. Hannah placed it on the corner table beside the basin, then smoothed a drying cloth near it. Satisfied that all was ready, she came over to the bed and waited until Catalin stood.

"The men were high in their cups when they left for the hunt this morn. The scamp you are to marry celebrated the night through at that lodge in the woods. He was in high spirits when he came back at dawn. Took a lot of teasing, he did." Hannah poured water into the basin for Catalin to splash her face. "Come along, young one."

Catalin stiffened. Hannah was staring at her thighs. She glanced down, horrified to see spots of blood. Now the servant was looking at the sheets. They, too, had splatters of red mingled in with some other strange stains. The bed had a musky smell, too. She gulped.

"My courses must have come. I was not prepared," she stammered. Her heart dropped, seeing understanding in Hannah's face. She knew better. Catalin's time never varied. Hannah well knew what happened, judging from the tightening of her lips.

"Aye. 'Twas the same when your father passed," Hannah lied. She hurriedly stripped the bed and handed the bundle of sheets to the servant.

Hannah latched the door behind her.

"Well, girl, let us hurry before anyone else discovers this."

"I'm sorry, Hannah. I should have resisted him." Catalin's voice was faint with shame.

"Nay, child. The fault was his. Do not fret overlong." She lathered a separate cloth and scrubbed over Catalin's legs, while Catalin washed her face. "I do not doubt many of the women under this castle's roof were tupped before their vows. Should he have made a baby, 'twill not be known for the wedding is but a day away."

It was the fastest Catalin had ever dressed in her life

She hurried down to the great hall. When offered porridge and scones, she smiled and said she had already broken her fast. She hoped no one could hear her stomach's hungry growl.

The thunder of hooves crossing the drawbridge and clattering on the cobblestones distracted her from her worries.

What were the men shouting? She raced to the window, hoping to get a glimpse of Moridac. She did not see him for all the men milling about. They jumped off their mounts and ran toward a group gathered around the entrance.

Chief Broccin had ridden his mount to the very steps. Why?

Hands reached up to him. Not to help him dismount. To take something from his arms. She did not have to see his white, strained face to know.

She gasped. The men carefully handled a bloodstained body. Her heart slammed against her ribs.

Moridac!

CHAPTER 4

Back at Kelso Abbey

"CHIEF BROCCIN MAY APPROACH, but dinna open the gate. He will return at once from whence he came." Ranald's lips thinned to a grim line. His dark, smoldering look revealed the fury, the hatred, kept banked for so many years.

"Hear him out, Ranald." Raik's eyes filled with sympathy for his cousin whose only wish was to be left alone.

For several heartbeats, Ranald sat his mount facing the Abbey gate, as still as if both man and horse were stone. Finally, he shoved the cowl back from his head, for it would interfere should he need to do battle. He did not mask his feelings as he eyed Raik. He fought to control his anger, his emotions. For if he did not, there was no telling what his temper could unleash. He squared his shoulders, stilled all expression from his face and watched the advancing army.

What need had they of so many numbers? A fool's question. Kelso was on the Scottish Border, and skirmishes happened more often here. He should know. 'Twas he who had the caring of the broken bodies, the dying men.

His father was many things. Careless was not one of them.

Ranald's horse sidestepped, nervous, as riders galloped toward them. They were close enough now that he scanned the men's faces, swept past Broccin, picked out his father's commander Domnall, the knights Fergus and Dubne.

His eyes continued their quest. A frown gathered between his brows. Where was Moridac? He had felt his presence much of late, even coming to him in his dreams. He would recognize him, for he would be the exact image of himself. He snorted in disgust. Aye. Like me. But then, *not* like me.

Sick fear twisted ugly fingers around his heart, dragging it to the pit of his stomach. He locked his mind from it. An arrogant voice brought his thoughts back.

"See the gates opened, boy," Broccin shouted, his face ruddy with anger.

"Boy?" Ranald looked at each of the men around him. "I see no boy, Chief Broccin. By yer own lips, that boy died near ten and five years past. If mayhap ye address me, ye are mistaken. I am Brother Ranald, Protector and Infirmarian of Kelso Abbey. If ye wish entrance, ye, Lord Raik's commander and yer own may enter. All weapons must remain outside these walls, or else surrendered upon entering. Armies are not welcome here. Yer warriors must camp outside the gates."

Broccin's mouth dropped. Ranald spied Domnall, riding beside his father, the corners of his lips twitching though he pressed them together. No one in many years had dared to dispute Chief Broccin.

Broccin, his eyes blazing, roared. "Open the damned gates. I have orders from King David that concern yer sorry arse."

Ranald's throaty snarl and the harsh rasp of his sword leaving its sheath answered his father. Though all else was still, wind began to stir and lift dirt and leaves into ever-increasing circles in front of Ranald as his horse stamped closer to the gate.

"Brother Ranald."

Ranald felt Prior Godric's serene presence nearby and the soft tug on his frock. He looked down to find he stood close.

"My son, allow Chief Broccin to enter." The prior fingered his cross, his eyes gentle with sympathy when they looked into Ranald's.

"Aye, Ranald. 'Tis best to get it over with. He's not about to leave."

Sweat trickled down Raik's temple. His jaw looked tense, too. What had he to fear? Ranald's stomach churned in dread.

He slapped his sword back into its scabbard then nodded at

the gatekeeper. The man's hands shook so badly it took several tries before he could free the lock and push the door halfway open. Broccin shoved through and rode to the center of the courtyard. He did not dismount in one smooth motion as was his custom, but laboriously climbed from his saddle.

Ranald stayed by the gate until Raik's two men and Domnall entered, along with a man attired in the king's livery. Ranald nodded and the gate clanged shut again. He rode over to where Brother Octavius waited and dismounted.

"After ye have secured their weapons, please see the men outside are given ample water. Ask if anyone needs aid." Ranald spoke quietly to the monk who had worked with him for the past five years. He handed his own sword to the young novice beside him.

As he strode over to the group waiting in front of the abbot's house, he watched the prior greet his father. His sire had not changed overmuch. Truth, his temples were gray and bitterness had etched lines beside his lips. His eyes had dimmed somewhat, no longer as piercing dark as before. He was tall, his muscles lean … a body much like Ranald would have when age crept up to meet him.

Raik stood, his posture stiff with displeasure radiating from every inch of his body as he, too, stared at Broccin.

The prior was a slight man below average height, and he could not see over the warriors around him. When he stood on the third step, his faded blue eyes found Ranald's. A delicate hand withdrew from the white sleeves to beckon him forward.

"Come, Abbot Aymer awaits you all." Prior Godric motioned Chief Broccin, Raik and the king's messenger to follow him.

Ranald frowned. The abbot had expected this visit? Why had he not warned him of it?

Raik strolled beside Ranald. Neither spoke as they followed the prior through the arched doorway, down the south arcade leading around the abbot's cloister gardens.

The open bays that faced the cloister were designed to look like huge arched windows with elaborate stonework latticed in the opening. Ranald watched Broccin greedily assessing everything, even gauging the wealth of the vaulted stone ceilings with their intricately carved patterns.

The men's boots striking the stone floor were foreign to this soothing place. Ranald grimaced and peered out into the cloister garden. At its center stood a marble fountain. Water flowed from a pitcher held in the hands of a stone monk and collected at the basin below. A bird fluttered to rest on the stone shoulder, its wings spread wide to catch the sun's rays. Benches surrounded the basin.

Lush flower gardens decorated the big square. He inhaled, enjoying the mixture of honeysuckle, roses, lavender, sweet violets, hyssop — too many scents for him to separate.

How many nights had he sat here with Abbot Aymer, his quiet words and prayers soothing Ranald's soul? He disliked his father seeing any of it.

Too soon, they reached the abbot's private offices. Sending a silent prayer for God to help him hold his temper, Ranald steeled himself to relax. Whatever his father wanted, he would have none of it.

Abbot Aymer waited patiently for everyone to enter his study. Books lined each wall and a heavy carpet covered the floor. Close to a large window stood a massive oak table, cluttered with work. Beside it, a brace of candles sat unlit, for the day was clear.

Prior Godric waited for everyone to take a seat then motioned to a lay brother who stood in a corner with a pitcher of wine and enough goblets for all. When he had served everyone, he retired. Prior Godric stood beside the door, his hands again thrust inside his sleeves. Ranald remained standing beside the abbot's chair, seeing to his protection.

"Mayhap you will tell me of your quest, Chief Broccin," Abbot Aymer started. He got no further before Broccin interrupted.

"I have come for my son, nothing more." Broccin glowered around the room as he downed his wine.

"Your son is at Raptor Castle. You declared his twin dead to you many years past. 'Twas printed on the missive attached to his litter when he arrived." The abbot leaned back in his chair and waited quietly.

"Dinna be a fool …"

Ranald was swift. He loomed threateningly over his sire. "Do not speak in such a tone, else ye will find yerself outside the gate." His tone was quiet. Deadly quiet. Only a fool would not have heeded the threat in it.

Broccin bolted up. His face turned purple, his eyes bulged in instant anger.

"Ye dare threaten yer father?" He shoved Ranald hard, thinking to knock him to the stones as he had so many times in the past.

Raik's man shot to his feet, ready to intervene should Ranald have need of it. He did not.

Ranald hadn't budged; he hadn't swayed. Broccin may as well have shoved a carved statue. Instead, a force pushed the Chief backward until the backs of his legs brushed his chair. He looked startled, for Ranald had not touched him.

When Broccin sat, Raik's man quietly resumed his seat.

"Please, Brother Ranald. I take no offense. Come. Stand beside me again."

Ranald reluctantly did as the abbot asked, though he did not relax his guard.

"Chief Broccin, be good enough to explain why you wish Brother Ranald to come to Raptor Castle. Is it for some family ceremony ye wish him to officiate?"

Broccin snorted. "Aye. A ceremony. 'Tis for a wedding."

"And whose wedding would this be?" The abbot tilted his head, curious as to why he would need one of his monks.

"His own." Broccin glared at Ranald and sat back in his chair.

"What? Are ye daft? I canna marry. If ye want heirs for Raptor Castle, Moridac will provide them." Ranald watched his father like he was a strange, talking creature.

"Moridac is dead."

Ranald's hands fisted, his nails cutting into his palms as he leaned forward and braced himself on the edge of the desk.

Pain shot through him hearing the words scream through his head. The doors burst open and slammed shut with a sharp bang while shutters beat against window openings then stilled. He couldn't control his grief much less rein in the turmoil it created.

He should have known. 'Twas why he had felt Moridac's presence these past weeks. He had thought 'twas because his twin still mourned for his lost brother. But nay. 'Twas Moridac trying to tell him he was gone.

The abbot gripped Ranald's hand and held tight, sending comfort. Broccin, Domnall and the king's man looked around them, puzzling what had caused the sudden chaos. Not Raik, the abbot or prior, though. Ranald straightened and locked his body rigid. He refused to show any feelings. His father would feed on it.

"He died, and 'tis yer fault." Broccin's voice grew to a shout. "Ye should have been there to heal him the way 'tis rumored ye do here."

"How could I have been? Ye are the one who abandoned me here, telling one and all I no longer lived." Ranald flinched and longed to be alone to grieve.

"What happened to your son, Chief Broccin? I had heard he was a healthy, strong man. Like his brother." The abbot strove to quiet the anger sizzling in the air.

"A hunt. Just a day afore his vows were to be said. He died in my arms three sennights ago."

Ranald was shocked to see tears dampen his father's lashes. Hurt filled him, for his sire had shown neither a look of sadness nor regret when he had lain near death.

"I am sorrowed by my brother's death." A dull, empty ached gnawed at his heart knowing his hopes of one day seeing Moridac walking through the abbey entrance was forever a lost dream. "I will say prayers daily for his soul."

"I don't want yer prayers. I want yer body at Raptor's church to wed Catalin of Hunter Castle. She was set to marry my son, and my son she will marry, though not the one she lusted after. Ye will return with me."

Ranald looked at Raik, and from his apologetic expression,

he knew there was more to it. For what reason did King David send Raik as his protector?

"I canna marry. I am a *monk*. Dinna ye ken? I have taken vows of celibacy." Ranald spoke slowly, as if instructing a child.

"Aye. Ye took vows. They are broken now." Broccin smirked when he said it.

"I have broken no vow."

"Ye had no need. I must have heirs for Raptor Castle. Ye will provide them. Ye are no longer a monk." Broccin snorted. "Have not been for the sennight it took the missives to reach me."

Ranald's lip curled with disgust looking at his father. Was the man brainsick? Then he remembered Raik's mention of King David and turned to him with raised brows.

"By what means is this?"

"Since Chief Broccin has no other sons, if he dies, the title devolves to you. Raptor Castle is vital to the safety of Scotland." Raik cleared his throat. "A castle without a lord is fair prey for a siege. King David does not want it to change hands. He petitioned the Pope. With ample incentive, the Pope granted a special dispensation."

Raik nodded to the king's representative, who laid a sealed parchment at the abbot's hand.

Everyone stilled as the abbot broke the seal and unrolled it. He smoothed it out on the desk and leaned forward, as close as he could get his failing eyes to the words.

Ranald's stomach churned, hoping there was some flaw the saintly man could find. His hopes dimmed when sad eyes peered up as he thrust the parchment at him.

His world of peace descended into the chaos of Hell. All in the time it took to read the Latin written there.

This was his home. His work was here. His peace was here. He wouldn't leave.

Slapping his hand atop the parchment, he straightened. "I may no longer be a monk, but I choose to remain here. If King David fears for Raptor Castle, let him appoint another lord. I dinna want it. I willna take it."

"Fool," Chief Broccin shouted. "Whether ye like it or no,

ye'll go. I thought ye'd be stubborn. 'Tis why an army awaits outside the gates. Return with me, else I'll raze this abbey to the ground."

Raik and his man bounded to their feet, along with the king's representative. Prior Godric hurried to stand on the other side of the abbot.

"I will not allow it, Chief Broccin." Raik ground out the words between clenched teeth.

"Mayhap ye will try. Do ye forget? We outnumber ye. How much damage, how many lives will bleed their last in trying to thwart me?"

The abbot stood, his hands upraised.

"Enough. We will settle this quietly, with the dignity God's house deserves." He rang a small gold-plaited bell setting on the corner of his desk. A novice immediately appeared.

"Please show these men to their quarters for the evening." He turned to them and smiled. "When it is time, someone will come to direct you to the dining hall. After lauds on the next sunrise, Ranald and I will give you our answer."

The prior opened the door wide. He and Raik hung back, making sure Broccin exited without causing any additional problems. Before Raik left the room, he turned to Ranald.

"I am sorry, cousin. I was to be given time to talk to ye and Abbot Aymer. Chief Broccin was not to arrive until two days hence. I should have known he would do something rash."

Ranald, his mind burning with emotions, nodded then turned away. The door quietly closed behind him.

CHAPTER 5

COLD SEEPED THROUGH TO Ranald's bones. He ignored it. His body ached; his muscles screamed. Stretched wide like a human cross on the chilly marble, he paid no heed. His forehead pressed hard onto unyielding stone, he prayed into the night. Through each liturgy of the hours, all within Kelso Abbey prayed with him. For him.

His heart filled with dread of leaving this place. Within Kelso, he could subdue his demons. He did not want to join the secular world. Doing so, how could he keep from becoming a beast like his sire? Or a slave to pleasure like he had learned his brother had become?

Aye, visitors had carried stories of Moridac. They had not known they spoke of the monk's brother. He knew of Moridac's drunken orgies held at a hunting lodge deep in the forest. And of his brutal fighting and cruelty.

Broccin thought he had stilled the talk, but men spoke of Moridac's eyes gleaming, his lips spread in a smile when he fought to the death. Over trivial things that meant nothing to him. He seized every chance to prove he was his father's son.

Though Ranald knew of these things, he still loved Moridac as his twin had been when last he saw him. Nothing could change that. What could change was himself, given enough time in that outside world with Broccin. It was his greatest fear.

The abbot and he had talked into the night. He knew he could defy his father, wanted to, even. But Broccin would wreak havoc in a few short hours should Ranald resist. And he must not defy an order from King David.

He had checked one last time on the Infirmary. Prior Godric, with Ranald's advice, had assigned the young monk who had worked the longest with him taking care of the sick and injured to become the next Infirmarian. The prior assured Ranald he would send word to him should they at any time need his help.

Footsteps drew near. It was time to rise.

He pressed his ruined cheek to the floor's coldness and tightened his body. It was as if he hugged the stones he had knelt upon too many times in the past to count.

A soothing hand brushed his temple. "My son, the time draws near for you to ride." Abbot Aymer waited while Ranald rose to his knees, crossed himself and stood.

When he walked out into the fog-filled courtyard, Broccin, Raik and the others already sat their mounts. Domnall held tight to a magnificent black horse's bridle. The horse stamped, threw his head about and tried to rear as Domnall led him.

"Moridac oft said this horse was too much for him. He believed you would have tamed him, had you lived. He didna ken you were here at Kelso," Domnall said.

Broccin rode over, a smirk on his face.

"Meet Satan's Spawn. Yer brother named him. A fitting mount to make a fool of a man who spent his night sprawled like a dead raven in front of an altar. No doubt ye'll be splattered on the cobblestones once ye mount."

Ranald let the words flow through the air, ignoring them. Brother Octavius handed him the belt, sword and scabbard given to Brother Ranald by a grateful knight. He fastened them around his waist before turning to kneel and kiss Abbot Aymer's ring. He took one last look around and blinked, seeing all the monks and laymen gathered there to see him off.

He cleared his throat, took hold of Satan's bridle and murmured to the horse. The beast jerked and strained. Ranald, his muscles rippling in his arms, kept him still. Again and again, he stroked down the shiny black head and long neck then rubbed between the beast's eyes, all the time talking and soothing him. Bit by bit, Satan quieted. He danced one last sidestep, shook his head to show he had the last word then stilled.

Broccin's jaw went slack when Ranald gained the saddle in a flash. Satan reared. Ranald did not budge. His firm hands and legs let the horse know the man was master, not the beast. Satan again stamped up and down with his forelegs. Ranald ignored him.

Each maneuver the horse tried, Ranald countered, until it shook and snorted then threw its head up and pranced. Regal. Proud. As if he deemed the black-robed man on his back worthy of him.

"Cover yer face. 'Tis as unsightly as the day I sent ye here."

"Nay, Broccin. Ye dinna like the design ye created? 'Tis a shame. Ye worked so hard at it."

"Yer fault. In yer drunken state, ye could have ruined a fine stead."

"Ah, yes. Yer mount was far more valuable than yer son. There is another problem ye are forgetting." Ranald's cold regard made Broccin twitch.

"What?"

"Are ye not afeared Moridac's bride will bolt with one look at her new husband-to-be?"

" 'Tis yer problem — not mine. Mayhap ye should blindfold her afore ye ram betwixt her legs." Broccin's laughter rang out as he rode toward the men waiting in the field beyond.

With Domnall riding beside him, Ranald led Satan through the opened gate and stopped. He twisted around, his hand rising in a farewell gesture to the men who ran behind them, waving.

Chief Broccin waited at the head of the long line of warriors facing them. Raik and the king's man were behind him.

"Take your place, Ranald." Domnall motioned with his chin for him to pull alongside the waiting Chief Broccin.

Ranald cantered over, knowing whether he liked it or no, he must show the warriors of Raptor Castle that he took his rightful place as their lord's heir. He drew in beside the man he despised, expecting to hear more hate spewing from his lips.

Instead, Broccin pulled a folded banner from inside the neck of his tunic and shook it out. Two shiny black eagles flew on a field of yellow; a red bar diagonally divided it. A waiting squire attached it to his pole and bobbed his head at Ranald, before pulling even with the other standard-bearers, their colorful banners cracking in a stiff breeze.

"'Twas *his* design," Broccin muttered. "He said 'twas for the two of ye separated by death. Should have been yer death. Not his." Broccin kicked his mount into action, heading for Raptor Castle.

"I know no more than you, Letia." At Raptor Castle, Catalin wrung her hands and paced back and forth at the foot of her bed.

"Moridac's twin Ranald has lived at Kelso Abbey all this time? I cannot understand why Chief Broccin said he died so many years ago."

Catalin blinked, clearing her eyes of the smoke from candles lit around every corner of the room. Since Moridac's death, she could not stand the gloom on cloudy days.

"Aye. 'Tis what he claimed. It does not seem right that a man would declare his son dead if he was not. I fear some terrible secret lies behind it."

Catalin's stomach heaved. She forced it back. 'Twas worry and fear that caused it.

"Letia, did he give any hint about Ranald when he sent notice to you?"

"Nay. His missive bidding our return took us by surprise. He said only that he wanted ample witnesses for a wedding betwixt his long absent son and you."

Hannah, ever close of late, brought a cold cloth and wiped Catalin's face. "You should eat more, child."

"I cannot keep it down. Every time I start to eat, Chief Broccin watches me with a strange look of glee. I fear he is brainsick."

"More likely too much wine." Letia grimaced with disgust and ran angry fingers through her dark brown curls.

"Late on the night before last, I heard the grinding of the portcullis rising. Mayhap twenty warriors escorted a messenger from King David."

Catalin pressed the cold cloth to her face and breathed in the soothing lavender oil Hannah had sprinkled on it.

"Could you make out who led the escort?"

"Nay. It was too dark. But before dawn even lightened the sky, Chief Broccin hammered on my door with his sword hilt." Catalin moved the cloth to her neck. "Afore I could don my robe, he burst in and announced there was to be a wedding. In three days. He was going to fetch his son. He waggled his finger at me and laughed. I think he had been in his cups all night. A short time later, he rode out with a large company of warriors."

"When we arrived, Warin was surprised to see he had left behind only men enough to patrol the walls."

"Aye." Catalin increased her pacing, worry in each footstep. "If he rode to fetch his son, why would he need an army?"

Letia shook her head, as puzzled as her friend.

Even as she did so, a bagpipe announced an arrival. Catalin and Letia ran to gape out the window as Chief Broccin's army approached the castle gates. The barbican guards ordered the drawbridge lowered, the portcullis raised. Their chains screeched in the evening air.

They watched the men thundering into the bailey. As they approached, Catalin's heart rang in her ears. Which man was Ranald? Surely, she would recognize him. When she last saw him, he was Moridac's mirror image.

"Moridac's standard flies. I see it. But where is Ranald?" Catalin rubbed her eyes and leaned further out the window to study the faces milling below.

"It is too dark to make him out," Letia decided. "They have not lit the torches for the evening."

"A monk rides alongside Chief Broccin. Do you think he comes to perform the vows?"

Catalin was secretly pleased, for she had much to confess.

She did not want to speak of it to the priest here at Raptor Castle. The man seemed much afeared of the castle's lord. No doubt, should Chief Broccin ask, the priest would tell all.

"Oh, Catalin. Is Ranald the knight riding alongside Sir Domnall? I can see no more than part of his face beneath his helmet. It is most comely."

"Nay ..." She stared and finally made out the face. "'Tis Raik, Ranald's cousin. We must have missed him." Catalin shivered and pulled her light robe across her chest.

"Why would his father not give you a day or two to meet each other? To have a wedding the day after he arrives seems hasty." Letia frowned, but seeing how upset Catalin appeared, went over and hugged her.

"Time enough on the morrow to see your husband." Hannah urged them away from the window and pulled the shutters closed.

A maid scratched at the door, guarding a candle's flames when Hannah opened it.

"Baron de Burgh said I was to see ye to yer bed, my lady, and to tell ye he would be late," she told Letia.

Letia held a dainty hand to cover her mouth and yawned.

"Do not fret, Catalin. After all, the two were twins. I'm sure you will see no difference between them when you meet." Letia crossed to the open door. "Rest well and do not worry."

Catalin sat on the side of the bed, her feet dangling above the floor. She ran a hand through her tousled hair. Her eyes burned for sleep yet it would not come. She slid off the bed. Her toes gripped the rug, enjoying the feel as she walked over to take a cloak off the wall peg. She slid her feet into her shoes then bent over to pull the ties tight.

One hand on the wall steadied her as she crept down the back stairwell. Mayhap if she sat in the gardens for a short time, she could relax her fears and sleep. She eased the door open and slipped out into the night. Rounding the side of the keep, she headed for the terraced gardens.

The sweet perfume of roses drifted with the night air. That Raptor Castle boasted such a lovely display of flowers startled most visitors. Catalin was used to it. The lord's sister Joneta was responsible. She was so unlike her brother. He was rude. Uncouth, even. Lady Joneta was quiet. Gentle. She oft looked at him as if she puzzled over what he did.

Catalin looked up at the cloud-wrapped sky and took a deep breath. Gravel crunched beneath a heavy foot. Startled, she looked toward the sound. A cloud drifted away from the moon, letting enough light filtering through an apple tree's leaves for her to see a robed man stood beneath it, his hands clasped something dark close to his chest, yet he seemed in prayer, his head bent.

A tonsure. It was the monk who had ridden beside Chief Broccin. Relief flooded her. Since the night Moridac had come to her bed, she had yearned to confess her sin. God would surely punish such a misdeed. Had that been why he had taken Moridac from her? How could she speak her vows on the morrow with such a weight on her chest?

She hurried down the path, afeared the monk would fade into the darkness before she had chance to speak with him.

Ranald sought peace in the garden, walking beneath the swaying branches of the trees, the rustling leaves giving voice to the slight wind. He had prayed long over his brother's tomb, had begged God to forgive Moridac of his sins. He prayed to Moridac, too, told him how he regretted he had no chance to be here with him, to mayhap help him. And if he could not, to ease him from this life. His tears had mingled with his words. His throat still ached with wanting to sob like some weakling of a woman.

His head jerked up. His eyes probed the shadows. A woman's graceful steps barely disturbed the stones, but it was enough to announce her. He whipped his cowl up to cover his head and hide his face in its shadows.

He moved to stand in the deep gloom where a thin shaft of moonlight split the darkness in front of it. He would see who hurried to him with such purpose in her stride.

"Please, I could not sleep. May I speak with you, Brother?"

He recognized Catalin at once, though she had changed much since last he saw her. Not everything, though. Some things had stayed the same. Curly hair the shade of a fading red sunset was as unruly as when she had skipped and scampered across the bailey, chasing first one piglet then another, trying to catch the squealing babies. Freckles trailed a path across her cheeks, crossing over a dainty nose. Her lips were full, pink, even in this gloom.

What had changed most was her spindly body. She had been all arms and legs beneath her flapping gowns. Now, her face looked pleasingly round, hinting that her body was no longer skinny but plump.

"... talk to a priest ... Moridac ... confess." He startled, realizing Catalin had been speaking, though he had heard little other than his brother's name.

"I am sorry, mistress. What is it ye wish from me?" 'Twas easy to look down at her, yet keep his face hidden.

"Has Chief Broccin brought you here to speak the vows this next morn?"

"Aye."

'Twas the truth, though she thought he would be doing the asking — not the answering.

"Chief Broccin has said I would not have time to talk with a priest before the ceremony, but I cannot marry with such sin on my conscience."

He heard Catalin take a quavering, deep breath as she stared up at him, her eyes probing the gloom.

"Will you hear my confession?"

CHAPTER 6

R ANALD GAVE THANKS THE clouds again hid the moon, for could she see, she would note his alarm. That she wanted to confess didn't surprise him. Most brides did so before they were to wed. What had she said about Moridac? About sin? He shuddered.

"My child, I canna hear your confession. 'Tis the dead of night." A lame excuse, but it was all he could think of at the time.

"I do not understand."

"Confessions should be made in the confessional, not amongst the apple trees." She would never believe such a thing. Most castle chapels did not have the small enclosed stalls.

"Is it not more fitting? Amongst all God has created, not closed within something built by man?"

Nay, Catalin had not changed overmuch. She was still stubborn and ready to argue, even with a man of God. Ah. But he was no longer a man of God. He had only to tell her the truth.

But not all of it.

"Aye, I believe God would prefer the outdoors as His house. I am sorry, Lady, but I canna help you. Just this last day, I was told by my abbot I could no longer hear confessions."

Catalin stilled. He could see her mind examine all her knowledge, seeking a reason for such a thing. Her look kept darting to Moridac's black hunting shirt clasped in his hand. No doubt, she caught his brother's scent that still lingered there, a scent they had shared. Juniper and spice.

"Oh."

She shifted from one foot to the next. Her head bobbed up. Her eyes tried to pierce the darkness.

"You have committed a sin? What offense is so great? You did not take a life else Chief Broccin would not bring you here. The next worse is breaking your vow of …" Her voice trailed off.

He had no need of light to see her blush. 'Twas clear the vow she decided was so forbidden to break was celibacy.

Her head shot back down. A playful breeze bared Ranald's toes. She tilted her head and stared. His toes bent, gripping the grass. He smoothed his hand down his robes, covering them. 'Twas foolish of him to feel exposed.

"Mayhap ye should seek yer bed, Lady, afore someone notes ye are gone?

"Aye." She nodded and halfway turned then twisted back. "'Tis his shirt," she blurted.

"Aye."

"What are you doing with it?"

"I sought to pray for Moridac's soul. Having his shirt aids me to feel close to him as I pray."

His hand tightened around it, pressing it to his chest.

Catalin remained silent, mulling his words over while her eyes probed the shadows. Finally, she gave a brief nod.

"I am pleased you are here. And about your vows? Mayhap it is strange, but 'tis a comfort knowing someone such as you also has a shameful secret."

When she twirled to leave, sweet violets scented the air. Ah. He breathed deep, surprised. Even as a young child, she had smelled of violets. It had been many long years since he had known a woman's scent.

Long after she disappeared in the night, one thought chased another through his head. She was an innocent. Wasn't she? What could she have done that she thought so shameful?

He would know afore too many moons. Catalin had never been able to keep a secret.

Footsteps behind him signaled another visitor to the gardens, but this time, it was an expected footfall. Without turning, he spoke into the night.

"Raik, come walk with me to the tanner's hut." He turned, his shoulders set, his back straight. He had made a decision the moment he had spied Catalin.

"What do ye need there? 'Tis not long afore the dawn. Ye took no rest last eve and have yet to seek yer bed."

"I would have him fashion a mask to spare Catalin my hideous sight."

"Hideous? There is naught hideous about yer scars. Harsh, aye. But hideous? Never." Raik's fists clenched. "My uncle does not speak truth about it. I would say he has forever envied ye as the boy and man he has never been."

Ranald shrugged, little caring what his sire thought of him. His own fingertips confirmed the stark contrast from one side of his face to the other.

After waking the tanner, it took a short time for that good man to come up with an idea for a mask. He sent his son to fetch the armorer. Between the two, they formed a metal frame for the mask. Once they fitted it to the contours of Ranald's face, the tanner would cover it with black leather cut from the ample bottom of Moridac's hunting shirt. The men promised to have the finished mask ready for him by first light.

Ranald and Raik slipped inside the keep and made their way to Moridac's room to seek what sleep they could. An overlarge bed stood against the far wall. Wind rattled the shutters of the large window beside it. Ranald strode over to enjoy the first raindrops on his face, before closing the shutters and latching them. The room boasted an ample fireplace with peat stacked ready to light. A table with two chairs stood nearby. Closely woven woolen rugs covered the floor, but fur rugs lay beside the bed and in front of the fireplace.

Ranald turned, a slight frown creasing his brows. Pegs on the walls held two cloaks, one black, the other red. Red? His brow shot up and he looked at Raik.

"Aye, Moridac had a love for the comforts of life. I believe ye will find all manner of garments within the clothing chest." Raik's hand lifted to gesture toward a heavy chest at the right of the doorway.

Lifting the lid, Ranald looked down at the many tunics, breeches and shirts folded there. Moridac must have been fonder of formfitting attire than the kilt. To be truthful, what surprised him most was that his brother had seemingly been enamored of comfort and fine cloth.

Ranald's hand smoothed down the heavy linen of his black monk's robe. His brother would have been most uncomfortable in such a simple garment.

"Well, now, seeing such an array, ye will have no need to go with a bare arse to yer wedding." Raik chuckled.

"Nay." All desire for sleep deserted Ranald. He prowled around the room, missing the nightly routine of Kelso. "My brother had more clothing in this one chest than I have seen in all these many years."

"Ye know not what to do with yerself, do ye, my friend?"

Raik's quiet remark eased the tension in Ranald's shoulders. His sigh was long and breathy.

"Aye. It will be long afore I learn to sleep as a man, not a monk. I am too used to short bits of slumber between services." He paced from the window to the door. If he had hair where there was now a tonsure, his fingers would have plowed through it. "Dinna mind me. Seek yer own rest. I will sleep when I find ease."

Raik nodded understanding and after undressing, settled his big body on the bed they would share for the night. Ranald was grateful that Raik knew he needed time alone.

Soon, soft snores signaled a deep sleep. He opened the shutters and knelt, his thoughts in turmoil. His head bent, his forehead rested on his clasped hands. He silently prayed. Seeing Catalin tonight had brought a long-fought reaction to his body, one ye had tried to conquer over the years.

What manner of man was he, that a woman's scent could draw him so quickly? Not even a sennight from the monastery, yet he felt himself already changed. He knelt there in the moonlight streaming in from a cleared sky and prayed he would not become like his brutal father, nor as lusty as Moridac.

He finally eased into bed. 'Twould not be long before dawn. He had promised the castle's priest Father Martin that he would chant the psalms of Matins when the sun began to rise. The priest's voice was hoarse, and if overused, chances are he would not be able to speak the wedding service. To Ranald's shame, he held a glimmer of hope that it would be so.

Catalin rose before dawn, surprising Hannah when she came to wake her. Dressed in a simple green kirtle and covered with a brown woolen cloak, she hurried up the stairwell to attend mass. The chapel was in the east tower where the sun's glorious rise greeted it.

Rays of light glinted through gems embedded in the cross hanging before the arched window. Colorful rays danced in every direction, adding to the beauty of an already sumptuous room. Did Broccin think to bribe God by giving prayer in such beauty? She stopped thinking on it, wanting, no needing, time to pray for forgiveness and hopefully bring peace to her mind.

Letia no sooner eased in beside her and knelt in prayer than a beautiful, strong voice chanting the liturgy came from the altar. Soft murmurs spread around the chapel. Letia's Warin leaned toward his wife and whispered, and she in turn inched close to Catalin.

"Warin has heard this done in his travels afore, but always in Rome. It is called plainsong," Letia whispered.

Catalin peeked above her clasped fingers, searching for its source. Only Father Martin stood there, his head bowed, silent.

"Where is the priest? I see no one but Father Martin," Catalin whispered back.

Letia shrugged, and she too looked around then nodded toward a screen placed at the left of the altar.

The sound of the deep voice, each melodic word precise, hastened Catalin's heartbeat. What manner of priest could have such an earthy tone? One that troubadours would envy? She gasped. The priest from the garden. So tightly did she grasp her hands together, her nails dug into her flesh.

Heaven help her. She was truly lost. Never to be saved.

How could God forgive her now? Last night had added

more sin to her already burdened soul, for her body had quivered when she drew close to the monk and caught his scent. Moridac's shirt and this disgraced monk smelled much alike. Now, his voice called to her senses.

"Have you seen Ranald?"

Letia's whisper barely disturbed the soft hair around Catalin's ear. She peered through her lashes thinking to see the man she was to wed. No. Nowhere in sight. Then her head sprang upright. Why did Ranald not appear at service? Shameless, her gaze roved over the small chapel. No, she saw only those men she knew or had seen last eve.

"Nay. How can he care so little for his faith that he does not deign to attend?"

Her sharp whisper drew Chief Broccin's baleful scowl to her. She slammed her head down so fast her chin bumped the wooden railing in front of her. 'Twas unfortunate her teeth snapped together catching the tip of her tongue. She pressed her lips tight to keep from crying out.

Ranald stood behind the screen. His hands lifted toward the glinting cross at the rear of the altar as he chanted the words in the eight tones used for plainsong. For the first time since coming to Raptor Castle, peace settled over him.

At the end of the mass, as his last words were fading and Father Martin took over, he slipped away. Few knew of the hidden passage there, and he was grateful for it. He wanted no one to see him, for he had yet to seek out the tanner and don his mask. He hurried down the circular stairwell and out into the open.

The sun spread over the top of the surrounding hills, its rays finding their way to a puddle in his path. He stopped, his muscles jerking, remembering another puddle all those years ago. He looked up, took a deep breath and glanced around. He had come to the very spot where Goliath had thrown him into the mud. The horse trough, a filled bucket perched atop a corner awaiting a stable hand, stood not twenty paces away. The stable doors gaped wide apart. Grooms scurried around inside fetching oats and hay, currying brushes clasped under their armpits.

A violent shudder wracked him. Remembering. His cheek twitched. Stung. He tensed, fancied he heard the whoosh of his father's whip.

His stomach lurched. Bile came to his throat. Burning.

Wind picked up around him. Tiny waves rippled in the puddle. He stared at the water in the trough, the memory of the terrible pain, the way the water had filled his nose when his mouth opened wide in a gurgling scream as fresh in his mind as if it were last morn.

"Ranald! Ranald!"

A hand touched his shoulder.

He blinked. Wind whistled. His robes whipped around his legs. A young boy stood, his mouth agape looking at the trough where water sloshed over the sides as if something heavy had dropped there. The bucket rocked, tipped, fell to the ground. It rolled and did not stop until it struck the stable's doorframe.

He gritted his teeth, shook his head.

"I kenned I held my feelings in check. What has happened?"

Raik squeezed his shoulder, giving acceptance.

Ranald took a deep breath, closed his eyes and waited. He had thought he had control over his anger. Had learned to hide the strange things that happened when he lost it.

His heartbeat slowed.

The fury in his mind softened, calmed.

The wind tapered. Fell.

Only then did he dare open his eyes.

"Come away from here. No one but the boy noted, and he didna sense the reason for it." Raik's gaze probed the bailey. "Ye have neither slept nor taken sustenance. Eat." He shoved a hefty chunk of cheese and the end off a loaf of hot bread at Ranald.

"Last eve it was too dark for ye to see anything. I expect bad memories besiege ye. Any man would lose control of his emotions. God knows, ye have much to forgive."

"Aye. And to forget." Ranald nodded, took a large bite of cheese, famished now. By the time they entered the tanner's hut built against the outer curtain wall, he had devoured the last of the bread.

Both the tanner and the armorer waited. The tanner handed him the finished mask, excitement sparkling in his eyes. Questions there, too, in both men's eyes. 'Twas eagerness to learn if their efforts were acceptable.

Ranald held the half-mask, turned it from one angle to the other. Examined it. Last eve, the armorer had formed a thin frame of metal used in making helmets, and shaped it to conform to Ranald's face. The tanner then covered it with black leather, even putting a soft pad on the inside to keep it from irritating his flesh.

The mask fitted from the hairline above his right brow, down through that small space between his eyes, around the edge of his right nostril, over the top of his lip then back across his jaw to end behind his ear. It hid all but the ridged scars trailing down his neck. For added safety, a thin leather strip pierced the mask at the hairline, another at the back of his ear. When tied, it would disappear amongst his black hair, once that hair grew back to normal style.

"Try it on, man," Raik urged, "though I still dinna see the need of it."

Ranald felt clumsy handling it, until the armorer held up a polished piece of metal for him to look into. He examined his reflection, at the sharp contrast between the two sides of his face. Truth to tell, from the feel of his scars, he had expected worse. Still, no woman or child should have to look upon such.

He fitted the mask to his face and adjusted it until it felt firmly in place then tied the leather straps. He had feared it would hinder his sight. It did not, for the opening conformed to the shape of his eye. Nor did he feel any discomfort from it. Raik looked at him his eyes alight with approval.

"Forsooth, man. The lasses will be beside themselves, it adds such mystery to yer face."

"Better that than having them shrieking with fear." Ranald

let out a long sigh. Part of his life was ending, another beginning.

He thanked both men for their hard work, and having no coins of his own yet, was grateful to Raik for providing them. He would set that matter aright when he had more time.

"Come, Ranald. We must find suitable attire amongst Moridac's things. Ye canna marry wearing a monk's cassock." Raik's eyes crinkled.

"Nay. Broccin's guests will have enough to shock them without that."

Out of habit, he pulled up his hood as they walked through the bailey and made their way to the keep. They took the long way around, wanting to see the castle in the light of day. God's truth, it seemed far more formidable than what he remembered.

They followed the contour of the outer curtain wall and went through into the inner bailey. Walking the terraced gardens paths, his muscles tightened recalling Catalin's upturned face, the questions in her eyes when she looked at him. What would she think when she saw him in the light of day? Would she run? Would she refuse to repeat her vows? He could not blame her if she did.

Using a back entrance, they entered the keep unnoticed. He still mused over what he would do if Catalin bolted at the altar. Once they entered the bedchamber, his brows raised so fast they near dislodged his new mask, for beside the right wall stood a flowered chest. Surely Catalin's, for it had not been there before.

It struck him like a cold dousing, this sign that he would no longer sleep alone. That he would share the room this night with his brother's intended. A strangled sound escaped his lips before he could stop it.

Raik's head tilted. He peered thoughtfully at him before speaking.

"Ah, Ranald. I can near hear yer thoughts. Ye are troubled about the night to come?"

"Aye." Raik cleared his throat. "I have not tupped a woman since Moridac's betrothal. Trying to outdo each other, we had a wild night of it, drinking and bedding every willing lass." He looked down, frowned then shifted. How could he ask what nagged and bit at the base of his thoughts?

"What if I canna, uh, perform my husbandly duties?" he blurted.

"Huh? What would hinder ye? Ye dinna find Catalin comely?"

"Oh, nay, 'tis not that. She has grown to a beautiful woman." His face heated. "Once I healed at Kelso, I was oft troubled with, um, a rampant tarse when I thought of women. 'Twas the same time I learned my injuries had left me with the strange happenings when my temper roiled."

"Did ye frighten the monks overmuch? Did they think ye bewitched?"

"Nay. The first time my temper raged was in private with Abbot Aymer. He showed me a missive from father that day in answer to learning I was well enough to return home. I read Father's answer. He declared I was of no use to him, that I was to become a monk and never to leave the monastery. He sent a pouch of gold coins to ensure it."

"The man rivals Satan for meanness." Raik's jaw jutted, his brows near met in the middle.

"Aye. Every chair in the abbot's office crashed against the far wall except the ones we used. The missive flew off his desk and landed against the door."

"Did he think ye a tool of the devil?"

"He put his hands on my head and began to pray. We knelt there long into the night." Ranald spied a pitcher of ale setting on the table, went over and poured a portion into two black leather goblets. He handed Raik one then sipped from his own as they each took a seat.

"The bells for Vigils at midnight rang. The abbot quieted and looked into my eyes. I thought he meant to tell me I was doomed. Instead, he declared God had spared me when all expected me to die. He believes my injuries and high fevers caused my strange abilities. But I must learn to control my temper so no harm would come because of it. Until Broccin arrived at Kelso, 'twas easy enough. Life was tranquil there."

"The abbot was an unusual man. Mayhap he had heard

before about the strange "gifts" that sometimes runs through our family? Though ye, Elyne and I are the only ones affected in this generation?"

"Elyne!" Ranald shot to his feet.

"Aye. Though 'tis strange with her."

"Is she like me? Does it happen only when she is angered? Or is she like ye, able to charm someone into doing things even against their will? When did she start?"

"I believe it must have been about the time she, uh, started her monthly courses. She often walks in her sleep at night. To see her, one would think her awake. She isna. She confided in me that when she does, 'tis then she dreams of a future happening."

"Do these things come to pass?"

Raik chuckled, his face merry. "She hasn't been right so far. Often what does occur is the opposite of her vision. Yer father has laughed and made sport of her warnings until now she keeps her dreams secret."

"I have not seen her this day. But then, I have kept away from everyone."

He startled when a servant called seeking entrance. Opening the door, he found two men carrying a wooden bathing tub, followed by a line of servants with buckets of water. Hearing the drone of people milling about below, he realized it was time he prepared for his wedding.

At first he was surprised at the heated water then remembered only monks denied themselves such pleasure. He looked down at his cassock and strode over to the big clothing chest. Everything there seemed too colorful, too unlike what he was used to wearing. Finally, ignoring Raik's raised brows, he took out the clothing he would be comfortable donning.

Never had he been so slow to remove his robe. Knowing it was for the last time, he folded it with care. Kneeling before the chest, he placed the monk's clothing inside.

What would be Catalin's expression when she saw him in the light of day, a short time hence?

Worse yet, would she fight him when darkness fell and he took her to his bed?

CHAPTER 7

"IF YOU DON'T CALM yourself and eat something, you'll not have the strength to walk to the church." Hannah clucked her tongue and pushed a bowl of gruel in front of Catalin.

It was well past the noon hour when a heavy fist banged on the door of Catalin's chamber, startling them both. Before Hannah could reach it, Chief Broccin shoved it wide, nearly toppling her and little caring if his son's bride was with or without her clothing. Fortunately, Catalin had finished dressing.

"If 'tis not too much to ask for yer appearance, the priest waits at the church to speak the vows." Broccin near bellowed with impatience.

"Begone, Broccin. 'Tis a bride's right to tarry." Lady Joneta flapped her hands at her brother to shoo him out. "You are quarrelsome because your guts are growling. Quit hollering and get you to the church. We will be down afore you know it."

Broccin, his mouth gaping down to his chin, turned like a testy lad, his boots ringing on the floor as he stomped away. Seeing Letia and Elyne sitting on the bed, their hands making poor work of containing the giggles that escaped between their fingers uplifted Catalin's spirits.

His stomping footsteps faded while they checked one last time to assure everything was aright. Catalin's sky-blue smock peeked between the slits in the sleeves of a peacock blue kirtle that heightened the color of her eyes. Moridac had purchased the rare, dark silk and bade her sew a gown of it. She swallowed. It was to have been for wedding him that she had made it.

A woven circlet of violets and rose buds kept her hair from

her eyes, though there was naught they could do about her unruly reddish-blond curls. A gold-plated girdle rode low on her hips, the ends near touching her shoes when she walked. She wished she were as tall and lithe as Letia, or even Elyne's height. She, too, was slender while Catalin felt plump as a fattened goose bedecked in bright feathers, ready to be the main course at a feast.

Ugh. 'Twas too apt a description, for Chief Broccin hungered to add Hunter Castle and her bulging coffers to his own. Why would he not wait a sennight? She swallowed, not able to shake the feeling she was marrying a specter, for Ranald had been dead to the world half her life. She shuddered. Her hands began to sweat. Her skin crawled. She rubbed her arms then wrapped them around beneath her breast, hugging herself.

Was Ranald the same height his twin had been? She had not even come as high as Moridac's nose ... she blinked. Why had he not come to see her this day? Worst yet, why did he not come when his twin lay dying? Moridac had called for him. Ranald's name was the last word from his lips. Had Moridac known his twin was not dead, but hiding away at Kelso, waited upon by the monks there? Anger straightened her shoulders.

The sun kissed her forehead with a warm beam. How came they to be outside the keep? When had they left her room? Here she was at the foot of the stairway into the inner bailey. Baron de Burgh smiled at her and offered his wrist. His skin felt comfortingly warm to her cold fingers.

"Thank you, my lord. You are most kind to act for my father this day." Thank heavens her voice was firm and without a quaver.

"My old friend would have been most happy for you. And 'tis my pleasure to escort such a lovely bride to her vows." His voice held warmth; his smile was gentle.

She glanced behind her. Letia and Elyne followed, with Joneta and Hannah behind them. She took a deep breath and pasted a smile on her face. Hopefully, no one would note she fought the urge to bolt and escape across the drawbridge.

God help her. Could a man tell when a woman had lain

with another man? Why had she not asked Hannah? What would Ranald do when he bedded her and found she was not intact? Would he cast her out, disgraced and shamed? Oh my. She wanted to spew. Trying to swallow bile back, she gurgled.

"Have no fear, Catalin. Ranald will be a kindly husband to you." De Burgh looked down at her and patted her hand.

Oh, for shame! Was her fear so easy to see?

Two of Broccin's squires held the church doors wide for them to step through. They would hold the ceremony inside. Not all the guests that had come for her wedding to Moridac three sennights ago had the means to return. When her eyes adjusted to the dimness, she saw rows of people stood, craning their necks to look at her.

All she could spy at the end of the aisle were flowers decorating the railing before the altar and Father Martin who waited there. Raik stood to the right. Was that Ranald between him and Father Martin? The nearer they approached, the better she could see him.

Saints! She moved three steps closer. The guests swarmed around, jostled each other, their murmurs loud. So many eyes inspected her face. What did they hope to see?

She caught glimpses of Ranald again. Why had he dressed in black? His hair was cut short. Why did he not turn to greet her?

Three more steps. That was all that remained. Those standing in the first two rows of benches swayed back, allowing her eyes better access to her husband-to-be.

He must have noted them stirring about, for he started to turn. She took another step. Outside, the clouds shifted from the sun, sending a shaft of light through the window beside him.

Her right foot lifted to step forward then jerked to a halt. The tall man awaiting there, his back to her, had hair as black as Moridac's, aye, but it surrounded a tonsure! 'Twas not her groom but the monk from the garden. It had to be. Was he to be part of the ceremony? Did he stand in for Ranald? Was it to be a wedding by proxy?

She tugged on the baron's sleeve until he leaned close enough she could whisper in his ear.

"My lord, why is Ranald not here?"

"Catalin, Ranald stands afore you." De Burgh nodded and patted her shoulder.

Her eyes felt near to bursting from their sockets. God in heaven! They could not mean it. The man standing there was a monk. Were they daft? She caught her breath as he stated to turn. She jerked hard on de Burgh's tunic. He leaned down again.

"That is not Ranald. Can you not see a monk stands there? Though he looks like Moridac, he cannot be. This is a man of the cloth. I saw him last eve, and he wore the cassock of the brotherhood." Catalin forgot to whisper.

Snickers filled the air, floated clean to the rafters. Catalin turned to scowl around her. Were they in her shoes, she'd like to see how they would react!

"'Tis all right, my dear. Truly, Ranald stands there. Though he has been a monk, he is one no longer."

"Nay, nay." She shook her head. This was not Ranald, but the monk she had spoken to not many hours before. "I talked to him. They would not toss him from the abbey because he committed a sin against," she rose high on tiptoes, her lips near brushing de Burgh's ear as she gulped and whispered, "celibacy."

"Nay, Catalin. He committed no sin. The Pope has forgiven him his vows. 'Tis why he is free to come here to wed you."

The man in black had turned to face her. Her first full sight of him held her speechless. How could this happen? He had to be Ranald, for the left side was the same as Moridac. A black mask covered the right.

She swallowed, remembering last eve. As she had approached him, graceful, long fingers had tugged his hood low to cover his face.

Saints! It *was* Ranald.

What secret lay beneath the black leather? A terrible one, of course. Else, why would he need to hide it? Oh my. Was she going to faint like some spineless ninny? She feared so. Spots swam in front of her eyes. The floor shifted. Her knees started to buckle. De Burgh slipped an arm around her waist.

Kept her from splattering to the unyielding oak floor like an overripe pear.

"Give her to me."

A deep voice, the tone rich and dark. Strong arms closed around her. A warm, large hand pressed her head against a solid chest. How strange. She felt safe. His chin brushed across the top of her head, his cheek came to rest against hers. She took a deep breath. His was a remembered scent.

"Catalin, ye have naught to fear by wedding me," he whispered. "I am no longer a monk. I will explain all when we have privacy."

She gurgled. Ha. Little did he know of what she had to fear from him.

"Get hold of yerself, lass. Speak yer vows so we can get on with the feast."

Broccin's booming voice nearby brought her attention back to the man whose arms surrounded her. His head jerked up.

"Enough!"

She felt as much as she heard it, for the word vibrated from the firm muscled chest beneath her cheek.

"Dinna dare order ..." Broccin began.

"Hold ... yer ... tongue." Each word slowly and coldly given. A sharp, inflexible order.

Anger churned in Ranald as he spat out the words, for his body tightened against her. Chief Broccin remained silent.

"Are ye all right, Catalin?" Ranald held her shoulders, supported her as he moved back.

She peered up at the face leaning toward her. Her breath hitched like she had cried for a lengthy time. 'Twas strange to view the eyes of a man behind a mask, though it did not hinder seeing that eye it surrounded. Compassion looked back at her.

She blinked then nodded, too surprised to speak more.

"Come." Ranald took her elbow and led her to stand before Father Martin. "'Twould be best to start the ceremony now, Father."

Fearing his frightened bride needed bracing, Ranald kept a firm hand on her elbow, aiding her as they knelt before the priest. He couldna blame Catalin's reaction. She had met a monk only to learn he was the man she was to marry. A man she believed dead for many years. A disfigured man, at that. Even a woman past her prime would be frightened, much less a lass of ten and eight.

From the corner of his eye, he watched her pale face, the freckles sprinkled across the bridge of her nose prominent. He noted her small, white teeth biting her lower lip till he feared she would injure herself. She clasped her trembling hands so tight her knuckles gleamed white. He brought his hand to cover hers, his fingers patting her hand, as a mother would comfort a small babe's back.

Bit by bit, her trembling eased. He darted a glance and was glad to see color returning to her face. He squeezed her hands one last time, before helping her to rise as they repeated their vows. Her voice was so soft, Broccin objected.

"Speak up, girl. We must hear if we are to bear witness yer vows were said."

Catalin huffed, her brows creased, her jaw firmed. He would venture a guess she was getting the measure of his father and didn't like what she learned. She had shown spirit as a child. Mayhap it wouldn't be too long before she stood up to Broccin.

He took his mother's wedding ring off the little finger of his right hand, grateful Aunt Joneta had searched him out after his bath to place it in his palm. "Your mother gave it into my keeping when she was ill with the fever. She asked that I keep it safe for the day one of her sons would pass it to his bride," she had said.

As he held it before each of Catalin's fingers and said the proper words, he watched her face.

He held the ring at her index finger. "With this ring, I wed thee." He moved the ring to touch the tip of her middle finger. "With my heart, I honor thee." As he slid it to rest firmly on her third finger, he intoned, "With this body, I worship thee."

Her face grew ashen. She watched his hands on hers with fascinated horror, as if they were some unknown form of life that she must closely observe to see they meant no harm.

Did Catalin fear how they would touch her this night? Had no one told her what passed between a man and woman in the marriage bed? Or, mayhap they had?

After they repeated the vows, Father Martin kept the mass brief. No doubt at Broccin's orders. His sire had never entered the small church unless it was of such import that he must do so, preferring short visits to the chapel within the tower.

"Well now, man, are ye not going to kiss yer bride so we may have a turn?"

Raik's chuckle behind him was a reminder he had not yet given his bride the expected kiss. His lips had not caressed a woman's for so long a time. Did he remember how? He grasped her shoulders. He hesitated. Would she pull away? Turn her face from him?

He worried for naught. He glanced down to see Catalin, her chin lifted high, eyes tightly shut and lovely lips pursed, awaiting him. Mayhap he was too hesitant, for one eyelid fluttered open enough for a curious eye to peer through gold-tipped lashes at him.

He couldn't stifle a chuckle as he lowered his head. As his lips met hers, a long-held burst of air passed through her lips into his mouth. Nay, he had not forgotten how to kiss. But he had forgotten how soft, how sweet a woman's lips were. His loins stirred in the way that had plagued his memory, his dreams, that had caused him to seek penance more times than he could count.

"Hmpf! Devour the girl later. 'Tis hot in here."

Feeling Catalin startle, Ranald raised his head to glare at his father.

Raik felt static air coming from Ranald, and knew he fought to keep his temper leashed. He shouldered Broccin aside to step between them.

"We are kissin' cousins now, Catalin." With a smile for Ranald, he bent to place a loud, smacking kiss on her pale cheeks. She blinked. A small smile tilted her lips.

Ranald stood back as men took this one opportunity to place a kiss on the bride's face. Most were content to kiss her forehead, her cheek, but one brazen young knight stole a quick kiss on her lips. He pulled a long face and hurried away when Ranald glared at him.

Feeling eyes boring into him, the hair on Raik's neck prickled. He moved back a pace and surveyed those standing nearby. Ah. It was the man who had walked with Catalin. Their eyes met. His eyes were the same blue as Raik's own. He frowned. Why did this man watch him so closely? What had Catalin called him? Warin?

Was the woman beside him his daughter? Hm, a beauty. She had felt his thoughts, for she pressed against this Warin. Not a daughter then, but a wife half his age? Now he remembered!

It was Warin de Burgh of Seton Castle. They had met when Raik crossed the border to retrieve cows taken from Douglas lands and ran into a patrol. He had given de Burgh that scar on his jaw. Aye. And the baron had returned the favor when he rode to take them back. The wound on his thigh had putrefied, had been the reason his men had taken him to Ranald for healing. He should thank him for it else he never would have known his cousin lived.

He nodded at de Burgh then bowed to the man's wife. While at Castle Raven, they would act as strangers. No doubt, they would meet again in the dead of night.

"Enough kissin' the bride," Broccin ordered. "Cook has prepared a feast. 'Tis well past time for the evening meal." He gave a pointed look to Catalin, blaming her for the delay that day.

Catalin stuck her chin out and refused the guilt her father-by-law tried to force on her. The man was hateful. She had seen the looks he cast at Ranald. Like he resented him. Hated him, even. Did he wish Ranald was the son lying in the tomb beneath the castle?

The sun shone bright, bathing her in warmth as they walked toward the keep. She glanced up at Ranald, at his beautiful profile. Such a strong, masculine jaw, bronzed like he was often out of doors. Did monks spend so much time in the open? She peeked again and near stopped in her tracks. She had not noted it before, but when he looked to the right, the top of his black shirt moved and revealed a ridged, white scar, a scar that had not healed easily. Saints! Were there more? She hesitated for a heartbeat.

"What is it, Catalin? Did ye see someone ye wished to have words with?" Ranald's voice was soft, polite, his eyes questioning her.

Catalin swallowed. "Oh, aye. Hannah. She is quite aged. I feared she would be left behind."

He patted her hand. "She has not changed overmuch. I spied her in the crowd outside the church door. She is likely within the keep by now."

Catalin nodded. She tried to smile at all the well-wishers lining the path, throwing flower petals. How she wished the day was done. She caught her breath. Empty-headed fool! What was she thinking? Were it nightfall, she would be in Ranald's bed. Within his arms.

Of a sudden, she was cold. Chill bumps formed on her arms. Yet her hands sweated. It was fear, plain and simple. What a coward she was. She who thought herself so strong. Why, she had bossed Moridac and Ranald around as if they were her servants when she was but a child. And all they had done was tease her about it. Huh! Oh, to be that sprite again.

The great hall teemed with people, though there were fewer than when she was to wed Moridac. But today, they sounded more boisterous, everyone asking questions. She heard them. So did Ranald, by the feel of the rigid muscles in his arm.

"At Kelso?" A sultry-eyed woman panting so fast her bosoms heaved, poked her friend as they passed. "A monk? And such a lusty lad he was. What a waste."

"Aye. Me daughter said he ne'er tired. She be giddy he is back."

'Twas a sharp-nosed woman Catalin had seen working in the weaver's hut. Never tired? Was that possible? That night with her, Moridac had panted as if he had run up a steep hill. She jumped when another spoke. No doubt, the woman was hard of hearing, by the volume of her voice.

"Psst, Maud! Did ye see that great bulge?" 'Twas one of the serving women whose back was to them. Her head was down, and she did not see her friend flapping her hands at her. "His rod be eager to poke ..." Her words cut off when she looked up and saw her friend. She squeaked and left in such a hurry that she disturbed the air.

Thankfully, they reached the high table. Ranald stood behind her chair until she sat.

"Ranald!" Elyne shoved people aside and jumped up at her brother, depending on him to catch her. "Why did ye not let us know ye lived? Now that's stupid, is it not? 'Tis our *adoring* sire that hid ye away." She rained kisses over his left cheek, drew back and frowned at the black leather. "I have missed ye. I oft thought ye would be the only one who wouldna laugh at my mistakes."

Ranald's arms folded around his sister. "Still the imp, eh? Are ye not yet wed?"

"Huh! Ye wouldna ask if ye saw the pitiful suitors father parades through here. All scrawny lads. Not a true man amongst them. Put me down. Ye're squashing me."

Ranald laughed. Such a rich sound. He lowered Elyne till her feet touched the floor. "Well, now, mayhap he doesna want ye to wed as yet?"

Elyne smoothed her skirts. "More likely he canna find a man with enough wealth to make it worth his while, is more like it."

"Sit!" Broccin's voice cut through the big room.

People chattered and scrambled for their seats like chickens avoiding a raging rooster.

Pairs of servants carrying empty basins, drying cloths and pitchers of warm, scented water afloat with rose petals, streamed in to approach the high table. They washed and dried the newly wedded couple's hands before anyone else.

Ranald's father barely allowed them to cleanse his hands before he waved off the drying cloth. He grasped a goblet of wine and drank it down without taking a breath. His hand flapped at the page behind his chair until the lad replenished his wine then brought it to his lips again.

The Chief stood and banged his empty vessel on the table. He waited, scowling, until the page again filled it.

"We drink to my son, who has long been in hiding beneath a monk's skirts! He fulfilled his duty as a man today by wedding the beautiful Catalin." He leered and waved his goblet in the air at her. "I am hopeful he isna so saintly he forgot how to swive!"

CHAPTER 8

CATALIN GROUND HER TEETH. Did Chief Broccin have to be so crude? Nervous laughter rustled among the guests.

One man stood and shouted, "A man's brain may fergit but his rod remembers!"

"Aye! Aye!" echoed above the din of stamping feet.

The ribald humor assailed Catalin's ears. Neither she nor Ranald took a sip of wine or acknowledged the toast in any way. Tension prickled the air around her new husband. The hair on her arms felt much like when lightning struck close-by.

Baron de Burgh cleared his throat and stood. One had only to look upon his lordly face to sense his dignity. The room quieted.

"I speak for Catalin's father, my dear friend Lord Harold, God rest his soul. Catalin has been most fortunate. She has pledged her life to a man who will deal with her tenderly, will protect and cherish her." He smiled at Ranald. "May you both be blessed."

Ranald nodded, and without hesitation offered the silver wedding chalice to Catalin before sipping from it himself. She watched his long, slender thumb rub over the eagles etched into the tall cup made large enough for two. Moridac had told her of it, how it had served at his parent's wedding feast, his grandparents, even beyond them so many years no one remembered when first it came into use.

Soon, there had been toasts aplenty. How could her father-by-law quaff such a great quantity of wine without slipping to the floor to snore the day away? Huh. Mayhap fighting in the early crusades had so hardened his body that the wine's effects could not make its way to his brain. Her tension eased on seeing servants laden with platters and bowls of steaming food approach.

The mouth-watering aroma stirred Catalin's appetite. Platters of roasted pork covered with crushed wild garlic, capons bedecked with a wild cherry sauce, venison, beef, salmon and trout, all arrived at the table. Not as many vegetable choices followed, but she welcomed the peas with chunks of onions mixed in, beans with mushrooms floating amidst them, baked onions and small purplish red carrots sweetened with honey.

Ranald, his left brow quirked, waited for her preference.

"Husband, might I have a sliver of pork? 'Tis my favorite." Applying that title to the man beside her sent a shiver creeping down her back.

Ranald blinked. Stirred. 'Twas strange hearing the term husband coming from her lips. He leaned toward her.

"Ye prefer pork?" He tilted his head and studied her. "Ye who were forever chasing and grabbing piglets to hide them in the woods?"

Catalin's cheeks turned a delightful pink.

"'Tis a shame when grown they taste so good." She raised guilty eyes to him. "But, would it not also be a shame if their great sacrifice was for naught?"

"Aye. There is that to consider." His lips twitched when he speared a succulent morsel. They did not use trenchers this day, but pewter plates engraved with flowering thistles around their rims. Most likely it was Aunt Joneta's doing, as was the festive flowers decorating the room.

He motioned a server to fetch a platter near so he could select a plump capon. He spooned extra cherry sauce over it, for if he remembered rightly, his bride also was fond of the fruit properly sweetened with honey.

Both picked at their food, and after a small space opened on the plate they shared, she nodded toward the bowls of vegetables.

"Peas and carrots, if you please."

He had not remembered her voice being so melodic. Nor so soft. Truth to tell, when she was a sprite, he had thought it shrill and demanding. More oft than not, she was running around the baileys behind him and Moridac, ordering them about.

He filled the empty space, tore off a chunk of hot bread and placed a small, warmed pitcher of honey beside the plate. Unused to such a bountiful array to select from, he chose salmon and a portion of bread.

Catalin made the motions of eating, but when he watched closely, he kenned she moved food around on the plate more than she placed it in her mouth. What portions she did eat were so scant it would not fill a child.

Her fingers trembled, too. And he noted her frequent swallows, though no food was in her mouth. She felt his regard, for she snatched her hands down to her lap. Fearing she was ill, he started to lean closer to ask but had no chance.

Broccin stood, the movement jarring a belch so blaring it startled Catalin. His father beamed and patted his gut.

"I wager wee Catalin will soon be breeding." His grating laugh cut through the room. He rolled his eyes and bobbed his head as he added, "Aye. She will."

Ranald's breath halted then quickened with each word from his sire's lips.

Broccin wagged a finger at him as if he admonished him.

"For truth, Ranald's ballocks should be weighty as a bull's." He turned a sly grin on his son, his voice boomed. "Have ye not hoarded yer seed there, hidden beneath yer monk's skirts, since leaving Raptor Castle?"

Ranald clenched his hands. One held the chalice. He lowered it back to the table, not daring to lift it, else he would spray what was left within over his father's face. He fought to control his racing heart. He took a deep breath, held it then eased it out, bit by bit.

Across from his father, a gust of wind rustled flower petals strewn on the floor. The white linen cloth covering the long table stirred.

"I expect a grandson ere too long. The bairn will look

much like Moridac." Broccin stopped to chuckle, a drunken, gleeful sound.

Ranald closed his eyes. Fought for peace. The room hushed. Not for long before Broccin continued.

"'Tis thankful I am Ranald canna pass on his unsightly scars ..."

The breeze picked up, whirled in a circle rising from the floor before Chief Broccin, bringing the petals with it. Faster and faster, it grew until it created an eerie whistle.

The lord's heaped platter wobbled, lifted and spun in a wild circle, colliding with the petals. Morsels of capon, globs of cherry sauce, red carrots thick with honey, flew off and struck Broccin's belly. 'Twas strange. They struck no one else.

Ranald drew in a deep breath. Fought for quiet control. He groped for the cross that hung around his neck, forgetting for the moment 'twas no longer there. He opened his eyes.

Broccin stared at the table. His gaze fixed on his goblet, full to the brim. It rocked back and forth in a crazy way. Wine splashed over the rim, leaving purple splotches on the white cloth. He gaped as the vessel flew toward him. It struck his right shoulder. Wine splattered his chest. The goblet crashed back to the table and rolled to stop against a basket of bread.

Broccin roared. Slapped at the mess on his best tunic. Startled chatter filled the air.

"Did ye see?"

"What goes here?"

"'Tis no wind without!"

"It took to the air like a hand tossed it."

Catalin's startled cry brought Ranald's thoughts to her. He turned his back to his father and saw her wide-eyed look.

"Ye have naught to fear, wife." Ranald reached to take her hand and found his own was none too steady. He slowed his heaving chest, kept his eyes on her lovely face and deliberately studied the pattern across her nose. Since she was a sprite, he had oft thought the sprinkling of freckles there lent such mischief to her face.

Raik, on her other side, spoke up so the room could

overhear.

"The wind has been much strange of late. Little puffs become strong, sometimes near to shaking leaves from the trees."

"Aye." Angus shouted from the farthest corner of the room. "One of me young stable lads told of a lone breeze that grew strong as a gale. It pushed water from the horse trough, it did."

"'Twas me son Donald. I thought the lad was telling an untruth till he pointed out the soaked ground." Hearing disbelieving chuckles, the man scowled. "Dinna laugh. I saw it with me own eyes."

"Broccin, I ken you need a change of clothing. Mayhap you had best hie yourself above?" Joneta's nose lifted high in a sniff.

"Hmpf! Dinna order me about."

Though he protested, he held the sticky tunic out from his body and thought better of keeping it on. To Ranald's disgust, his father cared not to leave the table but pulled the garment over his head and threw it to the floor, baring his hairy, muscled chest.

Elyne rolled her eyes and pursed her lips. Letia avoided looking in Broccin's direction. Catalin made a small sound, surprising Ranald, for she had sucked her teeth. Aye, 'twas in disapproval, though delicately done.

"Ye there," Broccin stabbed a finger at the closest squire. "Go above and bring me clean clothing."

The squire scampered off not chancing a harsh cuff for lingering.

Joneta's slight bob of her head signaled servants to clear the tables. By the time they finished, their lord was again properly clothed. Cheeses, baked apples nestled in custard, grapes, plums and pears arrived, as did dishes of baked tarts, custards, sugared delicacies and wafers.

Jugglers, acrobats and troubadours took turns filing in to entertain the diners after their heavy meal. Once everyone was enjoying the sweet offerings and kept occupied watching the center of the room where a young man strummed a lap harp and sang of a beautiful maiden, Ranald leaned close to Catalin.

"Mayhap ye should steal away while all are occupied?" he whispered. He knew not which smelled the sweeter, her silky hair or the violets in the garland of flowers around her forehead.

He caught Joneta's and Elyne's eyes and looked pointedly toward the doorway. Thankfully, they understood. He hoped his bride could leave afore his father embarrassed her further.

He hoped for naught. Catalin no more than stood, than Broccin's head lifted. His nose wrinkled, as if scenting game. His eyes gleamed; he rubbed his hands together. Ranald could near hear the thoughts going through the man's thick skull.

He didna like them.

Joneta, Elyne and Letia formed around Catalin. The ever-faithful Hannah stood waiting in the doorway. The first drunken man to stand, no doubt thinking to follow the women, earned her wrathful glare and sat back down.

Ranald didn't like his father's leering regard of Catalin. If he dared to rise, Ranald would not hesitate to stop him. His tense shoulders relaxed when Raik came to take Catalin's vacated space.

"Ye ate no more than a morsel of salmon." He tilted his head, his teasing eyes studying Ranald's face. "Are ye still hesitant of what faces ye this night?"

Ranald shifted in his seat, remembering his blood racing each time he caught Catalin's scent. The mere thought of it tightened his groin.

"Lucifer is having a good laugh, cousin. Not even a sennight from Kelso and already I forget."

"Forget?" Raik, lifted his shoulders, a hand raised, palm up.

"Aye. On how to turn my mind from lustful thoughts."

"Ye are troubled by it?"

"Should I stand, I will shame myself. I hardened before the words left my mouth for Catalin to go above."

Raik's laughter brought attention to them.

"'Tis a good thing, ye know." He spoke low for no other ears to hear. "How else can ye consummate this union? Limp as a wilted carrot willna work, as well ye ken."

"Hmpf. 'Tis no fear of that." He rubbed his chin. E'en though he had scraped his face smooth hours earlier, already bristles grew there.

"Well, then, ye worry for naught. Once abed, all will come natural again." Raik grinned at him. "I hope the baker's daughter still favors me. I plan to spend the hours until dawn warming her pallet."

"Dinna fill Raptor Castle with yer bastards, cousin. It will be my duty to feed and care for them. From the children I have glimpsed this day, Moridac had oft sown his seed."

"Do we not return to my own bedchamber?" Catalin gulped when Lady Joneta passed by it to push open a door a good fifteen footsteps down from the one she had used since coming here.

"Nay, child. We go to Ranald's room. 'Tis the room he shared with his brother since they were young lads." She smiled at Hannah, who arrived out of breath to close the door behind them. The two had become fast friends over the years.

Catalin's steps faltered on entering Ranald's chamber. She felt lost in it. Her heart fluttered seeing her clothing chest midway along the wall to the right. Though it was large, it looked small as a child's in this spacious room.

Hearing the door close, she glanced behind her and noted what must be a man's clothing chest, for it was large and sturdy, on the wall to the right of the door. Propped beside it was a sword and scabbard. It had not been Moridac's, for the hilt held no gold plate, nor was it adorned in any way. This sword was used by a man not driven by the trappings of wealth.

"I am to share my husband's room?" Her breath caught. She would have no privacy, no way to hide if sickness came early in the morn. Oh, dear saints.

Her toes curled thinking of her sin in deceiving Ranald.

Heaven help her. What could she have done? If she carried Moridac's bairn, she had to protect it. Would Ranald kill her for it?

Lady Joneta's voice distracted her as she eased the circlet

of flowers from Catalin's hair.

"Always have the wives shared their husband's bed at Raptor Castle." Her soft voice was kindness itself.

Noting the bed, Catalin's stomach flipped. More than twice the size of a normal one. Mayhap 'twas a good thing? Could she not put distance between them when they lay there?

A maid hustled to remove a green bedcover the shade of dense leaves as darkness fell, and placed heated stones between the sheets.

A thought struck. Perchance Ranald would not wish to claim his husbandly rights? Aye. Might he have a dislike for bed sport? Perchance 'twas why he became a monk? She clung to that hope.

"Hold your hands high, lovey," Hannah urged. She and Elyne gripped the hem of the blue kirtle and took care to lift it free of Catalin's head.

"Why do ye tremble?" Elyne's brows drew close together. "Ranald is a gentle man. Always he has been such. Many a lass greeted the sun with a smile following a night spent in his … Ack!"

A sharp pinch from Lady Joneta had halted her words.

Catalin was undressed except for the thin, sky blue smock.

"Come sit whilst I brush your hair." Letia placed a chair behind her friend. She grinned at Hannah as she filched the brush from her hands. "You have the chance to play with her hair every day. Do you know how much I envy your hair, Catalin?" She patted the shining hair in front of her. "'Tis a special color, neither red nor golden like the sun, a mixture of each at their finest, all soft and glowing." She picked up a curly hank and played with it. "The curls spring back when I stretch them out."

"For truth you like it? But curls are unruly, forever falling over my face."

As if making her point, one elfin curl crept over her forehead. She pushed out her bottom lip and huffed air upward, fluttering it from her eyes.

Elyne chuckled and bent to take Catalin's shoes from her

feet. She grinned up at her.

"Ranald always remarked about yer curls after ye returned home from a visit."

"No doubt to call them tangled knots like he was used to doing." Catalin wrinkled her nose.

"Nay. Bird's nests." Elyne laughed so hard she lost her balance and plopped down on the floor.

Amongst the laughter and giggles, the door creaked opened. Ranald stood framed there, the corners of his lips lifted a bit. Chief Broccin caused the women to scramble, though, for he shoved Ranald aside and stomped halfway across the room.

Catalin jumped to her feet and edged close to the bed, prepared to grab a pillow to shield herself did he come closer.

"'Tis time for a bedding, not for women's senseless cackles." Chief Broccin glared at Elyne. His hands rested on his waist, his fingers drummed there, impatient. "Why is she not nakit?"

"My wife is not for yer eyes, Broccin." Ranald's steely words cut through the room. "There will be no bedding ceremony."

"No bedding? How am I to know she has no flaws? No marks to mar my grandchild?" He stepped forward, a steely hand reached to grasp the smock from Catalin's cringing shoulders.

A strange sound filled the room, a buzz somewhat like angry words falling over themselves. Before Broccin could step closer, the chair Catalin had risen from scrapped forward and fell, blocking his path.

He scowled, reached to pick it up. His tunic flapped, whipped about his long legs and lifted clean to his shoulders. He snapped upright. Yanked it down in back, only to have the front fly up.

Catalin stepped back, near gagged. She could not mistake her father-by-law's member, swollen and upright, straining and near bursting his breeches in lewd excitement. She clamped her eyelids closed.

Broccin teeth snapped together. He grabbed hold of his tunic, trapping it against his thighs.

"You disgrace yourself, brother. Get from this room else

I'll take that chair across your nasty head." Lady Joneta's anger filled the room.

Catalin peeked in time to see her hit his shoulders with her fists, driving him toward the door whilst shooing everyone from the opening.

Broccin stamped through the doorway, yet tried for the last word.

"Dinna forget, Ranald. I would see the blood-stained sheet come dawn to prove ye are still a man!"

CHAPTER 9

CHIEF BROCCIN SLAMMED AGAINST the doorframe like a hand had pushed him. He caught hold of it and steadied himself, his eyes wide, then trod away, muttering.

Raik, his arm across Ranald's shoulders, laughed and playfully slapped his cousin's head before stepping away.

"I kenned it would come in handy."

Catalin frowned. What had come in handy? He talked in riddles. The strange sound dimmed. Had it been the men on the landing all talking at once?

"Turn yer backs," Elyne demanded, "so we may tuck the bride in bed."

She waited until Ranald, Raik and Baron de Burgh obediently faced the wall.

Letia pulled down the covers, Elyne thumped the pillow while Hannah lifted the smock over Catalin's head. She slid between the sheets. Naked. Vulnerable. Her arms blossomed with chill bumps.

Elyne bent to hug her and kiss her forehead.

Letia leaned close to whisper, "He is a good man. He will be gentle with you."

Hannah waited until they moved away. She pulled the covers up to Catalin's chin and bent close.

"Do not fear, lovey, all will be well," she whispered, patting the pillow, pretending to smooth it. "I secreted a small vial beneath your pillow. Once Ranald is done, empty it on the sheets without his seeing."

Empty what? She questioned Hannah with her eyes, but

had no chance to ask, for Baron de Burgh called to them.

"Come, ladies. We are needed here no longer." De Burgh smiled and held his hand out to his wife.

Catalin wished she could protest and ask the women to stay. But what could she ask of them? Would that she could pull her smock back on.

Her fingers itched to delve beneath the pillow. Perchance by the vial's shape, she could tell what it contained. While she pondered her problem, they left. She was alone.

Ack! No, not alone. Ranald stood at the bed's foot. Why did he not move?

He did. He straightened; his jaw squared. She noted shadows darkening his cheeks, his upper lip and chin. His raven black eyes glistened in the candlelight as he circled the room and snuffed the candles out, one by one. He left but one aglow, there on the table beside the bed, for it was a moonless night.

He strode over to the big chest. 'Twas a good distance from door to bed. She could see only his shadow. Glad of it, too, for he started removing his clothes. He took such care with each piece, seeming unfamiliar with it.

Of course. How foolish of her. He was unused to the trappings of a lord. Each item he removed, he folded and placed inside the chest. His belt he draped over the peg above it. He looked around, searching for something. Ah, his sword. It had fallen when the men had jostled into the room. He stepped over to it.

She bit her lip. He was naked, for she saw the outline of his body. Why did he bring the sword to the bed?

"Eep!"

"Is aught wrong?" He propped the sheathed sword near the head, even with his pillow, then stilled, awaiting her answer.

"Nay. I caught my hair in my ring. It startled me. Thank you for it."

"Ye thank me for the ring pulling yer hair?"

"Nay, for certes not. For the ring. 'Tis very beautiful."

In a graceful movement, he slid between the sheets whilst he spoke. "My mother would delight to know ye liked it. She was most fond of the blue stone at its center."

The bed ropes swayed a bit as he settled on his side, facing her. She grasped the edge of the bed so as not to roll toward him.

"It brings to mind the color of yer eyes," he continued.

She fidgeted. The stone was a beautiful shade of blue. Should she thank him for comparing her eyes to it? Mayhap she should keep him talking, and he would fall asleep? Ack, no chance of that, for his big hand came up to cup her face.

Ranald saw the whites of Catalin's eyes in the dim light, her pale face surrounded by sunlit hair on the white pillow. The closer he came to her, the more the faint scent of violets and woman's flesh quickened his breath. Which was sweeter? His nose brushed her cheek as his lips neared hers.

Hm, 'twas the scent of a woman, by far. Her lips were the softest of petals. His tongue traced their fullness, dipped in that small hollow at the corners. She didn't pull away.

'Twas a good sign.

His breath hitched. His tongue slid between her lips to brush over her teeth, to feel the softness inside her lips. She opened to him, let his tongue glide over hers, play with it. Hesitant at first, her tongue stirred against his. He took his time, not wanting to force anything from her. His mouth left hers, trailing kisses across her cheek, her jaw, to the hollow beneath her ear.

Her hair had warmth to it as it cradled his cheek. Life, too, for it clung to the top of his mask, to the leather straps holding it firm. For the moment, he ignored it, much preferring to nibble her ear.

He wanted to taste her. He licked a small spot there on her neck, then around to the hollow at its base. He kissed there, then across her collarbone and back again.

Raik had it aright. He hadna forgotten the thrill of making love. His abstinence made it all the more exciting. His heart's beating drummed in his ears. Could she hear it?

Slow, so not to startle her, he stole the sheet off her, pulling it across his body to land behind him. She shivered. Was she cold? Frightened? He slid his left arm under her neck and with his right hand on her left hip, turned her to face him. She was stiff at first, until he returned to kissing her.

Catalin greeted him, seemed eager even, for she parted her lips, inviting him. No doubt, she thought to delay more serious moves upon her body. His kisses were more demanding now, exploring deeper, becoming more urgent. She gasped, put her hands on the back of his head to bring him closer and opened wider. To his surprise, she suckled his tongue.

'Twas a verra good sign, for certes.

Pleasure shot through him. He stroked down her side, dipped in to her tiny waist then cupped her hip. Were his calloused fingers rough on her flesh? Did they scrape her? He hoped not. How wonderful she felt. He lingered on the softness of her thigh before easing back up again to knead her soft nether cheek. Cupping her firm bottom, he brought her closer to him. Against his own hips. She had felt his straining sex, for she flinched as if he had burned her.

His kisses became more urgent, demanded more. He stroked up the curve of her back, stopped and moved to outline gently the soft swell of her breast with his fingertips. She quivered when he bypassed her nipple to smooth over her shoulder and arm.

He nuzzled her ear. Took deep breaths in the hair behind it. Her arms moved down around his neck, hugging him.

"Ye should bear a flower's name, wife, for ne'er have I savored anyone so sweet." Her arms slackened.

'Twas not a good sign.

The years had not made him less the fool to mention making love to other women! He groaned and kissed her again. Soon she responded with growing fervor. He caressed her breasts, still avoiding her nipples, but running his fingertips around them, over her soft globes. She squirmed when he cupped and squeezed them.

He rolled, slipping her body beneath him. She ran her

hands over his shoulder to his back. They stopped, hesitated. Then explored. Inch by slow inch. Would the horror of his back repulse her?

Ranald rose up on his elbows to break the contact and giving room between their heated skins so he could feel every inch of her. How he had missed this! As his fingertips pressed the fullness of a breast, her nipple thrust against his palm. His head dipped. He wet his lips. He groaned when they formed around that hard bud. He rolled it between his lips, teased it. He lapped over it. It was like a small raspberry. She gasped and thrust up at him, urging him to suckle. He did.

She shivered then squirmed against him. Restless hands brushed over his head. His mask slid, the ties loosening. He started to raise his head. She grasped him tight to her breast. He reached up and stretched her arms to rest on the pillow above her head. With one hand holding them there, he tossed his mask aside. He could take no chances, though, and kept a firm grip on her wrists.

"Release me." She tugged, tried to free them.

"Nay, wife. Be still. I dinna want to bruise ye."

She shivered when he went from one breast to the other, sharing his kisses, his snuggling against them, while his hand roved. Her belly quivered when he brushed over it. He felt its soft roundness. It pleased him noting she was not all sharp angles, but ripe, soft curves down to the juncture of her body.

He groaned. So warm there in the crease of her thighs. His fingers played with the hair shielding her sex. He combed through it until he found what he sought. The full lips that guarded her core. 'Twas hot. Damp. Sliding between them, he welcomed the slickness.

Ah. 'Twas a verra good thing!

Ranald had deliberately ignored his body. Until now. It demanded attention, throbbed and strained. Every part of him was taut as a Welsh bow. His face. His neck. The muscles in his arms. His stomach. And, of course, his throbbing arousal.

He hesitated, for Catalin had not yet opened her legs to him. He reminded himself she was virgin still and knew naught of love play. He nudged his knee between her thighs. At first, she tensed. His gentle coaxing caused her to follow his lead until he could nestle his hips between her thighs.

"Please. Let me touch you." She was breathless in her request.

"Nay. This night I will touch you." He fondled her cheek with his unmarked one, being careful to stroke upward to keep his stubble from chafing her delicate skin. He moved against her, caressed her with his body. With each stroking movement, his tarse smoothed over her, teased her, until her feet dug into the bed and she lifted to him, groaning, seeking what she needed.

His impatient tarse nudged her cleft, entered slowly. Hot flesh closed around him. She was tight, delightfully so. He entered, then withdrew, each slow stroke dipped deeper. As he suckled her breasts, her wetness built easing his way. He thrust deep to seat himself. Though she flinched, naught hindered his way.

He stopped. Lifted his head to peer at her in the dark. Hesitated. Not for long, for that tight, hot silkiness surrounding his tarse called to him. He buried his face in her hair and rocked, faster with each stroke. Her body's heat scorched him. All her muscles tensed, were rigid. Then her stomach started to quiver.

Catalin writhed and thrashed beneath him. She jerked, twisted her hands, trying to free them. He clamped them tight, balanced himself and reached between them to touch there where he entered.

Catalin cried out. Her back arched. She exploded around him. While she throbbed and strained, he allowed his own release.

The two of them grappled each other until the bed sheets were near on the floor. Finally, their passion calmed. He dropped his head to her shoulder, panting, waiting for his heart to ease. When he was again in control, he rose up, released her hands and moved to her side.

He put his arms above his head, protecting his face should she decide to touch him. Catalin was very still. Stiff, even. He felt around for his mask, sat up, fitted it to his face and tied the leather. He padded over to the lone candle that was near to spluttering out. Holding it low before him, he gazed at his sex, his thighs.

He strolled over to the bed. Held it over the rumpled sheets. Over her. Catalin hugged her belly. Turned her back to him. A deep sigh burst from his lips. He lit two more candles afore the flame could die then set them on the table.

He stretched out alongside her. Knew why his father was so gleeful. Why he insisted he produce bloodstained sheets.

The candle flames flickered as anger thrummed through him. His fists clenched, his nails dug into his palms knowing why 'twas so urgent he leave Kelso. Why they couldna wait until he and Catalin could learn to know each other again. Why trick him so? That his father had was what angered him. And Catalin?

He turned to his side. His body was like a plank, so tense his waist did not dip into the bedding when he propped his head on his fist to study her. Grasping her shoulder, he rolled her to her back.

Catalin was fearful. Had reason to be. She had deceived *him*.

Her eyes shut. Tight. Not enough to keep the wetness from escaping, though. He felt more than saw it. His finger caught a tear as it slipped toward her ear, brought it to his lips. He tasted the saltiness of it.

He sighed, willing the anger to ease. He moved her arms from her belly. Rested his hand, splayed across it to feel her plump flesh.

"Moridac's child nestles here?" He rocked his hand on her flesh.

"I know not. 'Tis too soon to tell." Catalin's voice hitched, wobbled.

"On remembering my sire's triumphant laugh, I suspect he hopes 'tis so."

He fell back on the bed. It rocked like a small craft on a windy day. He stilled. Thought. He listened to her muffled sobs. He sprang from the bed. Padded across the cold floor. One by one, he lit the candles in the room.

"Come. Rise. I would see what we must deal with."

Catalin's chest ached, her neck strained, trying to hold back sobs. His voice was so cold, so harsh. How could she have been such a fool to yield to Moridac's lightest touch? What was to happen to her now? Ranald knew she was an impure bride. If only she had blurted out her confession in the garden. He could have refused to marry her and saved himself the shame of an unfaithful wife afore he even wed.

"Wife. I await."

Menace tinged Ranald's voice. The words so forced, as if through clenched teeth. She fought the urge to rise and flee, but did not. His hands would clamp around her neck afore she reached the door. She swiped her arms across her cheeks, trying to hide her tears. Bad enough she had come to him a tainted wife, but worse were she a coward too. Ranald stood beside the bed, his hand out-thrust. She rested her icy hand in his and stood, clutching the sheet to her chest.

Though every portion of his body had touched hers, she had no image of him. Had he not imprisoned her hands and she had felt him with them, he would not startle her so now. How came a monk to be so strong, so hardened? Did they not idle the day away in prayers?

This man looked every inch the warrior knight, from his massive shoulders to... Saints! She was cold no longer. Surely, her blush covered her from head to toe? If it had not before, it did now that he pulled the sheet from her fingers. It rustled to the floor.

Why was he silent? What she was staring at with her eyes finally registered in her brain. His body had strange scars, for they curved from his sides inward. What caused such heavy scarring? He shifted, bringing her thoughts back to him.

He again raked his fingers through the hair above his forehead. It did not help.

"Yer instinct led ye to protect yer belly, Catalin. I note it as an instinct of a breeding woman."

Her eyes followed where he looked. A torrent of melted snow could not have made her colder. She had thought grief had kept her woman's time away. It had before. In truth, fear had nagged at her. She should have known.

Her breasts were fuller, her nipples a slightly deeper hue. She raised her left arm to cover them. Her right went over her belly. She had ever been rounded, had felt like a plump goose. Her belly did not sink in like a slender woman's would. Both arms curled around herself, protecting her body should he beat her.

"Get back into bed. I'm not going to harm you."

She scrambled to sit back on the bed and clutched the sheet again. He shoved her down flat, then rounded the bed and went over to the basin and pitcher of water on a corner table. The candles he had brought to the bedside table lit his back to her view when he walked to his chest to hunt around in it.

Blessed Mary! His flesh looked as if some strange creature had burrowed beneath his skin, leaving thin, raised tunnels that crisscrossed each other. Her stomach heaved. She realized why the scars were so heavy. For truth, the mud had been nigh impossible to clean from his torn flesh. How had he not died? Surely, he had suffered long, hovering between life and death. Thinking on the man who had done this to his son, she felt a roiling hate for Chief Broccin of Raptor Castle.

"I need yer help, Catalin."

Ranald sat in the center of the bed. He bunched the sheets under his spread thighs. She blinked and shut her eyes.

"Ye canna help me with yer eyes shut, woman."

She opened them, stared. For the first time she saw a man's sex nested amongst the hair of his groin.

Where before his shaft had felt long and hard as pewter, now it appeared soft and boneless. What had happened to it? It rested atop two large, slightly hairy, vein-streaked ballocks, strange looking things that they were.

Oh God. He gripped a dirk! He meant to kill her. She scooted back against the head of the bed, slamming into it.

"What ails ye?" His head popped up.

The candlelight behind him threw his face in shadows. He looked wicked. Frightening, with his mask hiding so much of him.

She gurgled and nodded at the dirk.

"Dinna be a dolt. 'Tis for me."

"You? You would kill yourself for my sin?" She grasped her throat, about to gather breath for a hearty screech.

"Quiet. I dinna want to cut too deep."

He shook his head and huffed, then bent his right leg up to lay it back on the sheet, spreading it so he could reach an area at the edge of the hair nestled there. He laid open a slit no longer than to the first knuckle of her little finger. Blood welled. He did the same to his other groin.

"Come. Straddle me." He twisted at the waist to toss the blade on the table. He spread his legs wide and beckoned her.

She sat there, mute as a babe, not understanding what he wanted.

"Hurry, afore the bleeding stops."

She didn't budge. He grasped her waist and dragged her to his lap then placed her legs around him. Once he positioned her where he wanted her, he moved beneath her, rubbed her cleft over his intimate areas, her thighs over him.

Heat flirted with her again, for her woman's flesh felt every least bit of him. That thing was changing form again, too. She bent her head and peered at it. Aye. It did not look the same as earlier. Nor did if feel as hard as when he took her. She held to his shoulders. Why was he doing this? He did not seem inclined to kiss or touch her in any other way.

Finally he stopped, for the wounds stopped flowing. Bloodstains were on her thighs, her nether lips. Blood smeared the sheets, too, as well as his rod and ballocks. She nodded. Understood.

"Aye. My sire will have the stained sheets he demanded."

His voice was so very grim. He stood then wrung cold water from the cloth in the basin and approached her.

"Open."

"What?"

"I would cleanse ye as if 'twas ye who had bled. Just enough to show I aided ye."

"I can do it."

"Nay. Likely, ye would wash my hard-earned labors away. Fall back," he commanded.

She did, pulling her pillow to cover her face as he dabbed at her legs, her core. Though she had not been a virgin, the cold cloth soothed skin that had been unused to such activity. When he was done, she slapped the pillow down to cover her private parts. Something rolled and tangled in her curls.

"Ack! A varmint has nestled in my hair!"

She bolted up, swatting at her head, sure that some creature lodged there. Whatever it was, it bounced against Ranald.

"What the . . .?" He rolled it around in his hand then scowled at her. "Yer intent was to play the virgin?"

"Blessed Saints!" She craned her neck to see the object. 'Twas the forgotten vial Hannah had given her. It was red. "When you arrived at the door, Hannah secreted it under my pillow and told me to use it. I did not know what it was or when I was supposed to do something with it. Please, forgive me."

She watched his fist tighten around the vial until his knuckles gleamed white as a peeled onion. Did he think she told an untruth? She hoped not, for she already had much for him to forgive. To her surprise, he laughed. Was he daft?

"I stabbed myself for naught. 'Tis good the blade was clean. I would hate to die from a festering wound of my own making."

Catalin could not believe he was doing so much to save her from scorn.

"What will happen when a babe arrives afore it should?"

"When did Moridac come to yer bed?"

"The night before he went hunting and was gored."

"I will claim 'tis mine. If he looks like Moridac, he will look like me. If I say the child is mine, who can say me nay?"

"You would do this for Moridac's child? For me?"

Ranald heaved a sigh filled with sadness.

"Wife, I doubt ye have changed so verra much over the years. My brother had a silver tongue. As young men, I heard more than one lass talked into putting aside caution. I doubt not he argued what did it matter when ye were to wed?"

"Two days afore the wedding. But I should not have listened.

The sin is still mine."

Though he held his anger in check, she saw he seethed with it. His eyes blazed in a tight face, his jaw was rock-hard, his stance stiff. She swallowed before she reminded him.

" 'Twas that sin I wanted to confess and ask the monk, uh, you, in the garden for forgiveness and guidance." Her voice wobbled.

"Ye should have confessed to me, the man, afore we swived. We would still be wed. Though I am deeply angered, it is not at ye. Do ye think me so cruel I would not protect ye? Now come, we must sleep. 'Twill be dawn before ye know it."

With sharp bursts of air, he darkened the candles. He thumped his pillow and settled back on the bed. Of a sudden, he loomed up again. He hovered over her, studied her, before dropping back beside her. She had sniffled. The bed ropes creaked, strained then quieted.

"Sleep. I willna thrash ye."

A deep, drawn-in sigh exploded from him, before he spoke again.

"Yet!"

chapter 10

Yet? Catalin's eyelids flew high to near ruffle her brows. He was thinking on it? She shuddered. 'Twould be better to be done with now than dread waiting for the first blows to fall. She grabbed the sheet in her fists and clutched it tight to her neck.

Likely he would not be as heavy-handed as her Uncle Hamon, her only living relative, had been. Though Hamon was her mother's brother, he was nothing like that sweet woman had been. He had been furious when she refused to marry Moridac soon after her father died.

Moridac had noted the fading bruises on her arms when she foolishly wore a wide-sleeved tunic. He shook her uncle and threatened to flay him did he dare strike her again. So to heart did her uncle take it, he refused to again accompany her to Raptor Castle.

In case Ranald slept, she dared not move. She caught her breath and edged her head to the side to venture a peek at him in the dim light. She saw his profile, saw the white of his left eye shining. Saints! He did not sleep. He stared at the ceiling.

Fearful he would feel her gaze on him, she squeezed her eyes shut and sought sleep. Ha. As if that were possible. Her racing mind went back over their time in bed. With that one night with Moridac, she had not the experience to tell, but she had not expected a monk-turned-man to relish bed sport.

Ranald had not hesitated to touch her, had seemed to delight in it. Her body flushed, remembering. Moridac had not savored each touch like his brother had but had lingered only long enough to prepare her for him. Soon as he attained his release, he had moved away. She remembered wanting something more, but not knowing what it was.

She knew now.

Ranald had pleasured her until all strength had drained from her, so tumultuous had been her release. Judging from the fervor of his thrusts, his own explosive release, he had enjoyed their joining as much as she.

If not for his tonsure, never would she have believed he had lived as a monk. Her eyelids flew wide again. Could he have remembered how to make bed-sport from when he was a young man? Had he practiced? Mayhap he had not been celibate. Were there women housed in the abbey? By chance, a comely cook? How could she ask him?

"Go to sleep!"

Ranald had not thought a lass could startle so much she would near fall off the bed. Catalin clutched the sheet to her forehead and went so still he feared she had stopped breathing.

In his mind's eye, he could see his father sleeping with a grin spread wide on his face. No doubt gleefully anticipating telling one and all that the sheets had been snowflake white. No stains of lovemaking. No telltale red proving the bride had been untried. Knowing him, he would demand to see Ranald's arms, his legs, to spy evidence of a cut.

He would wear naught but a kilt when he rose, baring his arms. Would let the kilt ride up his thighs when he mounted Satin's Spawn. When he came into the bailey after a bout of sword practice with Raik, he would strip and rinse at the well. Naught would show that he was misleading them, for he had chosen his areas well. For them to be visible, he would have to balance on his head, his legs widespread to the sky.

Ah, to deceive Broccin! He burned knowing how his father had deceived him. He had given no hint Moridac had sampled his betrothed. His remark of the babe favoring his brother was dafty, since they were identical twins — except for the unsightly scars. Likely, Moridac had been the fool and bragged to his sire.

He clutched the vial tight in his fist. Once Catalin slept, he would conceal Hannah's token at the bottom of his scabbard.

'Twas enough room there for the sword to share. While with Raik, he would empty the vial, crush it and spread dirt over it. An uneasy thought struck. Had Raik known? He would find out. If he knew and had not warned him, he would pay for it.

Finally, the black sky gave way to the faintest hint of gray. He eased from the bed, and it took him but a blink in time to hide the vial. He padded over to the open window and knelt, letting cold air flow over his naked body as he prayed throughout what was left of the night.

'Twas near a penance.

He too had practiced deception.

All the years at Kelso he fought his body's craving for a woman's flesh. Had prayed and believed he was a pious monk. Until anger would shake him when someone sought to prey on his defenseless brethren. He had relished the fight. Guilt afterward had made him seek penance.

That first time after the killing was over, he had gone to the chapel in the dead of night. He had shrugged from his black robes, his rope belt holding them bunched around his waist. He gritted his teeth, took the monks' flagellum and scourged his back. He used all his force to strike the whip over his shoulders, down to his hips. Blood ran hot down his flesh.

Prior Godric came into the chapel to pray. The prior tried to stop him, but could not. Not until Abbot Aymer arrived, breathless from running with the prior, did he listen. The abbot's calm voice convinced him that though Ranald thought to deliver his own punishment in God's name, it was not what God demanded of him.

Nay. He was man. Not a monk. Had been all the time. His piety had been a lie. Else, how could his pleasure tonight have been so intense, so ecstatic?

His head sprang up, hearing a strange sound from across the room. Catalin sat upright, her eyes scrunched tight, holding both hands over her mouth. He didna puzzle overlong on it.

"Ye are ill?"

Her eyelids flung open. Distress and fear warred with each other there. Distress won. She scrambled from the bed and yanked forth a light wooden bucket from beneath, one most likely whose normal use was for collecting duck eggs. Her arms went around it. Hugged it.

"Ohhh." He heard a splash, a muffled, "I'm sorrryyy," quavered from her lips.

He couldna use the bloodstained water in the basin. He grabbed the half-full pitcher and cloth, grateful the water had chilled even more during the night. He went over to kneel on the cold floor by his bride. He slipped his arm around her for support, dipped the cloth in the water, then held it to her forehead, her eyes, while she wretched. Once done, he wiped her face. Shamed eyes asked his forgiveness.

"Ye are better now?"

A slight nod was answer. He pried her arms from the bucket and set it aside, then rose. Not until her face flushed did he remember they were both naked as babes. 'Twas a wonder his squatting beside her did not send her into a swoon.

"Come. Back into bed with ye."

He lifted her in his arms and placed her on the sheet, covered her, then folded the cold cloth over her eyes. It would help soothe her and shield her gaze from his body.

He poured water into the bucket, sloshed it around and flung the contents out the window. Too late, he looked to assure himself no one walked below. 'Twould not have been a pleasant way to start the day.

"Stay abed this morn. No one expects a bride to rise till well into the day."

"I am so sorry, Ranald."

The words made him stiffen.

"Did ye not know how babes are made when ye allowed Moridac into yer bed?"

"Aye. I knew. But I did not know but one time could make a babe. Letia has been a wife for years, and she is not breeding."

"Baron de Burgh isna a young, lusty man. Were he such, she would have a bairn at her breast afore now."

Seeing her cringe, he realized he had scowled at her all the while they talked. He went over to yank a wool tartan off a peg, slung it over his left shoulder, then bunched the rest around his waist and secured it with his belt. Instead of belting his long sword on as usual, he slung the belt over his head and drew his left arm through it. The sword rode on his back, the hilt available to his right hand.

He stilled. Listening. Someone crept outside their door.

"Pretend ye are sound asleep, wife," he hissed in Catalin's ear. He shoved her to her side and arranged the sheet to look like she had tossed it around in dreaming. He tilted his sword so as to enable him to sit on the edge of the bed, and took his slow time putting on his boots. The door eased open, footsteps neared. He sprang to his feet, his sword halfway out of its scabbard. He pretended surprise on seeing his sire, and let the weapon slide back into place.

"What do ye here?" he whispered.

Ha. As if he didn't know. His father's gaze devoured the bed. His eyes squinted to mere slits when he spied the rumpled sheets, for a bit of red showed there. Ranald, pretending to be helpful, slipped the top sheet over further to reveal them.

His sire examined the sheets, then Ranald's face. Ranald could near see his father's mind tumbling over all he had learned. Broccin's lips thinned. His brow furrowed. He stared again at his son, spun on his heels and left the room.

Ranald nodded, his own face formed a grim smile. He grunted, satisfied. He left the room and was about to ease the door shut when Hannah stepped out of the shadows. Worry etched lines beside her lips, her eyes, as she strained to study his face in the dim light. He gave one sharp nod and left the door ajar.

His long strides took him below and through the great hall.

"Ranald!

He ignored his father's sharp voice.

"Dinna walk away when I call to ye," Broccin shouted.

He stopped and turned with measured movements. He ignored the men who were breaking their fast.

"Dinna think to order what I do. I am not yers to command. If ye want words with me, ye will have to shout, for I aim to hone my fighting skills this morn."

Before Broccin could take his next breath, Raik came through the huge door leading down to the bailey.

"Ho, Ranald. Ye kept me awake much of the night. Ye need to change yer bed ropes, else I must sleep further from yer chamber."

He slapped Ranald on the back and winked broadly. The men eating nearby hooted and grinned at them.

"Come on, man. Let us see what skills ye acquired at Kelso. I should be able to take ye this day, seeing as how ye spent most of the night, uh, practicing with yer other weapon."

"Huh! Dinna count on it."

They were out and down in the bailey in short order, both eager to work up a sweat. Ranald sought mental relief and exhaustion, for with a broadsword in hand, he would not think on the way his ordered life had changed to one of chaos.

Raik sought pleasure. Wielding a sword and having a good fight to use it in was all he required of life. For most of the morn, they stamped and swung, each testing the other's skill, until they were running with sweat. Finally, Ranald was silent no longer and asked what he burned to know.

"What knew ye of Catalin and Moridac?"

He struck out at Raik.

"Knew?"

Raik's shield deflected Ranald's strike.

"Aye. Of he and Catalin."

Ranald raised his sword high, horizontal. Clang! Raik's return vibrated through Ranald's muscled arm.

"Naught."

"Did he not confide in ye?"

Ranald twisted to the side, out of range. His mask was shifting, sliding from the sweat streaming down his face.

"Nay."

Raik stamped back, pointed his sword downward to parry Ranald's swing.

"Only that he burned for her."

Ranald swiped his arm across his forehead, repositioning

the leather to clear his eye.

"Did he change in any way in the days afore he was to wed?"

Ranald struck his sword on his shield, signaling a halt. They both bent over and took great gasps of air. Raik spied the leather thong that had slipped from his hair. 'Twas beneath Ranald's boot. He flapped his fingers upward, and Ranald rocked his foot back on his heel, releasing the thong. After combing his fingers through his hair, Raik secured it back again.

"What mean ye by change? He said he planned to keep his tarse inside his breeches when Catalin arrived. Said he didna want his bride to stumble over him if she walked in her sleep as Elyne oft does."

"Did he seem different after she came to the keep? Confide anything to ye?"

Raik frowned, thinking, his unseeing eyes showing his mind searching over the hours he had been with Moridac. He finally shrugged his shoulders, held his palms out and frowned.

"Ask me plain out, man. I am no good at guessing."

"The morning of the hunt."

Hearing that, Raik looked up, his brows lifted in thought before speaking.

"He didna look like he had slept much. Looked right mindless he grinned so much. Never afore did he look the fool. I thought he had downed more than his usual cups before hunting. His chest was puffed. He looked about to burst with the need to gloat. I even asked what pleased him so."

"Did he tell ye?"

"Naught but that Catalin pleased him mightily."

"How?"

"I asked, but he only laughed and spurred his mount."

"Good. I dreaded killing ye for keeping silent."

Raik's face went still. He opened his mouth to speak then snapped it closed it. Shook his head. And burst out in anger.

"Cursed Satan! The fool. What would have happened to her had ye not been here? Her uncle would have killed her for sure."

"That fat old man Hamon who smelled of dung?"

"Aye. He beat her when she refused to wed right after her

father died. Moridac threatened to kill him for it."

"Best he never again comes to Raptor. He will leave head down across his mount, his eyes wide but seeing naught."

"Ah. Strong words for a monk-turned-man."

"Aye." Ranald's muscles bunched, his sword lashed out to clang against Raik's shield.

Raik returned the blow. Ranald nearly didn't block it in time.

"By heaven, man, take yer mask off when ye fight, else ye will take a serious injury. It has slipped over half yer eye. A man could take advantage and come at ye from that side." Raik shook his head when Ranald hesitated. "Never did I think ye vain, cousin."

"Nay, not that. I dinna want to frighten the bairns or women who may be about."

"Whilst we train? We are far from the keep. No one can see."

Ranald grunted and slid it up over his face, for the leather ties were loose. When Raik tilted his head, studying his face from all angles, Ranald scowled at him.

" 'Twill be an added weapon. Ye near scare the piss out of me when ye scowl. Put it back on, cousin." He burst into laughter when Ranald took a swing at him.

Hearing the sharp clang of weapons nearby, Ranald glanced around and noted his father training a young knight. Though he despised the man, he had to admire his finely honed body and skills. He was as taut and trim as when he returned from the Crusades. Not far from him, he spied Domnall and beckoned him over.

"Domnall, I have need of a squire. Which youth would be best suited?"

"Ah, I wish all requests were so easily filled. 'Tis Finn." He raised his voice and called to the youth he had been wrestling with. Finn sprang forward, an eager grin on his face.

"Aye, sir?"

Ranald watched him. The young man did not flinch on meeting his eyes, did not stare at his ruined cheek. And mayhap his fiery red hair lent him added temper for a good fighter.

Ranald nodded approval. He circled around him, taking in his strong arms, his tall stature and well-muscled body. The lad was about fifteen summers old. He would do.

"Fin, locate Lord Raik's squire and tell him to bring his mount, then saddle Satan and bring him to me."

Finn took off in a run.

"If he can handle Satan, he will do nicely."

The three warriors watched sturdy archers training with longbows in the field alongside theirs. Finn returned, Satan under control with the young man's firm hold. Raik's squire followed with his mount. Ranald leaned close to Finn's ear and gave him an order. The squire trotted off, his eyes wide, his mouth pursed like he was about to whistle.

Ranald took his time mounting, even flipped his tartan up and away from his thighs. He felt his father's eyes studying him, inching over his arms, his legs. Ranald near smiled, for his sire looked like he had bitten a cherry so unripe it shriveled his lips.

"What sight pleases ye, Ranald?"

"The look of a man thwarted." Ranald guided Satan to a far corner where he and Raik could hone their fighting skills while ahorse. What else did his father have spewing through his sick mind? In a short while, Finn would return, and he would bedevil his sire further.

Catalin was still awake when Hannah slipped into the bed-chamber. She went straight to Catalin and, seeing her eyes open staring at the ceiling, sat on the edge of the bed.

"Oh, Hannah. I was so shamed," Catalin wrapped her arms around her old nurse and rested her head on her shoulder.

"Why, lovey? Was Ranald not able to perform his husbandly duties?"

"Oh, nay! Had I not known, I would never have guessed he had been a man of God." Her face heated until she wondered if Hannah could feel it through her tunic.

"What, then? Did he suspect, even with the chicken blood?"

"Is that what it was? I never got to use it. He knew. Lit a candle and looked at the bed ... at me."

"Then where did the blood stains come from?" She went quiet. Lifted Catalin's head so she could see her face. "Are you hurt?"

"Nay. 'Tis Ranald's." Shame filled her.

"It will not work. Chief Broccin will note any slashes on his arms, his legs."

"Not where he placed them. They'll not be visible." Seeing Hannah's raised brows, she whispered where they were.

"Clever man." Hannah fell back on the bed, cackling. "I would give much to have witnessed what you described. If you knew little of a man's sex afore, you know it well now."

"I fear the cuts will fester." Catalin flushed again and rolled her eyes. She flopped back on the bed. "But I cannot ask Ranald to spread his legs to look at them."

"Oh, aye, you can. But you had best be ready to lie beneath him right after." Hannah uncovered the dry bread she had brought. "I though your stomach might be a little stressed this morn. Eat afore you sit up again."

"Before dawn, I was sick. I tried to swallow it back, but it came too fast. His face was so hard, though his words were gentle. He will never forgive me for not telling him."

"You did not trick Ranald. Broccin would not have let you get away. He wants your lands, your filled coffers." She eyed Catalin and frowned, looked at the sheets and nodded her head. "I think Moridac told his father what he had done."

"What?"

"I thought it strange when he insisted his own servant tend your laundry. 'Tis likely she is the one sent here to spy on you. She must have told him about the sheets that day. Ah. And told him that you had no bloody cloths, no woman's time after Moridac's passing."

Catalin gagged and grasped her mouth. A cold cloth on her neck soon calmed her.

"Hateful man. That is the reason he goaded Ranald. He came sneaking into the room afore dawn, but Ranald expected him."

They both hushed hearing a light scratch on the door. Hannah opened it a crack and whispered to someone, then closed it.

"Speak of the devil's helper, and the woman appears," Hannah whispered. "I told her Ranald had been so large that it was a hard deflowering. I asked she arrange for a hot bath, for you had need of it to wash the blood from your thighs. That should singe His Hatefulness' ears." Her giggle sounded much like a young woman.

Catalin's grin ended in a yawn. For truth, Hannah had not lied. Only about the deflowering part. They both looked surprised when someone else bade leave to enter. Hannah stepped out onto the landing, for it was a young squire. She returned, rubbing her hands and smiling.

"Yer husband is right quick with his thinking. He has sent his new squire, Finn, to guard your door to keep *anyone* from disturbing ye. He instructed Finn that when the bedding is gathered, he is to take it atop the keep and hang it below Ranald's pennant flying there. All will know his master's bride was pure!"

"Hannah, surely the man must hate me even more, for he must lie to protect me. He has been without sin, yet I have forced him into a lifetime of deceit."

Catalin could say no more, for her bath arrived. The servants quickly filled the tub and left, except for the woman they suspected her father-by-law had set to report to him. She stood on the far side of the bed, stripping the sheet, when Catalin stepped into the tub. The woman smiled, near looked pleased on seeing the stains on Catalin's thighs.

"Oh, my lady. 'Tis proof Sir Ranald is no less the man for having been a monk."

Catalin and Hannah looked at each other, surprised. Their spy did not relish the job Chief Broccin had given her? Mayhap she could become an aide instead?

"Your name is Ada, is it not? I have only seen you weaving with the other women." Catalin smiled at her and settled down in the water.

"Aye, mistress." She nodded and looked like she was about

to add something but feared to.

"Did the laird add to your duties because of the many guests?" Hannah went over to help her remake the bed. "Should that be so, it will ease, for he has been rushing them from the keep like he cannot abide feeding them another meal."

Ada laughed and nodded her head. "We had lasses aplenty." She bit her lip and looked vexed at her new duties.

"I am sorry for your extra work." Catalin smiled at her.

"Nay, dinna be. 'Tis not the work I mind." She banged her fists on a pillow, forcing the feathers around with vigor.

"Perchance it is what he asks of you while doing it?" Hannah asked.

"Ye know?" Ada's mouth dropped. She stood still as stone, staring at Hannah.

"Knowing Chief Broccin, I suspected." Hannah nodded her head, her lips pressed tight.

"Aye. It's not right." Ada glared at the pillow she had been punishing with her fists, opened her mouth to speak then closed it again. She grunted, slapped the pillow once more then words exploded from her. "Not right at all. He demands to have the stained sheet. No doubt to burn it."

"Do not worry. Lord Ranald has set a guard at the door for that very purpose. You can tell the laird you had no choice." Hannah grinned at Ada, bundled the stained sheet in her hands and marched over to the door.

"Here you go, Finn. You may tell your master the job is done."

She returned, smiled and dusted her hands together.

Ada walked around the chamber, setting the candles back where they belonged. Creases formed between her eyes. She stopped. Looked back at Hannah.

"I am no good at lying. My face turns red before a word leaves my mouth."

"If you tell him about Catalin's stained thighs, it will be the truth. What troubles you?" Hannah stopped rinsing Catalin's back to look at her.

"I am told to search the room. For trickery. He said I was

to find if the mistress used chicken blood or such."

"Then hunt away. Feel free to look everywhere. Under the bed. The clothing chest." Hannah thrust something at her. "Take Catalin's shift from last eve. You can fold it and put it away."

"I can truthfully say I opened her chests and found naught." Ada grinned and placed the folded garment inside without as much as a cursory glance.

"Uh-huh. Between us, we can provide His Hatefulness with enough tidbits. It may not be what he yearns to hear, but it will be most gratifying to tweak his nose a bit."

"I canna wait to tell him I saw proof afore my lady washed." She grinned again and winked at Hannah. "'Tis a shame we willna see his face when he spies the sheet flapping in the breeze."

The room was tidy by the time Catalin rose from her bath. Tossing aside the drying cloth, she ducked under the garments Hannah held out for her. She went to the bed, gave a little hop and climbed onto it. If ever she fell off during the night, she would no doubt break a bone or two. Once she had pulled her stockings and shoes to cover her feet, she heaved a sigh of relief.

Letia and Elyne arrived to collect her for the noon meal. When they entered the great hall, Catalin welcomed the absence of men.

"I have ne'er seen guests prodded to leave as fast as Father did this morn." Elyne's lips scrunched together. Her nose wrinkled. For a few heartbeats, she stared upward at the massive rafters, then huffed and shook her head. "He all but shoved them out into the bailey."

"Aye, the stable hands had their horses saddled and ready before they even finished breaking their fast." Letia's brow knit. "We had planned to leave with them, but Warin awoke this morn with pains in his chest. I told him I refused to go this day, telling him I did not feel well."

"You are feeling poorly also? Could it be tainted meat?" Elyne chewed her lower lip.

"Nay, I but told him that to keep him abed for a bit. I don't know what ails him. Though he coughs often of late."

Letia shook her head, a slight frown between her brows.

"The men are in the farthest corner of the castle grounds, training like they are about to do battle," Lady Joneta said as she came through the doorway. "It's best we eat. Cook will serve them a hot meal when they return to the keep."

"I, for one, am glad for the peace and quiet. How oft do we get the hall to ourselves?" Elyne grinned and hoisted a roasted chicken thigh high to brandish it above her plate.

Catalin released a deep breath, thankful she had time to compose herself before seeing Ranald again. She could not rid her mind of the picture of him standing over her with the candle, his cold eyes gazing at her naked thighs. Though he controlled it, his face showed his quiet rage, for his skin looked stretched over the bones there. Not even the mask could soften the anger. And his eyes? They had turned from dark plum to jet-black. Their stare had cut through her, sharp as any blade.

They soon finished their meal, and retired to the ladies solar. Several women sat there mending clothing, for training caused many a rent shirt or breeches. Coming through the doorway, a rough spot on the frame snagged Catalin's yellow gown.

"Blessed saints!" She picked the skirt up and noted a ragged tear. "Drats. 'Tis best I repair it now."

She pulled the gown over her head and sat on a chair near the light. They were no sooner settled with their sewing than hearty laughter and boisterous voices below drew them scrambling to the windows.

They made space for Catalin up front, since she was the shortest. Remembering too late that she was not fully clothed, she clutched her smock over her breasts. Letia, her eyes glistening with mirth, clasped her hand over her mouth. Elyne shook her head and rolled her eyes. Hannah and Ada crammed in with the other women at the window on the far side of the room, though they near had to hang out of it for as good a view.

'Twas Catalin who spoke first.

"Holy saints above. They are naked!"

CHAPTER 11

"COME, RAIK. I WOULD wash at the well. Dirt and grime cover me from head to toe."

Ranald slid from the saddle and handed Satan's reins and his weapons to Finn. "We canna spend the day reeking of sweat and horse." Though his muscles burned, he was well satisfied that he'd had a warrior as skilled as Raik to train with this morn.

The well stood in the inner bailey, not fifty paces to the right of the keep's entrance. He disliked baring his body for all to see, but it couldn't be helped. He knew his father strolled close, hoping to espy a telltale mark proving Ranald had lent his own blood for proof of a deflowering.

"The well? Why not wait and bathe with heated water?" Raik asked then thought better of it. "Ah, how soon I forget. Ye are not used to comfort."

Ranald turned his back to the keep, and with one quick move, his tartan was off and crumpled on a boulder so wide and heavy no one had attempted to move it from its original resting place. His back muscles twitched, whether from strain or shying away from prying eyes, he did not know.

Once Raik also was naked to the world, Ranald grinned at him.

"Ye know, cousin, 'twas not necessary for ye to strut yer bare arse before the keep?"

"Ha. Did ye not think I wish to show my goods to lure a lass to my bed this night?" Raik chuckled and lifted arms bent at the elbows then flexed his muscles.

"Aye, there is that." Ranald took a bar of hard lye soap,

dipped it in a bucket of water and rubbed it over his body.

"Huh." He frowned at the soap then sniffed it. "It's far harsher than we had at Kelso. Do ye think I should give them a better recipe for making it?"

Not expecting an answer, he pulled off his mask and took care to place it on the wide lip of the well, needing it close to hand yet far from the water splashed there. The skin on his back rippled, the cheeks of his arse tightened. He felt inquisitive eyes staring, their gazes roaming over him, and not the least of which was his sire. He took his time, seemingly occupied scrubbing the bloodstains off his sex and thighs.

Several lasses stopped their duties to approach close to the well. Watching the men, their lips lifted in appreciative grins.

Finn filled several buckets for rinsing. The squire upended two buckets of cold water over Ranald's head. Raising his face to the sun, he splashed the falling water with his hands to clear his eyes. He pressed his hands over his prickly dome, down his hair, his arms, chest, even his legs, clearing them of the excess water before taking a cloth to dry himself.

"Mayhap I should have worn a helmet. My pate is tender from the sun."

"From the looks of it, ye will soon have hair aplenty to shield it. Ye have the looks of a downy young raven. No doubt, a fortnight from now it will be covered."

All the while, Ranald knew his sire studied his flesh. He was used to the company of men, but his mind cringed at the display of his ruined back he was giving the women of the castle. He heard female titters, felt women's eyes combing his body. It couldn't be helped. He had best get used to it. After all, much of it would show when he wore a tartan without a tunic.

"Hurry with the bucket, Finn, else this soap will peel the skin off my body," Raik called.

Raik jumped when Finn sloshed the cold water over his heated skin. He danced about and shook like a hunting dog coming from a frigid loch. Ranald laughed for the first time since entering Raptor Castle. Come to think on it, he couldn't remember the last time he had laughed.

Had it been months? Mayhap, even years?

He spied his father so close now he could touch him. He stretched his arms wide and turned full circle, much as Raik had done in the Infirmary garden. He was cautious to lower his head a bit when he faced the keep.

"What think ye, sire? Did not God's work hone my body as well as mind?" Ranald narrowed his eyes to stare at Broccin when he completed his turn. He picked up his mask, slid it over his head and tightened the straps.

"Huh! God's work? To do God's work, ye need have been in the Crusades. Were ye too afeared of taking an injury that ye didna offer yer brawn to fight for God?"

"God had full measure from me. I healed the broken and torn men that came to Kelso. Seeing ye are so good at it, I left the maiming and killing to ye."

"'Tis likely ye would have bolted on seeing yer first Saracen."

Chief Broccin's cold regard crept over Ranald's skin like mice scampering and hunting for a crumb in every crevice of a floor.

"Did yer bride scream at the sight of ye when ye crept into bed?"

"Nay, she admired yer handiwork."

"Humph! I wouldna be surprised if that lance betwixt yer legs never rose to do its duty."

Ranald quirked his brow at his sire, lifted his tartan from the bolder and belted it on in short order.

"Hm. Did ye not note the new pennant this day?"

"New pennant? I gave no permission for another's standard to fly!" Broccin's head jerked up. He noted the sheet hung so the stains were evident. Anger, red and shiny as a summer sunset, mottled his face. The veins in his neck bulged.

Ranald was facing the well, his father's back to it. He narrowed his eyes until all he could see was a filled bucket resting on the well's ledge. He breathed deep. Held his breath.

Cold water splashed down Broccin's hips. He jumped forward, cursing.

"By Christ! Where's that boy! I'll bloody his nose for

splashing me!"

"It wasn't the lad's doing. He long since has left. Ye admired my night's handiwork with such awe ye backed into the bucket. Best ye have someone fetch dry clothing. Yer wet breeches cling so tight it's apparent ye have a boil on yer arse."

Ranald turned away, stamped into his boots and glanced to see Raik was also finishing, though his movements were clumsy. It was nigh impossible for Raik to latch his belt, for he held one hand clasping his mouth, his eyes alight with mirth.

"Come, cousin. I dinna know about ye, but after last eve's labors and this day's workout with ye, I am hungered enough to eat a boar." Ranald cuffed Raik on the shoulder.

Raik, his head tilted back, grinned like a fool. Ranald followed his gaze to see Catalin, with Elyne and Letia peering over her shoulders.

He frowned. His bride was near nakit! Though she clutched a butterfly yellow garment around her, it had slid from her shoulders leaving the soft swell atop her breasts bare to everyone's eyes.

It would seem she enjoyed peering at bare flesh as much as Letia. Letia he kenned, for she was not a new bride. Catalin and Elyne should have closed their eyes and turned from the window. He would have words with his sister about it.

And Catalin? His mouth tightened. He stared at her, putting his displeasure in his look. Why had she not turned on seeing nakit men before her eyes? Why had the sight not shamed her?

Did she relish it? Was she so used to it?

Sharp spears of doubt pricked his mind.

Catalin gasped as Ranald's dark gaze bored into her. She had earned her husband's added displeasure for certain. Though it was too late, she jumped back, stepping on Letia's toes, for being the tallest, she had stood behind Catalin and Elyne.

"Ow, Catalin. For one so small, you have a heavy foot."

"I sense my brother is none too pleased with us, for I too

felt his anger." Elyne grinned. Wide. "But it was worth it, dinna ye think?"

"Your cousin takes my breath away, Elyne," Letia said. "And, Catalin? You did not tell us Ranald has such a wondrous body."

"Aye. Never have these old eyes seen anything so, so ..." Hannah seemed for a loss for words. "When he bent over to shed the water on his legs ...!"

Ada did not have to speak more. Her smile said it all.

"Anyone so fortunate to lie with either man will be well-pleasured." Hannah rolled her eyes upward and let out a huge sigh. "Oh, to be a young lass. Though Ranald is taken, I would greet that Raik with my skirts hiked high did he come through my door at night!"

That set the women to laughing.

"Help me, Hannah. Run grab the first thing that comes to hand from my chest. I would dress before Ranald should chance to return here."

While the women talked, Catalin clutched her smock around her. She breathed a sigh of relief when Hannah returned carrying a kirtle that was the lightest hint of brown. It would have to do.

"My brother and Raik are much alike in body, yet one's skin is as dark as the bark of a tree, the other golden. Though his robes hid him from the sun, Ranald must oft have been without them," Elyne said. "He is white, uh, below. Likely he wore some sort of braies with less cloth than usual."

Ada chimed in. "During the feast last eve, I heard a servant say Sir Domnall told another the monk was also Kelso's Protector."

"Did you note the scars covering Ranald's back? They even curve to his sides." Catalin perched on the edge of the chair and rocked back and forth.

"Though he lowered his face when he turned for his sire, the sun streaked his cheek. I could see ... "—Letia tried for the right words to describe what the glimpse had hinted at,—"different types of skin are there. Raised like his back, though I do not see how?"

"Moridac told me he didna believe his twin could ever heal. The whip's tip had caught and pulled, tearing his flesh. Though Joneta tried, it was such agony for him, she couldna clear all of the damaged flesh from his wounds." Elyne shuddered and rubbed her arms.

Letia's brow knit, looking as if she viewed the vision deep in her mind.

"I caught just a flash before he tucked his head down. His eye is intact, of course. Three, mayhap four, stripes crossed from his nose and across his cheek and neck."

"Aye." Hannah put in. "I would have noted more, but the way his, uh, rod swung, I fixed on it."

Ada fanned her face. "I never got my sight higher than the waist on either man. The muscles lodged there were the ones I noted."

"Often, when Father hacked his way through the Crusades, I prayed somehow he would suffer in turn." Elyne's face was grim with distaste for her sire.

"Ranald will always hate me for having to enter the world again. He spied us looking. I should not have done it. He was angry." Catalin curled on the chair, one hand cupped her neck beneath her chin.

"Love, he does not blame ye. Father's greed tore Ranald from Kelso as surely as he thrust him there." Elyne smoothed Catalin's hair back from her cheek.

"Nay. He hates me. He was a monk, not a warrior. Now he will be forced to fight. Mayhap even to kill. And all because I am wealthy."

She tried hard not to wail. She despised weakling women. She had felt near tears for sennights now. All she seemed to do was pity herself. She would cry until her meals came up. Little good crying did, though. It did not even make her thin like Letia.

The women settled down to their mending. Every now and again Catalin glanced up to spy one of them looking into space, a grin on her lips. How she wished she could be that carefree again. The afternoon passed so quickly they did not notice until the sun's light was not enough for them to sew by.

They were folding the mended garments into neat piles, when the door burst open. It startled her so much Catalin dropped her yellow kirtle. She bent to retrieve it and glanced toward the doorway. Ranald stood there. He bestowed a look upon her that made her flinch. Had he known they had talked about him?

"If ye are through hanging out the window, it is time ye come below." He swung his gaze to Letia. "Lady, yer husband requests yer presence. He would come himself, but he trained hard and the stairs are many."

"Of course. We will come right away." Letia frowned on hearing Warin had been training.

"Come, wife." Ranald's stiff nod added to the command quickened Catalin's steps.

His lips tightened when he swung his gaze to study his sister. "Elyne. Do ye ken how foolish a lass is to stare at nakit men's flesh? All at Raptor could see yer grin. A warrior might mistake yer interest and think ye are not a maiden."

"Ha! 'Tis common at Raptor to see men unclothed. Often they come from hunts and strip in the rain to wash blood from their bodies. If men dinna wish to display their wares, they should keep their clothing about them," Elyne retorted.

"I had reason, Elyne. But what ye did may someday cause ye grief."

Catalin wished she had not raced to the window earlier. Had not stood there and stared, for shame and anger flashed in Ranald's eyes. And she knew why he had bared his flesh. To declare, though not in words, to his sire and the world that *she* had been pure.

When he touched her elbow, she did not need urging to follow beside him. She felt that strange static in the air around him that she had felt before. What caused it? Tension? Anger? Most likely a heaping of both.

Ranald did not press Catalin to his side, for the scent of her skin kept him from prudent thoughts. He needed to *know* his wife. Not in the way he had known her the night just passed.

Far more than that. If he was to forge any kind of life here at Raptor, he had to accept the fact he wed to his bother's... what? Moridac's love that he couldna wait but a few days longer to possess? Had he seduced her, or had *she* tempted him? He needed no mystic to tell him Catalin had loved Moridac, or that she loved him still.

His twin had been the one to take all, whether it was the finest sword, the best clothing or a lass who held Ranald's interest. He had proved over and again that as first born, though by only a matter of a few breaths, he *could* command it all.

Had Catalin seduced Moridac? He didna want to think too closely on why she chose to study his and Raik's bodies. It churned doubts about her through his mind. Never had he thought to marry, but now that Broccin had forced him to take a wife, he wanted what every man wanted.

A pure bride. One to bear his heir.

He had neither. Should the bairn be a boy, it would be Moridac's heir. His sons to come after would not hold Raptor Castle.

Mayhap that was a good thing.

Ranald's skin burned, though not from the sun. The looks cast his way when they entered the hall near singed the clothing from his body. When had women become so bold?

"Ho, Ranald. Yer frown is enough to scare magpies away. Do ye think to break Catalin's bones?" Raik glanced pointedly to where Ranald's fingers dug into her soft flesh.

Ranald fingers sprang open like he had grasped a staunch thistle.

"Forgive me, wife. I was deep in thought."

Catalin visibly swallowed and nodded. Her right hand twitched and half raised to no doubt rub her red skin then fell back to hide in the folds of her kirtle. He stared at the yellow smock peeking between the slits of the brown kirtle. So used to seeing and wearing plain, black habits, each new color was something to study. And admire. *On women*. He glanced at Raik's bright attire.

"Ye have changed, Raik. I thought the array of clothes in

Moridac's chest colorful, but they pale alongside yers. Crusaders biding their time at Kelso sometimes mentioned in their travels seeing birds with many brightly colored feathers. Do ye copy them?"

"Do ye not see how the lasses canna move their eyes from me? They are drawn to color like a bee to bright flowers." Raik waved his arms out at his side, mimicking wings lifting.

"Heh." Ranald looked to see Catalin had moved out of earshot. " 'Tis more likely they remember yer nakit body shining in the sun. They now picture that which is beneath yer plumage."

"Ah, there is that! Now, which one shall I favor this night? The alewife's black-haired daughter carrying a pitcher" He winked broadly at her. She tripped and near spilled ale on her skirts. "A might clumsy, do ye think? Or will it be the chandler's sister?"

Ranald's gaze strayed across the room to settle where Raik looked. For truth, the woman was most comely. Her hair was the color of wheat; her eyes a soft, light brown. She was a bold one, for she eyed him as closely as he did her. Surprise was his first thought, for surely she looked far too fine to be a workman's get? The closer he studied her, the more he puzzled that she was not a gentle woman.

"Nay, not the one ye are slavering over. I mean the chestnut-haired lass serving her. The tall sheave of wheat ye study is Muriele. Your father's ward. She is a mystery, though. Raiders slaughtered her family, and she was left without a protector. Lady Muriele sought sanctuary here."

"What is the mystery?" Ranald frowned. "Ye know from whence she came, and how she arrived. What else is there to know?"

"Ah, what else. Hmm, I have oft thought Chief Broccin sought to make her his leman. But Moridac hinted she was about to grant him that status, in exchange for protection from yer sire. The mystery is, whether she will be able to fend off another feint on her body by the Chief or if she still seeks a protector."

"Moridac would take advantage of a helpless lass?" Ranald

shuddered thinking of how wicked his family had become. "It is sinful my sire would misuse a woman in his care."

Though Ranald had heard of how his twin had changed, how could he have preyed on a gentle woman? He shared the same blood as Moridac, the same body, skin. All alike. Their stride had been identical, they savored the same foods, knew the same joy when they trained and rode. Even their tempers were similar, fast to burst forth and hard to control. Sometimes they had joked about having twin brains.

How long would it be? Before he became what Moridac had been?

How long? He feared it would be all too soon.

"If ye looked at me like that, cousin, I would have my hand on my dirk. Ye are scaring the lass, though until yer scowl, she was gazing at ye from head to toe, likely picturing yer naked body at the well."

Raik's words jolted him, for just then Muriele appeared to draw in on herself, making herself smaller. She dropped her head low and stared at her hands in her lap. He tried to relax his jaw, for it ached from having clamped it so tight. His hands had fisted, too. Feeling a sharp pinch, he startled and looked around. Elyne stood there, awaiting his attention.

"For all that is holy, brother, ye look about to pound yer fists on someone's nose. Look around ye. Half the men here look afeared ye will lash out at them."

Ranald studied the room. For truth, many uneasy glances flashed his way. Women had turned their faces, while some men sidled away to stand in the shadows of the walls. What had them so wary?

"Are they used to outbursts of temper, or is my face so ugly, so hard to look upon, that the slightest frown makes it fearsome?"

"Nay, yer face is far from ugly. The mask adds mystery. Afore yer scowl, women were eyeing ye like a hungry bird spotting the first worm after a long, frozen winter." Elyne grinned up at him.

"Hm, that statement makes me envious." Raik laughed. "No doubt the worm they hunger for lies beneath yer tunic."

"Huh! Ye'll not find yer pallet empty this eve either, cousin." Elyne shook her head at him. "Aye. 'Tis more likely ye'll have little space left to lie on."

"I can suffer that." Raik's grin made him look like a hungry wolf.

"But, ye say the slightest frown, Ranald? Ha. What makes yer face fearsome is the way yer eyes are near squinted shut. The way ye stare. And, too, when ye snarl, yer lips do look right mean." She ended her description with a chuckle and hugged his arm before leaving to join Catalin, standing with Letia and Baron de Burgh.

He watched as Elyne strode away and noted several knights admiring his sister. One hard glare from him turned their gazes elsewhere.

Catalin darted a glance his way. Doubt clouded her blue eyes. Her smiles were forced. She chewed her lips before quickly looking away.

Ah. No doubt, she worried what evening would bring.

She read his mood well.

Chapter 12

"Yet."

Catalin jumped hearing Ranald voice. Saints! He was not there. The word but echoed in her mind with such strength she had thought he spoke in her ear. He had said he would not thrash her. Yet. Had she angered him so much today he had changed his mind? Her cheeks flinched. How would she fare if he struck her? Uncle Hamon had dealt her more than one blow, near breaking the bones in her face.

Ranald's fists were much larger. His body, too. He held far more power than her piggish uncle.

She near bit her lips raw. She could not stop looking at him, either. He moved with such stealth. She feared he would suddenly appear and lift his hand before she had time to protect her face.

Heaven's above! He would not stop staring at her. She dropped her head to study her shoes peaking beneath her kirtle. She took deep breaths, squeezed her eyes tight, and tried to picture being in a quiet place with no one around.

Raik's voice calling Ranald intruded, and of a sudden, the prickling attention of Ranald's regard left her. Her breath escaped in a whoosh.

Ranald thoughts dwelled on every look, word and motion of Catalin's, filling him with doubt. She had best be wary. His blood seethed. 'Twas truth. How could he ever trust her?

Granted, as the monk in the garden, she had sought to confess her sins to him. But in their bedchamber, she should have confessed to him, the man. Aye. Her lie was letting him believe she was a virgin still.

Had she done it before? When he destroyed the small vial of chicken blood Hannah had provided her, he had thought hard about that.

Hearing Raik move beside him, Ranald brought his thoughts back to the hall.

"Ho, cousin. Catalin does not look the happy bride. She noted yer interest in Muriele. Mayhap she fears ye will take over where Moridac left off?"

"Do ye forget I was a monk until a few days past?"

"Oh, aye, I remember well. Still, ye have many years to make up for. And ye had a twin. That twin was a man of the earth, one in need of much female flesh. As ye were before going to Kelso. Mayhap she fears ye will hasten to have all the pleasures ye missed while ye were celibate?"

"Dinna talk daftie."

"Tsk. Ye're scaring the lass into the next world, ye know. She thinks yer scowl is meant for her." Raik chuckled, put his arm around Ranald's shoulders and urged him over to where Broccin had already settled with Domnall. Baron de Burgh sat across the table from him.

Catalin ignored him now and darted glances at his father. Broccin's steely black eyes stared at her body, no doubt looking for some sign that Moridac's seed had taken. 'Twas enough to make anyone uneasy, even a lass so brash she would marry a man she feared in order to protect her bairn.

Catalin had watched Ranald with his cousin. The two seemed taken with Muriele, for they stared and talked, not doubt, of how beautiful she was. Could Ranald be interested in her? Catalin had heard talk about Muriele and Moridac. Had heard hints that he wanted her. The woman had seemed most distressed when he died. So much so that Catalin had noted it even in her own grief.

Ranald's gaze often left the tall, willowy woman to fix on Catalin. She felt his anger clean through to her bones as he approached her.

Such a look was enough to make chill bumps creep over her arms. He had most likely thought all this day on how marrying had torn his life asunder like a winter's storm ripping trees from the forests. And all because of her.

"Do ye oft gaze at nakit warriors when they wash at the well?"

Catalin near jumped from her skin. Ranald's voice was so cold, so condemning. It stirred her anger.

"Only when they display themselves so freely."

Heaven help her. Why had she blurted that out? Her temper of late had flashed at the most unusual times. She grabbed a handful of grapes in a dish nearby and popped them into her mouth. Mayhap that would give her time to think before speaking.

"Display myself? Ye knew as well as I, my sire would suspect foul play. It was needed that he saw no wounds on my flesh."

All the defiance went out of her. She gulped the last of the grapes down, meaning to apologize. Too late, for Broccin demanded Ranald's attention.

"Once Catalin shows to be increasing, I expect ye to lead a foray across the borders. The time is ripe, for King Stephen's barons are angry and rebellious. They fight amongst themselves and are oft gone from their own lands to gather and bicker like dafty eejits."

Ranald skidded two chairs over to the table and waited for Catalin to sit before he spoke. " 'Tis truth then? Henry forced his barons to swear an oath to Empress Matilda after she married Geoffrey of Anjou, but many went back on it?"

"Aye. Men dinna like swearing to rally behind a woman." Raik leaned his hip against the table and crossed his arms. "Hmpf! What was Henry thinking? No woman can rule a castle, much less a country."

"The day will come when you will see more women doing such."

Catalin grinned hearing Letia's words. Raik was in for a surprise.

"Nay. Never. They have not the brains or skills to command men." Raik stiffened, near bristled with disapproval.

"Best not think so, Raik." Baron de Burgh chuckled then drew his wife down to sit on the arm of his chair. "Afore we married, Letia's father lay near death. He couldn't lift his arms much less give commands. Letia took charge, demanding much from the men."

"Why did they listen to a woman? Were the warriors so spineless?" Ranald jaws squared.

"She is an expert archer, and her men respected her skills. She kept her father's dire straits secret and gave commands as if she passed on his orders to the men. No one else knew she held the castle alone."

"Why did she not wait and petition the king for aid?" Ranald asked.

"It was needful she protect her lands before anyone found out. King Henry's bastard, Julian, had long coveted that which is hers. She knew he had spies amongst the workers. If he had learned of it, he would have besieged the castle.

"Did Julian not find out?" Ranald eyes narrowed as he studied Letia.

"Aye. He did. But by then she had sent for my help."

"Enough chatter. Do ye forget? I asked ye a simple question, Ranald." Broccin slammed his tankard of ale on the table. "Will ye raid across the border?"

"And I will give ye a simple answer: Nay."

"Nay? How can ye say 'nay'?"

Broccin shot to his feet, his face livid. Ranald rose to face him.

"Catalin's own lands are across the border, though they are nearly on it. We sit at table with Baron de Burgh. The lady Letia is Catalin and Elyne's closest friend. Do ye forget they, too, live across the border?"

"Once they return home, they are fair game. Mayhap even before they reach there." Broccin's eyes gleamed through narrowed lids, his elbows on the table, his fingers laced with his forefingers tapping his lips.

De Burgh steadied his wife on the armrest as he eased to his feet.

"You seek to threaten me? While I am a guest in your keep?"

Never once did he take his eyes off Chief Broccin. And never once did his hand leave the shaft of a short sword riding low on his belted waist.

Across the room, knights who had come with the baron rose, their hands fingering their own weapons.

Ranald bolted to his feet. "Never will Raptor Castle's men threaten yer land, Baron. I am lord over Hunter Castle, Catalin's home. It lies close to your own Seton Castle. My men at Hunter will ever be ready to aid ye."

"Ye may be lord over Hunter Castle, but Hamon of Cartington declared the castle is his by right of possession and as the only male of the family."

"How can he say 'tis his? He is not of my line." Catalin's face lost all color. "He is my mother's brother, not my father's."

"Did ye not hear afore? By right of possession. When last ye came here, he moved his men in with yers before the dust settled behind your escorts. The men either swore allegiance to him or were thrown in the dungeons until they relented."

Broccin rubbed his hands together, gleeful there was reason for another battle.

"Can he not be made to leave by King Stephan?"

"Dinna be dafty, girl." Broccin scowled at Catalin. "Had King Stephan cared, he would have already acted. Moridac and I had planned to leave with enough men to make Hamon shite his breeches when he saw us approach …"

"How long have ye known, Broccin?" Ranald interrupted.

"Broccin? I am Father or Sire to ye, ye ungrateful half-man." Broccin's lips lifted in a snarl.

"Ungrateful? Aye. I am that. Somehow, I could not learn to greet the day with a song of thanks on my lips for yer rearranging my face. My back. My life."

Broccin stood, the veins in his neck bulging as he shouted.

"Ye have Catalin. Her lands. Her castle. Her filled coffers. All waiting for ye to scoop them up. My son lies moldering in the vault whilst ye swive his betrothed and hide behind yer monkish ways."

Blood pounded in Ranald's ears, blocking all other sound from him. His lips curled, twitched. His fists clenched, stretched, then clenched again, until they tightened and would not release.

He took one slow step at a time toward Broccin. Ranald's tight fists drummed on his thighs. His right foot rose to the table's edge. Shoved. Raik and Domnall jumped aside. The table screeched on the stone floor afore it stopped against the wall.

For each step Ranald took, it forced his sire back. If Ranald trod with his right foot, Broccin's left shoulder jerked as if pummeled. He staggered back on his left leg. The same happened when Ranald stepped forward with his left foot. Broccin's right shoulder jerked; he staggered back again. 'Twas as if the air between them was solid.

Ranald did not touch him. Broccin's eyes blinked with disbelief. Finally, Ranald shook his head, clearing it. His shoulders, arms, hands … all his body relaxed.

"At Kelso I said ye have no son now. Ever have I known ye believed the old legends that if twin bairns were birthed, one child's soul was thought to be good, the other evil. Ye would only accept one of us. The first born."

His father's mouth opened to speak, but Ranald raised his hand, flat out, stopping him.

"Nay. Enough has been said."

Domnall slid a chair behind Broccin's knees. He plopped in it, his face white.

"Once I have learned the skills of each knight and warrior at Raptor, and ye and Domnall have told me what preparations have already been undertaken, we will make our final plans. That arse Hamon had best cherish his throat. He will soon be parted from it."

"Can we not start preparing this night?" Domnall asked.

"Nay. The morrow's dawn is soon enough." Ranald's left brow quirked. "Did ye not hear? My *sire* demands a grandson."

Ranald spun around. His kilt swirled, baring his thighs. He crooked one long, brown finger at his wife.

"Come."

chapter 13

CATALIN GULPED AND STARED at Ranald's large hands. Such long fingers, broad palms, the skin brown and calloused. Moridac's flesh had been pale, his hands smooth.

Not Ranald's, though. They looked strong enough to wield a broadsword with little effort. No doubt he could snap the life from a man should he grasp him by the head and twist.

She shuddered, shook her head. How could they have been so gentle, so exciting, only last eve? Would they ever be so again? Or would they be rough and cruel, seeking revenge?

Impatient now, he crooked his finger again demanding she come to him. She swallowed and squared her shoulders. Her feet lagged. His eyes flashed a warning when he grasped her elbow to urge her forward. She near had to skip to keep up with his long strides.

"Do ye want all to know things are not as they should be?" He snapped the words at her, and had he been an angry hound, he would have followed them with a feral growl and a nip.

"Do you think they would not guess when you stared at me all eve with looks near to loathing?" Her tone was every bit as irate as his.

Ranald's hand shifted from her elbow to clamp around her upper arm. The way he propelled her through the doorway and up the stairwell, all would think he was impatient indeed to have his wife abed. No doubt, if they glimpsed his face, they wondered if his intent was to ravish or to throttle her.

Hannah was in his chamber, preparing their bed for the night. Ranald paced the room while she placed warming stones wrapped in wool cloths between the sheets, far down on his side and higher for Catalin's own.

Catalin's face heated when Hannah came to draw her kirtle over her head. Ranald spoke, sounding close behind her.

"It is a strange outfit."

Catalin felt a slight tug and knew he fingered the garment.

"The gown feels of sturdy cloth, yet yer smock is so light it near has no weight. They dinna seem well matched."

She read the disapproval in his voice.

"They were not meant to be. I needed to mend the yellow kirtle I had donned with it."

Ranald dropped his hand, his gaze bored into her own.

"No doubt when ye made haste to gawk out the window. What happened? Did ye fight over who was to get the best view?" His lip near lifted in a snarl.

His eyes widened when Hannah giggled like a young lass. "No one shoved harder than I. 'Twas the most magnificent feast these eyes have had for many a year."

A flush started at Ranald's hairline and spread down his neck. Before he spoke again, he retreated to the far side of the room.

"All within sight saw Catalin, wife for but a day, staring like a dairy maid well-used to spying nakit men."

"Nay, not like a dairy maid. Like a wife who knows little of her husband," Catalin blurted out.

Seeing his back stiffen, she clambered up the two steps beside the bed and slipped between the covers. Why couldn't she keep her unruly mouth shut? Her feet searched for the comfort of the warm stones. She rubbed her toes over them, all the while regretting Hannah had no reason to linger.

"I placed wine and bread beside the bed, in case ye should hunger during the night." Though Hannah addressed Ranald, Catalin knew she supplied the bread to settle Catalin's stomach.

"I am sure my wife will be glad of it, should this day's food not set well with her. Ye may seek yer bed now."

Though his voice was quiet, sarcasm laced the words, knowing Hannah knew why she had spewed that morn. 'Twas wise

Hannah kept her lips sealed and left the room, for the tension sparking from him felt near enough to set light to a candle.

Ranald stalked around the room, nipping out each flame. She heard his clothing rustle as he removed and folded them like he had done the night before. Not all men were as careful. Her father had thought naught of leaving his clothing lay where he removed them, and Elyne had warned that Moridac left his clothes strewn from the door to the bed each night.

She held tight to the bed frame, for Ranald's weight dipped the feather bedding, making it rock on its ropes when he stretched full out on it. She waited. Held her breath, expecting him to reach for her. He did not.

In the dim light with his black hair against the pillow and the left side of his face toward her, he looked so like Moridac resting there that she held her breath. His eyes were open. He did not remove his mask. Could that ruined side be so horrible? Last eve, he had not allowed her to touch him. Most likely, it was the same as his back, though worse.

"Close yer eyes." Ranald's words were sharp, weighted with feeling. "Yer stares have probed me enough to last a lifetime."

She went totally still. Stopped breathing, even. When she realized it, she eased her breath out slowly so he would not hear. When next she inhaled, it was deep. His scent drifted to her, shooting a hot stab to her stomach. Not of pain. It was more like the heat that spread down to her belly when he kissed her last eve.

Though her heart had tripped with fear of his anger while climbing the stairwell, now her body yearned for his touch. She had not felt this way after Moridac's lovemaking. He had been intent on his own release, while Ranald had savored her, taking time to see she had pleasure too.

She shifted, restless now. The sheet teased nipples that had hardened further with each breath she took. How could a man smell so good when he had bathed with harsh soap at the well? She eased an arm up to her nose. Sniffed. She could barely tell her own soap had left the scent of sweet violets.

"Lucifer's pointy horns!"

Catalin near startled off the bed.

"Will ye stop sniffing and squirming? Ye're like a wriggling worm." Ranald sat up, thumped his pillow, turned his back to her and settled on his right side.

Catalin stiffened, her limbs at an awkward angle, for she was about to turn over. She did not dare move now. How could she go to sleep? She was not the slightest bit sleepy. Strange. All day, 'twas all she wanted to do and could not. Huh! Most likely, she would be awake when the sun next decided to rise.

Ranald burned with need. Knowing Catalin lay beside him hardened his tarse and made his ballocks ache. Then, too, there was her heady scent. She must like it herself, for he had heard her sniffs, seen her hold an arm to her nose.

Mayhap he should not have bellowed at her. Now she was so stiff he could feel her even more. His mind turned back to last eve. She had not been stiff then. No. Her body had yielded wherever he touched. Warm. Hot, even. Her belly had quivered when he caressed her there, had raked his fingers through her springy curls below. And her core? Like liquid fire when he had eased his shaft within, not stopping until he was seated all the way.

Cruddy Lucifer! He was afire. He gritted his teeth, stared at the ceiling. Catalin's light puffs of air told him she had found sleep faster than anyone he had ever known. Funny. She had been the one who was restless, while he had been exhausted, needing respite before the morrow. He had many plans to make. A castle to besiege. And all he could think about was his blarsted tarse staring up at him.

Excited. Pleading.

How quickly he had lost control of his body. Had he ever ruled it, or had he fooled himself? He sucked his teeth, disgusted. How could he lust after her? After a woman who likely grew his brother's seed in her belly? It was sick.

He eased from the bed, padded to the window and pushed

the shutters wide. Storm clouds hid the moon and the damp air held a hint of frost.

He stretched his bare body face down on the floor. His arms spread and legs stretched out as he had on Kelso's stones. His skin quivered, shrunk from the cold.

Good. 'Twas fortunate his tarse minded the cold. Mayhap, now he could keep his thoughts on his prayers.

Catalin awoke curled in a tight ball, feeling much colder than when she had gone to bed. Last eve, Ranald had pulled her close in his sleep, shared his warmth. It drew her now. Perhaps she could ease over to him? If she used caution with each move, he would not awaken.

She inched her right arm and leg across the cold sheets, then rolled as slowly as a cook turning a spit while roasting a leg of lamb. Hm. She reached out, fluttered her hand under the covers so as not to disturb them, trying to sense his heat. It was a huge bed. Though he did not want to touch her, surely he did not need to sleep so near the edge. She eased over one more turn. Still no enticing warmth. The sheets there were near cold as ice. She felt again. Her head lifted, her neck stretched. She frowned, seeing naught but bed covers.

No one rested beside her.

She sat up. Stared around the room. 'Twas empty. A cloud moved, baring the moon. Something was on the floor. She threw off the tangled covers and crawled closer to peer down.

Ranald lay sprawled like he had sustained a mortal injury.

"Saints help me. Ranald! He is dying!" Her screams echoed against the walls.

She scrambled over the side of the bed, tumbling pillows onto the floor. She drew in a great gasp of air and yelled again.

Ranald sprang upright, kicking pillows aside as he grasped her shoulders and gave her a shake.

"Woman, are ye dafty? Stop yer caterwauling, else ye will wake all in the keep."

Catalin's breath left in a heavy whoosh. Her husband stood before her, bathed in moonlight. She grasped her throat and stared. Her toes curled, and she began to hop like she danced on hot coals.

Ranald cocked his head and peered at her. Two perfect, full globes adorned with rosy tips bobbed and swayed in a most delightful way. Beckoning him. He tore his gaze from her, and dropped his hands like she scalded him. He was near losing the control he had prayed so long and hard for.

"Why do ye hop so? Do ye have to piss?"

"The shutters. They are open to the night, and the floor is like ice."

"Ranald!" Raik's voice. His fist pounding on the door.

"Cruddy Hell. Ye've waked the keep."

Ranald sucked his teeth and trod over to the door. Without paying heed to his naked flesh, he threw it open and bellowed.

"What?"

Whether it was the force of his yell, or the sight of his body, or mayhap both, the crowd gathered there thinned. He heard Elyne's laugh trailing down the hallway. From the corner of his eye, he saw Muriele's doe-like eyes peer, in one long, appreciative journey, over him before she ambled away, her hips swaying beneath her robe.

"I heard Catalin scream that ye were dying, cousin." Raik's lips split in a grin, his eyes gleamed with laughter when he glanced in the room. "Were ye fighting her for the pillows? Yer bed is a mess."

Ranald looked back over his shoulders. Saw the bed. But that wasn't where Raik's eyes dwelled. His wife stood there, her flaming curls spilling over her face, her creamy shoulders, while she held a pillow before her to cover her nakedness. Her bare feet vied with each other to see which one could leave the floor the fastest. He felt his blood heating, knowing what hid behind that pillow.

"Does she need to piss?" Raik's brows rose.

"Nay. Cold."

"Dinna waste it."

"Waste? Waste what? Ye speak in riddles." Ranald scowled to let his cousin know he was not pleased to stand there in the doorway for all to see, bare-arsed, while listening to senseless talk.

Raik's downward gaze explained his words.

"Shite!"

The ardor Ranald had thought to freeze into control had sprung to life again. All his good intentions fled with one quick glance at his nakit wife. He slammed the door in Raik's face and cursed again on hearing his burst of laughter.

In less than two full days, his wife caused half the keep to see him unclothed. Twice. His skin heated remembering Muriele's eyes studying him. She had not turned her gaze away, shy of seeing him. Nay. She had lingered. Had looked her fill.

Where was Catalin? She was standing close-by but a breath ago. His gaze darted to the bed. The lump in the covers must be her, for he could see the sheets shaking from across the room. His long strides took him to the window. He slammed the shutters together and latched them tight.

He was used to living in the abbey where men disciplined their bodies and did not seek a fireplace. Mayhap he had been thoughtless to let the fire die out and the night air in.

Catalin carefully shifted to give Ranald room when she heard him moving close-by. She shook all the harder after leaving the spot she had worked so hard to warm and found icy sheets.

She turned her back to him and clamped her teeth together, striving to still their chattering. On hearing him put more peat on the banked fire, she sighed with relief. After he worked over it for a while, Catalin finally noted a faint light through the sheet she had pulled over her face.

A cold blast of air hit her when Ranald lifted the covers to get back into bed. It didn't last long, for he turned toward her, hooked his arm around her waist, and pulled her close.

Warmth radiating from his skin was pure bliss.

"Are ye never still? Wiggle yer arse again, and I'll give ye a pinch ye'll long remember."

'Twas not an idle threat. It was not his way. She stilled. Now, more than ever, she felt his shaft, hard as tempered steel, nestled against her buttocks. It, too, was blessedly warm.

"I cannot help it. I have always liked a warm bed. Both nights you have banked the fire and thrown open the shutters."

"They're closed now." He pulled her tighter to him.

"Husband?"

"What now?" His heavy sigh ruffled the hair on the back of her neck.

"I will not permit you to destroy Hunter Castle."

"What?

"Hunter Castle. And my villages. You are not to destroy my people's lives. They have little, and what there is, is precious to them."

"I well understood the word destroy. It is not what I asked about." His body shifted as he rose on his elbow to stare down at her. "Explain this 'my', wife."

"Hunter Castle is my home, as Raptor is yours." She twisted her shoulders so she could frown up at him.

"Nay. Raptor Castle is not mine. Chief Broccin rules here. But did we not wed this past day? Aye or nay, wife?"

"Aye. You know we did. What has that to do with it?"

"There is no 'my' for a woman. Ye held Hunter Castle only until ye wed. What was yers is now mine. It is *my* Hunter Castle."

"But, you are a Scot. I am of Saxon stock. Your land is in Scotland. My land is in Northumbria."

"And?"

"What is in Scotland should be yours; what is in Northumbria should be mine." Catalin scowled up at him. Mayhap she should have thought twice about this before she spoke. She was not sure of the expression in his midnight eyes. Perchance it was surprise that she would assert her rights over her lands.

"Hm. I see yer point. But what was yers in Northumbria is now claimed by Hamon of Cartington. He holds it, not ye." Ranald rubbed his hand over the soft hair filling in his tonsure. "Since ye believe it rightfully belongs to ye and not me, I feel no need to wrest it from him."

He moved his arm and plopped his head back on the pillow making the ropes creak. He gave a great yawn.

"Since I have no need to plan for battle, I look forward to sleeping the morrow away." He stretched, yawned again. "Good eve, wife."

"What?" Catalin bolted upright.

"Good eve, wife. 'Tis sorry I am that I mumbled."

Ranald turned away, adjusted his mask so it would not slide, slid his arm under the pillow and thumped it around his head.

Catalin jiggled his shoulder and leaned over him. Her breasts tingled when brushed by the crisp hair of his arm. She jerked back, embarrassed.

"You can't let Uncle Hamon rule Hunter. He is cruel. If they do not cater to his every whim, the Lord only knows how many people he will beat and maim."

"I am not a mercenary. I dinna fight other people's battles. Only my own."

"You were the Protector of Kelso. That did not belong to you."

"Kelso was my home, was meant to be for the rest of my life. Of course, I defended it. Go to sleep and stop yammering."

Catalin turned away at his cold tone. She yanked the covers up to her chin, determined not to sidle close to seek his warmth. Mayhap she should have thought longer on trying to assert herself. Who would have thought a monk-turned-man would have such selfish, male beliefs? Would the day ever come when a woman wed that the man did not seize everything she owned? Surely not while the earth lasted.

Her mind flitted from one idea to the next. No matter how she looked at it, she could not allow her uncle to hold Hunter. When her father lived, he treated all the families there with kindness. He had been a just baron, was never cruel or starved out his peasants. Dratted Uncle Harmon! He would not care if they all died. Her eyes blurred from staring at the ceiling. Ranald had snored for what seemed a very long time. Was the midnight darkness showing between the shutters turning to gray?

Ranald was not stirring. Chief Broccin and the castle

knights would expect to meet with him before dawn. Could he have been serious about staying abed this day? Mayhap she should awake him.

She tapped Ranald's shoulder and waited. Nothing. She tried again. His snores halted a slight bit then changed tone. Expecting him to awaken, she pretended sleep. She breathed deep and counted each breath. Got all the way to twenty. Crud! He did not move.

She drummed her heels on the bed. Nothing. Sitting upright, she glared down at the sleeping man beside her.

"Have it your way. I yield! Hunter Castle is yours."

CHAPTER 14

"WHACK!"

Catalin emphasized her surrender with a thump on Ranald's back. Of a sudden, dizziness struck her.

"Ohhh, saints." She tried to keep from spewing. She gurgled and slapped a hand over her mouth.

Ranald's big hand darted out and grabbed the bread from the bedside table. He turned and shoved it at her, then took her shoulders to ease her down on the bed.

"Lie back. Take small bites. Have ye not learned to sit up slowly?"

She glared at him then clamped her eyes tight and took deep breaths before she brought the bread to her lips.

The way Catalin's small, white teeth nibbled the crust, searching out the driest parts, reminded him of a curious mouse.

He rose and rounded the foot of the bed, fully expecting what came next. Her eyes flew wide. Her hands clamped over her mouth. He leaped forward and drew forth the small bucket, just as her head stretched over the side.

Ranald wiped her face when she was done, and did as he had the morning afore. But this time, he checked to assure himself no one was doused with an unpleasant shower from the window.

"Could ye not try to greet yer husband in a more pleasant way?"

Catalin peeled the cold cloth back to glare at him with one eye.

"The gift of Hunter Castle is not a pleasant greeting?"

"Gift? Huh. It was mine when ye said yer vows. And I'm pleased ye finally saw the error of yer thinking." Ranald shrugged and dressed in quick movements. He left without again looking at his wife.

Sometime before the next dawn, he would seek out Aunt Joneta to find what herbs she had stored and what grew in the castle gardens. 'Twould be simple enough to make a potion to ease Catalin's sickness each morn.

He picked his way around people still sleeping on pallets in the great hall. Going out into the dark bailey, he made his way to the warriors' quarters. He had much to do before Father Martin rang the bells for Matins at dawn.

He gazed over the snoring warriors to select those he wanted. Satisfied, he walked amongst them to nudge them awake.

"Rise. We leave early this day."

Ranald selected each man he had noted leaving on yester morn's patrol. From this time hence, he would ride out with them. No lord with any pride left his castle's security wholly to others. Some men looked at him, reluctance flashing in their eyes. It was easy to see they doubted what skills a former monk would have.

His steely-eyed stare was enough to make them hustle. His barked orders sent them scrambling into their clothing and reaching for their weapons.

"Meet me at the stable, and be quick about it, else ye'll find yerself mucking out stalls."

He intended to know whether man or beast roamed the castle's perimeters each night. Marauding bands studied an area before they plundered it. Spotting anything unusual could mean the difference between a village thriving and one that burned to the ground.

This day, they would leave earlier than usual, for on his return, he must meet with his sire, Domnall and Raik to plan on how best to wrest Hunter back.

Ranald, hearing running footsteps behind him, fingered his sword hilt as he turned to see Finn, still belting on his short sword.

"I will saddle Satan's Spawn at once," he said as he dashed by him.

"Saddle yer own mount, also. I would have ye learn what I expect of ye each day."

Ranald was pleased with the lad. His body was more muscled than most at his age, and he had sprung from his pallet ready to ride afore the seasoned warriors.

On gathering in the bailey, Ranald eyed the leader of the patrol. He had oft trained with Dougald afore going to the abbey. He beckoned him forward to ride beside him.

"I would have ye show me what ye look for each day and what ye believe are our weakest areas."

Ranald set the pace, riding slowly until they cleared the drawbridge. Once they were far enough away they would not awaken all in the keep, he quickened their pace. Dougald outlined the route and the places where he thought Raptor Castle the most vulnerable. All the while, Ranald's gaze pierced the darkness, perusing everything in sight. On entering the woodland paths, he watched the trees ahead, seeking any signs of rustling amongst the branches that was more than normal for small critters and birds.

"I noted the villages looked in poor shape when we entered Raptor Castle lands a few days past. How long since the serfs had new thatching and time to redo their roofs?" His brows near met in a scowl. "I dinna like the looks of them. One spark and all here would be destroyed," he remarked as they rode through a village.

"By my reckoning, it has been a good many years," Dougald said. "Chief Broccin says he canna spare them time from working in the fields to take care of, what he calls, their petty repairs."

"Should the village burn, many lives could be lost. He'll not have enough workers to tend the fields, the cows or anything else."

On hearing hooves pounding outside their huts, startled men poked their heads out their doorways, oft with a shovel or rusty scythe clutched in one hand. On seeing it was naught but the castle patrol riding earlier than usual, they stared at the horsemen and scratched their nether parts.

The men eyed Ranald from head to feet. He wore naught but a tartan slung over his left shoulder and belted at his waist, his broadsword across his back. Some looked aside, no doubt afeared of his mask. Others stared more boldly as they studied his shoulders and arms before they nodded. What did their faces show when he rode past and they spied his back?

Ranald learned much on this early patrol. First of which was his sire did not take care of the cottagers as he should. 'Twas not enough to give protection in exchange for labor. Near every hut needed repair. The vegetables in their gardens looked in need of water, only a scrawny goat or two appeared to give milk, and they had but a handful of chickens for eggs. Every village was alike in need.

Not so when he approached the curtain walls, completing their search of the perimeter. Sheep dotted the far fields while fat, healthy cows grazed in pastures closer-by. Inside the curtain walls, the dovecotes near swayed with plump birds and chickens cackled while roosters crowed, though it was barely dawn.

"Squawk! Squawk!"

A large white hen launched itself off a fence post as they rode past and perched on Finn's shoulder.

"Jesu!" Finn sputtered and flailed his arms. "Get ye gone, ye brainsick bird!" The hen danced and squabbled, its wings striking the young man in the face as it fought for balance.

Finn finally leaned over the side of his horse to shoo the feathered attacker away.

"Yer head be crowned with feathers," one of the men yelled. "Best be wary. The rooster's eyeing ye."

"Best the rooster be careful, else his feathers will be stuffing for a new pillow. I dinna doubt a little boiling, some carrots and onions, and he'll make a tasty soup," Dougald said with a laugh in his voice.

Fat pigs grunted and poked their heads between the fence slats, followed by squealing piglets. The goose girls surely had their hands filled tending the large number of geese they spotted.

Ranald would start setting things aright in his own lands while he made plans for reclaiming Hunter Castle.

Catalin stood on the walkway of the gatehouse barbican, with Elyne beside her. The damp wind tousled her hair about her face, and she swiped it away from her eyes. She raised her arm and waved, for Letia had looked back and waved again. My, how she would miss her friend.

"Dinna fret, Catalin. Once Ranald wrests yer castle from smelly Hamon, ye'll spend more time at Hunter." Elyne looked down at Catalin and flashed a sunny grin. "Letia will be so close ye could travel there in a day."

"If there is a keep left at Hunter." Catalin frowned and rubbed her arms.

"Ranald will not destroy anything he is not forced to."

"I fear to think what damage fire and catapults pounding with every bolder from leagues around, will do to Hunter Castle," Catalin muttered. "They are my people, my friends that will suffer."

"Ye know Ranald isna like Father. Did yer husband not hand select twelve of our finest warriors to escort the de Burgh's?"

Elyne's unexpected peel of laughter startled Catalin.

"What do you laugh over? I see nothing to be merry about."

"Did ye not see Father's face? When he argued with Ranald that we couldna spare the men?" Elyne giggled again. "He was near to bursting when that egg splattered on his forehead."

"That was most strange. Never have I seen a chicken start laying an egg and suddenly fly through the air like a hand pushed it!" Catalin started laughing with Elyne.

"Raik said, 'Ye get better every day,' when he threw his arm around Ranald's shoulder. Know ye what he meant?"

"Nay. It is a puzzle." Catalin nibbled on her lower lip. "I

was pleased Ranald left off his planning to bid Letia and Warin Godspeed. He seems to like them both."

"Father does not, though."

"I doubt a man who cannot love his own son would like many people."

Catalin winced on remembering the hateful glares Chief Broccin foisted on Ranald. No wonder bitterness filled her husband's eyes.

She had always known her father loved her. Though he may not have kissed or hugged her like he had her mother, he found ways without saying so in words.

Mayhap it would be in summoning her to the stable where the mouser had birthed a new litter, and asking if she would like one of the kits when the mother cat weaned them. Or, taking her to a fair and noting if her eyes lingered on any special thing. If so, it would appear on her bed when Hannah took her above for the night.

Never once did she feel her sire regretted her birth, not even on his deathbed knowing his only heir was one very small woman. He had put his frail hand on her cheek, his voice barely strong enough to be heard when he spoke. "God blessed me with you, Catalin. You were the sun in my life."

Ranald stood and stretched. He glanced around the solar, noting the change in the room since his father had thrown open the door and ordered the women sewing and gossiping there to hie themselves elsewhere. Catalin and Elyne were not amongst them. When last he looked, he had seen their silhouettes atop the barbican long after Letia and Baron de Burgh had left.

The day had waned. Aunt Joneta had seen the men supplied with their evening meal, and servants had cleared everything away when the men finished.

"Then 'tis agreed." Ranald paced around the solar. "We send men to the countryside surrounding Hunter Castle, one to every nearby castle to start rumors afloat. They will burn a field, then pretend they are a traveler who happened by and hid in the woods when they spied men from the nearest neighboring castle torch the crop."

"Aye." Raik nodded, satisfied. "A word here, a word there. Soon all will think their neighbor plots against them. They will be so busy fighting each other, they willna have time to interfere with us when we lay siege to Hunter."

Broccin snorted. "Did the monks teach ye to be devious, Ranald?"

"Nay. I learned from a master of trickery afore going to Kelso," Ranald said.

They sat around a table, a parchment weighted down on the corners filling much of the space. On it, Raik had drawn simple pictures of streams and hills, villages, forests and castles. Ranald pulled a stool close and straddled it.

He bent over, took crude wooden spoons and placed them in a pattern in front of the gatehouse.

"We set up our siege engines within striking distance of the gatehouse. Ye say we have men well-trained to accurately gauge the range?"

Domnall grinned. "During summer months, we move a trebuchet inside the curtain wall then mark targets outside on the open fields. The men are most adept at sliding the counterpoise along the beam to adjust the range. Ye'll see."

"Down to as small a target as an ailing rooster," Raik added.

Ranald raised his brows at that. "Ye have tried?"

"Nay. Domnall did the deed. He murdered the little crower." Raik's tsk sounded like he thought Domnall a beast.

A scratch at the door caused them to halt. They wanted no one to leak what they were planning.

"Enter." Ranald did not disguise the impatience in his voice.

Lady Muriele swung the door wide. A servant entered carrying a tray laden with a large decanter and goblets.

"Cruddy Lucifer," Ranald muttered. He flinched for his mask lay on a small table beside the doorway far from his grasp. He stalked over to a window, his ruined cheek toward it.

"It is late in the eve. Ye have closeted yerselves away all this day. Lady Joneta thought ye might like cold ale for refreshment."

Muriele's voice was as soft and melodic as birds greeting the sun's rise. She lowered her eyes, appearing shy in a room solely of men. When she served everyone at the table, she filled another goblet. He watched her glide toward him with feline grace. His raised hand halted her when she was a step away. He spoke without turning to face her.

"Thank ye." He reached for the goblet, but noticed from the corner of his eye that she edged to her left to better spy his face. "Halt. Ye are close enough." He snatched the cup from her hand and turned his back to her.

"Ye are as handsome as Moridac," she whispered.

"Go."

He stiffened and did not turn until he heard the whisper of her shoes leaving, and a few heartbeats later, the door closing.

Raik let out a great whoosh of air before saying, "Would that the lady showed as much interest in me."

"It is only morbid interest." Ranald grimaced.

"Ye'll not take her to yer bed." Broccin's voice was cold, angry even.

"Best not think of her warming yers, sire," Ranald said as he approached the table. "She has placed her trust in us to protect her. I'll not see her soiled."

"Ye'll not? I am chief here. Till my death, ye have no say in what goes on at Raptor."

Ranald's eyelids narrowed. "Dinna tempt me."

On seeing his sire's mouth drop to his chin, he had some small satisfaction. He turned back to the table.

"Domnall, send two men inside Hunter Castle's curtain walls. If they listen under the eaves of the huts there, they might glean some bit of knowledge the people wouldn't freely speak of."

"Aye. I know the best men for the job. They can hear a feather drop on the training ground and are smaller than most. They can weave their way around in the dark shadows of night and escape notice." Domnall nodded and swallowed down his ale.

"What extra training should we have the men doing?" Raik leaned forward and studied Ranald's face.

"All warriors should be building their skills with bow, sword, mace, axe and pick. Double the patrols, Domnall. That will keep them busy when not working in the training fields. To build better muscles, they will work repairing the village huts still in reasonable shape, re-thatch where needed and build new ones. If that is not enough to make them sweat and build muscles, they can clear and plant a new field for herbs and vegetables within the curtain walls."

"Do ye think to spark a revolt?" Raik tilted back on his stool and laughed.

"Nay." Ranald shook his head, his face serious. "At Kelso, we didna have a minute when we were not doing something with our bodies. Ye saw the beauty there. We built it ourselves. Our only rest was during prayers. The work at the abbey honed my body. Why should our warriors do less?"

The plans they made that day was the start of all the days to follow for the next two months.

"Elyne, are the freckles across my nose unseemly? Is my face so plain it does not stir interest?"

Catalin stopped nibbling on her finger to look over at Elyne. It was a warm day, and they sat on a woolen blanket spread beneath the apple trees. "Moridac oft told me I was comely. Mayhap he did not speak the truth," she muttered.

"He spoke true, silly. Yer freckles make ye look like a faerie about to spring into some mischief." Her gaze roved over Catalin's face, searching. "I see naught unseemly about ye. Yer hair is an unusual shade that brings summer to mind, yer nose small, yer mouth just right, and yer blue eyes sparkle. What can ye find wrong about all that?"

Before her sister-by-law could answer, a stream of warriors returned from their duties dripping with sweat, looking like it took great effort to put one foot in front of the other.

Elyne balanced back on her elbows and studied the men as they trailed past, near dragging their weapons on the ground. Their barracks stood a short distance away, between the apple trees where the women sat and the stable.

"Catalin, have ye noted how tired they seem when returning after a day on the practice field with Ranald?"

"Aye. Look! Look at Sir Dougald. He's trying to drown himself in the water trough." Catalin stared at the man, wondering how long he could keep his head submerged before he needed air. "Saints! I counted to thirty before he came up."

"Raik said last eve that never has he worked so hard at training as he has under Ranald. We have seen little to nothing of my brother of late." Elyne looked at Catalin, a question in her eyes.

Even if Moridac had thought her comely, his twin did not seem to find her so. He had not touched her again in that way a husband should. Last eve, she had fought sleep until way past the midnight time, until Ranald quietly came into the room, undressed and eased into bed. She spoke to let him know she was awake. He did naught but snap at her to go to sleep.

"I know. He does not come to our chamber until way into the night. He never, uh, awakens me." Catalin's face heated.

"That is kind of him," Elyne said.

"Hmpf." Catalin could not stop the sound, for the more she thought on it, the more she worried.

"Oh. You mean he has not …?"

"Nay. I mean, aye. He has not." Catalin bent her knees up under her chin, settled her skirts for modesty, and wrapped her arms around them.

"Not even …?"

"Oh, he did. That first night." Catalin put her forehead down on her knees.

"Well, did he not, uh, enjoy himself?" Elyne looked up at the tree then down at a small bug struggling to climb atop a bent twig. "Hmm, I heard him shout. And I thought I heard ye moaning like ye were right pleased."

"Aye. We both were pleasured mightily."

"And the night ye thought he was dying? Was that not from his being overexcited? All thought he was having great bed sport, what with the pillows and sheets strewn across the floor."

"He was praying," Catalin whispered.

"What?" Elyne leaned closer. "I misheard ye."

"You heard me aright. Ranald was praying."

Elyne snorted. "Sure, and he was. I heard Raik telling Ranald 'Dinna waste it,' and Ranald looked down at himself then slammed the door.

"Nay, really. I awoke in the night near freezing. The shutters stood wide. I rolled close to find him, for we had not enough covers on the bed. Naught but cold sheets greeted me until I neared the edge of the bed. I threw everything off so I could peer over the side. I saw Ranald. I thought he was dying."

"Why? Did he moan and writhe about?"

Catalin shook her head.

"Clutch his belly, then?"

"Nay. He lay stretched out on the floor. Face downward, arms out like a bird."

"Huh? Had he fallen?"

"Nay. He was not hurt at all. He was praying! No doubt, he was hoping God would help him bear his wife. He finds me ugly." Catalin near died of shame.

"Surely ye jest? His eyes follow ye whenever ye are in sight." Elyne stared at Catalin and shook her head. "That does not sound like a man who finds his wife hard to look at."

"You may see him look, but you do not see the expression in his eyes." Catalin puffed a burst of air to dislodge a curl sliding down her forehead.

"Mayhap ye mistake a look of need for something else?"

"I would wish so. But, nay. He freezes me with one glance. If I turn my gaze to another man, he will stalk over and grasp my elbow. His mouth draws back like he is in pain, and his look singes all thought of anything else from my mind."

"Humph. Sounds like a man who suffers from air in the belly." She grinned then pulled a long face at Catalin. "Mayhap ye should offer to rub it for him?"

"I wish it could be so simple. I truly think he hates me. Why else would a man avoid his new wife?"

Catalin frowned and stared across the grass, only vaguely aware of the men trailing into the barracks. A flash of bright green cloth caught her eye. Hm. Muriele's kirtle. Why was she coming from the training grounds, a serving girl following her with a tray? The answer seemed clear, but why had she tended this duty?

"'Tis Muriele."

"Aye. Did ye think her someone else?" Elyne's brows raised in question.

"Nay. I have noted both Ranald and your cousin looking at her and talking. Some days ago, Raik laughed and thumped Ranald on the shoulder. Like he congratulated him for something. Ranald walked away and Raik near bent double with laughter."

"I ne'er thought I would use such crude words about my brother, but do ye think mayhap he is dipping his wick in another honey pot?"

"Huh?" Catalin frowned at her. What did she mean?

"Ye know. In bed sport. Are ye afeared he is giving some other woman what rightfully belongs to ye?"

Catalin's breath caught as if Elyne had dunked her into a cold loch. She barely nodded, thinking it over. Mayhap that was the cause Ranald didn't desire her. He was sated before he came to their bed. How could she fight his having a leman?

"Ye will have to lure him away from other interests." Elyne pressed her lips together, pondering.

Shame overcame Catalin. She knew nothing about men and what they desired in bed. Best she ask Elyne. She would have heard and learned more growing up with the three men. She hesitated, lowered her head and stared down at her hands grasped tight in her lap.

"If I would lure him to my bed, I must know what he likes in bed sport. How might I entice him?"

Elyne's loud gulp alerted her. Before her words faded, the hair on Catalin's arms prickled. She knew who stood behind her.

His words were cold and hard, each one dropping on her soul like heavy rocks on soft sand.

"Wife, do ye crave a man's flesh so strongly ye plot to snare another to yer bed?"

CHAPTER 15

"**I** AWAIT YER ANSWER, wife."

Catalin's stomach clenched and her arms drew her knees even closer to her chin, making herself as small as possible. She peeked sideways, half hoping she was brainsick and hearing things. Instead, her gaze met two heavily muscled calves. Dirt clung to the crisp curly hair there, and a streak of mud covered one knee down his shinbone. Both strong feet were bare but for mud coating them to his ankles.

"Which of my warriors have ye picked to grace yer bed when I leave for Hunter?"

Saints! Ranald's voice sounded mean. Seeing his feet shift, she knew he was not going to wait long for an answer. She took a deep breath.

"None, my lord."

Drats! Why had she worried that he did not find her comely? She should be glad. Moridac had been the only man she wanted to wed. For sure, vanity had pricked her pride, making her want Ranald to desire her as much as Moridac had. Now look where that foolishness brought her!

"Then 'tis someone higher? My captain of the guards? Cormac?"

"Do not be foolish. I have no interest in Sir Cormac. I am not even sure which man he is."

The grass around them started to move like waves on a lake when the wind was brisk.

"Oh? Then for what reason did ye stare at him but moments ago."

"I stared at no one." Catalin's anger began to stir that he so easily thought she would be unfaithful to him.

"At the water trough. Need I remind ye? Ye looked long and hard while he splashed water over his chest!"

'Twas a strange, hot wind that blew Catalin's hair back from her face, not the crisp coolness she had felt a short time afore. Branches overhead began to sway until dried leaves sprinkled down to snag in her hair.

"Dinna be foolish, Ranald." Elyne's voice cut in. "We were watching Sir Domnall." She reached up to shove her brown hair from her eyes and catch a falling leaf. "He kept his head dunked so long, Catalin but wondered if he might drown himself."

"Domnall?" Ranald moved a step closer, his toes anchoring her skirts to the ground. "Ye scheme to lure a man near old enough to be yer father? He is far too wise to succumb to the wiles of a foolish woman."

"Would that you became as wise as he." Catalin grabbed her skirt and tugged, but he shifted his weight forward to thwart her.

"He also desires to keep his head firmly above his shoulders," Ranald added.

"And you call *me* a foolish woman? What witless thought burrowed into *your* mind and caused it to leap from my watching Sir Domnall dunking his head to my scheming to take him to my bed?"

"Witless? Nay. I judge from what I see with my own eyes."

"Ha. Then what potion did Muriele slip into your ale that caused you to form such foolish imaginings about me?"

"Dinna defame the lass. Ye would do well to learn a woman's gentle ways from her."

"And you would do well to learn knightly ways from Sir Fergus. Move your foot!"

Was she brainsick? She'd done it again. Blathering when she should keep her mouth shut. Catalin's skin prickled with that strange feeling before lightning struck.

Thunk! An apple fell from branches thrashing wildly overhead and struck Elyne's lap. She bolted to her feet and shook out her skirts, dislodging it.

"Ack! Cruddy Lucifer. It was worm-eaten." Elyne studied the rustling grass and trees then looked up at the sky. Her narrowed eyes scanned Ranald's face, his lips drawn back in a snarl.

"Hm. There is no wind behind ye, Ranald, only in front. Since ye returned, it has become most unruly. Do ye contr ...?"

"Enough!" Ranald leaned down, grasped Catalin's wrist and hauled her upright.

Riiip! Her green kirtle parted at her right shoulder, revealing a sheer smock that did little to hide the beauty beneath it.

Too late, he stepped back, his gaze fixed on the creamy flesh of her right breast. His snarl slackened; he wet his lips before he swallowed. His face tightened in a different way. A hungry gleam burned in his eyes, much like a hound that stares at a juicy bone gripped in his master's fist.

"Let go of me, unless you want the whole of Raptor to see how *chivalrous* you are, dolt."

Catalin shook her wrist free from his now slack fingers. She grabbed the torn material and tugged it to her neck, then frowned down at the muddy footprint gracing her skirt.

He reached for her again, no doubt intent on dragging her off to let her know the full brunt of his anger.

"Ye would call me dolt? Do ye dare prick my anger anew?"

She gasped, for his nostrils flared, the muscles in his jaw twitched.

"Ranald," Raik shouted.

Ranald hesitated, his hand hovering close to her shoulder. He stopped and swung around to see Raik sprinting toward the drawbridge, his arm out gesturing for Ranald to follow. All thoughts of Catalin's foolish words fled his mind. For the moment. More important matters than teaching his wife he was not some callow youth she could lead by a string, needed his attention.

A man, battered and bleeding, rode through the gatehouse. His horse stumbled from fatigue, caught his footing and trudged on. Men ran out of the barracks and surrounded the horseman, parting to let Ranald and his cousin through.

Ranald reached the man in time to pluck him off the horse

before he fell to the ground.

"Get Domnall from the barracks. Tell him to meet me ... shite! Meet me in the solar." Ranald's long legs near ran to take the man inside. "Send a man to fetch Aunt Joneta. I have need of her herbs. Have another bring a fresh pallet to the solar. I will tend him there."

Raik pointed to two men, gave them their orders, and then ran to follow Ranald. He sprinted ahead of Ranald to open the heavy doors and order everyone out of the room.

"Clear the table, I'll need to see what we must deal with."

Ranald held the man in his arms like he was naught but a slight child. Once Raik had swiped everything off the table onto the floor, Ranald placed the injured man there.

"Help me cut his clothing away." He eyed the man's bloody head. Someone had hacked both ears off. "It is Gille, one of our listeners, isn't he?"

"Aye."

They worked together, cutting down the front of the man's ragged clothing so they could strip it back.

"More than one man did this damage. Never have I seen so many bruises. They must have kicked him with their boots." Raik sucked his teeth in sympathy.

"What are ye doing?" Broccin's voice boomed as he entered the room.

"I couldna take him to the barracks to tend." Ranald kept his voice calm, not wanting to startle the injured man. "In a castle as large as Raptor, there are bound to be spies amongst the warriors. I dinna want what he says to reach their ears."

"Tend him in the stables, then. Horses' dinna care what words he speaks. And what matters where he dies, as long as it is not where I come to take my ease."

"Gille will be cared for here." Ranald's tone left no doubt he would not allow Broccin to thwart him. "He sustained these wounds obeying our commands. We can do no less than care for him."

Ranald ignored his father's blustering. His fingers felt over the man's flesh, seeking for broken bones. Lady Joneta hurried into the room carrying a basket filled with vials, small earthenware pots and small bunches of herbs tied together. Catalin and Elyne followed, bringing two baskets of clean linen cut in long strips and rolled to keep them from collecting dust.

"I ordered hot water. It will be here in short order, Ranald." Lady Joneta waited while Elyne and Catalin brought over a small table and placed it handy to Ranald's hands. She unpacked her remedies, placing them in orderly lines across one side of the table, the linen cloths placed according to size on the rest of the space.

Raik glanced up and saw Catalin's white face, her lips pressed tight together. She stared at the man's battered body.

"Does he come from Hunter Castle? I do not recognize him." Her voice was so low he near had to strain to hear her.

"Nay. He belongs to Raptor."

"How can you be sure?" She came closer to peer around him and gasped when she spied the man's bloody head. "What manner of beast would cut off a man's ears?"

"Elyne, remove Catalin afore she spews over my back. Raik, clear the room and post a guard at the door. Keep everyone out but the man bringing the pallet."

He sighed, his tension easing when all had been ushered from the room but those he needed. His skills along with his aunt's would better the chances the man would live. The hot water arrived, and with the first basin, they cleansed their hands until not a speck of grime was on them or beneath their nails. Raik took charge of dumping soiled water out the window opening and refilling the basin with fresh hot water.

The man groaned. His eyes opened to stare fearfully up at Ranald. He twisted and fought, until Domnall's voice soothed him.

"Hold still, Gille. We are trying to clean yer wounds."

"I thought ye meant to slit me belly wide."

Ranald halted. His voice came out slow and even, with no hint of feeling.

"What happened? Were ye found out?"

"Aye. Found out. The cook's lass tried to sneak out last eve.

Through the window opening. She stepped on me head." He drew in a breath and hissed it out slowly. "She screamed like I had kilt her."

"Her father did this to you? He must prize his daughters high." Raik voice sounded surprised.

"Nay, 'twas the guard. Came running. Once't they finished with me, they left me fer dead." He near bit his lips through when Ranald cleaned filth away from the ragged skin around his ears.

"Domnall, help him drink some wine. Raik, roll a cloth tight and give it to him to bite on."

"Thank ye. I dinna want to shame meself screaming like a lass."

Ranald waited until the man downed the goblet of wine without even taking a breath. Where someone had sliced Gille's ears away, Ranald stitched the wound as best he could.

"At first, I kenned the cook would finish what the guards had thought done. But he knew I was not one of them. 'Twas him what helped me on me horse and led it out the postern gate." He flinched when Ranald started closing the wound. "He said he was sorry he couldna help me more."

"I take it ye heard some bit of news before ye were found out?"

"Aye. None likes the new master. They call this Hamon the 'smelly bastid.'" The man stopped and panted. "All are afeared. One eve, the hunter drank with the fletcher. Heard them whisper. He waits fer the day Hamon rises from his lazy arse and goes into the forest." He gritted his teeth and could not talk for a bit.

"Get on with it, man. I dinna want to stay up all night waiting for yer reports." Broccin scowled down at the man and reached out to jiggle his shoulder.

The injured man gasped and blinked. "Aye. The fletcher gave him an arrow."

"Hmpf. So he gave him an arrow. What is unusual about that?" Broccin's voice sounded impatient.

"'Twas coated with mandrake and shite and allowed to dry. If the arrow's flight isna true and misses his heart, the poison and a festering wound will make up fer it." His voice faded as he went limp.

Ranald felt his neck. The thready pulse beating there gave him hope.

They worked well together. His aunt covered the wounds with a healing salve then held pads of linen tightly over them while Ranald bandaged the dressing into place.

The light from the window had long since faded by the time they were satisfied all had been tended. Ranald nodded. He would return to sit with the man after he attended Vigils in the darkest time of the night.

That should give him enough time to show his restless wife that though he had been a monk, he was more than capable of fulfilling her shameful needs.

"Why would anyone cut that man's ears off? 'Tis barbaric," Catalin splashed cold water over her face, her own problems forgotten for the moment.

"No doubt he was sent to gather information by listening beneath window openings." Elyne held Catalin's curls back from her face. "Do ye feel better now?"

"Aye. I hate to admit it, but Ranald was right when he sent me from the room. Just a little while longer, and I truly would have spewed down his back."

"Ye are having trouble with sickness at dawn, are ye not?" Elyne leaned forward so she could peer around at Catalin's flushed face.

"And at eventide, too," Catalin confessed. "'Tis a good thing I have a hearty liking for food, else I would be naught but a shadow."

"I thought as much. Father was querying Ada this morn. It has been a month since ye wed, and he wanted to know if yer woman's time had come."

"Nay. Did you know your father has set Ada to spying for him?"

"Hmpf. It does not surprise me. Why have ye allowed her to

be yer chamber maid?" Seeing Catalin felt better, she released the handful of curls and handed Catalin a drying cloth.

"Hannah and I could tell right from the first that Ada had no liking for what he ordered. We formed a pact to feed him words of what we would have him know. By this next dawn, he will know Ranald's seed has taken."

"Um, Catalin?" Elyne lower lip came up to cover her upper. She hesitated while clearing her throat.

"What is it?" Catalin patted her face dry, took great care to fold the cloth and place it beside the basin.

"I never told ye, but I had one of my dreams before Moridac died." Elyne's piercing gaze locked with Catalin's. She sat on the edge of the bed and fiddled with her skirts, having them lay just so.

"One of your dreams? Moridac told me you oft had dreams you believed were glimpses into the future. Is this one of them?"

"Aye. It was a sennight before ye arrived at Raptor."

"Did it have to do with Moridac?" A horrible thought struck Catalin. "Oh no, pray do not tell me you dreamed of his death!"

"Nay. I dinna think I could have stood that, for I surely would have misread the dream and not have been able to save him."

"Well, then, tell me about your dream. Has it come true?"

Catalin waited eagerly, for she had heard of women whose dreams came true.

"It was verra dark in my dream, hazy like an early morn when ye can barely see the barbican? I heard footsteps outside my door, and when I opened it, I saw my brother carrying his shoes. I followed him as he walked to yer bedchamber door. He eased it open and disappeared inside."

"You dreamt such?" Catalin swallowed, feeling a flush of shame start from her neck and cover her face.

"Aye. And I heard him talking with ye, though that wouldna be possible, for the doors and walls are so thick anyone would have to shout to be heard on the other side."

"What did he say?"

"It wasna clear, but he was answering ye. I could hear only

his voice. He said, 'I am going to make pashing net love'. At least it sounded like pashing to me, though I have never heard the word. Then he said something like incense and sennight, and that ye were his, and that ye would have great bed sport together." Elyne blushed and twisted her rope girdle into knots.

Catalin stared at her, trying not to let her jaw drop open.

"Do ye think I am crazed?" Elyne's voice was hesitant. She ran a finger over her full lips and flashed Catalin a fearful look.

"Nay, you are far from being brainsick, Elyne." Catalin sat beside her on the bed, pulled her legs crosswise and settled her skirts around them. "When did you say you had this dream?"

"A sennight afore ye came to Raptor." She ran her fingers through her hair and started twisting a hank beside her ear as much as she had her poor tortured girdle.

"Have you had other dreams that came true?" Catalin voice was wobbly, and she cleared her throat to cover it up.

"It has always been a joke, for I will dream of events, but they dinna happen as I expect. Like seeing kits being born and running to the cow byre to find there were no new mousers, but the pig had birthed piglets." Elyne frowned and tugged her hair harder. "Aye, it does happen, but not the way I had envisioned. The event, that is, not the thing in the dream. The best way to explain it is the first dream long ago. 'Twas the night Father injured Ranald."

"Saints above! You were naught but a youngling then."

"Aye. In my dream, Ranald and Moridac were behind the cow byre. Ranald laughed and jumped atop a sleek, black cow, but a bull charged out of the dark and chased the cow. Ranald fell off right at the bull's hooves, and it ripped at him with his horns and stomped him till the ground turned red with blood."

Catalin squeezed Elyne's hand in sympathy. "What a horrid dream."

"Aye. I awoke screaming about cows smashing my Ray." She wrinkled her nose. "I couldna say his name. Strange as it may seem, from that night on, I have held a fear, and a, um, disgust for Father. I was always happiest when he was away on Crusades." She grimaced, shaking her head. "Years later,

Hannah told me he fought in the battle of Azaz and had recently returned. In the fighting, the Turks killed his favorite warhorse. When Father captured a Seljuk Turk riding a magnificent, black mount, he killed the man and took the horse for his own. He named it Goliath and forbade anyone but the stable master or his squire to touch the beast."

"Mayhap he feared Goliath would injure another?"

"Nay. 'Twas because Father canna stand anyone touching something that is his."

Not even a whisper of sound floated to Catalin, but her body tingled with sharp pricks over her skin. A voice taut with menace sounded from the doorway.

"As I will allow no other to touch that which is mine!"

CHAPTER 16

R ANALD'S PRESENCE FILLED THE room, though he stood but a step inside the bedchamber doorway. He moved with a stiff, angry gait toward Catalin. Like a man about to pounce.

Chills crept down her spine. She had not expected a man who had been a monk for so many years to say such or to feel the need to say it.

Her face grew hot, her lips clamped together and her nostrils flared. How could he insult her by even a thought that she would be unfaithful? Forgetting caution and the need to protect herself, her voice rose with bitter resentment.

"Until we wed, you had naught to call your own. Now you claim all that was mine. My manors, my wealth, my castle! Which of these do you speak of?"

"Ye forgot one thing else, wife. Though not as valuable as yer castle or yer other honors, yer body belongs to me."

Ranald's lips twitched in that lethal way, reminding Catalin of a hungry predator.

"Out!" He jerked a finger toward the door.

Though Catalin knew he did not mean the command for her, she glared at him and jumped up, ready to leave with Elyne. Not because she was affrighted. She was too angry for that. It would be best to leave, for she feared if she struck Ranald with the water pitcher, God would never forgive her.

"Humph! Did the monks teach ye to be so ill-mannered, brother?" Elyne stuck her tongue out at him on her way out of the room.

Catalin got as far as a step from the doorway before his

grip on her shoulder jolted her to a halt. She waited until Elyne pulled the door to before she spoke again.

"You do not own me like the cow in the byre or a horse in the pasture. Let go of me." She turned and jerked her shoulder, trying to dislodge his grip.

"Aye, but I do." His fingers tightened for a heartbeat, then released her.

"It is not the same! I am your wife, not some dumb animal who cannot think and talk. I belong to you because we are wed the same as you belong to me.

"It doesna work both ways. A woman's body belongs to her husband. She must hold herself only for him. A man shares his body with his wife, or with any woman he so chooses."

A vision of Muriele naked on a bed with Ranald sprawled at her side, his leg across hers, flashed in Catalin's mind. It near made her gag.

"Do you tell me you keep a leman?"

"I said no such thing. It is ye who were planning to lure a man to yer bed." Ranald stalked over to rest his sword against the bedside table. He turned slowly to stare at her. "I would sample this bed sport ye planned to entice him with. Take off yer clothes."

"I will not. It is not yet dark."

"Did ye plot with Elyne so long ye forgot to note the day has passed?" He spread his legs wide in a hostile manner and folded his arms across his chest. "I told ye to take of yer clothes."

"And I told *ye* I would not."

Catalin's chin jutted. Never had she felt as riled as she did now with Ranald. And she did not know why. Nay, she lied to herself. She did know why. 'Twas because he near accused her of taking a lover, while with her own eyes she had seen more than once that he was enamored of Muriele.

"Take them off!"

The words bounced off the walls, as Ranald moved to stand beside the window opening.

Catalin flinched. Shook her head.

The muscles in Ranald's jaw twitched. Blazing anger shot

from his eyes. His gaze raked down her body to the hem of the blue kirtle she had donned for the evening meal. A cold gust of wind blew in from the window. It did not ruffle even a hair on his head.

The cloth about Catalin's ankles moved and began to flap, cooling them. Faster and faster it moved. The kirtle whipped about her calves, forcing the wind beneath the cloth until it billowed and reached her knees.

She batted her skirts trying to control them, but it was no use. Suddenly, linen swaddled her head. She fought against it and thrust it off. It landed on the floor in a rumpled, blue pile.

She gulped and eyed the window. All the wind outside seemed aimed at that one small opening. Ranald did not seem bothered, but ignored it.

His lips lifted in a thin smile, no doubt sensing her fear as he slowly unbuckled his belt. She released her breath when he let it drop to the floor. The end of his tartan slipped down from his massive shoulder.

Fascinated, she watched. Freed, the folded length around his waist clung to his flesh as it took its slow time leaving his body to join his belt. The wind did not rustle even the smallest part of his clothing.

Ranald was bare but for the scant braies worn for battle practice. He had drawn the white linen around his waist, up between his thighs to cover his sex, and joined it at his belly.

It was the first time Catalin had seen him in this scant garb. Somehow, it drew her gaze far more than his naked flesh would, for it tempted her to envision what was beneath the linen.

Moving to the foot of the bed, he sat on the edge and drew off his boots. Not once did he shift his regard from her. She felt rooted to the spot where she stood.

When he rose, his gaze fixed on her shoulders. Catalin clutched her thin smock. Why did he not pull the shutters closed? Wind could not untie the ribbons at her neck, could it?

Soon, she felt as if warm, strong fingers lingered there. Her lids flew wide when the thin strips of silk began to slide and the bow came untied. She grasped for the ends, but they eluded her. The smock slithered from her shoulders. She wrapped her arms around her waist, trying to anchor it there. She darted a look downward.

Saints! Her arms clasped around her waist thrusting her breasts upward made it look as if she offered them to him. She dared not move, for what little she had left on would join that on the floor.

It would expose her body to his heated eyes.

Every spot Ranald's gaze touched felt like warm hands caressing her flesh. Her body heated. She swallowed and fidgeted when he studied her stomach beneath the sheer smock.

"Yer babe has grown much these past fortnights." He wet his lips and stared at her breasts.

Her nipples tightened and strained toward him. Shamed, she moved her hands to cover them. Wisk! Her startled gaze followed her smock as it near flew to the ground.

Saints! His bare toes near met her shoes. When had he moved? She felt even more indecent standing there naked with naught but her shoes and stockings to cover her. The thought made her breasts swell.

Of a sudden, his arms slid beneath her knees and around her waist. He lifted her against his chest. A frizzle of excitement built when the crisp hair on his chest scraped her nipples. A gasp of pleasure slipped out before she could stifle it.

His skin felt so warm. Hot, even. The feel of his bunching shoulder muscles, the hard warmth of his chest, all sent anticipation through her. Her hip pressed against the hard slab of his belly, and when he bent to lay her on the bed, she missed the intimate contact with his flesh.

She near clutched his arm when he slid it from her. Her mouth went dry, for he straddled her, wearing his braies still. His aroused flesh bulged against the clothing. She dragged her gaze upward and saw he chuckled.

Drats!

Was he a sorcerer that he could inflame her with one look? She had been furious at his high-handed remarks, and what had she done? She had melted like butter on a hot iron grill the minute his flesh touched hers.

minute his flesh touched hers.

Devil take it! She needed him. Had Moridac turned her into a lust-crazed slattern? Nay, not Moridac. She had not craved man-flesh after her time with him. 'Twas only after the first night with Ranald that she could not stop the feelings only he had brought forth from her.

"Ye stare, wife. Ah. Ye are impatient? If ye would sample what is beneath the braies, ye would do well to tempt it with a display of this bed sport ye were planning."

"I planned no bed sport. How oft must I say it?"

His only response was to bend his knees and lower himself to press against the bare flesh at her legs' joining. She tried hard not to look at him cuddled there. Her breathing quickened, and when he wiggled his arse, the heat from his groin against the red curls between her legs seared her. Her gaze flew to his braies.

She could not mistake the hard pulse of his full arousal beneath the scant cloth. His long, slender fingers ever so slowly reached for the knot at his waist. Her breath quickened, her fingers twitched, and her body flushed from the top of her head to her smallest toes.

What took him so long? Why did he stop? She shivered and raised her eyes to peer at him. His mask did not hide his eyes or the animal lust there. Blazing black eyes flashed at her. Were they green and not black, she would feel it was a hungry wolf who kept her pinned.

He looked down. Her gaze followed. His blatant, aggressive arousal stood free. She shamed herself with a low moan, and arched her shoulders, thrusting her breasts upward in invitation. He leaned forward and flicked her straining nipples with the tip of his tongue, sending excitement flooding to her moist, needy place.

He rubbed his face against her breast and began to suckle. Using his knee, he spread her legs so he could burrow his body there. After he aroused both breasts until she found herself digging her fingers into his scarred shoulders, she clamped her legs around his buttocks, urging him toward what she needed.

"Aye, ye are needy, lass." Ranald rubbed his tarse against

her, teasing her flesh. Catalin cried out and grasped him tighter. He nudged the slick wet heat of her, entered slowly and buried himself until the springy, black curls of his groin mingled with the red at hers. Her sharp gasp of satisfaction heated Ranald's blood the way no practiced tricks of bed sport could.

She answered each thrust with her own.

If he lifted his chest and did not touch her, she arched her body until her breasts brushed the hair on his chest.

He teased her with subtle, circling movements of his hips. She clamped him all the tighter.

Each rock of his buttocks she met and matched with an answer, until she writhed beneath him and cried out, begging for release. He arched his back up enough to slip his hand between them. He teased her slick flesh around where he plunged, until she thrashed and grabbed his hair. She pulled it, crying out near senseless with passion. Feeling his mask slipping, he stroked upward over her swollen nub.

Catalin's scream drowned out his shout as they convulsed together until both were limp.

Ranald buried his face against her neck, inhaling her violet-scented flesh. His breathing finally slowed, and sanity returned. With it came guilt.

He pushed away from her and fell over on his back, the cold sheet dampening his ardor even more.

What manner of man was he? Surely the weakest of kinds. He had resolved not to touch Catalin while she was carrying his brother's bairn. His will lasted little over a month. He raked his fingers through thick, wavy hair that now covered his head. He bit off a groan and dropped an arm over his eyes.

Tonight he had near gone crazed with lust. Was this how Moridac, how his father lived? With a constant turmoil of wanting? Of craving female flesh? Of strong drink? He had changed much. How long would it be afore he, too, became battle crazed and drunk with killing?

He bolted up, grabbed his woolen tartan from the floor and his belt in one hand, his sword in the other. He was still belting the tartan around his waist when he burst out into the front bailey and the cold, wet night. His long strides carried him silently across the ground and into the empty church.

Would that he could scourge himself as his father had punished him those many years gone by. At Kelso, when his body cried out for the pleasures of the flesh, he had made use of the flagellum to distract himself with pain. Until the night when Prior Godric had fetched the abbot who had talked sense into him. Would that they were with him now.

He knelt in front of the altar, his arms uplifted, his eyes focused on the cross hanging before the arched window.

His voice rose softly in plainsong, singing the words of the Psalms, becoming stronger with each verse until his deep baritone filled the small chapel and drifted on the still night.

Catalin, clutching a blanket around her body, stared down at the church bathed in moonlight.

Listening.

Hearing the pain in her husband's beautiful voice, tears blurred her vision.

Before the midnight hour of Vigils, Ranald's voice faded. For a space, not a sound drifted from the church, and then his voice rang out in a plea.

"Jesu!"

CHAPTER 17

"WHY DO YE TORTURE yerself so?" Raik's big hand squeezed Ranald's shoulder, giving comfort.

"Why?"

Ranald blinked. He rose slowly, stiff from kneeling on the cold stones. He started to think of some tale he could tell his cousin but did not, needing someone to voice his worries to. He sorely missed having midnight talks with Abbot Aymer. He released a long, unsteady sigh.

"Soon all will know Catalin is increasing."

"That is reason for giving thanks, not grieving. Why would it cause the pain in yer voice?" Raik's blue gaze bored into Ranald eyes, like he would read his soul.

"Because I," Ranald struck himself in the chest, "a man who was once pious, am forced to live a lie for the rest of my life."

"Why would ye ... ? Ye canna mean ... ?" Raik's jaw clamped. He shook his head, understanding now what plagued his cousin and hoping to hear it was not so.

"Aye. My sire rid himself of me, paid the Abbot to take me, hoping I would die. I made peace with my life and became a monk. But that wasna enough penance for surviving. My father. King David. King Stephen. The Pope. All thrust me from Kelso to make haste and marry my brother's intended."

Ranald jerked off his mask and roughed his hands over his unshaven face, the black stubbles making a rasping sound.

"I have sinned against the church's laws of marriage."

"Ye suggest the laws of consanguinity?"

Ranald dipped his head a mite, acknowledging it.

"But Catalin and Moridac were not yet wed."

Ranald's lips tightened; Raik's jaw dropped.

"Jesu! She was breeding. She did not tell ye before ye consummated the union?"

"Nay."

"Ah! That's why Broccin was so intent on a hasty ceremony, why he threatened to raze the abbey if ye did not agree. He guessed, aye?"

"Aye. Never speak of this, or so help me, I will slit yer throat for saying of it."

"Do ye think me dafty? How will ye protect the babe from being a bastard? Like me?"

"The babe will come afore it's time, but who can say me nay, if I say it is mine? Thank the blessed Lord we were twins alike, not with different color hair or eyes."

"It is a fine thing ye are doing for the bairn, Ranald. Knowing all yer life ye are a bastard does not lie easy on a man's soul."

"Never have I thought of ye as such." Ranald's anger cooled as he put his hand on Raik's back and urged him toward the church doorway. "Let us leave. I would be gone before Vigils. It's time for me to check on Gille."

Their boots rang out on the stone steps leading from the church. Brisk, cold air hit their faces. The grass was beginning to grow again after the hard winter. Ranald glanced at the sky and hoped it would clear. If he didn't know better, he would have thought it looked suspiciously like a storm threatened. He breathed deep and pulled the end of the woolen tartan from beneath his belt to spread it across his back and shoulders.

"I have always known ye as our cousin. Is not yer mother a distant relative of father's? Have ye learned who yer sire was?" Ranald asked as they made their way across the courtyard.

"Ye didna ken my mother?" Raik's brows rose in surprise when he glanced at Ranald.

"Do ye forget I was a youth when I left Raptor Castle? Ye were still fostered at Castle Douglas and spent only short fortnights here with us."

"Ah, true." Raik nodded and yawned, then scratched behind

his ear, much like a hound did on awakening. "Soon after ye left, a squire called me bastard one time too many at Castle Douglas. I broke his nose and near choked the life from him. Laird Douglas pulled me to my feet and asked how the fight started. I told him the squire claimed my mother was a slut who followed Laird Douglas' army. The laird thrashed me, not because I beat the boy, but because I near throttled him into the next life. He was fair, though. He also thrashed the fool."

"Seems no more than yer right to pummel the mouthy squire. I would have done the same."

"Aye, but the laird said I should have ceased when I broke his nose, then come to him and asked who my parents were."

"Did ye ask?"

"Aye. He told me what he knew. Which was not all of it. Far from a camp slut, my mother was the youngest daughter of a nearby laird. She was in love with a Saxon across the border. Laird Douglas would not tell me who, only that her father threatened to kill the man, as did her brother."

"A nearby laird? But Raptor Castle is nearest Douglas'..." Ranald stopped in his tracks. "She was no distant relative. It was Aunt Joneta? Do ye tell me ye are Aunt Joneta's bairn?"

"Aye. Dinna ever speak of it. She has gone to great lengths to hide her shame. Most likely at Broccin's orders."

"Always was she watching ye when ye stayed with us. She made yer shirts and breeches. Why did we not sense it? Remember? She had cook bake yer favorite pies, the meals ye favored. Never did we have plum pudding when ye were not about!"

"It has been hard to pretend I kenned nothing. One day, when the time is right, I will speak to her of it."

"As much as ye have suffered being called bastard, she must have grieved not having her son. It's no wonder she never wed."

Raik nodded. "Aye. She is comely still. I had oft wondered why she never married."

"Likely she feared being wed to someone far from Castle Douglas. She would never see ye."

"Living with yer sire has made her strong." Raik grinned at

Ranald. "Have ye noted she does not take any shite from him?"

"I think mayhap he has some small bruises on his back where she shoved him last." Ranald chuckled, remembering her feisty anger.

"One day, I will have my own keep where I can take her from yer father's care and ease her life." Raik's jaw set.

Ranald did not doubt that he would make it happen, no matter how impossible the task sounded.

Aunt Joneta was spooning water into the injured man's mouth when they entered the solar. Why had he not noted before the look in her eyes when she spied Raik? It was so easy to read the love there now that he knew her secret. And his cousin was especially gentle when he helped her rise from the stool and insisted he walk with her to her chambers.

Ranald held his hands over a brazier while he studied the flushed face of his wounded warrior. It would not be a kindness to put cold hands on him, for if it caused him to flinch, it would disturb his raw injuries. Ranald smoothed the back of his warmed fingers over the man's cheeks. On reaching his neck, he stopped there to feel his heartbeat. It was weak but steady.

He jostled a young warrior sleeping on a pallet, ready to fetch whatever they needed.

"Bring red wine from the kitchen and a small pot of honey. If anyone asks, tell them I have sent ye."

"Aye, sir." He sprang up and raced out of the solar, making enough noise to wake all in his path.

Ranald studied the rows of stopper vials and earthenware pots on the nearby table. Selecting the ones he wanted, he pinched small amounts of powdered cloves and cinnamon into a small bowl. He took careful measures of Feverfew and Borage from tightly stoppered, dark bottles and mixed them with the spices. Careful to avoid waste, he emptied the mixture into a pewter tankard. The lad raced back into the room and handed him the wine.

"Thank you. You may return to sleep now."

"Do ye mind me asking, sir?" His brown eyes were watching Ranald as he poured wine into the tankard. "Can he hear us?"

He glanced uneasily at the man, whose eyes were following their every movement.

"Aye. His inner ears are unharmed. His hearing is softened by the bandages, but if we speak loudly enough, he can hear us."

The boy leaned close to whisper, "Why did they not kill him as well as hack off his ears?"

Ranald bent over to pick up a latticework of small iron strips leaning against a leg of the brazier and placed it over the coals.

"They thought they had." He raised his voice to normal, so Gille could hear him. "No doubt, the churls believed, because of his height, he would not have the heart of such a brave warrior. One day, he will have the comfort of seeing them breathe their last."

From the corner of his eye, he watched Gille's lips lift in a small, hopeful smile. He poured a portion of wine into the mixture and stirred it with a wooden spoon, then placed the cup on the grid and watched carefully until it was the right heat. He carried it back to the table, added a dollop of honey and pulled a stool close.

"'Tis normal to burn with heat when a wound is fresh," he murmured, then smiled and added, "This will warm yer belly and bring yer fever down. It will ease ye back to sleep if ye drink it all."

Ranald talked soft and low to the man as he coaxed the warm potion past his lips. When he glanced to see the squire had returned to his pallet and was snoring with the blanket over his head, he began questioning his patient.

What he learned was enough to help plan several forays a month or more before they started the siege of Hunter Castle.

Catalin watched Raik's dark form cross the courtyard to the door of the church. He stood, listening, before he entered. Would Ranald be angered that his cousin intruded on his sanctuary? She nibbled at her lips and waited. It seemed a long while before they both emerged and appeared deep in conversation as they strode back to the keep. She latched the shutters and kept the blanket grasped around her shoulders while she crawled back between the sheets. Even so, it seemed to take forever before she stopped shivering.

Ranald was like another man when he made love to her, a man who was earthier than she would ever have imagined. He fought his need, but once he gave in to it, she could not imagine that he had ever been a man of the cloth. Mayhap those years of physical denial was why he made love with such ravenous hunger.

And he hated her for it.

He could barely stand to be in her presence outside their chamber. He could have rejected her that first morn, but did not. He had taken pains to make it appear she was untouched before he came to her. But why had he protected her person, yet rejected her emotionally?

Both times they were intimate had been powerful, heart-stopping experiences she had never expected to have in her life. How could she protect herself? Her heart? She could not be with Ranald and remain unaffected by all he did. She found herself conscious of his every movement when he was in sight, would hold her breath when he approached, and her skin tingled waiting for his slightest touch. Just thinking of his hands on her flesh earlier made her heart thump and pound like a war drum.

With excitement came guilt, too. It was her fault Chief Broccin had forced him from the peace and solitude he preferred. Now, not only was a wife thrust upon him, but fatherhood too. Saints! For certes, she had earned his hatred.

Would his anger build until he turned on her? Her bairn? Cold chills washed over her from her thoughts.

Catalin's dreams were violent when she finally slept. She walked down a dark passageway and heard booted feet ringing on the stones behind her. It was Broccin, looking wild and lethal. She ran, screaming, but he cornered her when she came to a massive door at the end of the passage. No matter how hard she jerked at it, it would not open. His big fists slammed her against the wall. Spittle flew from his mouth as he bellowed it was her fault Moridac died. His beloved son had been giddy and careless, thinking on bedding her instead of watching for danger. Then a huge, dark shape jerked her away, back against a hard body.

She had screamed and struggled around to find a horrid face looming over her. From the glittering eyes, she knew it was Ranald, his mask gone. That ruined side was all she could see. The skin was missing from under his right eye, and the white cheekbone gleamed. His right nostril was near cut away, his cheek thick with shocking, inflamed scars.

His twisted lips grinned. "Is this what ye wanted to see? Are ye happy now, wife?" His mouth lowered until he was a breath away. Catalin flinched. He jerked back and thrust her from him.

"Nay. I dinna want ye. Another does not scorn my wounds."

He crooked his finger. A woman flew from the shadows to lock her arms around his neck. Lady Muriele looked back over her shoulder, triumph gleaming from her eyes. She whispered a word Catalin read on her lips.

"Mine."

One balmy May afternoon, Ranald settled back on his heels beneath a gnarled oak far to the rear of the training field. Gille, now healed as best as he would ever be, crouched by his side. While Ranald stripped the leaves from a small branch, he listened to his sire, Raik and Domnall discussing the men best suited for quick forays. After the last leaf fell to the ground, he began to sketch a map in the dirt.

"I have no doubt now. Our second listener must have made a fatal mistake, for he has not returned. It is turning summer and we canna wait longer. We must send men to each village Gille spoke of. Some to Hunter Castle, others to neighboring barons."

Satisfied when he had a reasonable outline of Northumbria south of the border, he began placing large rocks where special castles were located.

"Hunter Castle lies here." He settled the largest rock east of Raptor across the border. "De Burgh's Seton Castle," he said as he placed the next rock south of Hunter. He picked up and palmed the last of the rocks. "Ridley Castle northeast of Hunter belongs to relatives of the Morgan's of Blackthorn. No one is to touch even a fallow field of these two estates." He eyed each man as he spoke.

"The targets we seek are here, here, here, here, and here." Ranald identified and placed stones at five different locations until the ground had pebbles in all directions. "These smaller stones mark castles where we plan to rouse trouble for Hamon."

"Ye marked a castle north of the border to Hunter." Broccin grinned and rubbed his hands. "Hm, right sneaky of ye to include a Scot's holdings. They will ken it is more proof of discontent from King Stephen's reign."

Ranald tilted his head and studied his father. Was that a glint of approval in his sire's eyes?

"There is a fallow field there filled with overgrowth. We will set it alight. They will rant about the burnt ground, but no harm will come to the families there. They will blame Hamon, of course, as will the others." He stuck a twig in the ground next to the stone.

"South and southwest of Hunter are neglected fields that could do with a good burning." Ranald positioned two more twigs. "Their lords are so busy causing Stephen strife, that they neglected them. The southwest holding also has two huts that naught but rats and curious pigs enter."

"What of this land southwest of Hunter?" Domnall rubbed his chin, where a busy ant scampered amongst the bristles there. "Gille, ye didna venture there, did ye?"

"Nay, 'tis said to be an evil place," Gille replied, his eyes wide in his gaunt face.

Ranald nodded. "Aye, it is. Baron Rupert holds it. Send three men within the west curtain wall. Ye will find a thatched hut set apart from everything else. Check to see no one is within, then burn it, the fields and whatever else ye can get to."

"And if someone is there?" Domnall asked.

"Take care to bring them to safety. They will likely need help." Ranald frowned down at the dirt. He lifted his eyes to study each man's face. "Baron Rupert is known for his cruelty. I tended three men in as many years who had fallen from his *special* favor. He tortured them all. After he used dull knives to cut off their ballocks, he left them in the woods to fend for themselves. Two died, for by the time their family or friends found and brought them to Kelso, it was too late."

"Better they died than live as half-men," Broccin muttered.

"How fared the third?" Raik's raised brows helped ask the question.

"His cousin followed Baron Rupert's men when they took him deep into the forest. Once they left, he slung the injured man over an old nag and made haste to bring him to me. Ye met him, cousin, as did ye all."

"I saw no ill man," Broccin said.

"None but men of the cloth," Domnall added.

"It was the young novice, Clement, who took charge of yer weapons." Ranald's lips thinned, his lids near closed over his eyes. "One day, I will take pleasure in maiming Baron Rupert in the same way. And I will see to it he survives."

Broccin's laughter caused warriors to pause and glance their way. One in particular had been watching Ranald closely all morn.

"So, ye are more man than yer pious manners show," Broccin said when he stopped laughing.

"If cruelty makes me a man, than ye have little to worry of."

Ranald nodded toward two of the men who lingered over-long returning to battle practice. They talked together, motioning and snickering when they glanced at Ranald.

"Who are those two?" he asked Domnall.

"Giric and Kerr. Both enjoyed hunting with Moridac. Yer brother was right fond of them both."

Domnall's face did not give Ranald any clue to what he was thinking, but Broccin frowned.

Ranald turned back to the dirt map and, using his hand, roughed up the ground so it left no trace. One of the watching men laughed, then spoke with a sneer in his voice.

"Huh, Giric. What knows a monk of battle plans and fighting? Most likely, he will piss his breeches and run at the first sight of blood. Mayhap he should have been a lass."

"It is unlikely, Kerr. He is Moridac's twin, without doubt."

Ranald's lips twitched and bared his teeth. The man Kerr had called him monk several times before, always when he was with other men. For truth, he wanted Ranald to hear for he did not say it quietly. Kerr turned and started to walk away.

Ranald sprang to his feet. He jerked his tunic off and let it drop to the ground, leaving naught but his scant braies to cover him. Before Kerr could speak again, Ranald's hand shot out, grasped his shoulder and spun him around. His hand closed around Kerr's throat, the rock hard muscles of his biceps bulged, and his back muscles tightened as he lifted Kerr off the ground. Wisely, Giric stepped away.

"Ye talk a good deal, Sir Kerr. Mayhap ye feel I could learn from ye?" He lowered the man until his feet stood firmly on the ground. "Get yer weapon. Since I am so poorly trained from living at Kelso, I need the exercise."

"Aye. And if I scratch yer delicate skin, no doubt ye will kneel all night praying in the church, begging God to help ye be a man." Kerr laughed as he strutted over to take his sword from his squire.

Ranald nodded at Raik, who grabbed Ranald's sword from against the oak and tossed it to him. Keeping his eyes on Kerr's back, Ranald threw his mask to the left, where he knew Raik stood. Kerr turned with an arrogant smile on his face. It faded when he found Ranald's sword tip just a finger's width from his nose.

"Are ye finished stalling, Kerr?" Ranald grinned at the surprised man.

"It isn't fair. I had not yet armed myself," Kerr blustered.

"Ye are ready now, are ye not? I wait to be taught how to fight like a man." Ranald stepped back several paces, pretending to be as inept as the man supposed, his sword held slackly at his side.

Hearing the exchange, those training close-by formed a ring around them. He paid them no heed, though he sensed his father's eyes watching him.

Kerr no doubt thought Ranald lacked the skills of a squire, for his eyes lit with delight as he lunged for Ranald's right shoulder. Ranald's blade whipped up, deflected the blow then dropped again. Kerr again struck, this time aiming left, expecting the same maneuver. Ranald turned sideways, leaning back at the waist. Kerr's blade met thin air. Ranald did not lower his sword again. It whistled as he reached up to slice the ribbons on Kerr's shirt. The cloth gaped open, revealing the sweat glistening on his neck.

Their blades rang out as they parried and thrust, and though Kerr was more than an adequate fighter, Ranald read each strike correctly. Both men had thin strips of red glistening on their sweaty flesh, though Kerr's cuts far outnumbered Ranald's.

Ranald had long since learned to note expressions on an opponent's face. He watched as Kerr's eyes widened after an especially effective maneuver, then narrowed as he more closely studied Ranald's moves, a small smile of appreciation beginning at the corners of his lips.

Before long, Kerr's laughter rang out in pure delight when Ranald swiftly parried an unexpected maneuver. Ranald, some nine to ten moves later, repeated the pattern. This time it was he who laughed, for Kerr was an apt pupil and showed he had learned his lesson. What started as a battle of dislike turned into a sparring match, each enjoying the testing of the other's skills.

Soon, Ranald began to tell Kerr what he was doing wrong, becoming the instructor, not the supposed hapless monk.

"Dinna watch only my hands, my body."

Ranald made as if to strike on Kerr's right, but at the last moment, whipped his blade to Kerr's left. Before Kerr recovered, he again feigned an attack, this time on Kerr's shoulder, but struck at his thigh instead.

"If not yer hands, how then will I know what ye are planning?" Kerr's brows near met. His gaze switched from Ranald's hands to his face.

"There ye have it. Ye must watch my face, my eyes, and ye will see in what direction I will swing the blade next."

They worked until both dripped with sweat, their breath bursting loudly from lungs working hard as any blacksmith's bellows.

"I cry defeat, *Sir* Ranald," Kerr called out. He stepped back, stuck his sword into the ground and leaned over, laughing and coughing. "Ye canna tell me ye were only a monk. Not when yer sword flashes like lightning."

"I didna say I was. Ye named me a man used to only kneeling in prayer. Ye failed to learn I was also Kelso's Protector. I had ample time to hone my skills, for the abbey is often raided from across the border."

Sweat ran down his temples and stung the corners of his eyes. He swiped it away and pushed back his wet hair, its length now grown long enough to fall over his brow. Of a sudden, his skin prickled. Surprise marked Kerr's face as he stared beyond Ranald's shoulder.

Ranald breathed deep. He picked up the scent of another, one not bathed in sweat.

He crouched ready to spring. A feral growl rumbled from his throat.

CHAPTER 18

RANALD'S LIPS LIFTED WITH a snarl and his feet kicked up a cloud of dirt as he whirled around and came face to face with Lady Muriele. And her probing stare. Expecting her to screech with disgust, he rose to his full height and stiffened his spine. She did not. Instead, she held out a sweating pewter goblet of cold well water, all the while studying his face as if it were as any other man's.

"What do ye here? It is no place for a lady, and well ye know it." Ranald ground out the words through a jaw locked near closed.

She flinched, but instead of fleeing like he had expected after his harsh tone, she squared her shoulders and thrust out her chin.

"Why cannot a lady admire your skills? There are lasses aplenty gawking from behind the wash house."

"Lasses, aye. Not ladies of the keep." Had Catalin ever watched when he trained? Had she stayed away, fearful of coming upon him without his mask?

Muriele dropped her gaze to his chest. The tip of her tongue stole out to wet her upper lip. Her breasts rose and fell with her quickened breathing. Each intake of breath made the round, creamy swell of inviting flesh visible there at the opening of her kirtle, stirring his loins.

"I watched from the wall walk atop the north tower. Even from that distance, I sensed you were in dire need of a cooling drink."

Her gaze studied the breadth of his shoulders, lingered on

the sweat snaking through the hair on his chest as it made its slow way down to his stomach. His muscles tightened. Her eyes were as enticing as warm fingertips whispering down his body.

His stomach muscles corded, loosening the cloth at his waist. A heartbeat after, her brazen gaze studied the hair disappearing beneath the gap at the top of his braies.

She blinked and moved her head slightly forward. Closer. A wave of heat rushed to that part of him which was easily interested of late. He feared his body was more than willing to show her how she affected him.

Aye. She was well aware of it. He did not miss the way she shivered and gave his groin one more quick study. Seeing the change there, she started and her regard slid upward.

Ranald grabbed the goblet from her hands. Never had he expected to see her face flush and desire cloud her eyes on looking at him.

"Get ye back to the keep." His arm flung out and he pointed across the wide expanse.

His voice was grating, abrupt, and must have hit her like a physical force for she jumped back and spun. Her skirts trailed behind her like she faced a driving wind, so fast were her feet leading her away.

"Cousin, mayhap I should comfort the lass. Yer snarl near scared the curl from her hair," Raik said.

"I didna snarl."

"Aye, ye did." Raik nodded his head and grinned. "And she has interest in ye."

"Ye imagine things that are not there." Ranald's brows near touched. "Her only concern was learning what lies behind the mask."

"Ha!" Raik's lips quirked as he tried to still them. He gave up as laughter rumbled from his chest. "More likely it's what lies behind that linen wrapped around yer loins that peaks her interests!"

Domnall came up behind Ranald and cuffed him on the shoulder.

"Had a lass looked at me so eagerly, we would be behind

the nearest tree, her legs clamping my waist while I plowed her like a needy hare."

High on the battlements, Catalin stood at an embrasure studying the men squatting in the dirt beneath an ancient tree. Were they playing some battle game? She easily recognized Ranald's form, for who else at Raptor had a body so imposing?

He scratched in the dirt. His father and the other men leaned forward to study what he did there. After a bit, she noted his head turned toward two men nearby, then he stood to join them.

Join them? Nay. His body looked as hard as the merlon she leaned against, for his hands jerked up to yank off his tunic. His mask followed. When he slammed it to the ground, it sent up a small cloud of dust.

She felt his tension as if he were but a hand's-width away. Seeing their swords flash in the sun, her fingers went to her throat. Too far to see, but she knew they both drew blood by the way their bodies curved away from the strike. Not serious, though, for neither seemed to note it.

The man was a good fighter, but Ranald was ready for his every move. Unexpected pride filled her chest as she watched.

A flash below drew her gaze away. Lady Muriele was at the well filling a tall pewter goblet from a freshly raised bucket. She must be thirsty indeed to require so much water.

It was not for her to drink? The lithe figure hurried across the courtyard, past the orchards, the barracks, the stables and on toward the men's training ground. She did not intend to intrude, did she? Why, Ranald was near naked, his muscled body gleaming with sweat, his braies his only covering.

Her eyes narrowed to mere slits. She ground her teeth until her jaw ached. Why did Lady Muriele stand so close? Ranald took the offered water. Huh, the nerve of her. She stood nearly touching a man almost as bare as the day he was born! Catalin snorted. No doubt, Ranald gloried in the woman's inspection.

Seeing Ranald fling his arm in a gesture toward the keep, she smiled with satisfaction. Humph! 'Twas good she hurried, else Catalin would be tempted to stomp out there after her.

She swallowed. This anger was not jealousy. How could she be jealous of a man she had not wished to marry?

Her babe took that moment to give her a resounding kick, the strongest one so far. Her hands firmly cupped her rounded belly, hidden by her loose-fitting, yellow tunic. The babe reminded her of a kindness she had not acknowledged.

Not long after they wed, a potion appeared on her bedside table each morn. Hannah told her Ranald had mixed the herbs and claimed he had much success in the Abbey Infirmary with the brew for easing upset stomachs. Once Catalin swallowed it and rested a short time, she was delighted to find no trace of dizziness or nausea remained.

It shamed her that she had yet to thank him for it. She bit her lip and stared out into the bailey, not really seeing. Her cupped hands felt the soft movements beneath. By the size of her stomach, she feared it would be a large bairn.

This morn, Ada had leaked the news of her breeding to Ranald's father. How would they get away with claiming it as Ranald's when Moridac had bedded her in December? It was early February when Ranald appeared, and by Hannah's reckoning, the babe would be due in September. Everyone was bound to know it was not his when she gave birth to a fully formed babe afore time.

She remembered his determined face that first morn when he had said, "If he looks like Moridac, he will look like me. If I say the child is mine, who can say me nay?" The memory soothed her, but unease swept her anew when her nape prickled.

"I thought as much."

Catalin jumped so hard she nearly lost her balance. Chief Broccin grabbed her shoulders and pulled her back from the open embrasure. Once she stood firm, he released her and rubbed his hands with glee.

"Ye carry a bairn. But who is the father? Moridac or Ranald?"

"Ranald, of course." Catalin made her voice hard and firm, and buried her hands in her tunic pockets to hide their trembling.

"Hmpf. I saw ye cup yer belly. By its size, it would have to be a giant to be Ranald's." He reached forward as if to feel her stomach for himself, a gleam in his eye.

"You will not touch me!" Catalin folded her arms across her waist. Blood rushed from her face, leaving her slightly dizzy.

"Dinna be foolish, lass. I would not harm ye. Ye carry my son's seed." He stepped back, hands held up waggling back and forth showing he was keeping away.

"Why are ye not resting, Catalin?" Ranald appeared on the last step leading up to the wall walk. He was at her side in a heartbeat, placing a firm arm around her shoulders for support.

Tension flowed like physical waves from his skin. He had thrown his tunic over his head, for it had not settled in position over his shoulders. Though he smelled of sweat and dust, leather and weapons, she was thankful for his close presence.

"I thought to take the sun. It is warmer here than inside the keep."

Feeling Ranald's muscled leg pressed against her own and his hard body so close, she shivered and envisioned his bare flesh beneath the tunic. Catalin looked up into dark eyes, eyes that changed from black to the color of a dark plum when in the sunlight. She reached up to free a hank of midnight hair, damp and wavy, imprisoned by the top of his mask.

Ranald flinched, then held steady until she finished.

"Catalin is breeding, yet ye did not tell me." Chief Broccin glared at him. "Dinna think to claim it. The seed is Moridac's. Her belly grows too large for it to be yers."

"I do claim the seed as mine, not his."

"Ye are a fool. The proof will be at the birthing." Chief Broccin, his chest stuck out, scowled. "When ye take Hunter Castle, ye will both reside there. The child will remain with me."

Catalin gasped and gripped her stomach, as if to protect the babe yet to be born.

"The bairn remains with its mother." Ranald's voice was

cold as ice. "When it is birthed, I will claim it as mine."

"Not if I dispute its parentage, ye willna," his father shouted. "This bairn is all I have left of my son!"

"Listen, and listen well. If ye dispute my claim, do ye know what will happen?" Ranald's voice was soft, silky. Menacing.

Catalin shivered as cold dread swept her.

"Happen? Aye! I will raise it as my son to take over Raptor after me. *That* is what will happen." Chief Broccin planted his fists on his hips and glared at Ranald.

"Nay, ye willna. Catalin is *my* wife. Though betrothed to Moridac, they had not said the final vows. If ye name the child a bastard, I will see it sent to the church." He stopped and spoke slowly, deliberately. His nostrils flared, and a snarl curled his lips. "If a boy, I will rid myself of him as ye did me. The Abbot at Kelso will raise him to become a monk. Be it a girl, she will live at Saint Anne's Abbey with the good sisters."

Catalin gasped and tried to wrench away from him. Ranald clamped her tight against his side. He felt her draw breath to speak, but he would not allow it.

"Be silent, woman! I have not given ye leave to speak."

She felt as rigid as if he grasped a young apple tree tight to his side. He stared into his father's eyes, not flinching at the hate radiating there. His father wanted this bairn because it was Moridac's. If it were Ranald's seed, he wouldna care, would shrug at Ranald's threat to cast it away as he had done him. He held tight to his anger, fearing what could happen there atop the highest point of the keep. In times of peace, the merlons had no protective shutters fastened between them. A person could easily fall if nudged by an angry wind. He tightened his arm around Catalin.

"Jesu, Ranald! From the look on yer face, it's no wonder the villagers have named ye the Black Raptor."

Raik stepped up behind Broccin, drawing Ranald's gaze to him. Elyne followed, panting, from running up the steep wooden stairs. She took one look at her father, then at Ranald and Catalin, and moved to stand between them and the laird.

"Come, Catalin. We have the solar to ourselves again. We

should start garments for the babe, but I need ye to tell me what ye would prefer."

Ranald released his arm around Catalin and glanced down at her face. Her eyes were wide, fear and horror warring with each other. He watched Elyne lead her down the stairs, one hand behind her making sure Catalin stayed close to the wall. The stairway had only a flimsy railing meant for steadying a person, not supporting them. Once the women were on firm ground, he relaxed.

"I willna stay and listen to the ranting of a fool," Chief Broccin blustered. "Ye canna do as ye say."

"I have no use for another man's seed to take from what rightfully belongs to my own. Do ye remember the last words I heard from yer lips those many years ago? Nay?"

His father, silent, glared at him. Ranald roughened his voice, doing a fair imitation. "'He is of no use to me now … dump him at Kelso and return.'"

Ranald spread his legs farther apart and folded his arms across his chest. His chin lifted, jutted. His voice softened to near a whisper.

"Ye want to chance I will not do it? Hm?"

Chief Broccin glared at him, his chin jutting.

Ranald's voice lifted to near a snarl.

"Try me."

Chapter 19

Raik studied Ranald's set face, curious as to what unusual feat his anger would unleash. His cousin's dark eyes gleamed between lowered lids as he stared at his father's left ear as if it fascinated him. Raik's lips quivered as he held back a grin. He rocked back on his heels to watch events unfold.

"Dinna think to threaten me!" Broccin snorted, his head lowered like an angry bull.

Ranald's chin dipped, his lips twitched, baring his teeth. His gaze took on such an added intensity you could near see heat shimmering from his eyes. It would take but a few foolish prods from the laird, and they would lock horns and fight as savagely as any beasts.

One had to listen closely and watch Ranald's lips, for his voice was like a whisper of silk on the air.

"Ye heard what I said. Nay, not only said, but promised if ye thwart me in this."

Broccin shook his head to the left, frowned. One hand rose to brush his ear. It had turned shiny pink.

The air around his uncle sweltered. Raik stepped back a pace where it was as delightfully cool as any May afternoon. Strange. But then, knowing from whence the heat came, maybe not.

Ranald's form looked to waver and glow, not unlike heat waves rising from a plowed field in the distance. The knuckles strained white on his fisted hands as Ranald held tight to his soaring temper. Broccin would be lucky to come away from this challenge with only a bit of reddened flesh.

"Ye see, *my loving sire*, I have naught to lose if ye prove the bairn is not mine." Ranald scraped one hand over his chin, mulling over his words while still staring at Broccin's ear. "Why would I wish to claim a son who is not of my seed? To give him first rights to Raptor, leaving my own future son without?"

"Hell's pests!" Broccin swatted the air around his head. His ear was fiery red and beginning to swell. "How have bees flown so high?"

"Mayhap ye brought one from the orchard on yer clothing? It looks like the small pest has feasted on yer flesh." Raik tried his best not to chuckle.

"Best ye seek Aunt Joneta for something to soothe it," Ranald said in an emotionless voice.

"Dinna think this is settled," Broccin spluttered and stomped over to the landing, his arms flapping like wings as he swatted the air around him. "We will see who has the last word here."

His voice faded as he pounded down the stairs.

"Interesting." Raik nodded his head. "So, that is how it was done."

"What was done?"

Ranald opened his clenched hands, rolled his shoulders and took deep, cleansing breaths, as he relaxed and cooled his anger.

"How ye lit the candles that night in the Infirmary. I wasna as fevered as I thought."

Ranald's gaze flickered to him.

Suddenly, Raik laughed.

"Satan's rotten teeth!" Ranald's temper had yet to cool to normal. "What do ye find so amusing?"

"Ye." Raik grinned at his cousin. "Knowing ye, I would be willing to bet not once did ye use yer temper to stay warm on the most frigid nights at Kelso."

Ranald's face relaxed. His lips twitched at the corners. Raik laughed all the harder.

"Ye would win." Ranald shook his head and grinned. "I didna even think of it, since no one prodded my temper."

"Yer father seems smitten by Satan, the way he is determined to get his hands on Catalin's child." Raik shook his head and frowned.

"Aye. He would label the child a bastard in order to keep him close." Ranald snorted. "He ne'er concerned himself with Moridac or me for years on end, leaving Domnall to fill in the gap as father."

"Aye. Though, after he threw ye away, he kept Moridac forever in his sight."

Ranald heaved a sigh then pressed his lips together. He glanced at Raik, then across the curtain walls toward the darkening forests beyond the castle. So many things he wanted to learn about those years he was away. It was best he sought answers now.

"I often felt a pull from Moridac. It was like he called to me, yet he never came to see how I fared." His chest ached, reliving the loneliness and fear in those early months at Kelso.

"Aye, he called to ye. In his deepest sleep, he would cry out yer name. He grieved over yer separation, got so lean from not eating that the laird near forced food down his throat."

"Why did he not come to me?"

Ranald turned his head away, his shoulders slumped with the memory of how abandoned he had felt.

"He slipped away more than once. He was near to Kelso one night when Dougald caught up to him. That next morn, the laird sent a letter to the Abbot. When the messenger returned, yer sire made a great show of saying he had word that his second son had died of a fever and was already buried."

Ranald smacked his hand against the cold stone beside him and fought for calm.

"He has Satan's own cold heart to claim that a son who still breathes is dead!" His words hissed through near clamped teeth.

Raik snorted. "Heart? Are ye certain he has one? I oft wondered."

"I heard many tales of Moridac. I could not ken the wild things he did. The men he killed. That he gloried in it?"

"Aye, ye can say he did." Raik nodded and hesitated but a heartbeat. "Yer brother threw himself into fighting and killing, mayhap with reason. Most times, it was after a rousing argument with the laird."

Raik frowned and steadied a foot on an open crenelation, then leaned over to brace his arms on his knee. He heaved a regretful sigh before he continued.

"More than once, I came upon him unaware and saw fear flash in his eyes when he looked at yer sire."

"What had he to fear? My sire loved him since his birth."

"Likely, he thought if his father could maim and discard his twin like so much offal, he could do the same to Moridac if he displeased him." Raik raised his brows and studied Ranald's face.

Ranald nodded.

"Moridac was weak; ye were strong. Mayhap ye were destined to be the second son, because ye could face what life had in store for ye."

"Nay. Moridac was not weak. He was far more daring than I. 'Twas he who thought up most of our ventures. We were so much alike. We fed on each other's strengths." He lowered his head, then lifted it and glanced aside at Raik. "Had I been strong, I would have returned here after I healed. I was the weak one."

Raik shook his head.

"I ken yer twin was afeared. In the years growing up together, was it not ye who defied yer sire? Ye who took all the chances, who claimed the guilt to protect Moridac when he got into trouble?"

Ranald grimaced and shrugged. It had been second nature for him to step between his sire and his brother.

"Once he no longer had ye to protect him, he made himself into the image of yer father. The more he became like him, the more the Chief praised him."

"Ne'er did I think on it that way." Ranald closed his eyes, picturing Moridac lost and fearful. "Hm. Moridac drank the most when our sire was in a temper."

"Aye. He did. After they took ye away, Moridac locked himself in the bedchamber ye shared. He let no one in until your father threatened to take an axe to the door."

"Many times, in those brief spaces between sleeping potions, I felt him calling to me." Ranald sighed, and his impatient fingers jerked off his mask. "'Tis nice to feel the air on my face."

"It is not necessary to use it." Raik picked up a stone from beside his foot and tossed it far out into the open bailey.

"Mayhap not with men. I have no wish to see the look of horror on Catalin's face should she come upon me without it." His fingers shoved through his hair as he lifted his face to the waning sun.

"Ye give her too little credit."

"Mayhap because I gave her too much before."

Ranald gave his hair one last tug and shrugged. Both were silent for a space, thinking.

"Ye said ye felt Moridac call to ye those years ago. Did this feeling fade over the years?"

"Aye. Somewhat. Not all. There were times when out of nowhere I would glimpse his face."

He shuddered, remembering. He had thought himself daft, at the time. Was certain of it that day in December when he heard Moridac's voice scream his name, begging his aid. Should he ask? He cleared his throat.

"The day he was injured. Were ye there?" His heart pounded, waiting.

"Aye. Not close, though. I heard shouts, horses crashing through the brush and screams. Domnall, Giric and I arrived as Kerr slit the boar's throat and dragged him off Moridac." Raik clasped Ranald's shoulder. "Until he was not able to speak, yer brother begged for yer help, asking ye to greet him and guide his way when he breathed his last."

Ranald's eyes stung. He straightened, and as he slid his mask on, furtively swiped the moisture from his eyes. He growled softly, deep in his throat, and nodded.

"Thank ye." He stopped to clear his husky voice.

Eyes normally as blue as the sky now held a hint of gray as Raik studied Ranald's face. It was always thus when Raik delved into a person's thoughts.

"What?" Raik asked.

"I understand now."

"Understand?"

"Aye. My father."

"Ye do? I expect God shakes his head at Broccin's thinking."

"Nay, I dinna ken Broccin, only his anger at Kelso."

Raik tilted his head, drew his shoulders up and held his hands up.

"Eh? He was in a temper from the moment we left Raptor. Remind me so I can follow yer thinking."

"Do ye not remember him shouting it was my fault Moridac died? That I should have been there to heal him?"

"Aye. I think I see yer drift."

"He had to blame me else he must admit it was his fault I was not there." A glimmer of sympathy pried at Ranald's mind. "Can ye imagine the guilt, the horror that something ye had done made the passing of a loved one so terrible?"

"That's the monk in ye talking. I feel no sympathy for him. He earned all the anguish he feels now."

Ranald shrugged, then straightened and cocked his head to listen as he studied the open field leading to the drawbridge. Two men on horseback galloped out of the far woods toward the castle. The way they leaned forward in the saddle lent urgency to their appearance. He pointed to them and turned.

"Come. Cormac and Duncan return from Baron Rupert's castle. They are one man short. I dinna see Egan with them."

Raik followed at his heels as they bolted down the stairway to meet the men clattering through the barbican.

Catalin could not stop the shivers that shook her. They were more from what Ranald had said than from the cold air blowing on her back. On the last of the wooden steps, Elyne grasped Catalin's hand and tucked it in the crook of her arm.

"Come, your hand is like ice. It's turning wet and windy again. A warmed cup of mead will be just the thing to chase the dampness from us."

"Did you hear what they were fighting over? Do you think he really meant it?" Catalin bit her lip and glanced sideways at Elyne.

"Who meant what? Ranald or Father?"

"Both, really. Either way, I will mayhap lose this child I carry because of one of them."

Had all in the castle heard Broccin's yells and Ranald's responses? No matter where she looked, people peered at her from the corner of their eyes. Even the goose girl found a reason to herd her charges closer. Was she trying to overhear what she said to Elyne?

She stumbled, and Elyne tightened her grip on her arm.

"Lose to one of them? What crazy thing were they fighting over?" Elyne's head cocked to the side, her brow creased with thought.

"Your father declares that if this babe is proven to be Moridac's, Ranald and I will live at Hunter Castle, but the child will stay here to be raised by him."

"What? Moridac's?"

Surprised, Elyne tripped over her own feet. Had not Catalin grabbed tight to her arm and steadied them both, they would have landed on their bottoms in the dust.

"Aye. Your father says he will prove the child is Moridac's and will take it from us. But Ranald said if your father names the child a bastard, then Ranald will see it sent to the church." She gulped and let out a wavering breath.

"Huh! They are brainsick to think such a thing." Elyne frowned, her eyes puzzled as she pondered the idea. "Sent to the church for what?"

"If it is a boy, he will be given to Kelso and raised to become a monk."

"What if it's a girl? Will they still fight over her?"

"Your father cared naught about a girl. Ranald did. He claims a bastard girl child will live at Saint Anne's Abbey with the good sisters." Catalin's last words trailed off like the wind had taken the sound from her. "Oh, heavenly saints. Whoever wins, they will take my child from me."

"I canna believe Ranald would do such." Elyne sucked her teeth and shook her head. "By God's love, how could a man who has lived a life of prayer and healing think of such an evil thing?"

"Because that same evil thing was done to him. He believes it would be a fitting revenge, since your father wants this child so badly. But I will not let them take my babe from me." Catalin lips pursed with anger and her chin lifted. Afore this child was born, she would make her way to Letia and Warin for safety. They would help her petition King Stephen for protection.

She remained silent as they approached the keep's entrance, for young and old men alike were gathered around the well flirting with cleaning maids and cook's helpers who were drawing water. Before he hoisted water to fill the small bucket she clutched, Sir Fergus flourished a bow to a blushing lass. The girl was near stumbling over herself, she was so flustered.

Sirs Giric and Kerr leaned back against the boulder next to the well and watched, smirks lifting the corners of their lips. 'Twas certain they had been well-sated the night just passed, for neither attempted to favor any of the lasses.

Catalin recognized Sir Kerr as the warrior Ranald had fought with earlier. He looked most pleased with himself, and although his green tunic bore blood stained rips, he wore it as if it were a badge of honor. He bowed with respect, while Sir Giric lounged back and eyed them as they passed. On straightening, Kerr frowned and muttered something to him Catalin could not hear. Giric shrugged and made a slight bow. His probing regard searched her form much as Broccin's had, and as they went past him, he chuckled as if he had learned a nasty secret.

She quickened her steps, wanting to be away from so much speculation.

"Ada, fetch hot mead to Lady Catalin's bedchamber," Elyne called out as they passed her in the hall. "It's likely she has taken a chill."

She hustled Catalin up the stairs. Neither spoke until they reached the room and closed the door behind them.

"Oh, Elyne, the wind must have carried Ranald and your father's voices throughout the bailey, and now their words are being spread to all within the castle walls."

"They squabble and fight like two hounds over a meaty bone." Elyne sucked her teeth and pulled a stool over. "Sit. Ye need the rest," she said as she lightly pressed Catalin's shoulders down.

Catalin sat, her teeth worrying her lips. What was she to do? Her stomach roiled, and she took a slow, soothing breath and let it out.

"I won't have it! This babe is not scraps from a table for them to fight over. It is mine. I bear it, not they."

"Aye, but how will we stop them?" Elyne pressed her lips together, her forehead furrowed in thought. "Hm. When it comes time to start the siege, I shall beg Ranald to allow us to go to Letia's. I will say we canna trust Father, and yer bairn will be safer away from him."

"It is a good idea. Once we are at Letia's, I will persuade the baron to send an escort with me to King Stephen's court."

Catalin shuddered, fearing the time when the babe fought to come into the world. She had heard the screams of laboring women; had seen the bloodied sheets. She would have no loving husband anxiously waiting to learn if he had a son, or if it was a daughter. And what would she do if the babe came afore she could get to the English court? She would have to rely on Letia and Warin to protect it.

She squeaked and near jumped off her stool when someone scratched at the door and immediately opened it.

Hannah held the door wide while Ada entered with a tray filled with hot, freshly baked scones and a pot of honey. Beside them was a thick earthenware jug filled with hot mead. A wooden stopper held in the heat. Hannah looked back over her shoulders and pulled the door shut.

"Ada no sooner had the words of your morning sickness out of her mouth afore Broccin was charging out the door. I thought mayhap he would fall over the stairway to the battlements, so fast did he take the steps." Hannah shook her head as she helped Ada set the food on the small table.

"Aye. The master was near aside himself, he was so gleeful." Ada sniffed and muttered under her breath while she poured mead into two cups. "He near drove me dafty with all his questions. I lost track of how many times he asked when yer signs started. I told him again and again! It was a month after ye wed."

"Knowing my sire, he will ask ye again later to be sure ye say the same. Dinna change yer story." Elyne took one of the cups and handed it to Catalin. "Drink this, love. There is nothing like warm mead to chase a chill away."

Catalin cradled the cup close to her face and sniffed the steam. Hannah handed her a scone, but she shook her head. Her stomach would not welcome food now.

Hannah was so aware of her mistress' feelings that she went over to Catalin's side of the bed and pulled out the wooden bucket.

"Just in case you have need of it," she said and beckoned to Ada. They left the two young women alone.

As Catalin took the last swallow of mead, they heard hooves clattering across the wooden drawbridge.

"Umm, Catalin, come look." Elyne leaned out the bedchamber window, the better to see the man sliding from his lathered horse. "That handsome captain of the guards is below."

"Cormac? Is he not the man Ranald accused me of lusting after?" Catalin leaned over Elyne's shoulder to see what so engaged her sister-by-law's interest.

"Aye. Oh, saints! Hide." Elyne groaned and jerked at Catalin's sleeve, urging her downward. "Too late. Ranald spotted us. Does the man have a special sense that warns him when ye are at a window? Likely, he will think ye enamored of the captain."

"Huh! As if any man would look at a woman as round as a barrel. Even my face looks like a piglet's."

"Are ye blind? Ye are more beautiful than ever."

"Not from this view." She looked down, then back up and waggled her brows at Elyne.

"Oh, aye. Ye canna see yerself as other's do." Elyne shrugged and chuckled. "Ye will have to take my word for it, and mayhap the men who watch yer every move when ye walk into the hall? Especially Sir Giric, Moridac's friend. He canna take his eyes off ye."

Unease swept Catalin, for she had noted his interest. Giric was Moridac's friend, had always been close to his side. They had often thumped each other on the shoulder. Had Moridac told him about seducing her in her bed?

She slapped her hand over her mouth and raced to the other side of the bed. 'Twas the first time since taking Ranald's potions that she had felt so ill. She plunked down on the floor and grabbed the bucket, curling her legs around it.

"Oh," she gasped, then gurgled and tried to take deep breaths. It did not seem to work.

Elyne knelt beside her and grabbed the tumbling red curls back from Catalin's face, clucking in sympathy for her plight.

"Ugh. I dinna think I care to have bairns." She held the handful or hair high as she rose on her knees to reach for the ribbon dangling from Catalin's hair. She made short work of re-tying it. "There. That will hold you while I get a wet cloth."

"A wet cloth? What do you on the floor, Elyne?"

Catalin groaned hearing Ranald's demanding voice coming closer with each word, until she saw his leather shoes rounding the edge of the bed. Elyne jumped up and rushed over to the water basin in the far corner.

Ranald squatted in front of Catalin. His tunic rode up high on his thighs. Catalin's gaze traveled from hairy calves, up past strong, solid knees, even higher to thick, muscled thighs.

And beyond.

'Twas the *beyond* that shocked her mind off her plight and turned it to anger.

CHAPTER 20

CATALIN SPUTTERED AND GURGLED. Ranald huffed and snorted, then leaned forward on his knees, pulling his tunic to hide his manly attributes, mumbling all the while.

"Must ye gawk at a man's sex?"

"Ha. You have no shame. You welcomed Lady Muriele's gaze pawing over your flesh." Catalin's words snapped sharp as a whip, bringing a scowl to his face.

"I have no time for such foolish talk."

Elyne crept up behind him and placed a well-aimed foot on his arse. He tottered forward.

"If ye canna be of help, Elyne, go to yer chambers."

"I aim to please, brother. Here. Catalin has need of this."

Splat! A wet cloth plopped over his head down to his chin. Water sloshed over his face, trickled beneath his mask, and a stream traveled a chilly trail down the back of his neck.

"Lucifer's fetid breath!" So loud was his curse that the wet cloth puffed out with each word. He slung it off, nearly displacing his mask.

A giggle from Catalin drew his attention. There sat his wife, the bucket cradled between her legs, her eyes round as an egg yolk and a hand over her mouth trying to stifle her mirth. Elyne stood beside her, a basin of water cradled in her arms, grinning.

What was best? Rant and scream his outrage at Elyne, or leave the room with what little dignity he had left? He chose the latter, for truth to tell the truth, he deserved the dunking. He rose to his feet and stalked over to his clothing chest. 'Twas fortunate a black tunic was the first thing that came to hand. He grabbed it, slammed the lid down and was out the door before either woman could speak.

"Jesu, Ranald. Did ye forget to take off yer clothing afore ye bathed?" Raik stood, a hand uplifted, for he had been about to seek entrance.

"Make yerself useful, cousin." Ranald threw the dry tunic over Raik's raised arm, then stripped off his wet clothing and dropped it at his feet.

"Er, Ranald? Ye might want to cover yerself with as much haste as ye stripped." Raik's laughing eyes looked beyond Ranald's back in the dim corridor.

Ranald jerked his head around to find Aunt Joneta standing there, her hands on her hips, shaking her head.

"Shame on ye, Ranald. Is that any way to go about? I see more of yer bare arse than I see of ye clothed."

Feeling like a chastised youth, Ranald yanked the black tunic over his head and fought to find the opening. He pulled and tugged, until suddenly Raik's hand came through the cloth and waggled his fingers. He groaned, realizing he was fighting his way through a sleeve opening.

Aunt Joneta's tsk was so loud it would be a wonder if she still had teeth left firmly in her jaw. By the time he had the tunic settled on his shoulders, Ranald's dignity was nearly trampled to dust.

"For truth, Raik, there is much to be said for living in an abbey," Ranald muttered.

"Hm. Name something."

"The absence of people everywhere ye turn."

"By people, ye mean women, do ye not?"

Ranald had already started down the circular stairway leading below. He looked back over his shoulder and grimaced at Raik.

"Aye. Elyne near dumped a basin over my head, and I forgot all I went in there to say."

"Mayhap ye can tell Hannah or Ada what ye wished?"

Ranald nodded and glanced around the hall as they hurried through to the doorway. Neither woman was there.

They clattered down the outer stairway to the keep, his eyes searching for the women amongst the warriors assembled there awaiting them.

"Ah, Lady Muriele is closest. She will have to do."

He motioned with his hand for her to come to him. Finn strapped Ranald's short sword around his waist and his broadsword on his back where he could reach up and draw it for battle.

"Go to my lady wife and tell her to keep within the castle grounds. I go to Baron Rupert's lands to avenge a great wrong."

"And when should I tell her to expect your return?"

"When she sees me, of course," he muttered.

He flexed his arms and moved his shoulders to see that all felt right before he turned to her. Her worried look surprised him.

"I canna help but ask, sir, if you have a word of comfort for your lady wife? 'Tis likely an increasing woman needs assurance you will return safely." Lady Muriele frowned up at him.

Ranald shrugged and glanced up at the keep's windows.

"She has no need of words. Do ye think my battle skills so puny I canna overcome a man whose only combat is against helpless men trussed like pigs for slaughter?"

Would Catalin truly worry about him taking an injury? Or would her real fear be of facing his father alone with a babe born before it's time, proving it Moridac's?

He shook his head as he took the reins from Finn and sprang onto Satan's back. Raik, mounted on Storm, trotted over as Ranald started to ride off. About a horse length away, he twisted around in the saddle and looked upward. He glimpsed Catalin's face at the window before she darted back out of sight.

Swinging Satan around, he faced the Lady Muriele, scowled and jabbed a finger at her. "Tell Lady Catalin to stay away from window openings."

As they rode past the line of warriors, Ranald gestured to visibly tired Sirs Cormac and Duncan to join them at the head of the line as they galloped over the drawbridge and out into the open field beyond.

His gut twisted thinking of young Egan who had scaled the walls to burn down the torture hut at Baron Rupert's castle. No sooner had he set it ablaze and near gained his freedom, than guards discovered him.

Catalin peered out the window as Ranald prepared to leave. He glanced around the courtyard, searching for someone. She pressed her lips together seeing him nod, as if pleased he found the one he sought.

"Why, he has beckoned Lady Muriele to him! Drats! He seeks her out more times than he does me."

Clouds of dust rose from the men and stomping horses milling about. It was a wonder the warriors did not sustain crushed legs when their horse sidled away from another, only to come too close to one on its other side. The creak of their leather saddles and harnesses, the clanking of swords against shields, the clatter of hooves on the cobblestone paths all lent an air of urgency.

"What could they be talking about?" Elyne propped her head on Catalin's shoulder and stared down at the warriors restraining their mounts as they waited for Ranald.

Catalin's teeth grated together. She had best stop the foolish habit or they would be naught but mere stubs.

"The nerve of him. He forever grouses at me, accusing me of looking with favor upon other men. He is the one openly toying with another woman."

"What could they be yammering about?" Elyne pursed her lips as she watched. "Hmm. Lady Muriele seems vexed. She looks to be arguing with him."

"Oh saints. Duck."

As Elyne ducked, Catalin moved quickly to the side of the opening where he could not see her. She hugged the wall and peeked around it to see below.

"He started to ride off and then turned and pointed at her. He said something more. She looks surprised, doesn't she? I wonder what it was."

Catalin glared down at the woman. As Ranald galloped to take the lead, she leaned out to watch. She couldn't take her eyes off his back as the horsemen clattered over the wooden planks of the drawbridge. Though she could no longer see him, she kept watch until the warriors cleared the bridge and came out into the open land beyond. She did not move until they were out of sight in the woods beyond.

"Did ye know Ranald planned to ride out today?" Elyne's brows creased as she studied Catalin's face.

"Nay. Why did he not tell me?"

"Uh oh. Mayhap that was why he sought ye out. No doubt the sopping cloth on his head washed all thoughts from his mind." Elyne giggled. "My poor brother. Did ye see his surprise?"

"Surprise? More likely he was stunned." Catalin smiled, remembering Ranald's face.

"He has been from the company of women far too long. He does not know what to make of us." Elyne grinned at her. "I was ready to run. Afore he went to Kelso, he would have chased me down and dunked my head in the horse trough."

"I feared he would strike out in anger, but he did not." Catalin shook her head, puzzled that he held his temper. "Had I done such to Uncle Hamon, no doubt I would soon be covered with bruises."

"Ranald would ne'er strike a woman.

"Mmm."

Catalin was not so sure he would not. More than once, his eyes had smoldered with anger when he stared at her. His hands had tightened to fists, too.

She hugged her belly, shielding it. Even a light blow could have a terrible affect on her babe. The thought of Ranald lifting his fists against her made her shudder in fear. She squeezed her eyes tight and forced her mind to remember the youth he had always been. He teased her but was never unkind. For truth, he could not have changed so terribly that he would harm a woman, much less an unborn child.

"Elyne? The pennant. 'Twas not Raptor Castle's. I did not

see your father ride out. The page flew the black eagles on the yellow silk."

"Aye. The twin's banner. And the men. In full battle gear." Elyne's eyes widened. "'Tis no special patrol. They ride expecting to fight.

Catalin frowned and chewed her lip. Where was Ranald going?

"'Tis not to Hunter Castle. They could not take it with so few men."

"Nay, they wouldn't be so brainsick." Elyne narrowed her eyes, thinking. "I didn't see Sir Giric. Mayhap I can find out from him."

Elyne's skirts flew behind her as she went out the door.

Catalin rubbed her arms, trying to warm them as emptiness filled her. Raptor Castle no longer felt secure. Turning, she stared at the foot of the bed. It was far too big for one person. Why, it was ample enough for three, so large Ranald easily kept space between them when they slept.

He avoided her by day, rising early and riding with the patrol before the sun even thought of rising. He returned only to disappear into the far practice area for the rest of the day and did not come back to the keep until darkness fell.

Most evenings, he sent her up to bed with a stern nod of his head and a finger pointing to the stairwell. He did not join her in the big bed until she slept. If she by chance rolled too close and touched his hot skin, he flinched and moved nearer the edge.

Did he dislike anyone touching his scarred back?

Or was it her he avoided even in sleep?

The other evenings truly puzzled her the most. The evenings when Ranald's eyes grew hot and stormy, and he did not take his gaze from her. No stern nod then, but a firm hand on her back guiding her up the stairwell and hurrying her into the room.

Her clothes were so speedily taken from her that they near flew across the room, their breeze blowing the flame from the candles. He surrounded her with his heated body, falling with her onto the bed. Those nights, he made love to her with wild abandon, his heart thudding against her own.

For days afterward, he avoided her even more.

She dreaded being between the cold sheets alone. How many days would he be gone? She shuddered and wrapped her arms around her stomach, getting comfort from holding it.

If only she could keep the babe there. Snug and warm, where no one could wrench it from her arms.

Safe from Broccin.

Safe from Ranald.

CHAPTER 21

RANALD SET A FAST pace, galloping whenever possible, for Baron Rupert's lands were only half a day away. Mayhap if they arrived as night fell, they had a chance Egan still lived. The baron preferred his *sport* in the evening hours, for no doubt the anguished wails in the dead of night were a more potent threat to all who heard them.

"Tell me again what happened." Ranald lips thinned as he listened to Cormac retell the last three days for at least the fourth time.

"The land around the castle is cleared beyond the curtain walls, enough so that anyone coming from the forest beyond can be easily seen. We climbed trees on the western side. I watched the barbican while Duncan studied the rear bailey from high atop an old oak. Egan noted the fields, for we needed to know when the workers went in for the night." He shuddered and glanced back at Duncan, who took up the tale.

"Aye. I ne'er took my eyes off that hut. Before we went there, I wondered why the baron used it instead of his dungeon." He ran a hand over his face, as if hoping to wipe what he had seen from his memory. "All could hear what happened if they dared to anger their lord."

"Then the hut wasna empty when ye got there?" Raik's lips pressed together in a thin line.

"At first it was," Duncan continued. "Late last eve, Egan noted an old man weeding the rows of carrots. Several times, he glanced around at the other workers but kept on pulling the weeds. The last time, no one else was on the same row. He dug up two scrawny carrots and slipped them inside his breeches, hidden from view."

The muscles in Duncan's tense face twitched. "A corner tower guard turned and saw him. He gave an order, and the next thing we knew, men were dragging the old man inside the walls."

"The pour soul didna have a chance," Raik muttered.

"Aye. I joined Duncan and Egan once night fell." Cormac ground out the words between clenched teeth. "Never have I heard such pitiful wails. In the darkest time of the night, Baron Rupert came out of the hut laughing and joking so loud all could hear, that the old man's tarse was so small it near disappeared when he stuffed it into his toothless mouth." He leaned to the side and retched, then shamefaced, wiped his mouth.

"We waited until Rupert and his men went inside the keep. Egan and I were over the wall in a trice, while Duncan waited at the edge of the woods with the horses. The hut was empty except for the old man's body. The fire pit still had hot embers, so we had no trouble starting the fire. We went back up to the wall walk, but a sentry saw us and put an arrow in Egan's back.

"He fell to the inside bailey. He never had a chance. The next thing I knew, arrows were flying and the walkway was swarming with guards. Duncan was below with our horses. I dropped when I was near halfway down."

"I suspect the guards put out the fire." Duncan scratched the stubble of whiskers on his jaw. "When I looked back, naught but wisps of smoke drifted on the air."

"We are a few leagues away." Ranald motion to Cormac. "Stay with me. I would have ye take me to the spot where we can scale the walls. Duncan, fall back and tell the men that when we are within sight of the castle, keep to the shadows and walk their horses. I want no warning that we are there."

Duncan edged his horse to the side of the path then made his way back down the line.

Ranald tugged off his mask. The ever-watchful Finn galloped up to take it from him, then handed Ranald the helmet he preferred when fighting for Kelso. Made in the Norman style, it was open-faced but for a narrow gold-plated nose guard jutting down from the rim. His nostrils flared, remembering the added fear his mangled face caused — the only good thing that came from his unsightly scars.

"Raik, what think ye we take Dubne, Cormac and two others to greet Baron Rupert?"

"Sounds like a meeting I will relish." Raik patted a dagger hilt protruding from the top of his left boot.

Ranald caught glimpses of the castle in the distance and held up his open hand, stopping the men. They were far enough away no one would hear them stand down off their mounts and lead the horses through the woods to the west of the looming castle.

When they drew opposite the wall where they would enter, he whispered to Dougald to take charge. Dougald was to watch for an arrow shot over the area of the postern gate. At that time, he was to have five men charge the gate bringing the extra horses. The rest of the warriors were to defend Ranald and his men leaving.

Fortunately, the moon was only a sliver and clouds covered what light there was. Ranald pointed out the men to go with him and Raik, and they silently ran from bush to bush, advancing on the curtain wall.

Cormac led them to the corner tower and silently pointed. Ranald squinted, studying the old wall where the round tower met the curtain wall. Evidently, Baron Rupert thought more of his *pleasures* than he did in the upkeep of his castle.

A hoarse scream split the air. Ranald sucked in his breath. Rupert would have much to pay for when they met. He motioned for Cormac to start up the wall. He followed, his hands and feet feeling for the holds he had seen Cormac use. Soon they came to an area where he could draw alongside him, so badly did the wall need repair.

Now and again, one of his men's feet scraped the wall when his toehold crumbled, and he heard the faint sound of a breathed curse.

When they heard the sharp striking of the guards' boots

on the stone walkway above them, they halted.

"The sick bastid ne'er tires of his games," a gruff voice said above them.

"Aye. 'Tis a shame he doesna slip and slit his own wrists," a man answered.

"Shh. Should anyone hear, we wud be doing the hollerin."

"'Tis time for the changing. I will be right glad to stuff me ears and hug me pillow this night."

"Drink with me first. I canna sleep till I have downed more than a few." Their voices grew more distant.

Soon, footsteps clamored on the stairway leading from the ground up to the wall walk, a sign the new guards had arrived. Ranald pointed at Cormac and then to the left. He touched his own chest and then gestured to the right. They inched their heads between merlons and waited. Hearing the new footsteps fade, they peeked out and saw the two guards' backs going in opposite directions.

Not five breaths later, Ranald's left arm whipped around a man's neck, he grasped his head with his right hand and snapped it so quickly the man had no chance to scream. He eased him to the ground and saw Cormac had done the same. They stripped the tunics off the bodies and drew them over their own heads.

Raik and the other three Raptor men joined them. Ranald's head dipped toward a dark corner and motioned for them to stay. He and Cormac sauntered over to the next two guards, and soon Raik and the next man had the proper tunics. They in turn acquired the guards' clothing for the last two men.

Ranald and Raik boldly started down the stairway to the bailey. Ranald motioned to Cormac and Dubne to keep to the shadows as they followed him. The last two men were to stay atop the walkway and pretend they were guarding it. He and Raik jostled each other like any other men happy to be at the end of their day's work.

The hut was no more than ten footsteps away to the right of the stairway, with the postern gate to the left. Anyone looking their way would have seen what appeared to be Baron Rupert's guards entering the hut, but leaving the door open. Two other men entered and quietly pulled the door closed.

Ranald's gaze scanned the inside of the hut. The attempts to burn it down the previous night had blackened the walls, but they were still standing. Foul odors assaulted his senses, from burnt wood to the heavy, sickening smell of blood and burnt flesh. A post stood at the center of the room with crosspieces across the top and bottom to secure a man's arms and legs.

His stomach clenched, for never would he have known Egan. The poor lad barely had strength to moan from what was left of his face.

"Ho, there! Who gave ye leave to enter?" Baron Rupert swung around from where he perched on a stool.

Ranald leapt, his arm swung around the baron's neck, cutting off his breath. Cormac and Dubne subdued the other two men, whose only purpose must have been to do whatever pleased the baron.

Their blood mingled amidst that already soaking the ground.

Ranald tightened his grip on the struggling Rupert, depriving him of air until he went limp in his arms.

"Gag the bastard afore I release him."

Raik tore off the bottom of his stolen tunic and stuffed it in Rupert's mouth before tying a strip to keep it there. Ranald dropped him on the ground and stepped over to Egan.

Though they tried to be gentle, the suffering lad cried out with each touch until they lowered him gently onto a blanket found beside the door.

Ranald removed his helmet and knelt beside Egan, his hands skimming lightly over his body. His sightless face jerked back and forth, for his eyes were gone.

"Egan, lad, it's me, Ranald. I have come for ye."

Egan's throat worked, trying to answer.

Ranald kept speaking in a soft voice as Raik knelt across from him. His eyebrows rose, questioning Ranald. Ranald shook his head, nodding to the rest of Egan's body.

Egan's intestines protruded, trying to spring free from a deep gash in his left side. No place on the lad was without a mark. They had mutilated his nether parts as well. The lad was dying with each agonized breath.

Ranald rested his right hand gently on Egan's forehead and started to pray. He prayed as he had at Kelso when a soul was soon to enter heaven. And, when the formal prayers were done, he prayed with all his heart, asking God's forgiveness for what he was about to do. Finally, he leaned close, for Egan's lips moved.

"Please ... hel ..."

It was all Egan had the strength to whisper.

"Aye, lad." Tears streamed down Ranald's face, their paths straight down from his left eye to his chin, but making a jagged course from the right before finally dropping on Egan's chest.

Ranald's face twisted in anguish as he reached inside the sleeve of his shirt and drew forth a thin misericord. 'Twas used by knights to bring a quick and merciful end to a suffering life that couldn't be saved.

"Go to God, Egan. He waits to hold ye in his arms."

In a flash, he ended the young man's suffering.

Raik watched Ranald rip off the guard's borrowed tunic, and with one last blessing, he covered the body. Slowly, like a wolf awakening from a long sleep, he stood and turned, moving one foot and hesitating before he moved the next. Raik rose to join him.

Ranald's face looked as hardened as any bread baked a deep brown and kept for forming into trenchers. His head swung to where Rupert lay trussed on the floor.

"Tie him to the post. We wouldna want the castle to think he tired of playing with Egan." His nostrils flared, his lip lifted and bared his teeth. Sounds as feral as any maddened beast came from his lips. He waited, his hands slapping his thighs.

If Raik had not known Ranald since they were young lads, he would not have recognized him now. Before him stood, not the monk-turned-man, but a man who looked never to have seen the inside of a chapel.

Ranald's impatient slaps changed as his hands fisted and drummed against his thighs. Dubne, a knight stronger than most, held Rupert aloft while Cormac and another man tied his arms and legs to the crosspieces.

"If he does aught but scream, stop him."

Ranald freed the baron's mouth then stepped back and waited for Rupert to awaken.

"What do ye plan, Ranald?" Raik was truly curious as to what his cousin would do.

"Did I not vow that one day I would do to him what he did to others?"

"Aye. That ye did. But do ye not think death is too easy?" Raik's mouth set in a grim line.

"Ah, but did I not also say I would make sure he didna die?" A gleam shot through Ranald's hooded eyes. He reached a hand to pull forth a small object — an oiled cloth tied with a string.

Raik near laughed aloud. What fitting punishment for a man like Rupert. It would be far worse than death, for Ranald had brought what was necessary to keep the man's wounds from festering and killing him.

Cormac cut and ripped away Rupert's clothing. He was no sooner done than Rupert's eyelids fluttered. Ranald moved so close his nose near touched the bound man's. A scream rose from Rupert, shrill as any lass near scared out of her wits.

"Ah. Ye are a comely man. But yer eyes tell me you find me fascinating. Ye relish my face, do ye? Would ye like yer's to be like it?"

Rupert screamed when he saw Ranald's dagger approach his cheek.

Ranald had his answer.

His weapon flashed. Rupert bellowed and blubbered, trying to call for his guards. Cormac slapped a stick between his lips, tied a cloth to each end and then knotted it in back of his head to keep it there. The man could still scream, but he couldn't utter any intelligible words. The veins in his temple were livid ridges, his neck swelled.

Cormac built up the fire, and held a knife over it, waiting.

Ranald worked swiftly on the baron's face. When done, he held out his hand for the hot blade. He motioned Dubne to hold Rupert's head still while he sealed each wound with it. The man's muscles bunched and strained, his body stiffened.

He moved calmly from Rupert's face down and around his thrashing body. It would have pleased him to copy every horror Egan had received, and had they been at Raptor, he would have. Even so, he took precious time to stitch an occasional wound that bled too freely or gaped too wide. He didn't want the man to have ease in death.

Before long, the baron fainted.

Ranald shuddered at what he was doing. Each time he faltered, he envisioned Egan's young body covered with the bloody tunic and steeled himself to finish. He had but one last thing to do.

He stood back. His jaw jutted, determined. His teeth clamped tight. Waiting.

CHAPTER 22

"I DIDNA THINK YE could do it."

Ranald flinched at Raik's words and drew in a long, slow breath. What he had so feared was happening. He had changed much in these last months.

Raik's gaze studied Ranald's hands. When he looked back up, Ranald noted the blue of his eyes had deepened and tinged with dark gray. Ranald answered their unspoken question.

"Aye. Were this any other man, I could not. The bastard deserves no less than he gave."

Ranald's skin prickled. Bile threatened to choke him. He stiffened his spine and swallowed. He wished to be leagues away from this place, never to see it again.

"We must be gone afore the sky lightens." He took a deep breath and stepped forward to finish what he had promised he would do.

Rupert awoke, biting the stick so hard it was a wonder it did not crack in half. Ranald held his bloodied hands close to the man's eyes, so he could see what Ranald held aloft.

Rupert sucked in a breath and gurgled in disbelief. His eyes told Ranald all he needed to know. He stared with fascinated horror, shaking his head back and forth, trying to convince himself he saw wrong.

"Aye, Baron Rupert. Ye are as ye made Egan and so many other men these past years. But ye should thank me and be grateful I didna take yer tarse, as ye did the old man."

He waited until Rupert's garbled sounds quieted. His eyes bulged, reminding Ranald. He held his blade close to the outer tip of Rupert's left eye. He blubbered and jerked in horror.

"Nay, dinna worry. Ye took young Egan's eyes, but I want ye to have yer sight. Each day ye live, ye will know the stares of others when they look upon yer face. And, too, ye will wish to admire my handiwork on yer nether parts. I have stitched yer wounds and packed herbs there. The wound will heal nicely."

"I still think you should slit his throat," Cormac muttered.

"Too easy." Ranald tilted his head and stared into Rupert's eyes. "When yer men find ye, ye are to order this hut burned to the ground. Should ye live to walk again and ever torture another man, I will return when ye least expect it. When I finish with ye, ye will have no eyes, no hands, no tarse."

Ranald threw what he had in his hands onto the coals. Grimacing with disgust, he wiped his hands on his clothing.

"Dubne, take our poor lad across yer shoulders and let us be gone from this hellish place."

Raik wrapped Egan in the blanket and helped sling him over the big man's shoulder. Ranald edged the door open to peer out the crack. He couldn't believe his luck. It was as if the devil had deserted Rupert. They eased out of the hut and moved to stand in the shadows.

The two Raptor men left on the walkway spied them. One notched an arrow and shot it in the air. They pretended to take their time coming down the stairs.

Raik and Cormac subdued the guards at the postern door and pulled it open. The sound of hooves pounding the earth alerted Rupert's men patrolling above. Amidst the shouts and clamor of guards racing down the stairs, Ranald and the men raced out the door then slammed it shut behind them.

Seeing two sturdy branches lying close-by, Cormac and Ranald seized them and shoved the edges under the door, seating them so firmly that if anyone tried to open the door they couldn't without a struggle.

They sprinted as fast as their legs could take them. Six men galloped toward them leading their horses. Arrows whooshed through the air, but none did more than tear a tunic or nick a bit of skin on a man's arm. 'Twas a half-hearted response from the confused castle guards. Trained to stop raiders from entering the castle grounds, they were confused on seeing men in Rupert's colors leaving. Dougald's archers harried the guards while Ranald's men leapt into their saddles.

Astride Satan, Ranald slapped Finn's horse on the rear, making sure the lad went on ahead. At the edge of the clearing, he held back, waiting until each man passed him and entered the woods. Dubne had slung Egan's body across his lap, and holding him with one arm, he urged his horse to a gallop. As soon as he passed, Ranald spurred Satan and followed.

They rode hard to distance themselves from their pursuers. Little by little, the sounds of drumming hoof beats and shouts of uncertainty faded. Raptor Castle's men slipped away as if swallowed by the black night.

Catalin worked hard to avoid Lady Muriele after Ranald left, for the woman seemed determined to have words with her. She was equally determined not to let her near.

At the noon meal, Lady Muriele sat to the right of the Chief Broccin and Lady Joneta. From the corner of her eye, Catalin noted now and again the beauty leaned forward and tried to catch her eye.

She sighed and pushed food around on her trencher. Could it be the babe was draining her good nature? Every time she saw the beautiful woman, she longed to dump a pitcher of sticky mead over her head.

"Do ye not feel well?"

Elyne, sitting beside her, leaned forward to peek at her face.

"Um. Well enough."

Catalin stabbed a sliver of pork like she needed to kill it before she took a bite, then scooted it from one side of the sopping trencher to the other.

"I thought ye loved pork. It's why I asked cook to prepare it today." Elyne's brows quirked. "Ye have lost yer taste for it?

"I do love pork. Since Sir Giric told you Ranald was riding

to that horrid Baron Rupert's, I have been too angry to eat," she muttered.

"Angry? But why? Rupert is a cruel man who needs a sample of what he has dealt out. If I read my brother aright, Ranald is the perfect man to teach him."

Catalin's unladylike snort turned curious gazes in her direction.

"What was that about?" Elyne grinned at Catalin's scowling face.

"The perfect man? Saints alive, Elyne. Ranald was a monk. What does a monk know of warfare?"

This whole day, wherever she walked, she overhead someone speaking of the hideous things accredited to Rupert. What if the baron captured Ranald? He wouldn't be able to defend himself properly.

"Did he not tell ye?"

"Tell me? Must I forever ask 'what'!?"

Saints help her. She was near ready to scream. Her stomach churned with worry. Ranald had not spent these last years training for battle. He'd been locked away in a dismal abbey, most likely spending his days on his knees. And all because of the hateful wretch seated beside her who called himself Ranald's father.

Wherever she turned, she felt Broccin stare at where her breasts thrust against the top of her kirtle. Such calculating looks, too. Like he weighed her flesh beneath the cloth. Thank the saints her skirts were loose and he could not see her expanding middle. The gleam in his eyes made her flesh crawl. She wanted to slam her eating knife into his thigh.

She fingered the knife, near tempted to use it. She looked down at the muscular leg so near her own. Humph. The blade would surely break before it pierced his thick skin. Mayhap that stony hide was why he had survived battling the Turks.

"... why they called him The Protector."

Elyne leaned close to tap Catalin's nose with her forefinger. "Ye didna hear a word I said, did ye?"

"Aye, I did. Who is a protector?"

"Was, not is. Ranald."

"Ranald? He was the protector of what?"

Elyne rolled her eyes and shook her head.

"If ye want the regard of my brother, ye will have to sharpen yer wits. Now, pay heed to what I say. Border abbeys are favorite targets for raids from across the border. There is always someone ready to risk their life for the riches found in abbeys."

"Why would a man risk his soul stealing from God's places?" Catalin shrugged her shoulders.

"Greedy men will do anything to have their hands on the coffers of coins and jewels given to an abbey as gifts, or by men seeking favors from the church. Huh! Father would have sent a goodly amount of coins with Ranald to Kelso."

"Ranald was not a warrior. He is only now learning to be one. He was a monk. Monks do not wear swords or heft broadswords."

"Aye, not usually. But did ye expect a monk to have the muscles and hardened body my brother has? He did not get that way by kneeling in prayer or by digging in the gardens. All these past years, he defended Kelso. He is well used to fighting and holding his own with sword and shield."

Catalin frowned, thinking of Ranald at Kelso.

"Elyne, if Ranald defended Kelso with his fighting skills, is it not likely he could have killed someone? I cannot imagine they would allow him to do such." Catalin grimaced, wondering what penance they would give a monk in the confessional.

"It's different. Ranald was defending God by protecting the abbey. Crusaders take lives. It's not considered the same as murder." Elyne sighed.

"That is what we believe. I pray God feels the same way." Catalin, very much worried that mayhap God was not pleased with the way men defended him, shifted uneasily in her seat.

Lady Joneta rose, crooking a finger at the servants, signaling it was time for them to clear the tables. Catalin had been so engrossed in her worries she had not noted the large bowls of fruits and cheeses. Her stomach grumbled, reminding her she had not eaten enough to feed the small babe nestled beneath her heart. She grabbed a pear before a servant could whisk it away.

"Lady Catalin, I have need of words with you."

Catalin jerked her head to the side, her eyes narrowed. Oh, Saints! Muriele. She had not seen the woman approach. A rush of heat flooded her face. Her hand tightened, her fingers dug into the ripe pear. From the wary look on the lady's face, was the beauty intent on telling her she also carried a babe? Ranald's babe?

If it was so, Ranald could easily denounce his wife and gain his freedom. Freedom to marry a woman whose babe was truly his and would inherit Raptor Castle and all its lands. Sticky liquid dripped from her fingernails mangling the succulent fruit.

Muriele's soft voice finally caught her attention.

"... speedily as possible." Lady Muriele looked concerned as she watched Catalin's face.

"Mmm. Sorry. I could not hear. The fools are so rowdy I can barely hear mine own thinking."

Catalin did not feel it was truly a lie, for the men were playing Hot Cockles in the far corner. The rough game would surely do someone a serious injury one of these nights.

"Nay, I spoke too softly. Sir Ranald had to leave before he could talk to you. He wished me to tell you not to worry about him. He needed to correct a wrong at Baron Rupert's castle. He wanted to assure you he will return as speedily as possible." Muriele shifted her feet and clasped her hands behind her back.

"He wished me not to worry?" Catalin's heart lifted. Her fingers around the pear lightened their strangle hold.

"Aye. And he was concerned for you. He added that you were to take care around window openings, for fear you might do yourself or the babe some harm." Lady Muriele cleared her throat and looked about to move away.

"Ranald said all of that?"

He had not seemed concerned for her safety when he berated her about gawking at men.

"Mayhap not in those exact words. He was in such a hurry to ride out that he may have said more than I can recollect." Lady Muriele gave a shy smile.

"It was most kind of you to tell me."

Advancing footsteps behind them made Muriele glance over her shoulder. Chief Broccin was charging around the table, a determined look on his face.

"Good eve," Lady Muriele whispered.

She slipped around Catalin and Elyne. Her hasty strides took her across the room and out the doorway into the shadows of the stairwell. He hurried in pursuit until Lady Joneta stepped out of the shadows of the stairwell. Lips pressed together, she stared him dead in the eye before she turned to follow the young woman.

Curious, Catalin watched the laird. He halted in his tracks and scowled at where they disappeared. He muttered under his breath and whirled on his heels to join the rowdy men across the room.

"Hmm. It was nice of her to relay his words. I didna ken Ranald talked long enough to say so much." Elyne tapped her finger on her chin.

"Oh." Catalin's shoulders slumped. She dumped the mangled pear on the nearest tabletop and stared at her gooey hands. She looked around for something to wipe them dry. The ewer and basins for washing before the meal had long since gone. Naught remained but her own clothing. She sighed and used her skirts.

'Twas foolish of her to have been pleased on hearing Lady Muriele's words. What was the matter with her? Why should she care if Ranald thought to send words of comfort? It wasn't as if he loved her, or if she loved him. If she lost her heart to him, he would break it again by not loving her back. A deep sigh slipped out before she had sense enough to stop it.

Elyne hugged Catalin's shoulders.

"I'm sure she relayed his message correctly, Catalin, now I think of it. We could not see his lips clearly. He likely talked fast being he was so pressed for time."

"It does not matter. Our marriage was not forged in love. He had no choice. I am happy enough to be away from Uncle Hamon, so I have no need for silly words of love or gestures of affection."

"It's a good thing. I doubt Ranald learned either one while living amongst monks and traveling knights." Elyne chuckled and squeezed Catalin's hand. "Saints. What soap did ye use when ye washed last?" She sniffed the palm of her hand and laughed.

Catalin nodded at the table where she had dumped the pear.

"I will know Ranald's feelings by the way he treats me, not by words easily said and not meant." She stood straighter, her head held higher. She did not pine for love. As long as her bairn was safe, 'twas all she asked. If Ranald thought to take her babe from her, he would have to fight her for it.

Elyne tugged Catalin's hand. "Come. Aunt Joneta had the laundress color a length of linen as a surprise for ye. It's a soft yellow made from boiled Comfrey leaves. What think ye of making a sleeping garment from it for the babe?"

"A fitting color, whether it is a girl or boy."

Catalin welcomed the hours spent away from the laird's watchful eyes, though plying a needle was not her favorite thing.

The muffled sound of pounding hooves on the damp leaves carpeting the forest broke the stillness of the night. Harnesses jingled and clanked, and leather saddles creaked as warriors shifted their tired bodies. Now and again, a horse snorted or huffed.

Ranald rode, his teeth clamped tight behind lips that held back bile.

What kind of man was he becoming? Had become, was more like it. Cold chills made his shoulders twitch. He ignored it and squared them again. What bothered him most about what had happened this night was that he didn't regret it.

He had not struck at Rupert in the heat of anger. It was not the type of anger that unleashed the power to stir the wind or radiate heat. It was far deeper than that, a cold anger that chilled his soul.

They rode in silence, broken now and again by grunted

curses and muffled moans coming from men who had the misfortune to be in an arrow's path when fleeing Baron Rupert's castle. The curses were most alike, all aimed at the baron. More often than not, orders to God to allow the man to die an agonizing death accompanied them.

Ranald held up his hand and slowed Satan to a trot. Beyond the next curve was an area where they could rest until dawn.

"We will stop here. If I remember rightly, a stream lies beyond the willow trees." Ranald stared up at the sky, thankful that clouds covered the sliver of a moon.

"Aye. The trees will make an ample blanket for a small fire. Ye will need a bit of light to tend injuries," Raik murmured.

Ranald glanced sideways at him, for his cousin was usually one with his mount. Not so now. He looked awkward.

"Did ye take an injury, Raik?"

"Too small to worry with until the men are treated."

"Oh? And where would this *small* injury be?"

For a bit, Raik did not speak. Then a husky growl rumbled from his throat.

"I am sitting on it."

"I thought as much. Left nether cheek, eh?" Ranald could not keep the amusement from his voice.

"How did ye know? I kenned I rode as hard as the next man."

"Ha. Never have I seen ye sit a saddle so far to the side ye were likely to spill from it." Ranald wiped a hand over his mouth, erasing the grin spreading there. It was not kind of him to tease Raik about an injury.

"Not likely. My foot is firmly in the stirrup. I wanted no weight on the tip, else it would dig deeper." Raik sighed with relief when they pulled to a halt.

Ranald near jumped off Satan's back and was beside Raik, ready to lend a hand if he needed it.

Raik shook his head, stood upright in the stirrups and released his right foot. When he slung his leg over his mounts rear, he grasped the pommel and back of the saddle. With straight arms, he lifted his body enough to kick his left foot free before jolting to the ground. His left leg buckled, protesting the weight put on his hip.

Ranald braced him, one arm around his waist, and called to his squire.

"Finn, gather tinder and build a fire." Ranald turned and pointed his chin to the ground where he wanted Finn to start the fire and led Raik over to it.

"Sit."

"Huh! That's easy for ye to say," Raik grumbled.

Ranald watched as he lowered himself to the ground and stretched out on his right side. He braced his arm on the carpet of leaves, his head on his hand, so he could keep an eye on their surroundings.

"Dubne, check the men. I would know what injuries need tending," Ranald said as he untied a leather pouch from his saddle and placed it beside Raik.

As Ranald washed his hands and arms at the stream, he spied a good-sized flat stone an arm's length from the shore. He stepped into the rushing water and hefted the stone, then sloshed it around making sure it was clean. He carried it over and set it on the ground near Raik.

It was ample enough to hold the herbs and supplies he had brought with him. Truth be told, he begrudged the care he had given Rupert's injuries to keep them from festering. He hoped his men would not suffer for what Rupert now lacked betwixt his legs.

"Dinna think to touch me until ye tend the men." Raik scowled at Ranald and scooted a bit away.

"Huh! I dinna yearn to touch yer sorry rump, cousin. Since ye are not yelling and screaming, I figure yer injury can bide a while."

Ranald eyed the few men Dubne brought over. All had wounds that needed binding, but none serious enough for stitches. When they noted Ranald's equipment spread out on the rock, they straightened and declared they had no need of tending. When they started to sidle away, one flex of Dubne's shoulders stilled them.

"I had expected a heartier defense than the baron's men offered." Ranald checked an arrow's injury on Cormac's right arm that had near stopped bleeding on its own.

"Aye. I dinna think their hearts were in it." Cormac watched Ranald smear ointment on it and bind it with clean linen.

"He has been most lax in his training. Never have I seen such poor aim from archers." Ranald glanced sideways at Raik. "Of course, Raik's broad arse made a target hard to miss."

Raik snorted and raised up to rake his fingers through the leaves at his elbow until he found a stone and tossed it aside. He sighed and leaned back again, resting his cheek on his palm.

"Many a lass has admired the same arse ye are talking about."

Ranald finished with the men and bent over the stream to cleanse his hands. He returned to kneel beside Raik and slit his breeches from the waist down in a vertical line to the broken arrow shaft, then made a horizontal cut across on either side so he could peel aside the black cloth. He probed Raik's flesh, seeing how far the arrow had entered.

"It's good ye didna try to pull it out yerself. The head would have angled and caught yer flesh, ripping it further. Do ye need a biting stick before I remove it?" Ranald looked around for something Raik could clamp between his teeth.

"Nay. This will do." Raik pulled his dirk from the sheath strapped to his leg and bit down on the dagger's hilt.

Ranald gripped the wood shaft and rocked the arrow gently back and forth, each time reaching his smallest finger inside the wound to force the flesh away from the top as he tugged. He stopped when Raik took the dirk from between his teeth and spat on the ground.

"Lucifer's warty balls! It tastes like dog shite. Wrench the arrow out and be done with it." Raik clamped his teeth back on the dirk's handle.

"I aim to please." Ranald grasped the arrow, and before Raik could take the next breath, yanked it free.

"If I didn't know better, I would think ye took yer time just to bedevil me." Raik's eyes lit when he saw Ranald reach for a flask and remove the stopper.

"Ye can have it after I cleanse yer wound."

Ranald grasped Raik's flesh at the widest part of the wound and pressed them gently toward the center, making a small well. Raik jerked and near came off the ground when Ranald poured the fiery liquid into the wound.

"Ye can have that drink now." He handed the flask to Raik. Ranald prepared a needle and began to sew. "Hm. 'Tis most interesting."

"My arse?" Raik took another swallow of the potent Scottish brew.

"Not yer arse. The birthmark on it. I thought it would fade with age, but it hasna."

"It's the same as it always was." Raik closed his eyes and rolled the liquid around in his mouth.

"Nay. Now it is not." Ranald's brow furrowed as he stitched. "Remember how I used to tease ye and say it looked like a plump bird staring at yer crack?"

Raik grunted. "Ye were a fool then and an even bigger one now. 'Tis a brown blotch, nay a bird."

"Ye canna see it. Dougald agreed that day we swam in the loch together." Ranald placed the last stitch. Taking a large glob of herbs mixed into a salve on his finger, he smeared it over the stitches.

"It was Moridac's idea to swim that day. That loch was almost frozen." Raik offered the flask to Ranald, and seeing his shrug, took another large swallow.

"Aye. It was a good thing no lass was near to see yer proud tarse looking more like a limp worm."

"Ha." Raik waved the flask at him. "*Yer* ballocks shriveled to near disappear before our eyes."

Ranald frowned down at his handiwork. He could see no way to bind it.

"Hm. It will leave an unusual scar. Yer brown bird now sits on a perch."

"Ye are seeing things." Raik twisted his head to look, to no avail.

"Dinna take my word for it." Ranald glanced around, saw the men had wrapped themselves in tartans and were fast asleep. All but Dubne and Fergus who were standing watch. He beckoned Fergus over and pointed at his handiwork. "What does this look like to ye?"

"A blood-stained arse with stitches, what else?"

"Told ye." Raik crowed.

"Nay, above the stitches." Ranald pointed directly at the brown birthmark.

Fergus stared. He tilted his head back and forth to judge it from different angles.

"Ah! It's a fat quail walking on a path." He grinned and went back to standing watch.

"Close enough." Ranald packed away his medicines and banked the fire. "Sleep. We leave before first light."

He made his way through the snoring men and lowered himself to his knees beside the blanket-wrapped body of young Egan. The banter with Raik had eased his mind for a bit, but the nights happenings flooded back, filling his soul with black thoughts.

Ranald prayed into the night, stopping only when the darkness eased and told of a dawn soon to come.

CHAPTER 23

"THE BLACK RAPTOR! THE Black Raptor!"

Ranald's lips set in a grim line as the shouts followed him through village after village. He did not mind the name so much as men crossing themselves and women snatching their young ones and scurrying to hide in their huts.

"Dinna scowl so, cousin. It's good to be feared." Raik rode beside him, not quite sitting squarely on his saddle. He tilted his head and studied Ranald's profile. "Hm. I ken the name suits."

Ranald swung his head to stare at him. "Suits? Mayhap the black garb. It was all I wore for so many years I would feel like a gawky flower in the bright colors ye favor."

"Aye. And raptor fits ye as well."

Ranald snorted and shook his head.

"What raptor have ye seen with half a face?"

"It's not that. Ye canna see yerself in that Norman helmet."

"What bird of prey have ye seen with a helm?"

"Naught. It's the nose guard. It makes an apt beak. Even the color suits."

"Huh!"

"Aye, it does. Like now. Yer eyes flashing fire on either side causes a man to feel trapped."

Ranald shook his head. His cousin surprised him with such fanciful imaginings. His shoulders and neck ached. His bowed head through all last night's prayer vigil was likely the cause. He turned his head side to side, stretching his stiff neck.

"Aha!" Raik pointed at him and grinned.

"What now," Ranald grumbled.

"The way ye did yer head. I have seen many a bird do such. Most times, they were seeking for worms. Ye are hungry, Ranald?"

"Addlepated fool."

Ranald kicked Satan into a gallop, the horse's hooves slinging clods of wet earth behind them. Raik's rumbling laughter mingled with the pounding of Storm's hooves as he raced to join him.

They rode hard for near half a league, until Ranald spied a grimace of pain on Raik's face. He slowed Satan to a smoother gait. How could he have been so thoughtless? It was hard enough for his cousin to sit his horse in any comfort, but the drubbing his wound received now must be sheer torture.

He caught his breath at the thought. For the time they had been talking, Ranald's mind had turned from agonizing over what he had done last eve. As he had prayed over Egan, he knew he had to seek out Abbot Aymer.

It was as he had feared. Never had he heard of Moridac doing any deed as harsh as what he had done. He drew in a ragged breath at the thought. And his sire? Mayhap he had. He had talked much of how the Seljuk Turks were less than men. That to subdue a crafty animal, ye had to use more than physical force. Ye had to spread fear of the Crusaders.

He knew what that fear was. What he had done to Rupert was far less than what his father bragged of doing in the name of God.

"I said ye were the image of a bird of prey. Did ye think to fly home to prove ye *were* one?" Raik forced a grin with taught lips pinched white with pain.

"Forgive me. 'Twas brainless to push such a fast pace."

"Ye look troubled. Want to talk?"

"Dinna worry yerself. 'Tis my problem, not yers."

"Me worry? I have not the patience for it." Raik glanced at Ranald's face. "But I am curious."

"Of?"

"Yer anger. I felt no heat coming from ye. No winds blew. No fires lit. No things flying' through the air." He shook his head. "Naught but cold surrounded ye."

Ranald clenched his teeth together, trying to find the words.

"Why?" Raik prodded.

"Why the cold?" Ranald saw Raik nod from the corner of his eye. "Anger is like passion. Hot. Sometimes violent. I was beyond anger. I steeled my mind to what I needed to do. Rupert had to pay for all the torment he caused his victims and all the grieving families of the men he mutilated. It was payment to them. Had I merely fought with him ....," he hesitated, trying to explain. "I could have killed him. But it would have been an honorable death."

Raik nodded. "No doubt today he wishes ye had."

"Aye. To do battle would have been easier for me, too, even had I suffered a serious injury." Ranald blinked and cleared his voice.

"He is not worth risking yer life."

"Nay? Instead, I risked my *soul!*" Ranald pressed his lips together. His shoulders slumped for but a heartbeat before he consciously squared them.

"Ye think sparing his life was worse than slicing yer sword through his heart?" Raik's brows rose.

"For me, aye. What I dreaded most when I left Kelso is steadily coming true."

"Ah. Ye fear being like Broccin. Even Moridac?"

Ranald's lips hardened. He had certainly been like his father this past day. Heedless of the suffering he caused. And he thought of Moridac and his hunting lodge. The lust his brother fed there. Ranald could not deny Lady Muriele had heated his loins. Every time her gaze explored down his body, he had felt it as potent as warm lips sliding down his flesh. He could not deny the desire to experience them on his body had been strong. He finally nodded.

"Living at Kelso kept ye from the world, Ranald. It is as it always was. Men fight and hold on with tooth and nail else another will steal all from under him. If that means risking yer soul, then all in Scotland, England and Normandy have likely lost theirs." He flashed a grin at Ranald.

"I fear I will never be the same." Ranald straightened in the saddle.

Mayhap being ruthless was the only way he could survive. He no longer lived in a peaceful community, though there were times he had to be the warrior there. Aye. He had killed. But always Abbot Aymer had been there to listen as Ranald emptied his mind to him.

He nodded, coming to a decision. Once he assured himself all was as it should be at Raptor, he would go to Kelso.

Catalin watched, curious, when a peasant came running across the drawbridge. He looked excited, yet fearful, for his movements were tense.

"Elyne, why is that man waving his arms around and gesturing toward the south?"

"He is yelling something. A crowd is gathering around him. Come! Let us see what he has to say."

Elyne jumped to her feet as sprightly as a young doe. When she glanced at Catalin, she held out her hand to help her rise.

Catalin grasped it and carefully pushed to her feet, for she was not as agile as she had been before her belly had become her central point.

"I expect he saw someone coming. It canna be foe, for the guards have not dropped the portcullis or raised the drawbridge."

"It is most curious. Do you think mayhap your brother is returning from tending to Baron Rupert?"

"Aye. I feel him near." She turned puzzled eyes on Catalin. "Why is it always *yer brother* when ye speak to me of Ranald, and never husband?"

Catalin felt heat flush her face. "Calling him husband feels far too intimate. I do not feel like I thought a wife would when we are together. I fear he is pretending to be a husband to me, nothing more."

"Hm. Have ye not learned how to entice him to yer bed

as yet?"

"Of late, he pushes himself way into the night and rises afore dawn. If I stay awake until he comes into the room, the next eve he comes even later. He avoids me still." She looked down at the toe of her shoes peeking beneath her skirts as they walked, before glancing at Elyne.

"Always? How does a man go so long without satisfying his male urges?" Elyne's eyes flashed with curiosity.

"Sometimes during that darkest time of night, he will roll toward me. When his flesh touches mine, he groans in his sleep and reaches out."

Catalin would not speak more of those times when Ranald's arms surrounded her, his body hot as any warming brick could be. Each time, it was mostly the same.

His lips would claim hers so rough and eager their teeth clashed together, his tongue stabbed through her lips until she opened for him. He would comb his fingers through her hair and closed them into fists that held her head so tightly she could not move the slightest bit. When he finally lifted his lips to gasp in a breath, she would call his name.

It was at this point he awakened enough to know what he was doing. He hesitated before he began to part from her. As their flesh separated and the cold air slid between them, a deep groan rumbled from his throat. His arms returned to pull her so close she feared he would crush her breasts against her ribs.

Her slightest gasp brought gentleness. His lips caressed hers, a feathered touch. He devoured their softness, waiting until she parted her own before his velvet tongue entered.

Gentle hands searched for a breast to cup, his calloused thumb teasing her nipple till it thrust for more attention. Always, when his lips claimed her breast to suckle, it was with tantalizing possession. Such deep pleasure shot through her body down to where she longed for his touch that she began to thrash beneath him.

She ached to touch him. He let her hold his head, to clutch him tighter to her breast. The hair atop his head where it filled in at his tonsure felt warm and silky. His hair had grown long enough he tied a leather strip around it to keep it from hindering his sight.

If she dared slide her fingers onto his cheek, he was quick to grasp her wrists in warning.

She longed to cup his face, to feel his lips with her thumbs the way he smoothed over hers. Her body responded to his slightest touch, leaving her skin burning with fire. His impatience built until his hands and lips moved so demandingly over hers she caught fire from his heat.

She opened, inviting him. When he entered, she clasped her legs around his waist and met him thrust for thrust as they fought each other to end that impossible tension which near threatened to shatter her into little pieces. His head would nestle there at the joining of her neck and left shoulder, his undamaged cheek against hers. She loved his scent, the feel of his skin against her face. She caressed him with her cheek, feeling the light stubble of hair there.

In loving, Ranald was two people.

One, a fierce man who hungered so deeply he could not wait.

The other, a gentle man who thought only of pleasuring her before taking his own.

The sounds of people gathering brought Catalin from her musings. She glanced aside at Elyne, fearing to see that she had known what occupied Catalin's thoughts. Thankfully, she stood high on her toes, peering over shoulders while gripping Catalin's hand.

Elyne tugged Catalin along as she used her elbow to part the last two people in front of them. No sooner did they have a clear view to the cobblestone path leading in from the drawbridge than they heard the approaching thunder of hooves coming from the forest.

Catalin's stomach tripped with fear of what she would see when the men came bursting through the barbican. Would

Ranald's body be slung over Satan's back, broken and bloody? Cold icy fear coursed through her veins. Though she might fear Ranald and what he would do once the babe was born, she feared even more being alone under Chief Broccin's care.

"The standard bearer comes first. Sir Dubne is at his side!" The guard shouted from above the barbican. His next words were subdued. "He carries a body across his lap."

Suddenly, the crowd gathered there quieted. Tension filled the air, making the hairs on Catalin's arm stand.

She felt that airy sensation when her stomach slowly forced bitter fluid up through her chest to her throat. She swallowed, and swallowed again, forcing it back. She clutched Elyne's hand. Something was terribly wrong.

Was it Ranald's body carried home in the position of honor, the first to enter the castle after the standard-bearer? She flattened her hand over her mouth to suppress any sounds of horror.

"Wait! Satan's Spawn has burst from the woods. Light flashed off Sir Ranald's nose piece."

Catalin's held in breath tore loose with a whoosh. The ground rumbled with the force of the returning men, accompanied by sounds of thunder in the distance. It seemed to take forever before the first horses' hooves clattered over the wooden drawbridge. Once they came close, she could barely hear herself think.

Young Finn carried Ranald's banner high, his back stiff, his face solemn. Anguished cries broke from women not knowing whose body Dubne carried so carefully across his lap.

Sounds of "The Black Raptor, The Black Raptor" whispered over the crowd, floated with the wind. It got stronger when Ranald's black horse burst through the long corridor of the barbican after Dubne. Storm, with Raik seated awkwardly on his back, danced across the cobblestones.

Catalin's eyes widened as she watched Satan advance. Ranald's black clothing bore large blotches of a color near as dark as the material beside them. Her gaze flashed back to Dubne, then Raik. Their tunics bore witness that they had spent a night where blood flowed freely. Her stomach tumbled. Ranald looked to have near bathed in blood. She almost gagged.

Hearing a burst of pleased laughter, she followed the sound to see Chief Broccin, arms on his hips and legs spread wide, watching Ranald from atop a wooden mounting block placed in the middle of the path.

Satan's hooves clopped over the cobblestones, near opposite Catalin and Elyne, when Broccin spoke.

"If yer pious friends could see ye now, they would scurry to the altar to give prayers of thanks that ye are no longer their brother." His hard eyes combed over his son. "Ye have never looked more the man than ye do now!"

A cloud moved in the sky as if a hand had reached up to clear a spot, sending light to bathe Ranald's face. The sun glinted off his helmet, his nosepiece.

It drew Catalin's gaze to his face. He looked straight ahead at his father atop the mounting block. All she could see of her husband was the ruined right side of his face. She could smell the blood on his clothing. She gasped. Held her breath. Impressions flashed quickly at her. Blood splattered his face. Not Ranald's blood. Another's. He had attempted to wipe it off, but telltale marks lingered in the creases of his scars.

Broccin laughed again. "Yer lady wife looks sickened by yer bloody clothing. Or is it that ye returned in one piece?" Broccin looked pointedly at Catalin.

Ranald's eyes followed his father's gaze to look down on her. His black eyes pinned her. Blinding light bathed his face.

Every scar stood out. Bold. Telling.

Catalin couldn't breathe; she couldn't tear her gaze away.

Looking at him straight on, to the left of the nosepiece, that half that was as Moridac, showed the dominant, handsome man she married. To the right was a man she did not know.

She knew the eyes, though. They were the same. Their deep purple-black gaze pinned hers. They bored into her thoughts, her mind. He must have found his answer, though it was the wrong one. His scarred lip lifted on the right, baring gleaming teeth.

All Ranald lacked was the growl of a wolf.

Ranald's hold on his wife broke when crackling thunder crashed overhead and lightning struck outside the curtain wall. Satan reared, pawing the air. Ranald clamped his legs tight to the horse's flanks, refusing to come unseated. All his muscles bunched as sheer strength controlled the frightened warhorse. Finally, he forced Satan's head down, and his hooves came jarring back to earth.

He wanted to bolt from this place as surely as Satan's Spawn wanted to race back out the barbican and into the open fields beyond. He would not. It was the coward's way to run, to hide from Catalin's startled look. He heard a strangled cry and looked to the left to see young Finn, tears of remorse welling as he felt inside the neck of his tunic where he had secured Ranald's mask.

'Twas not the lad's fault, but Ranald's own. He was the one who had insisted on shielding women from his ravaged face. He scattered a glance around the crowd that had quieted after no added outbursts from the sky accompanied the first.

His stare scraped over Catalin, not deigning to linger. He'd had his answer there. Elyne's clear eyes never flickered. Many women looked away. Some did not. Ah, the Lady Muriele. Her regard held steadfast, understanding shining from their depths.

He ignored all as he dismounted and walked over to stand beside Dubne while the big man handed down Egan's body to two waiting men. Egan's young widow stood alongside the stairs leading into the keep, an infant clutched tight in her arms. Tears rolled down her face. Knowing all hope faded that they had rescued her husband in time, a high keening rose from her lips. Soon, sympathetic wails from other women joined her.

His heart twisted. He blamed himself for having accepted the lad's wish to join the men at Rupert's castle. He had said he was the most agile of the lot and could make his way over any wall or through any maze of hazards. And he had. The least Ranald could do was to look after his widow and child. He would find a way.

The first thing he could do would be a kindness to the widow. He did not want her to see her beloved as he was now. He turned to Raik at his elbow, and drew him aside but a few paces.

"Seek Elyne and Catalin. Have them take Egan's wife to her dwelling."

"She will want to prepare her husband's body for burial." Raik raised a brow, hesitating.

"No loving wife should see her husband in such a state of horror. I have tended many a man for burial. Go through Moridac's finest garments and bring clothing for a fitting tribute. Her last sight of him willna be the terrible thing she would see now."

Ranald watched as Raik went over to Catalin and Elyne and whispered to them. Both women sprang forward, and in speedy fashion, they whisked the woman and child off, leading her to the men's barracks, where a corner tower housed the men who had families. Raik turned and bounded up the stairs to the keep, intent on carrying out Ranald's second request.

It took but a short time for the men to carry the body to the solar and to ask Aunt Joneta to assist him. By the time she fell in step with him, he had heard her order adequate warm water, soap kept for esteemed guests and drying cloths.

"Ye prefer no other eyes see the lad?" She nodded as she asked, not expecting an answer.

They entered the solar, and before they uncovered the body, he sent everyone but his father and Aunt Joneta from the room. Once the supplies and Raik returned with the clothing, they bathed the body. Before Ranald and Aunt Joneta set to stitching and closing all gaping wounds, they cleansed all traces of blood away. Never had he worked so hard to make a man presentable for burial.

His sire surprised him by remaining silent. When Ranald repaired the gap in Egan's side, his sire turned on his heels and fled. Ranald glanced up, and seeing Raik nod, knew the wound reminded Broccin of Moridac's injury.

As they were clothing the lad in Moridac's finery, he acknowledged a voice filling the room that had been there from his first touch on the battered body. The voice hesitated for a beat, then resumed. Ranald had unconsciously been singing the prayers for the dead.

They clothed the body in a pale blue shirt, beneath a long, two-toned suede tunic, one side a brilliant blue, the other as light as the sky in spring. A seamstress had decorated the tunic with crosses done in colorful threads in opposite color of blue on either side. Soft stockings covered his feet. Raik had gone to the lad's home and brought his shoes, for they were smaller than most.

Clean black hair crowned the pale, peaceful face. All the wounds were sealed. Ranald's work on his face was so skilful no one would have known Egan had been sightless before death.

"We can do no more," Ranald said as he stood back. "Have them bring in the carrier."

Raik opened the door to allow men to carry in a flat board with three wooden rods protruding from either side. They transferred the body to it, and at Ranald's nod, carefully made their way to the church.

Ranald gazed at Raik, then down at his own clothing. "Am I as unsightly as ye?"

"Hm, now, if that which ye call unsightly was ten times more, then I would say aye. Ye need a good bath, cousin." Raik rolled his eyes. "Come to think on it, ye may need more than one."

Hearing someone approach behind him, Ranald turned.

"Ahem." Finn cleared his throat, fidgeting from one foot to the other, his hands behind his back. "Lady Catalin has already ordered a hot bath for ye." He brought his hands forward and handed Ranald his mask. He had freshly cleaned it. "If ye no longer wish me to be yer squire, I ken it would be no more than right."

"Nay. 'Twas not yer fault I did not remove my helm before

we came to the drawbridge. I canna wear them both." He reached over and took the mask. "Go join the lasses. I noted cook's daughter with a special look in her eye on seeing ye. Be gentle."

Ranald strode from the room and climbed the stairs. Outside his bedchamber, he took a deep breath and stiffened before he thrust the door wide.

"Would you like me to stand betwixt ye and my brother? He looked to be in a sour mood." Elyne glanced sideways at Catalin as they returned across the bailey after tending the new widow until her family arrived from the village.

"Sour mood? It is not me who needs protecting. If you stand between us, it will be to protect your prideful brother." Catalin kicked a stone for added emphasis.

"Truly? Prideful? In what way?" Elyne laughed at Catalin's scowling face.

"That fool mask he has worn since returning home."

"Ye dinna think he has need of it?"

"Need? It's naught but vanity. All these months I thought he must be frightful beyond thinking." She kicked out again, thinking it was but a small stick in her path. "Ow! Lucifer's ba ..." She hopped up and down. Her words cut off. She near repeated a curse Ranald muttered afore dawn one day when he rammed his bare foot into the edge of his clothing chest.

"Ye were not affrighted? I heard ye gasp when ye saw him."

"Hmpf. The smell of blood was so strong I thought he had sustained an injury."

"Aye. I feared so too."

"I was not truly honest afore," Catalin blurted.

"Oh. So you did find his face, uh, terrible?" Elyne's voice was low, with hints of disappointment.

"Not at first. His scars were not the cause. Seeing blood splattered over his flesh did turn my stomach. What made my heart cringe was the utter ruthlessness of his face. He looked at me with such anger and disgust."

A puff of wind blew over the terraced gardens, wafting the sweet smell of roses and honeysuckle to them. She took a deep breath, hoping to dampen the anger building in her.

"And did you note how he looked from me to Lady Muriele? He's in love with her."

"What? Ye read that from a look?" Elyne's brows shot up.

"Aye. From the look! His face lost that taut, mean way he scowled at me. It softened. He did not turn from her. Oh, no! He let *her* look him full in the face! He never has allowed me to."

Catalin stopped in her tracks. She did not like this strange feeling. If her words came from someone else, she would have accused them of being jealous. It was not possible. She did not love Ranald. Had only followed through with the wedding to save her child. How could she be jealous?

Catalin took another step, then stopped again and shook her head. But if she were not jealous, would she not be gently shoving him in the beauty's direction to satisfy his manly needs?

Wouldn't she? She had her answer. She kicked the ground again.

"Crud!"

Hearing Elyne chuckle, she frowned over at her and decided it was best to keep her tongue clamped behind her teeth, as these Scots were fond of saying. She squared her shoulders and thrust out her chin. She beckoned the first servant she spied.

"Have heated water and the big bathing tub brought to Lord Ranald's bedchamber."

"Aye, mistress." The servant bobbed and started off.

"Um, wait." Catalin touched the woman's shoulder, and she stopped and turned. "Best they bring extra water. It's likely he will have need of it."

She sighed and watched the woman turn and take several steps to do her bidding. Mayhap he had not eaten? She followed the servant and grabbed her shoulder again.

"Yes, me lady?"

"Food. Tell cook to prepare a platter of the capons we had at the noon meal, some fresh bread, cheese and wine." She tilted her head and thought of what else had been on the table. "Fruit. Apples and pears."

Why did the woman not hurry to carry out her requests? Catalin looked at her and raised her brows.

"I thought mayhap ye were nae done with yer lists, me lady."

"That will be all, thank you." Catalin felt heat rise to flush her face.

"Um, ye are really angry at him, aren't ye?" Elyne dared to grin. "Do ye plan to push his head beneath the water and drown him? Nay? Mayhap ye will kill him with mouthfuls of food, then?"

Catalin sniffed. "He had an odor. I hate the smell of blood, and I could smell it above horse sweat, leather and metal."

"Oh, aye. He must be clean when ye feed him to death, right? A fitting end for a man who looked mean." Elyne's laughter floated out behind her when she strolled over to Joneta, who had beckoned her.

Catalin hurried off to their bedchamber, for she wanted to be there to see they placed the tub near a brazier of coals. Though the weather had been warm of late, inside the keep was always as cold as a winter's day outside.

She waited by the window opening and spied the men carrying Egan's body to the church. She had the servants place the tub where she wanted it, and made sure they had brought an ample supply of hot water.

Maids brought the food she had ordered. She arrayed it on the table, appreciating the delicious aroma wafting from the warmed capons and the hot bread.

Ranald's savage mood would ease once he had a hot bath, warm food and wine, wouldn't it?

Heavy footsteps approached the door. Hesitated. Mayhap it was not Ranald?

The door jerked open. Aye, it was Ranald. And from the looks of him, he was still in a fury over her supposed horror. He spied her standing there and jerked up his hand to stab a finger at her.

"Get out!"

CHAPTER 24

"**N**AY!"

Catalin steeled herself to defy him. His angry words felt like a solid presence, for their force pushed at her shoulders much like his hands buffeted her there.

"Ye dare defy me?" Ranald's eyes narrowed, his nostrils thinned, as he took a threatening step toward her.

Catalin swallowed and set her feet firmly, for the closer he came, the more she felt his force.

"I do not defy. My duty as your wife is to be here. Your bath is waiting, and I doubt you had aught to eat or drink this past day."

"Ah. A bath." Ranald stalked another step closer. "Why do ye flinch? Do ye fear me, or is it the odor of blood that is not to yer liking?"

"Nay, I do not." Catalin swallowed and gazed down at her feet, unable to look him in the eyes when she lied.

"Nay? Nay to which? Fear me or the odor of blood?"

Her head jerked up at the sound of his voice, so quiet, near a purr and far more menacing than any shout. Had he been a wild animal stalking her, he could not have looked more menacing. Oh, aye, she feared him. The name Black Raptor well suited him. If his black clad arm rose to smite her alongside the head, it would be like an eagle's capture of a field mouse in his talons.

"Well? Do ye not have an answer?" Ranald's eyes shot heated sparks, his lips jerked as he stalked ever closer.

Catalin's heart tripped. Aye, she feared. She feared so much she could not move. His eyes pinned her, waiting for his answer.

Ever she had heard not to let a wild animal scent your terror. But how could one not? His nostrils flared. He knew, as surely as a beast would know.

"It is the blood," she near shouted.

Ah, it was better the odor she hated than that she feared he would hurt her.

Ranald stopped in his tracks. His eyes narrowed. He turned his face slightly to the right, the better to see her more clearly with his left eye without the mask narrowing his vision.

Catalin's face blanched, and had the blood that left it been freed of the veins holding it, it would have drenched her yellow tunic. There was one way to find out what she feared most, him or his bloodied garments.

He braced his legs apart, grabbed the hem of his tunic and whisked it over his head. His eyes bored into the fabric as it sailed across the space between them and thudded against her chest. Without hesitation, she caught it.

Nay, she didna fear blood. He watched her eyes widen with horror when she noted his bloodstained chest. Her gaze searched. Did she seek wounds? When she found none, she clasped a hand to her lips, no doubt to keep from screeching.

"Aye. Ye fear me. Would ye hear from my lips what horror I have done this past eve?" His voice was near a whisper.

He watched Catalin struggle to swallow. He held her eyes with his gaze, not allowing her to look away. If she found him so loathsome when looking upon his face below in the courtyard, then she had best know all of him.

"Ye dinna answer again, so I take it as an aye." He moved his hand in a slow, circular motion over his body. "So much blood, I dinna ken where one man's started and another's ended." His breath hitched, remembering. "Young Egan didna bleed much, for Rupert's attentions had near drained the lad's body."

Catalin's hands fisted tightly around the foul tunic.

"Now, Rupert. Hm, he is another matter." He tilted his

head again. "The streaks near my shoulders? 'Tis his. I thought mayhap he was envious of my father's work, the way he stared at me. I obliged him."

Catalin moved back one small step. He advanced the same measured step forward.

"Dinna worry. He will heal nicely and should not scar overmuch. I was most careful that no dirt fouled his wounds."

Why would she not leave? He wanted to scream at her to leave before he spilled his mind of all the things he had done.

"I wanted Rupert to carry the same wounds he had carved into the young man's flesh, but we couldna chance such a lengthy visit. Too, I needed to keep him alive, always to remember my tender ministrations."

She gulped again, no doubt hoping he had said all he would reveal.

"Would ye like to know the last carving that sent blood dripping to my elbows ...?

He did not need another word. Catalin spun and near flew to the door; her hand clutched the latch. He sprang forward and was behind her when she tried to jerk it open. He slapped his hand over hers on the latch, held it closed. He pressed himself against her back and nuzzled his lips at her ear

"Aye. Ye fear me," he whispered. "I knew it was so when ye caught the tunic." He squeezed his eyes shut, sighed and opened them again. "Ah, Catalin. Rupert is Lucifer himself. Had I been a comely man, a man still with Moridac's face, ye would not have flinched on hearing what justice I meted out."

He stepped back from her, moved her aside and took the tunic from her slack hand. With a mighty heave, he slung the door open.

"Go!"

Catalin wanted to run, but she did not. Not until the door slammed behind her. Elyne's bedchamber was only two rooms away. Without asking leave, she burst into the room most likely looking like a brainsick woman from the surprise on Elyne's face.

"Saints! Catalin, ye near startled me out the window." Elyne's hand was at her throat.

"Elyne," Catalin halted and held her hand over her trembling lips hoping to still them.

"What is it? Ye look like ye have seen a ghost."

"Nay, not a simple ghost. Mayhap the specter of a man bent on living up to his ruined face. Though, from the agony in his eyes, he is fighting it."

Catalin held on to that flicker in the deep blackness of Ranald's eyes. The look of torment.

"I canna believe Ranald would ever do anything near as vile as Father's cruelty." Elyne shook her head, frowning.

"You have been amongst everyone below. Are they not whispering of the terrible things they claim he has done?"

"Terrible? Aye, mayhap if done by a man like Rupert who takes joy in them. Nay, all are bragging that *their* Black Raptor is a cunning master. They say that when word of his vengeance spreads, never will another man dare to anger him."

"He spoke to me of the horrors he has done, of the blood spilled by his hands."

Catalin's flesh tingled, still feeling his soft breath on her ear when he accused her of flinching from him in fear.

"Ranald heard the gasp I uttered when I saw his face beneath the helm. Elyne, my horror was from knowing what terrible hate had caused his father to ruin him so."

"Aye, I knew. But he didn't see the look of scorn ye aimed at Father."

Catalin frowned, trying to put her feelings in words. "Ranald and Moridac were so comely that had they not been male, all would deem them beautiful."

Elyne laughed and nodded. "More than once, a lad teased me saying I was the spotted hen and the twins were peacocks. Especially Moridac with his love of bright colors!"

The sharp noise of a door slamming and the striking of booted feet in the hallway startled them. Catalin knew. Ranald was leaving. Had he time to bathe and eat? Mayhap one, but not the other. She opened the door and stepped out of the room in time to see his black cape billow behind him as he plunged into the stairway's darkness.

Inside their chamber, both window shutters stood wide. A crisp breeze fought the foul odors lingering in the room as smoke made its way out into the night.

"What burns here?" Elyne stared at the brazier standing close to the window. "Ah. His tunic. Weighted down with hot coals."

"'Tis likely he would never want to wear it again." Catalin knew that had he not destroyed it but asked to have it washed, afterward she would have packed it deep at the bottom of his clothing chest in hopes it would forever stay unworn.

"He didn't eat." She frowned at the table. Not a bite was gone, nor had a drop of wine passed his lips.

Hearing voices below, she almost leapt to peer down into the darkening bailey. Finn was leading Satan to Ranald, who stood speaking with Raik. The wind lifted their words now and again.

"Did he say aught to ye about leaving?" Elyne turned to study Catalin's face.

"Nay." Her nape tingled, instinct warning her. She jerked back from the opening.

Satan stomped and snorted, the way he did when Ranald mounted. She waited until she heard the sharp clop, clop, clop of Satan's hooves on the cobblestones before she dared look again. Ranald's cape flew behind him as he disappeared through the barbican.

When Satan burst out on the other side onto the draw-bridge, Ranald's cape billowed wide on either side. For truth, it appeared like the wings of a giant black bird that sat on the steed's back.

Ranald pushed Satan hard, riding into the night. It was fortunate the only dangerous part of the ride was the forested lands west of Raptor. He traveled them before true darkness fell. The rest of the way to Kelso, the land was near clear of hazards.

After dawn, he heard other horsemen and thought it wise to leave the road. He walked Satan over to wait behind the sheltering trees. He listened to the boastful talk of men returning to their cottages after carousing all night in a village east of Castle Douglas. They seemed peaceful enough. Nonetheless, he thought it wise to bide his time until they were far ahead before he mounted Satan and continued.

He ignored the black clouds and steady drizzle that fell all morn. Mayhap he was a coward to run from Raptor. He could have made his confession to Father Martin, but it would not do. The priest was far too timid from years of dealing with the laird. Ranald didn't want to brush off his sins as if they meant naught. If he asked if he was doomed to suffer the agonies of Hell when he died, Abbot Aymer would tell him the truth.

Through the night, his mind had stumbled over all he wished to confess to the abbot. He didn't know which misdeed to speak of first. He had no sooner decided to relay the events in the order they happened, than he spied Kelso Abbey looming against the black sky.

Rain had darkened the walls surrounding the abbey, making it mysterious and forbidding.

To Ranald, it was a beckoning refuge.

"Catalin, ye have been pacing the wall walk near most of the morn. Ye don't even blink yer eyes. Peering at the woods beyond won't make my foolish brother appear." Elyne sighed and patted Catalin's shoulder.

"Drats! He has been gone three days. You are a fine one to tell me not to worry. Whenever I come atop the barbican, you have been here with me all but for a wee bit of time." Catalin made shushing noises and patted her stomach. "The babe is not sleeping much this day."

"Could it be because his mother is standing overlong?" Elyne grinned down at her. "Come, Cook made blueberry scones. She knows how ye like them hot out of the oven so the clotted cream ye pile on them drips over yer chin. She says ye near purr when ye lick yer lips."

"Cook is as fanciful as the lot of you," Catalin grumbled. She caught herself, for she near flicked out her tongue to wet her lips thinking of the hot scones.

Wind flirted with their skirts as they went down the stairs into the bailey, blending Elyne's forest green kirtle with Catalin's sunny yellow. Catalin took a deep breath, savoring the scent of pines sweetening the air. She made a face when the wind fell, for the odor of the stable boys carting horse droppings away was most pungent on warm days.

She ambled for another few steps, stopped and looked aside at Elyne. "Have you noted the size of Ranald's bed?"

"Aye. It's most ample."

They stopped to watch children laughing and chasing a squawking chicken away from the well. Elyne jumped aside when its flapping wings lifted it near as high as their waists as it flew between them. Catalin grinned and flicked off a stray feather stuck on her skirt.

"If I lie across it and stretch my arms above my head, my fingers still do not reach the other side."

"Aye. Ranald must feel swallowed in it. From what he has said, a monk's pallet is meager."

"He has talked to you of Kelso?" Other than the herb garden, not once had he mentioned his surroundings at Kelso to her.

"Aye. He said his bed was a wood frame with slats, covered with a straw-stuffed pallet. The room had a small table and stool, and a peg or two on the wall to hold a cloak and mayhap a wide-brimmed hat to shield their tonsures during summer."

"Hm. Did you note Ranald's head?" Catalin sidestepped to avoid treading on the tail of a scrawny dog sunning himself.

"Aye, of course. How could I not. His shaved pate was there for all to see." Elyne grinned at her.

"I meant the color of it. It was a glowing brown like his face. I do not think he bothered much with a hat." Catalin frowned, and looked daggers at the ground as she walked. "All those years, he saw no need to wear a mask."

"How did ye know?" Elyne's eyes helped ask the question.

"Ada learned it from the tanner. He and the armorer made the mask. They said both sides of his face were golden brown. She told Aunt Joneta, who then told Hannah, who in turn told me."

"That does not seem strange to me. A man would not feel the need to hide from other men." Elyne shrugged.

"He does not hide from Lady Muriele. He met her eyes after giving me a look of scorn. He let her gaze at his face without even so much as a flinch." Catalin clamped her lips together and swallowed a curse.

"Hm. Mayhap he feels naught for her and does not care how she sees him."

Catalin reached for the handle on the massive door of the keep, only to have a man's arm snake around her to pull it wide. She glanced over her shoulder to see who it was.

"Thank you, Sir Kerr." Catalin nodded at him as she passed through. Kerr continued on, heading for the stairwell leading below to the storage rooms.

"There you be, lovey." Hannah bustled over in the great hall and peered down at her face. "You look pinched. Too much standing in the wind and not enough food in your belly, that's what it is. Sit yourself down and rest while I fetch those scones you favor." She turned and was gone, walking as fast and agile as a woman half her age.

Catalin wanted to stretch her arms and yawn, but did not. Sir Giric and several men came in behind them, buffeting and jostling each other to benches alongside the wall. Giric called for a servant to bring them ale, his slurred words sounding as if he had already had several cups too many.

Elyne frowned and led Catalin over to the fireplace, where several chairs occupied the cleared space before it. The men were talking, their voices muted. Catalin's flesh prickled. Every time she glanced up, Sir Giric smiled at her. Was it her fault? On his first smile, she had hesitatingly returned it. Did he believe she was seeking his attention? She lowered her head and kept it there until Hannah returned with a tray of hot blueberry scones, clotted cream and cold milk.

Catalin rose, pretending it was only to save Hannah having to serve her, and went to the round table between them for her repast.

"Here you go, lovey. You feed that wee one now else he will give your belly a proper kick." Hannah brushed her hands together, ridding them of crumbs before hustling from the room.

Catalin took her scones and milk and chose another chair, its back to the men. She was glad when the men lowered their voices to a whisper.

"Do you think a babe can taste what a mother eats?" Catalin eyed her fingers dripping with blueberry-stained clotted cream and licked them. She tilted her head at Elyne and waited for her answer.

"I dinna know. Does he wiggle with pleasure like ye do when ye eat something ye like above all else?"

Catalin's brows rose. "I do not wiggle."

"Aye. Ye do. And ye licked yer fingers just moments ago, too. Like a contented barn cat after feasting on a plump mouse."

"Did not." Catalin sat motionless, concentrating to feel the bairn's movements. Elyne's gasp drew her attention at the same time a man's words seeped in.

"Giric, did ye ever hear of a monk cutting the ballocks off a man? Then holding the bloody balls afore the man's eyes?" The man's voice sounded deliberately loud and clear. "I heard Rupert near choked on his tongue, trying to scream. It's a shame I wasna there."

"Aye," Giric answered. "He did what Rupert has done to many another. Ha! It was most fitting."

"Our Chief's son earned being dubbed the Black Raptor. Not a man in fifty leagues will dare anger him." The bearded warrior rubbed his hands together. "I'm right glad to follow him."

Catalin swallowed and near choked. She held her breath, staring at Elyne. Did the man say what she thought she heard?

She shook her head. Ranald could not do such a thing. Could he? Even these rough men, whose deeds she never wanted to hear about, seemed in awe of Ranald.

Mayhap they were wrong. Should she confront them and demand to know where they had heard such?

"Come." Elyne held out her hand, urging Catalin to rise. She glared over at the boisterous warriors. "Ye men should nae be talking of such where a lass can hear."

Sir Giric rose and came to stand beside Catalin. He offered his wrist to her. "Come, my lady. I would escort ye from the sounds of such crudeness."

Catalin placed her hand on his sleeve, the warmth of his flesh beneath soothing to her cold fingers.

"Thank you, Sir Giric."

Catalin hurried her footsteps, wishing she could cleanse her mind of all she had heard. At the door, she nodded her thanks and dropped her hand from his arm. As she and Elyne passed an arrow slit on their way up the stairwell, chills chased down her back. Was it from the stiff breeze passing through, or was it learning of Ranald's cruelty?

Reaching her bedchamber, she hurried Elyne through the door, and for the first time in her life here at Raptor, shut the door with such force it made a hearty slam.

"I do not know which man is the most fearful, your father or your brother. For certes, I cannot trust either one. I must persuade Ranald to send me to Letia's afore Hunter Castle's siege."

"What if he says nay? Ye must have a plan in case he denies it." Elyne paced around the room, shaking her head. "I canna ken Ranald being so brutal, though truth be told, were I a man I would not think it harsh. Rupert's cruelty is well known."

"Sir Giric seems most courtly. Do you think I could trust him to escort me to Letia's should Ranald refuse? I cannot stay here with the laird."

"Hmpf. I dinna trust Father either. He tore Ranald from the abbey solely to be a husband to ye. He required his seed for an heir." She sighed and shook her head. "I think if the babe is a girl, Father wouldna keep Ranald from doing as he promised.

He would still need him to, umm, plant another seed. Hopefully a male child the next time."

"It's disgusting. I am naught to them but a breeding mare hopefully carrying a lusty stallion." Catalin climbed the two steps to the side of the bed and plopped back on it, her arms outstretched, hitting the bedding in anger. "Be most careful of any man's attentions, Elyne. And if he declares his undying love and prevails with his words that it is right and proper to lie with you before the vows, kick his randy arse from the …"

Oh, Saints! Had Elyne noted she spoke of Moridac? Hearing Elyne clear her throat, she had.

"Mayhap ye should drop a hint to Sir Giric and see if he would chance helping ye? It may not be possible to ask his aid once the siege plans are set in motion." Elyne sat on the edge of the bed.

It was two stressful days later afore Catalin chanced to be close enough to Sir Giric that she did not look to be seeking him out.

Fortunately, the weather cleared soon after Ranald left the abbey and turned Satan's Spawn toward Raptor Castle.

He thought long and hard over Abbot Aymer's advice as he rode for home. The abbot had been hesitant at first, but then confided to Ranald that once he too had been married to a beautiful woman.

One lone night, he and his men had ridden out to drive raiders from burning a close-by village. It had been naught but a lure for his enemy to steal into his keep and abduct his wife. He would gladly have paid any ransom to have her back, but it was not to be. His sweet love had fled from her abductor and tumbled down the stone stairway, breaking her neck.

On learning of it, he had gone on an orgy of killing for which he spent the rest of his life doing penance.

No doubt, the abbot meant Ranald to take a different lesson from his story, but Ranald decided a cautious man kept his wife where he could see her. He did not trust his father, and truth be told, he knew it was best he not allow himself to love Catalin.

His brow furrowed, his eyes squinted, thinking on it. It was with some surprise when he noted the frightened looks of an old man and his son pushing a small barrow of peat. They scurried so close to the slope bordering the road they near tumbled into the muddy ground alongside. Not until the lad's whisper of "Raptor" floated to him did he ken why. Hmpf. He must be growing a thicker hide, for it didn't bother him.

Later that day when he arrived at the keep, he had reason to think himself wrong. He was still batting the dust from his tunic as he entered the great hall and found his wife so close to a man she looked about to embrace him.

CHAPTER 25

"SIR GIRIC, YOU WILL be richly rewarded for your help." Uneasy, Catalin stepped back a pace. She did not care for the triumphant gleam in his regard on hearing her proposal.

He quickly shuttered his eyes and advanced a step, so close now his leg brushed against her skirts. She edged away again.

"I dinna seek rewards for helping a beauteous lady."

His hand stole around to her nape and stroked slowly down her back. She near jumped out of her kirtle.

He grunted after her elbow rammed his ribs. She glared at him, before again moving to put distance between them.

"Keep your hands to yourself, sir," she hissed through her teeth. Her fingers flexed, wishing to strike out at him. "I do not seek a man for any purpose other than safe escort to King Stephen's court. It is best you understand that."

Giric, his hands held high, waved them back and forth before clasping them behind his back. "Forgive me, Lady. I meant no disrespect."

Huh. His eyes told her different. They edged from her face to her breasts thrusting against her kirtle. What ailed the man to look on an increasing woman with such interest? She frowned, realizing the boisterous room had quieted.

She stretched her neck to peer around his formidable body. Her gaze collided with Ranald's scowl. Framed in the doorway, her husband appeared larger than life with his head held high, his squinted eyes and firm jaw leaving no doubt of his displeasure at seeing her talking with another man. Drat him. His mind leapt to conclude she had sought Sir Giric's company.

Well, saints, it was true. But not for the purpose of, of, um …
certainly not for the purpose Ranald thought.

She stared down at her shifting feet. Ack! What was she
doing? Looking guilty, that's what. She flung her head up and
squared her shoulders. She had naught to feel guilt about.
Protecting her unborn babe from two foolish men determined
to take it from her justified her intent to flee her husband.

She pasted a wifely smile on her face. Mayhap Ranald would
agree to see her to Letia's for safety, whilst he proceeded with
the siege of Hunter Castle. She would far prefer it.

She watched him walk, nay, not walk, it was more like
stalking with the fierce expression on his determined face,
toward her. People parted before him, giving him a clear path.
How could so large a man move with such grace? His broad
shoulders filled his long-sleeved, black tunic. No cloth could
hide the powerful muscles beneath it.

His clothing did conceal much, though. 'Twas like his face,
one side so comely she fought the urge to stroke her fingertips
over it, while the other side was dangerous, hidden. His body
was the same. Her mouth went dry thinking of his beautiful,
muscled chest dusted with crisp, black hair narrowing over the
hard slab of his belly. In the dark shadows of their room, she
had trailed her hands down the bunching muscles of his back,
over all the crisscrossed scars there. Her fingers had traveled
down to grasp his buttocks, loving the restrained power as they
flexed and relaxed with his thrusts.

Oh, saints. Heat filled her. The plump juncture of her thighs
throbbed and dampened. She shifted her feet again, near crossing her legs. Mayhap he would only think she'd had too much
to drink and needed relief.

Ranald stood in front of her, his scowl every bit as mean as
before, but his head tilted in question. Well, Hell. Had he known
what she and Sir Giric had been talking about? For truth, his
hearing could not be as keen as the raptor people called him.

"You are well, husband?" Catalin's voice squeaked when his
strong fingers grasped her elbow. They softened as he hauled
her from Giric's side up against his own.

"I am well. And ye, wife? The bairn thrives?"

Did he suffer an infection? His body heat was feverish. He had left the keep after sending her from the room when he bathed. Mayhap he had sustained an injury not yet healed. She tilted her head back to study his face.

His stony gaze bored into Sir Giric's eyes. Saints! If a look could be felt, the young knight would have bruises around his eyes every bit as dark as from a fisted hand. Why, Ranald's high body heat was anger. If she did not know better, she would venture to think he was jealous.

"Ranald, where have ye been?" Elyne came close to buffet her brother on the shoulder, turning his attention from Sir Giric.

Catalin watched the knight slip away, making haste to leave the room. More fool he, if he thought Ranald did not note. He did. His nostrils flared and his narrowed gaze followed the man until he disappeared from sight.

"Away." Ranald looked at Elyne, his voice thoughtful.

"Aye. We knew that since ye were not here. Ye have become a man of few words." Elyne grinned up at him.

"Ye asked. I answered. What more needs be said?" Ranald's left brow arched.

"Well, now, ye could say ye were hunting, or that ye were riding Satan's Spawn and fairies lured ye to their fern castle and had their way with ye. Or ye can tell us where ye truly went." Elyne pinched his arm. She laughed in surprise when she could not grasp his firm flesh.

"Kelso." He nodded at Raik, who came up in back of Elyne. "All was well with Egan's burial?"

"Aye," Raik answered.

Elyne rolled her eyes at Catalin. "One word answers must be a sickness caught by men. Father Martin's mass was most soothing, Ranald. All seeing Egan laid out for viewing said he looked to be asleep. His widow was much comforted for she had feared to look upon him until Catalin assured her he looked most peaceful.

"Did that not mean, aye, all went well with Egan's burial?" Ranald peered down at Elyne. A slight twitch showed at the corners of his mouth.

"True." Elyne nodded, her face serious.

"Come?" Catalin shrugged from Ranald's side and held her hand out to Elyne.

"Surely." Elyne stuck her tongue out at Ranald as she and Catalin made their way over to sit with Joneta and Hannah.

"All weapons have been gathered and counted?" Ranald asked as he nodded toward the solar door and started towards it.

"Aye. The armorer and his helpers have been busy from sun up to sun down. The squires have worked like busy ants to check hauberks, shields, chain mail and helmets. The men have seen all swords, axes, picks, daggers, maces, hammers and other weapons sharpened. The blacksmith's hammers ring out well into the night."

"The men using crossbows and longbows? Have the archers been practicing? I want no arrows wasted by landing short of their man." Ranald frowned, thinking of the distance needed to reach men atop the battlements. The defenders had the advantage of added height.

Sir Domnall answered as Ranald strolled into the solar. "Aye. We've crossbow bolts aplenty. Cormac has the archers going over every inch of their bows for cracks, splinters or chips on the notches. They gathered arrows together in bundles of twenty and five. Dinna be surprised if chickens, geese, and anything else with a feather, squawk and scurry away on sight of the fletcher."

Ranald near smiled at the picture.

Chief Broccin hitched up his belt around his still-trim middle, straddled a stool and reached for an apple amongst the fruit piled at the center of the table. "Angus has seen that all horses have adequate shoes. Ye best check that beast of yer own."

"Lady Joneta and I are going through the storage rooms with Cook," Brodie, the man who took charge of the food when they were away from the keep, said. "We will have ample supplies. The harvest is plentiful this year and the vegetable gardens are flourishing. We should be able to replenish supplies as we need them."

"That leaves battering rams and trebuchets." Raik frowned. Pulling the unwieldy siege engines was the most difficult part of any battle preparation. He paced the solar like a hound impatient for the hunter to set him free.

"Aye. The oxen are fat and healthy. It's about time they earned their food." Broccin grunted and took a large, crackling bite of the apple. Juice ran down his chin, and he scrubbed it away with the back of his hand. As he chewed, his calculating gaze studied Ranald like he tried to search his mind.

"What?" Ranald was tired of people's gazes on him. He would welcome the dark of his bedchamber.

"Yer wife?" The laird took another bite, talking as he chewed. "Have ye questioned the little spitfire about Hunter Castle's layout? She has only to see me and she darts around a corner, her red hair and bright clothing looking like one of those barn cats with all shades of color on their backs. She takes off like she's running before the hounds." He wiped his chin on his sleeve.

"And ye wonder why?" Ranald could not believe the innocent look his father returned in reply.

No doubt, Catalin feared his sire would prove the bairn a bastard. He would not allow his father to make him a fool by having one and all know his wife presented him with his brother's get.

They sat there in the solar going over all the battle preparations. Darkness had long since fallen by the time they assured themselves that all men and equipment, and what they needed to sustain them, was accounted for.

Ranald stretched, relieving his stiff muscles. He thought with longing about the luxury of a hot bath. He shook his head. Last year at this same time, he wouldn't *have* thought twice about bathing with cold water.

He must be getting soft.

Catalin eyed the buckets setting close to the fireplace. She'd had the servants build a small fire, for she knew Ranald did not like a warm room. Whilst he had been away, she had enjoyed the lit fireplace, for the sheets were too cold for her to sleep comfortably without his big body to heat them.

She twisted her fingers together. While he besieged her castle, what if he refused to allow her to leave Raptor? She'd almost made herself dizzy darting around corners avoiding his father. In the great hall, she hated the laird's calculating stare at her swelling breasts. Could a person judge when a babe would be born by the growth of a woman's breasts? Ada said he was forever asking questions about her.

Saints! How had Ranald entered the room without her hearing his footsteps? He looked as surprised as she.

"Catalin, I thought ye would be asleep and snoring by now." Ranald looked hesitant, his hands resting on the belt holding his scabbard. He glanced around, his eyes widening when he spied the tub and steaming buckets of water.

Was that a look of pleasure? Had she for once done something to please him?

"I thought it likely you would be tired from your travels. Too, you spent a deal of time with your father planning the siege." For truth, any time spent with Chief Broccin would tire the strongest of men.

Could he hear her heart pounding when she moved close to him? Hopefully not. Why did his mere presence make her blood race, her nose flare to catch the familiar scent of juniper and spice mingled with leather?

She waited as he carefully placed his sword beside the bed and draped his belt on a chair back. "Let me." Catalin held up her hands when he grasped the hem of his tunic and started to pull it off. He hesitated before he let her grasp the black linen. He bent forward, his arms outstretched, for her to pull it over his head.

The neck opening was ample enough it did not interfere

with his mask. What would he do if she snatched it from his face and threw it into the fire? Her fingers itched to do so. Let them itch. She was no fool. She did not want to unleash that anger she had seen when his father provoked him. Would Ranald ever trust her enough to let her gaze upon his face?

"Do ye read minds, wife?"

"Read minds?" Catalin looked over her shoulder at him as she hung his tunic on a wall peg.

"Aye. Ye looked like ye try to see into my skull."

"That would be an interesting gift to have. Elyne mentioned once that she thought mayhap Raik could."

"Hm. More likely he studies people and knows what they will do."

She shivered watching Ranald remove the rest of his clothing while they talked. He was as nakit as any man could get. In this light, he reminded her of a sleek animal, his hair falling beside his face and down to his shoulders. Black hair furred his chest and narrowed down the lean slab of his belly, where his slender hips framed loins nested in a bed of thick, black hair. With wolfish grace and the soundless padding of his feet, he moved to fetch the hot water. Firm buttocks above massive legs drew her gaze. She swallowed again.

The fire's glow molded his form in light; darkness hid his scarred back.

She startled, for he hesitated, his hands holding a bucket over the tub, his eyes studying her face. Questioning her. She tried to hold his gaze, tried to pretend she was unaffected by his body. Could he see her flushed face?

"Would ye wash my back, wife?" Ranald dumped the hot water in the tub and walked to fetch another bucket.

For answer, she walked over to wait beside the stool where she had placed the soap. It's aroma of Scot's pine and spices reminded her of his scent. As he stepped into the tub, she tried not to stare. Heaven help her, she was no saint! Her breath caught in her throat when he lifted his left leg and put his foot into the tub. It was only natural that his sex was even more obvious. After all, it hung there betwixt his legs with the soft glow from the embers behind him.

How could she plan to flee from him at the first chance she found, yet all she could think about was how she wanted him? Mayhap she was sex-crazed. Ha! That had to be it.

"Ahem."

She near jumped across the tub. Ranald's hand holding a wet cloth flashed up, spraying water over the side, reminding her why he was in the water and she was kneeling beside the tub.

"Lean back." She gathered his black hair to the sides and guided his head to avoid the rim of the wooden tub. She hesitated.

"Uh, Ranald?" She peered down to see he had shut his eyes. "Aye?"

She tapped his forehead on the right, where leather covered it. His eyes flew open and stared into hers.

"Move to my left." He waited until she went to stand between the tub and the fireplace.

Looking down, she saw his shoulders were in shadows. Still, a brace of candles stood but a few paces away, between the table and the bed. He stared at them. Why was he so still?

"What are you thinking?" Was he deciding he did not want her help with his bath?

"A soft breeze." Not a muscle twitched.

He stared, looking fascinated, at the candles. Why had she not noticed their flames stirring? Had she left a shutter unlatched? She started to rise to go over to it. Without taking his eyes from the candles, his wet hand reached out to clasp her wrist. The flames leaned, almost level, and then there were no flames at all. The room was near dark

He reached up, slid off his mask and placed it on the stool beside the bowl of soap. With a sigh of pleasure, he propped his feet on the foot of the tub. Sliding forward, he leaned back and dunked his head beneath the water then lifted it. He reached for another cloth and wiped his eyes. Huh. It was just to fool her, though. She noted he did not put it down but clutched it in his right fist.

She enjoyed lathering his hair and running her fingers

through the thick, healthy strands. She scrubbed then massaged his taut scalp, savoring the feel of his strong skull beneath her fingertips.

"You were at Kelso?" She near whispered the question, her fingers still.

"Aye."

Ranald pressed his head into her hands like a small dog would nudge her palm. He was so many men piled into one. The teasing lad who had chased her around the bailey with an ugly toad. The gentle monk in the garden. The grim husband learning she had deceived him. The man filled with such fury that Chief Broccin stepped back. The shadowy image of that man who could maim and disfigure an enemy then turn and prepare a savaged man for burial, making him look like he slept peacefully.

Ranald's many contrasts made her head spin.

"Your friend, the abbot. He is well?"

"As well as any man his age can be."

At her urging, he leaned back again and waited until she swished his hair in the water, then used a wooden cup to complete the rinsing. He reached up and swiped the water from his hair, then soaped his face and rinsed it.

"I have noted warriors come and go, but hesitated to ask Chief Broccin about them."

She soaped the cloth and washed his shoulders and back, kneading the muscles as she worked. Unconsciously, she eased her touch over each scar as she encountered them. Why, there were too many to count, for they crossed over each other.

"The men you noted were watching Hunter Castle and the surrounding countryside." He rolled his shoulders, relaxing.

"Have you heard anything about Uncle Hamon? Is there a chance he will flee the castle when he sees your army?" Catalin hoped that somehow no one would be injured because of the hateful man.

"Nay. Greed makes a man hang onto what he covets till his fingers are pried from it."

She patted his shoulder. He reached to take the cloth, ready to finish bathing on his own, but she held on to it and shook her head. He relaxed and rested back against the tub's rim. Without looking above his chin, she washed his neck and arms.

"Catalin, are ye familiar with the whole of Hunter Castle? Not just the keep?"

She loved the dark, smooth sound of his voice. He looked quickly upward when she didn't answer, and sighed. His breath ruffled an unruly lock falling onto her forehead.

"The whole? Hm. The baileys and land within the walls?" Her soapy hands ventured around his collarbone and smoothed down over his furred chest, her fingers combed through the hair, exploring his flesh. Every now and again, his hot skin quivered so lightly she wondered if she imagined it.

"Aye." His voice was little above a murmur.

"Hunter is a formidable castle. My great-great-grandfather built it on flat ground near woodlands where wild pigs, deer and grouse are abundant. The hunters will find plentiful game to supplement your supplies." She stopped and grinned. "When Uncle Hamon learns you hunt what he considers his, he will screech loud as a cat with its tail beneath your boot till he has no voice at all."

With a soft giggle, she resumed her task of cleaning his body with her soapy hands. Would now be a good time to petition him about staying with Letia? How should she start? She could not say she wished to flee from him, so please be so kind as to take her to Letia's where she would beg for an escort to King Stephen.

He was very quiet. In the dim light, she noted his left eye squeezed shut. His jaw was rock hard, too. Saints! Was he in pain? She relaxed her labors. Not until then did she realize where she scrubbed. She gave a startled squeak and jerked her hands back.

Ranald had noticed sooner. It was his groin she attacked with such vigor, his erect manhood that bobbed against her hands.

She dared to breathe again when he cleared his throat. His voice was husky and dark, but he made no mention of her activity.

"Are there any weak spots in the curtain wall's defenses? Mayhap crumbling stone that needs tending, or an area guarded with only a handful of men?"

"Nay ... not that comes to mind."

Catalin moved to the end of the tub, thinking about it while she soaped a foot propped against the wood. She had never noticed what strong feet he had or what handsome toes. Straight and narrow, without a crooked one on either foot. Seeing that slight distance between each toe reminded her of something that caused her to caress them fondly. Her brows drew together, trying to recollect what it was.

"Elyne and I talked about what would be best for us while you are busy ousting Uncle Hamon."

"Oh? What might that be?"

She saw his left brow arch, but he did not open his eyes.

"Ranald, I fear your father. Should the bairn come before you defeat my uncle, Chief Broccin could wrest the babe from me and even throw me outside the castle grounds."

Her back quivered with the thought of him snatching the babe from her arms and telling her she had fulfilled her usefulness to him.

"And? What scheme did ye and Elyne dream up?"

She had his attention. She saw the faint gleam of his eyes.

"You should take me to Letia and Warin's for safety. It is about fifteen leagues south of Hunter Castle. If you could not take me there, mayhap once we get near Hunter, one of your men would be good enough to escort me the rest of the way." She surprised herself saying such a jumble of words all in one breath.

"Nay." He ended it with a healthy snort.

"Nay? But you have not even thought about it. I think it an excellent plan."

Catalin stopped playing with his feet long enough to dart a look at him. He stared her in the eye. She about decided he was not going to answer when he finally sighed.

"I have thought about it at some length. Abbot Aymer suggested I bring ye to Kelso. He could house ye with the women for protection."

"Kelso? What if no women are there at the time? Do they not stop but overnight in their travels?" Saints! She had never seen inside an abbey, but she pictured their cold, barren cells with hard pallets and scant furnishing.

"Aye. I mentioned the chance to the abbot. The nearest convent is the Sisters of Mary Magdalen southeast of Kelso. It lies slightly north between Douglas Castle and de Burgh's Seton."

"Mayhap you should take me there instead? I would fare better amongst women at a convent." If she was at the good sisters, she could make her way on her own to Seton.

"Nay. Baron Rupert's lands are close-by. I have decided on another plan." Ranald dropped his head back against the rim and closed his eyes.

She squeezed water from the bathing cloth to keep from pinching him. In the years their parents met to work out the terms for her betrothal to Moridac, Ranald used to torment her with this sort of dominant behavior. It was his way of letting her know he considered a woman's opinion less wise than the twisted rambling of a man long in his cups.

What if he took her where Sir Giric could not help her? Waiting for him to speak stoked her anger. She counted each heartbeat thudding in her ears, trying to hold tight to her temper. Her count lasted until five.

"Drats, Ranald! Must I pull every word from your lips? You drain my patience."

"As ye do mine."

Ranald's relaxed stance disappeared when he surged to sit upright. Water flowed from his massive shoulders down his arms and chest.

"Ye will come with me. I have ordered a large tent and commissioned the carpenter to build a bed frame. Ye will have every comfort I can secure."

"I will not spend months in a battle camp with naught but dust, noise and smelly warriors tromping about." Mayhap her voice was commanding enough he would bow to her wishes, for he sighed. She waited for his nod, but his lips set in a determined line.

"Elyne and Lady Muriele will accompany ye, as will Hannah and Ada." He gave her a ye-should-be-grateful look.

Catalin, her mouth agape, dropped the cloth in the water. Was the man dafty? He may as well scream Lady Muriele was his leman, if he thought to take her along with his wife. She took several astonished breaths. Why, the randy blockhead shrugged and swiped water from his arms as he talked, his voice slow and patient, like he was reassuring a silly, timid woman.

" 'Tis not uncommon. Many a Scotsman keeps his wife close for fear of her being abducted whilst he is gone." He leaned back in the tub and sighed. "Even some of yer dainty English kings have taken their wives on campaign."

Huh. More than likely, he feared his father would attack his lovely Lady Muriele whilst he was gone! Her breath came in angry spurts. Her nostrils flared so wide she noted them when she looked down at her soapy cloth.

Ranald wriggled his toes against her hand inviting her to massage them again. She nodded and lifted the cloth.

Splat!

Her aim was accurate.

CHAPTER 26

"JESU!"

Ranald grabbed the cloth and slung it across the room. Blinded by the soapy water, he swiped at his eyes and spat so hard bubbles floated from his lips. She had no time to admire it, for she likened his rising out of the tub to descriptions of how Nessie surfaced in Loch Ness. The violent shake of his head sprayed water so far it sizzled on the hot peat.

"Are ye daft?" His voice crashed against her ears.

"Daft? 'Tis you who have lost your mind."

Catalin glared at him, her hands on her hips. No doubt, he had planned to have Lady Muriele with him all along. She had heard women saying that once they were with child, their spouse shunned their marital duties. They were even pleased when the men spent their lust on willing servants and the many widows at the castle.

Huh! She was not pleased. She had near thumped a pitcher of ale against more than one sighing, curvaceous tart's head after hearing them giggling about lustful bouts with the twins before Ranald left Raptor. Humph! They planned to lure him to their beds. What man could find a woman appealing when her belly looked like a round loaf of bread rising on the baker's table?

Water surged over the rim as he slowly stepped to the end of the tub and lifted one foot to the floor.

"Ever ye were quick to pick a fight. Do ye not recall the last time ye riled my anger on purpose? In case yer memory is faulty, it was the day before yer betrothal."

Oh, blessed saints! The picture of the goose girl and Ranald behind the stable that sunny day flashed to her mind. The girl was on her hands and knees. Ranald, grasping her skirts hiked up around her waist, knelt behind her. As he had pumped away, his bare arse flashed in and out of the building's shadows. His pale flesh gleamed when the sun hit it but faded when in the shadows. Catalin had scooped up a handful of horse droppings. Paying no mind to the stench or disgusting feel of it, she threw it as hard as she could. Her aim was good. His arse no longer gleamed in the sun.

She had admired her handiwork for only a breath then ran for her life. Hearing his thudding footfalls behind her, she could still feel her heart racing. Suddenly, an arm snapped around her waist and jerked her off her feet. He'd carried her like a bag of wheat at his hip. For truth, the water in the horse trough was frosty cold. He dunked her beneath it then tugged her upright. Aye, she remembered his stony face, before he spun on his heels and stalked away.

Water splashing her skirts as his left foot joined the other on the floor, brought her mind back to her present peril. In the darkened room, he looked like a dark predator taking measured steps toward her. She backed away. He followed. He slowly closed the distance. His raspy breathing charged the air between them. She spun and made a mad dash for the door. Just as she grasped the handle, his powerful hands slammed the wood on either side of her shoulders.

"Going somewhere?"

His husky voice caressed her nape like warm wool. She gulped. And lied.

"I thought a cup of hot milk would warm you after your bath."

She banged her forehead on the door. Ugh. How stupid. He was no youngling craving milk.

He swept her up in his arms, cradling her like a child. She grabbed his shoulders as his purposeful tread took them back across the big room. Toward the bed? Nay. To the tub! Her hands slid off his still soapy shoulders when he bent close over the water and ever so gently dropped her.

"Eeep!" Splash!

Unlike before, he did not submerge her head. He stood back, arms folded across his chests, and scowled down at her.

"Dinna think to question my plans to protect ye. Now, get out of that water." He stood back, waiting for her to rise.

She muttered curses and tried to gather her legs beneath her. She needed to get to her knees and use her hands on the tub's sides to stand.

"Blessed St. Michael. Why are ye so gawky?"

Ranald leaned down and grasped under Catalin's arms to haul her out onto the soaked floor. Feeling her shivers, he turned his gaze on the brace of candles behind her and stared, thinking all the while of flame leaping from the wick. His body heated. The water dripping from him dried in a heartbeat. A spark flickered on the wick. He stared all the harder. A candle flamed to life. The others rapidly followed.

Catalin craned her head to look behind her when the room lightened. "When did you light the candles?"

"While ye were paddling in the water."

Catalin's form drew his gaze. The loose-fitting kirtle clung to her like another skin. He stared, entranced by her body's changes. Where before her breasts were soft mounds and her stomach gently rounded, now there could be no hiding the growing bairn. These past weeks, he'd been occupied avoiding her and didn't note the rapid changes.

He grabbed the large drying towel set out for his use and wrapped it around her shoulders. Long, purposeful strides took him to the fireplace, where he added a block of peat to the embers. His back to her, it was not difficult to encourage it to flame with thoughts of heat and fire.

Catalin's eyes rounded and she bit her lip when he turned and advanced on her. Clutching the cloth to her neck, she watched him like she thought he meant to dunk her again.

"Come. Do ye want to take a chill? Get out of yer wet clothes."

"Huh! Do you not remember how I got this way?"

He brushed her hands away, drew the drying cloth from her

and slung it over his shoulder while he whisked her wet clothing over her head. She muttered so low he couldn't hear the words, but he kenned they were of him being a lout of a husband, a churl of the worst sort who would dunk his increasing wife. He rubbed briskly over her back, her arms and legs before gently patting droplets from her breasts. He felt the blush heating her skin while he brushed the cloth over her belly.

He studied her stomach. If the babe stirred, would he see its movements? Never had she been more beautiful. Not even that day when she and Moridac stood before the priest and spoke their betrothal vows.

He had ached then, knowing that had he been first to leave their mother's body, it would be he and not Moridac beside her.

He ached now, knowing that had he been first, it would be his bairn, not Moridac's, nested there.

And had it been his, he would not think on sending it to Kelso — away from himself . . . from Catalin . . . from his father. He would have no need, for the laird would not waste even one breath to claim a bairn from Ranald's loins.

'Twas only Moridac his father had loved. Still loved. He had felt naught but hate for Ranald since his first breath.

Moridac's child was the sole thing on this earth that Broccin wanted. And Ranald had the power to make him suffer for all the pain and loss he had felt from the first time he reached up his arms and asked, "Da?" begging to be picked up and cuddled. Instead, Broccin's booted foot had knocked him to the cold floor, before he stomped away with Moridac in his arms.

Ranald shook. When had he dropped the towel? Gently, he cupped Catalin's breasts and enjoyed their warm weight in his palms. He nuzzled his face against their creamy softness, and it was feeling that silken swell caress his scarred cheek that reminded him his face was bare. His heart near stopped beating. He swept her into his arms and tucked her face beneath his chin as he strode over to lay her on his side of the bed. Turning to the right so all she'd note was his unmarked left profile, he pinched out the candles before pulling the fire screen in front of the fireplace. Satisfied the room was again in shadows, he turned to her.

"I am not moving from this spot, husband. It has just now turned warm."

Naught but Catalin's eyes showed above the blanket she clutched beneath her nose. He padded over to the far side of the bed and crawled between the sheets, stretching his length alongside her. Snaking his right arm beneath her, he pulled her close so his heated flesh would warm her.

He brushed his lips over her cheek before he nibbled gently at her full, lower lip. Stopping to place little kisses at the corners of her mouth, his tongue explored the outline of her lips. His mouth captured hers in hungry, lingering kisses. She sighed, her lips parting to entice him. His tongue slipped between, exploring the silky haven of her mouth. Hesitant at first, her tongue touched his then skittered away, before it returned to stroke and dance with it.

As his lips glided over her cheek, down her lovely neck and further to again nestle between her breasts, he listened to her soft sighs, the uneven pounding of her heart. Her nipples hardened against his cheek, inviting him. Open-mouthed, he slid over her silky flesh and captured one. She gasped and strained to pull his face tighter to her flesh until he gripped the hard nub softly with his lips. While suckling one breast, he rubbed his rough palm over the other, liking the feel of the straining nipple tickling his hand. He lifted his lips to blow soft puffs of air on her glistening flesh, fascinated by her shivers. Capturing the other breast, he lavished it with the same sweet treatment.

Catalin gasped and squirmed. Her hands rubbed feverishly over his arms and shoulders. When his lips started to wander, her fingers gripped his head, holding it tight to her breast. He was happy to oblige her. Rolling, he pulled her atop him. She gulped and braced her arms beside his head, her lovely, glistening breasts hovering over him. He moved freely from one pebbled nipple to the other, suckling and drawing it to fill his mouth.

His hands roved freely over her shoulders, across her shoulder blades, then tickled their way down her delightfully sloped back. When he reached her firm nether cheeks, he traced the crease, tickling up and down its length until she squirmed.

He reached down to grasp her thighs and opened them to straddle him, then coaxed her to her knees. His fingers explored the moist, tender flesh between her legs and stroked until she arched her head. He teased her breasts, letting one go then flicked it with his tongue when she offered it to him again.

"Ranald."

Ah, such pleading in that whispered word. He had not the heart to tease her further. Reaching between them, he guided his straining arousal to ease up into her. New to this position, he needed to grip her waist to show her the rhythm. Awkward at first, she soon set the pace, sometimes stopping entirely. He watched her tense face, her eyes unseeing, concentrating on feeling him buck inside her. His teeth clamped together, subduing his rising passion, until he could no longer stand it. He surged up into her and quickened his pace.

He abandoned himself to the heated pleasure. Wanting her to reach her peak with him, he slipped his hand between them and found where he entered her. He rubbed her flesh where it hugged around him until she whimpered even louder, then slid his thumb over and over her hard, slick nub until she throbbed around him.

She stiffened and gripped him with her legs. Eyes squeezed tight, her body strained as she uttered warbling cries until she lowered her mouth to his shoulder. Opening wide, she clamped her teeth on him and held on, never so hard as to pierce his flesh.

He rode the frenzied wave with her and groaned as he joined her climax. Spent, he wrapped her in his arms and turned to the side, exhausted.

Catalin awoke and peered through strands of red hair near covering her left eye. A thin line of light crept through the window opening, warning her it wasn't long before the full-blown dawn. She shoved the curly hair aside and looked to find Ranald had already left the room.

She rolled over the rumpled bed to where he'd lain. He had been long gone, for the sheets held no warmth. Seeing the imprint of his head on his pillow, she pulled it into her arms and nuzzled her face on the white linen. Inhaling deeply, she closed her eyes to savor his scent.

Memories of their heated discussion of last eve flashed in her mind. Aggravated at herself for being such a willing slave to his lightest touch, she thumped the pillow and scrambled out of bed. Hopefully, Elyne would still be in the great hall breaking her fast.

Catalin dressed with all speed, not waiting for Hannah to appear and help her. Though impatient, she was not such a fool as to go hurtling down the stairwell. Her reduced speed 'fashed' her, as Ranald had said once. She giggled. *Fashed* did sound more satisfying than *bothered*.

Once she reached the safety of the great hall, she hastened to take a seat beside Elyne at the high table.

"Elyne, why can I not talk to your brother without becoming so angry I could spit?" Catalin smiled up at the young servant who placed a steaming bowl of porridge before her.

"Hm. Sounded to me like ye did a whole lot of that *spitting* in yer room last eve." Elyne grinned and waved a wooden spoon at her.

Catalin, busily selecting cherries and arranging them in colorful circles atop her porridge, jerked her head up to look at Elyne and missed her bowl. As plump, red cherries bounced and rolled toward the edge of the table, she jumped up to cup her arms and surrounded them. Surely, her heated face was as red as her hair.

"Do ye think? I thought it sounded more like a cat howling," Raik's deep voice said behind her.

Oh, cruddy worms! She dropped back down onto the seat. How had she missed seeing him close-by? She ignored him and busied herself trying to herd the fruit close so she could add it to her porridge.

"Nay. Ye didna hear her up close. I thought it the sweetest

music, though my ears did ring now and again." Ranald stopped behind her to lean down and nuzzle her neck. On his way back up, his teeth nipped her ear lobe.

Drats. The men must have been in the solar. From the sounds of footsteps and chuckles, it was not just the two of them. She dared peek up to see no less than ten men leaving the great hall. Ranald paused at the doorway and winked, then chuckled as he walked away.

Mayhap she could crawl beneath the table. But to what end, since they were now gone?

"I am sorry, lovey. I didn't know they were near, else I would have held my tongue."

Catalin shrugged, her mind busy searching to remember making any sounds when Ranald's magical fingers had teased her. Hm. Oh, Blessed Saints! She remembered hearing her loud groans. It did not take too much of a stretch to say they were wails. Not being able to silence them, she had bit down on his shoulder. Next time, she would stuff her mouth with the sheet.

"Ye said Ranald made ye angry last eve? Why?"

Catalin's stomach reminded her she had yet to eat. In between spoons of porridge, she whispered to Elyne.

"I told him I was fearful of staying here at Raptor, in case the babe came before Hunter's surrender. I asked him to let me go to Letia's during that time."

"From the look on yer face, he said nay right away?"

She shook her head. "He said he talked to Abbot Aymer about me staying at Kelso, but fearing no women could attend me there, he decided against it. He mentioned a convent, but he discarded that idea because Baron Rupert's lands are too close."

"Then ye are to stay here at Raptor?" Elyne brows rose, not liking the idea.

"He wasn't finished. He said I would go with him. He has had a large tent made and a bed frame. When I protested, he said you, Lady Muriele, Hannah and Ada would also be going."

"What?"

"You heard aright. We are all to accompany him there."

Catalin sighed and searched around in her porridge until

a small red spot peeped up amongst the creamy gruel. She scooped the cherry up and plopped it in her mouth.

"Why is he taking Lady Muriele along?" Elyne frowned.

"Huh. What do *you* think? I fear he has made her his leman."

She fished out another cherry, but it rolled off her spoon and bounced on the table. Grabbing for it, she smashed it in trying.

"Yuck." She took a small piece of linen from her kirtle pocket and wiped her hand. "I will tell Sir Giric that we must plan to leave from the siege camp instead."

"That might work just as well. I will go with ye." Elyne tilted her head, thinking. "The men will be too busy to even think of us during the day. We could leave soon after dawn one morn and be leagues away in a day's ride."

Catalin frowned and looked down at her expanding middle.

"It will be much harder to make good time. If we were going to Seton from here, we could take our time. Once at Letia's and I had de Burgh's escort, I would have no need to travel fast. Ranald would not know what was amiss."

"Oh! I was so distracted teasing ye, I near forgot about how I came to hear yer, uh, um, ye know." Elyne grinned, looking most satisfied.

"What happened? Do not tell me you listened at the door."

"Nay. I was sleep walking, until yer wailing woke me."

"Elyne!"

Elyne snickered. "I was dreaming a handsome knight was taking us to King Stephen, but someone chased us. The knight took us to this secluded place. Stone walls surrounded a building filled with women. Thirty knights led by a man with a dreadfully scarred face, threatened to tear down the walls."

"You dreamt Ranald discovered our plan?" Catalin swallowed, fearing Elyne's dream would come true.

Elyne waved her hand in front of Catalin's face, motioning her to wait. "Nay. Hovering overhead was a *black* eagle as big as a man. I think *it* may have been Ranald."

"Did the dream end there?"

"Nay. The eagle swooped from the sky. The evil man tried to kill it, but the bird's talons tore into the man. The man's broadsword sliced into one of the eagle's legs." She shuddered, and continued. "The eagle's beak plucked the man's eyes out afore it killed him."

Elyne stopped when Catalin put her hand to her mouth and swallowed back stomach acids surging up her throat. She took several deep breaths before nodding for Elyne to finish.

"Dinna worry. The eagle hopped on one foot over to me. It turned into Ranald." She shrugged her shoulders and looked sheepish. "Raik's hands touched my shoulder and I awoke. He was grinning at me because I was clutching the latch, ready to burst through the doorway."

"Oh, saints. We should pay heed to your dream. For truth, Sir Giric is a comely man and Ranald did mention the convent. But I wonder who the terrible man could be?"

"Aye. I dinna think we have anything to fear as long as Sir Giric takes us to Seton and not the convent." Elyne frowned at the people milling about. "Come, we must plan what clothing to take, and I must find a weapon for ye."

"Weapon? How could I carry a bow or sword?"

"Nay. I will have my bow and quiver of arrows. And a short sword, too, come to think on it. What we need for ye is a good sized dagger, and mayhap a small one hidden inside yer kirtle."

Catalin's mouth was still agape when they left the hall.

Ranald fought to keep a grin off his face as he left the keep. It wasn't chivalrous of him to tease Catalin, but she amazed him. He had expected lusty behavior from the women he bedded in the past, for he was a young man with sexual appetites and stamina enough to pleasure even the most demanding lass.

Many times, he'd heard the married warriors at the castle grumbling about their wives not enjoying sex, much less delighting in it. One man had grumbled that 'twas like bedding a cold, giant fish that long since had stopped flapping its tail up to meet him.

He barely had to touch Catalin for her body to get as hot

and wet as any young lass he plowed in his youth. Truthfully, she was the most responsive woman he had ever bedded.

"My lord Ranald?"

A voice at his side and a soft hand on his arm turned his thoughts back from his bed. Raik pulled a long face at him, and with eyes twinkling and mouth fighting a smile, he dropped back to walk with Domnall and Cormac. Ranald stepped to the side to let the men pass, before he turned to frown down at Muriele.

"Did ye wish to have words with me?"

He had no idea what the lass wanted, thought she looked hesitant about speaking. For certain, she seemed to be rethinking her reason for stopping him. While he waited, his gaze traveled over her from head to toes. It was a most pleasant wait. She was more comely than most women at the keep. Other than his Catalin and Elyne, of course. Still, he grew impatient.

"Speak up, lass. I have much that needs to be done."

"Please, sir, walk with me amongst the apple trees. I would speak where none would overhear."

Muriele lifted her hand in a gesture that invited his arm to rise and let it rest upon his sleeve. Cold swept from her fingers through the cloth. He kept silent until they were well into the grove. She looked around, appearing hesitant. Taking a deep breath, she turned to face him.

"My lord Ranald, I know not what tale others have told ye, but lest they be untrue, I thought it best to speak with ye."

"I have heard little. Only that my brother was thought to, uh, have a special interest in your protection."

Muriele flushed and lowered her eyes. He could not very well come right out and ask if she had been Moridac's leman. She must have read his mind, though.

"Ye have no doubt heard that I am without family and fled the Highlands to come here. I needed to escape a man who would have done me great bodily harm. My horse was too old and tired to carry me, so I resorted to walking, hoping to give her a chance to recover. Sir Moridac came across me whilst she was dying, her head on my lap. He was kind enough to wait until she breathed her last before he helped me to rise."

"It was considerate of my brother." Ranald could not keep his brow from arching, wondering what Moridac was after.

"He promised his men would bury my faithful old horse, and he offered me protection at Raptor Castle."

"Most fortunate, truly, that ye met a patrol from Raptor."

What had this to do with him?

"He took me up in back of him and brought me to the castle." She blushed and lowered her head.

"I am pleased my brother acted with honor." This was the type of tale he had expected of his twin, not all the stories of his excesses that filtered through even to the abbey.

"As was I. He brought me to Raptor and told everyone I was his father's ward. Chief Broccin was not quite pleased with this. But Moridac stood between me and all others who would prey on a helpless woman. Everything was well until that fateful day when Moridac again went hunting."

"Ah. A woman alone is sure to draw the Chief's *regard*." Ranald's lips thinned.

His sire thought nothing of picking up a lass and carting her off to his bed when the mood struck. More oft than not, he paid off her angry father or brother the next morn.

"I am weary of this cat and mouse game with the chief. Lady Joneta has been most kind. She shares her bedchamber with me and has been diligent in her protection."

Muriele startled him when she stepped close and placed her long slender fingers on his shoulders and boldly raised her gaze to search his.

"Have ye not noted I have tried to bring myself to yer attention? It has been many long months since I have had the, um, attentions of a man. Since the day ye returned to Raptor, I have craved ye as my lover."

CHAPTER 27

RANALD STARED AT LADY Muriele's face, trying to read her intent. These past months, he had thought she gathered her nerve to ask for his protection. Not as a lover. As a warrior to stand between her and any male who sought favors she didn't want to give. Now, she boldly sought him as a man between her thighs. He grasped her wrists to remove her hands from his shoulders. She stopped him with her pleading.

"I will be most discrete. I vow I will not come between ye and Lady Catalin. I do not seek love from ye, nor do I wish gifts for my favors. Ye will have no need of yer mask, for yer scars add strength to a face more comely than most. I will wield no ties to bind ye. Should yer seed take, mayhap ye could find a warrior to be a husband to me."

Releasing his shirt, she ran her hands down his arms. She studied his face, though he didn't know what he saw there, if anything. When he did not venture to embrace her, he noted the moment she changed from hesitation to determination.

She rose on her toes, and as she molded her body to his, the soft mounds of her breasts brushed over his pounding heart. Could she feel it? Arms soft as warm velvet circled his neck. Long fingers combed through his hair, touched and caressed him, while she kissed him with skilled passion. His skin threatened to burst into fire beneath her lightest touch. His loins hardened and stirred when her tongue sought to pry between his teeth.

Near panting with rising hunger, he determinedly unwound her arms from his neck and stepped back, taking deep breaths to calm himself.

"Nay, Lady. I have no desire for a leman."

"No desire? Ye deny what my body felt? What my eyes can see?" Her gaze trailed down his length and stopped where his flesh betrayed his words.

"Nay. I canna deny my response to ye, but ye insult me by thinking I can't control temptation. Do ye forget I was without the pleasures of a woman's flesh until I left Kelso?" Ranald shook his head.

Muriele's reaction puzzled him. Where he expected teary eyes and protests, she beamed at him like he had given her a handful of gold coins. He studied her through narrowed eyes. Was she daft?

"What game do ye play, Lady?" He glowered down at her.

"No game. I prayed ye would give me the right answer. And ye did." She nodded and looked him square in the eye.

"And what would ye have done had I thrown ye to the ground and burrowed myself between yer legs?"

"This."

One hand darted into the folds of her kirtle. Her eyes widened with shock when he gripped her wrist and they tumbled to the ground together. He straddled her, then gathered both her hands above her head and anchored them there with one of his.

Swiftly, he felt over her form until satisfied she had no other blades. His grip on the hand holding the dagger tightened. With a soft cry, she dropped the weapon.

"Ye intended to stab me?" Astonishment sent his brows so high they near dislodged his mask. "Lady, had ye hidden blades aplenty over yer length, I would have taken them all from ye," he growled.

Muriele nodded gravely at him. "And had that happened, I would have summoned aid."

She puckered her lips like a woman inviting a kiss. Instead, a piercingly loud whistle rent the air.

Ranald twirled off her and crouched, the dagger at the ready, as someone charged from amongst the drooping apple tree branches. He near dropped the blade as Aunt Joneta, both hands waving a hefty stick over her head, charged toward him.

"Aunt Joneta!" He jumped up, his mouth agape on seeing her angry glare.

Muriele scrambled to her feet and stepped between them. His aunt halted, looking surprised the young woman was not in distress.

"I am sorry, Lady. Sir Ranald demanded to know what I would have done if he had accepted my offer."

The stricken look faded from his aunt's eyes and relief spread over her face. Her pent-up breath escaped in a great whoosh as she dropped the heavy stick.

"I feared I had been wrong when I told Muriele you would aid her, Ranald." She raised a shaky hand to wipe it across her sweating forehead.

"Ye knew Lady Muriele would plead to be my leman? What game do ye play?" He shook his head. "Aunt, how could ye?"

Annoyed that they had tricked him, he scowled and glared down at her discarded weapon. "Huh! Ye meant to hit me over the head with that?"

"Only if you took advantage of Muriele's offer." She grimaced. "And I would only have whacked your arse to make you let her be."

His left brow rose. His mouth twitched. "Would that not have aided a rutting man?" He shook his head, ridding the thought from it. "Ye are both making my head ache. What was this about? Make haste with the telling. I dinna have time to waste."

Muriele shifted her feet, looking ashamed. "I had to know if you were as honorable as I thought and as Lady Joneta told me. The quickest way was to find if you were easily swayed by lust." A blush swept over her creamy cheeks and spread down her neck. "What I told you before was true. I had to flee my home. I fear those who threaten me will comb all of Scotland until I am run to ground."

"Ye expect me to protect ye from an unknown force?"

Ranald eyed the beauty. She had said she was without family. Was she fleeing a lover? A cruel husband? Someone who would not cease hunting for her until she was back in his possession. The thought made him pause.

"Is it yer husband ye seek to escape?" If so, he would have no choice but to release her to him if he found her.

"Nay. I have no husband." She shook her head, her gaze not wavering from his eyes. "Ye must cross the border. I have heard Lady Elyne and I are to accompany yer wife."

"How have ye learned of this so quickly?"

His aunt chuckled and smiled at him. "More than a few people heard you argue with Catalin last eve, Ranald. Those who did have told the rest."

Cruddy Lucifer! Did the entire castle know each time he had words with his wife? As vocal as Catalin was in her pleasure, they for certain knew when he swived her. Mayhap he should move their bedchamber to a remote area. Like atop the wall tower that housed the supplies and weapons. By night, it would be most private.

"I would ask yer help once we cross the border." Fear lurked in the depths of Muriele's eyes as she twisted her fingers into knots. Her quivering lips made her appear even more vulnerable. "I plan to seek refuge in a convent where no one would dare follow me."

"Jesu! A convent? What bug worms its way into a woman's mind that makes her beg lodging with the good sisters? Do ye think ye will live a life of plenty? Ye must have an ample dowry to enter there else ye will be scrubbing floors, cleaning pig sties and grubbing in the earth squashing worms."

He doubted Catalin had not known of Muriele's plight when she mentioned biding with the good sisters. If he had correctly read his wife's expressions when sighting Muriele, she had no sisterly love for this slender beauty. They were as unlike as a spitting wild cat and a sleek white wolf, though both leapt to do battle when danger threatened.

"If it meant I would be where no Highlander could ever find me, I would joyfully do so."

Muriele's chin thrust out, her face determined, as she stood tall and squared her shoulders. She had changed before his eyes from helpless lass to a warrior woman ready to take up a sword and flay it about her — should she have need. He sighed and turned to Joneta.

"Ye shielded her from Moridac? And now Father?"

"Aye, Ranald. Though it is my brother who proves most persistent. After ye take Hunter Castle back from Smelly Hamon," Joneta's eyes twinkled saying the name, "it would take no great effort to provide Muriele with an escort to the nearest convent."

She nodded and smiled as if he had already agreed to their plan.

He shook his head and glared back, showing them he didn't like their wily stunt and his was the final say.

"The Sisters of Mary Magdalen lies south of Hunter between it and de Burgh's Seton." Ranald rubbed his chin, thinking.

"Why, it would take only a day once we are at Hunter." Muriele's eyes brightened like some inner sun had risen behind them.

"Hmpf. For truth, a most treacherous day's travel. One needs to take a roundabout way around Baron Rupert's lands to reach the convent. It's why I sent twelve of our own men to supplement de Burgh's escorts when they returned home."

Shadows faded the light in Muriele's eyes as her shoulders slumped. That glimmer of fear lurking in their depths broke through again.

"I didn't say I would not see ye safely there, Lady. Once all has been set aright at Hunter and I can spare a goodly escort, I will see ye settled at the Sisters with an ample dowry. Ye won't have to pinch worms for yer keep."

Her reaction pleased him, for hope lit her face again. What could this comely woman have done to cause a man to hunt her like a wild animal?

"Thank you, Sir Ranald."

Before he thought to fend her off, Muriele sprang forward and placed a hearty kiss on his cheek, near knocking off his mask in her eagerness. He jumped back like she had bit him. His hand covered the mask as he swiftly settled it into place. All the while, his left eye glared at his aunt. The kiss was not his doing, in case she thought of retrieving the branch and whacking him with it.

"Enough of wasting my time. If I dinna see to the men, there will be no army crossing the border once we get word, no siege will start and certainly no escort to any convent."

He frowned and looked each woman in the eye, pausing a moment doing so. Noting by their hesitant faces that they had grasped his message, he nodded and strode away grumbling about annoying women taking up his much-needed time.

"Monday?" Catalin could not believe Elyne. "We leave in less than two days, yet your brother said not one word of it until now!"

Catalin kicked a shoe so hard it slammed against the just-closed door. She jumped when it crashed back open and Ranald stood there, his hands propped at his waist, scowling at her.

"If ye would rather indulge yer anger than prepare to leave, I am sure Father would be glad to have company these next months."

"Could you not have told me yesterday? Or even earlier today? Or were you too busy rutting with Lady Muriele amongst the apple trees to think of it?"

Ranald's cold stare was like adding tinder to a blaze that had started after seeing him stride from the darkness of the trees brushing dirt, leaves and twigs from his knees. A scant two heartbeats later, Lady Muriele had appeared.

Catalin's nostrils thinned; her hands clenched.

"Moridac would never have flaunted his leman in front of his wife," she yelled.

A heated force, much like someone's hands on her shoulders, pushed her back until she near staggered.

A bestial growl rumbled from Ranald's chest. Eyes narrowed with contempt, he spun and stalked out of the half-opened door. The force of its slam made Catalin's ears ring.

Ranald's boots striking the steps gave warning of his anger as he stormed down the stairwell.

chapter 28

ANGER SIZZLING THROUGH RANALD'S veins sent waves of tension so strong its energy would shove tables, make chairs fly against the walls or, God forbid, might even direct itself against Catalin herself.

His temper had not cooled by the time he burst out into the courtyard swarming with soldiers, horses, carts and even oxen.

Ahead of Ranald's every step, dust rippled in waves and lifted into the air. Feathers flew about as fowls squawked in fright, flapping their wings and taking great running leaps to escape him. Buckets toppled, and as they rolled, the splashing water formed muddy rivulets. Startled horses, their eyes rolling in fear, stomped and shied away until their surprised riders brought them under control.

Ranald heard only blurred sounds. When a hound yipped and sprang out of his path, he took note of footsteps pounding behind him.

"Hold, Ranald. Hold!"

Ranald stopped. Squeezed his eyes tight.

"What has ye in such a fury ye near destroyed all in yer path?" Raik's ready grin spread across his lips, but his eyes flashed concern.

"Naught that would keep me from my duty." Ranald's eyes hardened; his mouth set in a grim line. He scanned all around him, taking note of the turmoil and uneasy glances cast his way.

Cormac left his position in line and rode over to him, a question in his eyes.

"Start out," Ranald ordered. "I will join ye soon."

"Aye, sir." Cormac whirled his destrier, its great hooves

stamping as he led it to the head of the column winding toward the barbican.

Ranald studied the line passing before him to see everything was as it should be. Wagons filled with food, supplies and equipment for building a tent village, rolled ahead of others filled with weapons and armor. Sturdier wagons lugged battering rams, and finally, fatted oxen slowly tugged wagons laden with sections of trebuchets and catapults they would assemble at the siege camp. Foot soldiers marched beside and between them, ready to lend a hand. To the rear of the long row, mounted warriors waited to file in, their spirits high as they looked forward to a good brawl.

"'Twas right kind of King Stephan's subjects to be fighting amongst themselves." Ranald rubbed the back of his neck, easing his tense muscles.

"Aye. Our men did a thorough job of pricking their tempers." Raik grinned and nodded toward the moving line in front of them. "Cormac, and the men needed to set up the siege camp, will soon pass the heavy equipment. Dubne will guard the oxen and keep them moving."

"That leaves Father and Domnall to protect Raptor, though Lucifer himself knows Father is feared enough no one dares venture close." Ranald gave a wry smile.

Hearing Finn clear his voice, he turned to find him and another squire waiting to help him don his battle gear. He nodded and leaned over for them to pull on his heavy hauberk. Once it was in place, he stood tall and rolled his shoulders to help settle it more comfortably around his body.

Ha. As if comfort was possible while wearing mail. He hooked his thumb beneath the mask, lifting it off. He handed it to Finn then slipped the helmet over his head. Holding the nasal guard and the back of the helmet, he adjusted it before nodding his satisfaction.

Ranald had gone to their bedchamber to tell Catalin he would lead this first siege party.

His cousin could tell her instead.

"Make sure the women are ready to leave before dawn on

Sunday. Dinna let them dally and delay ye." Ranald turned his face aside.

"I thought ye set out to tell Catalin earlier? Surely she didn't say anything so worrisome it pricked yer temper?"

Ranald snorted. "I had not the chance to tell her. And would ye not be angry to find ye came up lacking when yer wife compared ye to ..." He stopped the words he had not meant to say. Looking down, he noted Raik's surprised expression and scowled.

"Tsk. Do ye forget I lack a wife, cousin?"

His mouth set in a grim line, Ranald jerked his sword belt so it would not hinder his mounting. "If Catalin wants to think the worst of me, she is a fool. I dinna easily abide fools."

The stable master handed him Satan's reins. As soon as Ranald swung up into the saddle, he began to relax. This was where he belonged. Where everyone accepted him for what he was, for what he could do. He was away from foolish women and their prying eyes.

"See ye leave on time."

Ranald jerked his head in a nod to Raik and led Satan's Spawn over to Dougald patiently waiting at the passage through the barbican. Soon they had galloped over the drawbridge and into the cloud of dust kicked up by the advance army. As he passed them, Ranald's critical eyes scanned the men and supplies trailing across the land beyond the curtain walls. He and Dougald fell in with Cormac behind the standard-bearer flying Ranald's snapping yellow banner with the twin black eagles.

Before dawn fully arose two days later, Catalin glanced up at the walkway over the barbican. Chief Broccin was not pleased to see her leave, though he had provided her with a small cart with brightly colored cushions and thickly padded seats. She had thanked him for his thoughtfulness and assured him she would fare well riding in it. She waved at him, for he had seemed truly worried over her.

Elyne sat opposite her, her face uplifted as the sun sent its first weak rays over a distant mountain. Lady Muriele rode in another cart bigger than the first, carrying Hannah, Aunt Joneta and Ada. Thick cushions and padding covered the two benches along its sides. Stacked on one end were blankets aplenty for their comfort.

"If Father could have kept ye at Raptor, he would have done so." Elyne grinned at her. "It isn't often that I have heard Raik yell as loudly as Father."

"Aye. With each breath, your father's words softened until they faded away. You were standing close. What did Raik say that convinced him?"

"He didn't speak. He went very still; not a muscle moved, not even in his face." Elyne frowned and tilted her head, looking puzzled. "He stared into Father's eyes so long I didn't know how he kept from blinking. Father relaxed and said Raik should not set too fast a pace, for it would cause ye discomfort and harm the babe."

"Hm. I have heard others speak of Raik staring at a man until the fellow did what he vowed he would not do. I thought mayhap he spoke so quietly none could hear." Catalin wondered if he sensed they spoke about him, for he turned halfway in his saddle. His intense blue eyes stared into hers and he smiled before he turned back to face forward.

Catalin took a deep breath of pine-scented air and shivered, for it reminded her of Ranald's exciting scent.

"I look forward to spending these next days in the open." It had rained late in the night, but the dawn was clear with nary a cloud to mar the crystal blue sky. She glanced down and patted her expanding middle, for the babe had awakened early and seemed as excited as she.

"Uh huh. I hope we feel the same tomorrow, and the next day, and the next."

And those next days passed without any untoward incidents. It was as if Ranald had swept all problems away, leaving them clear passage to Hunter Castle. That last day, Catalin lifted her face to the sun. Mayhap the beauty of the day was a sign that all would go well. Several leagues later, they rode out of the forest to see softly rolling hills in the distance with beech and rowan trees mingled with the pines covering them. Shimmering waterfalls interrupted the swaying green branches now and again. What most brought a smile to her lips was the sun turning droplets in the cascading water's mist into sparkling jewels. Water crashing at the foot of the hill added to the roar of the rapids.

Catalin tilted her head and listened to thunder in the distance, yet the sky showed not even a hint of clouds. She first noted it earlier when they stopped to water the horses. It had been thus for the last league or more. A storm approached. She watched the sky for the streak of lightning that should soon follow.

Nothing. The heavy forest thinned as they drew near Hunter. They rode out onto a grassy area, providing a clear view of the sky near the edge of the forest. Yet another boom sounded. This time, the sky did show the change. Her brows near met in the middle as she studied it. Dust? Or smoke? Why, it must be both!

The more fool she. It wasn't thunder but the sound of battle, though she had never before heard it. She shivered knowing her home was under siege. Dratted Uncle Hamon! She would like to ring his hateful neck for putting the people of Hunter Castle in such dreadful straits.

In the distance ahead, a sea of white surrounded Hunter Castle's lands. The white turned into a village of tents lined in neat rows like streets. Every third row ended with a larger tent, a banner flying above it.

She recognized Ranald's tent from afar. The yellow silk banner caught the wind and flew as if the raptors took flight on their own.

Far enough away that the castle archers were unable to pick off the men operating them, trebuchets battered the tops of Hunter's curtain walls. After each toss of the trebuchets, catapults filled with heavy stones harassed the men left standing there. Great clouds of dust and smoke rose over the grounds.

Sitting closest to the front lines of tents was what looked to be a large storage area for provisions. The constant stream of warriors coming and going afforded protection for it. Up and down the rows, men built cooking fires, and sturdy women took pots from the carts and preparing food.

Now and again, she saw a familiar face and stopped to ask if they needed help or if they fared well. Hannah near jumped out of the cart when she spied an old friend. The woman walked alongside, chattering and laughing up at Hannah, her hefty bulk swaying with each step. It struck Catalin that her old nurse's eyes lit with laughter for the first time in many months.

Hannah and her friend aided Catalin when they reached Ranald's tent. Finn and Raik's squire carried in two small chests Catalin had brought with her. One held clean kirtles and under-clothing; the babe's supplies filled the other.

Inside the tent flap, she skidded to a halt and gawked around her. She had expected a dirt floor, a rude frame with a pallet atop for sleeping, and perhaps a small table with stools set around it.

Instead, carpets covered the floor. At back and to the right stood a bed ample for two filled with a thick down mattress. Pillows and wool blankets, and animal skins for extra warmth, covered it. More animal pelts were at the foot and sides of the bed. Against the back wall to the left, Finn placed the two chests alongside Ranald's own.

A good-sized table held two large pewter plates, mugs and a heavy iron candleholder. A pitcher filled with cold water, beads of moisture covering its sides, stood to one corner. In the middle was an earthenware platter filled with bread, cheese and cold meat. Instead of stools, two chairs stood on either side. At the center of the tent, a stout pole added support to the roof.

She stared, dumbfounded.

"Ye are pleased, Lady?" Finn's face split in a wide grin.

"You have done a wonderful job, Finn. Thank you."

"Not me, Lady. Sir Ranald ordered every comfort we could provide."

Daylight was near gone when Finn brought the evening meal. As he readied the table, she sighed and stood, her cloak slung over her shoulders, to peer out the tent opening. Was that Ranald? Talking with Lady Muriele? It was not a lover's meeting. Aunt Joneta stood behind the lovely woman. Whatever it was, he was denying her something, for he shook his head. Lady Muriele's shoulders slumped, but she nodded and returned to her tent. When he strode over to Catalin, she was pleased.

"Wife, how fared ye on yer journey?"

Ranald's gaze lacked warmth as he scanned down her form then searched her face.

"It was as pleasant as possible. The Chief provided a comfortable cart." She fidgeted, sensing the bitter resentment her words had caused the last time they spoke. Ranald had spent a lifetime knowing he came up far short of Moridac in his father's eyes. Why had she been so foolish as to compare him to his twin?

"How did you fare with Hunter's villagers?" From the people she had seen and talked to, Ranald had been exceedingly kind, going out of his way to soothe her people.

"Ye need not fear for them, Catalin," Ranald helped her to sit across from him. "I met with them and offered safe passage if they wished to leave. I made it clear I had no intention of burning their homes, but I did intend to oust Baron Hamon."

"How many left? Did you advise them to go to Letia's?"

"I had no need. They pledged loyalty to me. The women and older men supply us with water and do other chores. The young men put their backs to supplying stones and debris for the siege engines. It frees more of Raptor's men to fight."

Catalin near sighed with relief. She eyed Ranald as he wolfed down his food. From what she could tell, the blood splatters over his form were not his own. They finished the tense meal with polite questions and equally polite answers between them. Ranald nodded formally when he left and returned to the field.

For a fortnight, the steady thump of siege engines at dawn awakened her. The dullness of the days made them endless. Long after Catalin slept each night, Ranald quietly entered the tent. Exhausted, he slid into bed. If she awoke and started to speak, he put his fingertips on her lips and fell into a restless slumber. When she awoke the next morn, he had long since gone.

One evening, she tossed and turned, unable to get comfortable, until she fell into an exhausted sleep. She knew not what roused her, for the night sounds were no different. The steady drone of men talking, laughing and arguing as men do, was all too familiar now. She paced the tent then went to look outside.

She spied Ranald riding toward her. The way he sat his saddle betrayed his fatigue. Unfortunately, Cormac called to him and the two turned their horses back toward Hunter Castle looming in the night sky. She returned to bed and had every intention to remain awake, but her body finally demanded she sleep.

Catalin dreamt, of all things, about Ranald's handsome toes as they had been that day she assisted with his bath. But this time, as she admired them, they turned into bars in a window.

A window that was the key to Hunter Castle's defeat.

CHAPTER 29

CATALIN JOLTED AWAKE IN that false darkness before dawn. She closed her eyes, picturing the bars in her dream and remembering where they were. More than once she had sought solitude in the crypt below the chapel where her beloved mother and father rested, for Uncle Hamon was fearful of the dead and never once entered there.

Ranald has asked if she knew of any weakness in Hunter Castle. She looked over at his pillow. No dent showed that he had found his way there. She fumbled around on the fur rug to find her shoes. Wrapped in a cloak, she stepped out of the tent. The guard snapped to attention.

"Lady Catalin, is aught wrong?" His eyes were stretched wide, no doubt fearful she was about to give birth.

"Please seek out Sir Ranald and tell him I must speak to him."

"Aye, Lady. He is with his sire." The man started to turn.

"Wait. Chief Broccin is within the camp?"

The man nodded. "The Chief arrived late last eve. They have been closeted together since."

Catalin nodded, and he started out in a trot toward Raik's tent. His banner now flew with a dark one alongside it. No doubt, it was Chief Broccin's yellow eagle that flew on the black silk.

She hastened with her dressing, for her father-by-law was bound to come with Ranald. No sooner had she pulled her kirtle over her head than Hannah and Ada burst into the tent.

"Lovey, are you in pain?" Hannah took hold of Catalin's

shoulders and studied her face for signs of stress.

"Nay, it's not the babe." Before she could speak further, Ranald's voice sounded outside the tent.

"Ye canna enter until I find what Catalin needs. I willna allow ye to make her more fearful than she already is."

"Me? Ye are the one likely to set the tent aflame with yer temper." Broccin snorted, but did not try to enter.

Ranald burst into the tent and eyed her from head to toe. "Wife? What caused yer call for me? Are ye in, uh, distress?"

Catalin shook her head, frowning. She looked at him as carefully, for even with naught but candlelight, she noted the dark circle under his left eye. No doubt, the masked eye gave the same evidence of a lack of sleep. He looked beyond tired. Her gaze probed over his body for blood or new injuries. Blood there was, though thankfully, still not his own. Her heart squeezed knowing after she left he might sustain a serious injury. More than likely, he would make light of his wounds and might not receive the proper care in time.

The corners of his mouth twitched the slightest bit. "Aye, we are both as we last saw each other, though are ye sure ye have not stuffed a pillow beneath yer clothing for the bairn to lie against? He seems to grow even at a blink in time."

"And you look as if you have neither slept nor eaten this past sennight." She turned to Hannah and Ada. "I am sorry they awakened you, but before you return to your rest, would you have food sent?"

"No need. I didna hear screams of labor, Ranald," Chief Broccin said as he entered the tent, "so I sent a lad to bring food enough to break our fast. Catalin, ye are well?" He stepped aside to allow Hannah and Ada to pass through.

"I am most healthy, my lord." She nodded at him. It was strange, but Chief Broccin, though he looked tired, appeared happier and more relaxed than she had ever seen him.

"Were ye frightened that ye called for me?" Ranald's gaze again searched her face for signs of pain.

"Nay. You once asked if I knew of a weakness in Hunter Castle. At the time, I did not recall any. Your toes teased my memory, but I could not understand why until I had a dream tonight."

"You dreamt of Ranald's toes?" Broccin snorted with a surprised laugh.

"It was seeing light between them when I bathed his feet." Catalin heat spread over her cheeks, for the men pulled long faces to keep from grinning. She wrinkled her nose at them. "They reminded me of the crypt beneath the chapel. The rising sun threw five shadows across the room, for there is a window set high in the wall with five bars guarding it."

"In what area is this crypt, and how high?" Ranald's eyes lit with interest.

"The chapel is on the third floor of the keep. It is easy to see. The window is in the shape of an arch; a stone cross near fills the space. The crypt lies directly beneath it. The window is very near the corner."

They stopped talking when Finn and a servant hurried in with ale, platters of bread, cheese, hard cooked eggs and apples. Once they left, Ranald filled a pewter plate with ample amounts of each and shoved it in front of Catalin.

"Eat. Now, those bars. We would need ropes tied to horses to dislodge them. I dinna think we could do that and not be seen." Creases formed between his brows as he thought.

"You would not need ropes. I have stood there atop a bench to look out over the hills. One day, I lost my balance and grabbed the bars. They wiggled. The stone around them was beginning to crumble."

"Could they have …?" Chief Broccin's eyes were alight with interest.

Catalin shook her head, silencing him. "No one will have noted it. Since my parents' deaths, only I ventured to pray there. Uncle fears crypts. He even refused to see the stone likeness of my father atop his tomb."

Ranald and his father talked and planned in between bites of food. Judging from the way Ranald rubbed his belly and stretched after he'd eaten the last bite, he was well satisfied.

"Will ye come with us, Catalin?" He looked at his squire,

who stood at the tent opening. "Finn, I would have Lady Catalin wear yer cape. Hamon's men are used to seeing ye beside me, so they willna note her."

Before he finished speaking, Finn had handed him the cloak, and Ranald settled it about her shoulders. He pulled the hood up to cover her hair, then leaned back and studied her.

"Aye. It will do." He glanced at the edges bunched on the floor and shook his head. "Once ye are on the horse, no one will note it is too big for ye."

"Ha! They will note if she does not ride astride." Broccin frowned. "Lass, do ye think ye can handle it?"

"Astride? I would relish it." The idea appealed to her, for she had oft thought men looked far more comfortable than women on a horse.

Soon after, they had mounted and were slowly weaving their way around the village of tents. Men scurried about in every direction, readying for the days work. Others must have worked throughout the night, for they had piled so many mounds of heavy rocks and debris high behind each siege engine that she wondered if they left any stone in the ground.

Ranald was seeing his father in a different light. He appeared relaxed and looking forward to these next days. He surprised Ranald with his jovial and bracing greetings to warriors as they passed.

His sire fretted over Catalin's exposure to any danger. He had even attempted to help him lift her onto Finn's saddle. Ranald did not allow it. She had needed to hike her clothing high beneath the cloak in order to straddle the horse, and his wife's creamy thighs were for no other eyes than his. After he adjusted the stirrups, she looked as comfortable as any lad in the saddle.

By the time the first rays lightened the sky, Ranald had led them across the field facing the chapel window. Without pointing or looking directly at the castle, Catalin described where they would find the crypt window.

"Hm. Had ye not pointed it out, I doubt I would have noted it was a window and not two guarded arrow slits close together."

"Is that not a drain? There in the shadows of the corner?" Excitement sounded in Chief Broccin's voice.

"Aye. We will make a great show today of being unsure of where to aim our efforts." Ranald rubbed his chin and grinned at his father. "We could pretend a great dispute and come to blows over it. Think ye we could be convincing?"

"Ha! That will be an easy performance."

"Aye. I judge it should take the better part of two days to prepare for Hunter's fall. We must draw much of their defense to another area, so when we are ready, the men can climb undetected at night. Once they enter and disable the guards at the gates, they will open them for us." Ranald's face set with resolve. "Come, Catalin. We return to the tent. While ye describe the keep and grounds, Cormac will draw the route the men must take once they are within."

Already the newly stoked cooking fires sent a haze of smoke over the endless rows of tents. As they made their way, he gestured to Raik, Cormac, Dougald and Fergus to follow them.

The sun was high long afore he was satisfied his men could find their way around Hunter Castle in the dark, which was precisely what he intended.

Seeing Catalin hide a small yawn and blink sleep from her eyes, he ordered her to bed.

When the sun again set, they would force out Baron Hamon.

CHAPTER 30

"**P**SST. WAKE UP," ELYNE hissed in Catalin's ear that next night then jumped when Catalin's arm flew out, almost toppling her to the floor.

"Saints, Elyne. You near scared me into the next world." Catalin pushed up from her side and stared at Elyne. "Is aught wrong?"

"Nay. Not unless ye canna get yer wits together so we can leave."

"Leave?" Catalin blinked and tilted her head, not sure she was awake and not still dreaming she was locked inside a strange room and heard men fighting and screaming on the other side of the door. The steady thunder of the siege engines gave her the reason for the dream.

"Ranald has stepped up the bombardment at Hunter. Sir Giric said we must leave while Ranald and Father are staging a great fight over which end of the castle to attack."

Catalin shivered and hugged her arms around her body. Now the time to leave was upon them, she feared what would happen if they did not succeed in getting to Letia's without pursuit. She gulped and clamped her teeth together. Now was not the time to become weak-kneed. She must stiffen her spine and protect the little body growing within her.

Hurriedly, she pulled on a heavy beige smock and deep green kirtle, dark enough not to stand out in the moonlight. She had finished lacing her shoes and knotting a ribbon around her hair when she heard Sir Giric speaking outside her tent. He softly called to them.

"Make haste! I have sent your guard on an errand and told him I would keep you safe until he returns." He kept his back to the tent flap, his head turned to the side so they could hear him. "Make your way to the back end of the camp and step within the first ring of trees. Men and horses are awaiting there."

"We are ready." Catalin grabbed her cloak around her shoulders and pulled the hood low over her face.

"Now," Giric hissed. He opened the flap only wide enough for them to slip through then pointed toward the line of trees in the distance. "Hurry. Dinna talk."

Catalin started off at a fast pace, feeling more confident with Elyne close behind her. Keeping to the shadows, they skirted the row of tents. She near shrieked when a man coughed so close to her she thought she smelled his sweat. She thrust her arm backward warning Elyne, for the man was relieving himself behind his tent. While his back was turned, they tiptoed backward and scurried away.

Never did she think it would be so hard to go unnoticed when all should be asleep. But when several warriors slept within the same tent, she could hear a man thumping the hard ground and grousing at another for snoring so loudly it kept him from his slumber.

Catalin frowned and kept glancing behind them. Was that other than Elyne's footsteps following? She pulled Elyne close, her fingertips on her lips. She probed the darkness but saw only shadows. She hoped clouds, owls or anything other than man caused them.

Had they been able to take a straight path to their destination, they would have been there in a flash. Having to dart in and around, sometimes going back further than they progressed, Catalin despaired of reaching the horses and men afore someone found them.

Some time later, Elyne whispered in Catalin's ear, "I dinna see them. Do ye?"

"Mayhap we entered the woods beyond where they await us?" Catalin wished her heart would slow its pounding so she could hear something other than it in her ear.

"Hsst! Halt yer blabber. Ye will draw every man in the camp," a man grumbled. "Hurry. There is but one spare mount. Ye must be ahorse afore Sir Giric arrives."

Not recognizing the voice, Catalin was uneasy. Elyne did not hesitate. She put an arm around Catalin's shoulders and they followed the shadow in front of them deeper into the woods. Four men waited at a small clearing, their hands patting horses' necks and whispering into their ears to keep them quiet.

One man led a mount to Elyne, and she swung up to straddle the saddle as easily as any man would. In what looked like modesty, she jerked her cloak about her to cover her legs. But Catalin, seeing Elyne's hand steal to pat her thigh, knew Elyne assured herself that her knife was firmly strapped in place.

She bit back a gasp when someone grabbed her elbow. It was Sir Giric. Where had he come from? She had not heard even a leaf move, much less a man's feet. He led her behind a tree where he had tethered his horse. In silence, he mounted while another man boosted her up to him.

It seemed forever before they were far enough from the camp that only faint sounds reached them. It was slow going at first, but whenever they broke out onto a level area, the men gave their horses leave to lengthen their strides to eat up the ground.

Catalin sat as straight and as far from Sir Giric as was possible, which wasn't very far. Her nose wrinkled with distaste, for stale sweat was not her favorite scent. It was unkind of her. The men were fighting a battle to take back her castle. They had no time for baths and fresh clothing, and too, they were aiding her and the babe. She rolled her eyes. She was an ungrateful wretch.

When had she fallen asleep? And why had they stopped? She soon found out when two men came crashing through the trees, pulling a figure that was fighting, scratching and kicking like a vicious cat.

"Idiots! Barbarians!"

Was that a woman's voice? Though raised in anger louder

than Catalin had ever heard it, she knew the cornered cat was Lady Muriele.

"Shite! Bite me again, witch, and I'll rap ye alongside yer head!" The man pulled back his hand, threatening her with his fist, then brought it to his mouth to suck clear the blood oozing from crescent wounds.

"Dinna dare strike her! That is the Lady Muriele ye are threatening." Elyne's cold voice stilled the man in his tracks.

"Lady, what are you doing here?" Catalin couldn't believe Muriele had left Ranald and the camp to follow them.

Lady Muriele jerked her arm at the same time she kicked the man's shins. He dropped his hand from her like she was a hot ember. Catalin fought a grin seeing her swat the side of her cloak like she meant to brush his touch from it. With the murderous look in her glare, undoubtedly she would have liked to skewer him.

"I followed ye, of course. I have long looked for a chance to go deeper into England." She smiled up at Elyne. "When I saw ye slip from the tent, I guessed what was afoot. I took a horse and started out after ye."

"You stole a horse?" Sir Giric's eyes widened with admiration.

"Not stole. Borrowed. 'Tis a trade for my horse left at Raptor." She nodded, making an end to the queries. "Now do ye not think we should set out again? Where do we head?"

"To Seton Castle and the de Burgh's." Catalin could only imagine the uproar when morning showed not only two, but three, women missing from the camp. "Hurry, we must be very near Seton. We should be within the gates and hidden before they search for us there."

"Seton Castle?" Muriele narrowed her eyes and studied Sir Giric's face. "Should ye not have turned south by now? Ye have been riding directly west. I kenned de Burgh's was to the south?"

"Heh! You know little of direction, Lady." Sir Giric jerked a finger at her. "Get on your horse." His squinted eyes shot sparks at her. "Your *stolen* horse. And keep your mouth shut."

Catalin saw a look pass between Muriele and Elyne. Elyne's lips thinned. She stared Catalin in the eye, and then looked pointedly up at the sky. As they started out, Catalin pretended to peer behind Sir Giric to see they all followed. A quick glance proved the sun at their backs. Had they been going toward Seton, it would have been slightly to their left.

She had not long to worry over it. In less than a league, she noted the men scanning the forest around them then glancing over their shoulders. Sir Giric held up a hand, bringing them to a halt. When she would have spoken, he covered her mouth and shook his head. He pointed to the woods around them, and they quietly melded into the trees.

He motioned to the wiry man Muriele had bitten and then at a tree. The man was up it in a flash and down again in short time, his face pasty. He glanced at the women. Moved close to Sir Giric. Had Ranald discovered their absence?

Wondering, Catalin swallowed. Would Ranald be able to control his rage? He might hold his hand with her, but the men would surely feel the bite of his sword. She studied their faces and saw raw fear. She did not want to be the cause of their deaths.

"Sir Giric, leave us here. We will await Sir Ranald. Mayhap you can disappear and circle around to return to Hunter. We will tell him we left on our own."

"Aye. Dinna fight my brother. He will be in a rage and willna listen to reason," Elyne added.

"Lady, it is not Sir Ranald who picked up our scent."

"Oh, saints! Chief Broccin?" Catalin shivered.

"Nay, Lady. I wish it were so." Sir Giric swallowed and kicked his horse into action, crashing out of the woods and back onto the path in a full gallop.

"Baron Rupert is stalking us!"

Giric's lips pressed into a thin line. He tightened his left arm around Lady Catalin to hold her more securely.

"Baron Rupert? He heads toward Seton Castle?" Lady Catalin shouted close to his ear. "Surely we can safely reach there afore he can venture close?"

"Nay, Lady."

Regret filled his soul that his greed for a vast ransom would end with this comely woman in Rupert's hands. No doubt, he would take glee in ridding her of the bairn then sending it to the Black Raptor. Rupert had suffered from Sir Ranald's hands before, but after such a monstrous deed, for certain the bastard would die an agonizingly slow death.

Giric's only prayer to save the women was to distance themselves enough from the pursuing baron that he could send the women ahead to seek sanctuary at the nearest habitat while he and his men fought to the death.

Aye, they were dead men riding now. By late day, they would have spent their blood on English soil. The men could not allow the baron to capture them. Once they could no longer fight, it was best to slit their own throats or throw themselves on their opponent's blade.

At the top of the rise, he jerked his horse to a frantic halt. Standing in the stirrups, he studied the ground ahead, than dared to have a glimmer of hope for the women. He jumped down, snatched Lady Catalin off his horse and tossed her up behind Lady Elyne.

"A monastery or an abbey is ahead at the base of the next rise. Clamp your legs as tight as you can to the horses' sides, else you will become unseated in a gallop. Stay hidden alongside the trees. No matter the reason, do not stop! Once close to the gates, scream to alert them."

Lady Catalin's stricken face showed a moment of panic before she nodded and set her lips in determination. He slapped both horses' rumps sending them on at a swift pace, then spun and leapt atop his own mount. With any luck at all, the baron would not see the two horses following the tree line. Pray God, he and his men could hold Rupert long enough for them to escape.

Huh. It was strange to pray for one's own death. Mayhap he would take the baron with him to meet Lucifer.

In Hell.

Catalin clung to the horse like a burr. Her arms around Elyne's waist ached with strain. Once they were hurtling down the hillside, Elyne bent close to her mount's neck. Catalin leaned with her. Wind tore off their hoods and freed their hair. She feared for the babe with each pounding leap the horse took. Muriele inched up alongside. It was the first time she had ever seen the cool beauty's face in other than calm repose. Her lips drew back in a snarl near as fierce as Ranald's. She dared a glance backward and saw a lone horseman galloped toward them.

One of the baron's men! The devil's beast likely didn't need him in the fight but sent him to capture women instead. She swallowed to keep from spewing down Elyne's back.

The horses must have sensed their terror, for their strides lengthened until they near flew across the level ground. Elyne and Muriele started screaming at the same time. At first she thought someone had circled around and was about to attack them. She darted a glance backward and added her screams to the others. Ahead loomed what had to be a house of God, for she made out a cross atop the gateway.

They shouted and waved one arm. They made as much noise as possible and prayed someone would notice. Oh, God! No one would open the gate in time! The distance between them and the man galloping in pursuit slowly closed.

She glimpsed his face. And wished she had not.

Had she thought Ranald looked cruel when angered? Though the thunder of the horses' hooves drowned out other sounds, this lout surely gnashed his teeth and snarled as loudly as a greedy beast.

Was someone on the small tower over the gate? Aye! It looked like a man ringing a bell and people scurrying about.

For God's love! Open the gate. There! It started to move. They had at least twenty horse-lengths to reach it. Time slowed. Near stopped. When their horses' hooves left the ground, they seemed to float at a standstill. She shot another look back.

Oh, my God! So close. He was sure to overtake them before

they reached sanctuary.

Muriele, too, kept glancing back. Why did her mount slow? The horses had been nose to nose. What happened? She edged her horse closer. Her mount's nose was now alongside Elyne … then at their mount's rump … now his tail. Muriele dropped behind.

But five more lengths to go. Catalin's heart thudded and leaped. The gate was wide enough now for one horse to enter at a time. They hurtled on toward it. She dared to check on Muriele.

The beauty had hiked her skirts up around her waist, baring her thighs. Her hand reached to whip a wicked blade from a sheath strapped there. For truth, the devil pulled alongside her. He reached out a burly fist and grabbed Muriele's hair. He twisted it around his wrist. When he jerked on it, he nearly ripped her off her horse.

Lord Jesus, help her! Catalin lost sight of them as their horse streaked through the opening gate. Women yelled and male voices shouted. Then Elyne jolted the horse to a stop and pried Catalin's arms from her waist and eased her down into caring hands.

Elyne turned the horse, her dagger gripped tight, and raced back out the gate, avoiding three running men in flapping black robes. Catalin's voice caught on a sob as she started to run toward them, but someone grasped her shoulders and stopped her.

She covered her mouth to stifle a scream. Muriele, her long legs locked around her rearing horse, clung to its mane with one hand. The man was not finding it easy to yank her to his horse.

"She witch! Mother of Satan!" He shouted and let his reins go to strike her head with his fist. The motion turned his chest to Muriele. Both his arms raised and he tried to force her from the horse before the running men could reach them.

"Agggg!"

Blood arched high in pulsing spurts. Red soon splattered Muriele's lovely, pale hair and face. Blood covered her chest and arms. His hand fisted tightly in her hair. Both toppled to the ground. Muriele's foot fell free of the stirrup. His foot remained firmly lodged, his twisted boot wedged in the stirrup iron. The horses shied, their eyes rolling, their mouths wide. Screaming, as panicked horses do. Her mount bolted away. His horse, its eyes rolling and its ears laid back, jerked then leaped to pull forward.

Catalin twisted and pried the fingers from her shoulders that held her back. She ran, grabbed her skirts high about her knees as she followed Elyne.

The horse pulled away. Elyne leaned forward on her horse's neck and galloped after it. The monks chased after them, their swords raised. The horse drug the man, Muriele's hair tangled and caught in the dead man's glove. Even in death, he held her prisoner. Elyne caught up to the horse and made frantic grabs for the reins. Catalin gasped. Muriele's hands rose. One went to her head to grab her hair. Sun flashed against steel as the dagger rose.

The blade flashed back and forth, stopping when she bounced from her back to her side then back again. Suddenly, with one desperate swipe, she cut her hair free. The horse, still dragging the man, screamed and raced onward. With crazed eyes, it often looked behind then galloped faster back toward the hill.

Elyne, seeing Muriele had freed herself, leapt off her mount as the monks caught up to them. The men yelled for her to get back on the horse. Two monks lifted Muriele up to her waiting arms.

"Baron Rupert pursues us," Elyne shouted before she prodded her mount toward the gate. "Run!"

Catalin turned and hurried back through the gateway, watching over her shoulder to assure herself the others were still safe. She did not pay heed to anyone around her, only those following. She wrung her hands watching as Elyne's horse galloped through the portal. The monks, their black robes lifted to their knees, soon ran through to safety. The heavy gates clanged into place.

Her pounding heart filled her chest, near closed her throat. She watched an old man help the monks to place a heavy wooden bar across the gate. Two younger men hurried to a platform on the right side of the door where another heftier bar waited. They struggled to lift and slide it within the iron holders, while the old man guided it. Fear made it seem like it took forever, but she knew they had done it swiftly.

"Never have I seen so much blood." Catalin took slow, even breaths, and settled her stomach as she cleaned the dagger in a basin. The water quickly turned red. Muriele had held tight to her weapon until Catalin had coaxed it from her hand. "I thought it was hers."

"Aye. I did also." Elyne settled a blanket closer around Muriele's shoulders.

This was a rare room for a convent, more spacious than most. Carpenters had built two wooden frames and laced them with strong rope. Pallets stuffed with feathers rested atop, covered with a sheet and a wool blanket. Two smiling but silent women had brought in an extra pallet and linens and placed it near Muriele's bed.

"Muriele's blade found his throat." Catalin glanced at the unconscious woman. "Had she not struck at the right time, he would have carried her away."

"Aye. And if she had not chopped at her hair, she would be dead or Baron Rupert's prisoner." Elyne reached for the cleaned weapon, a white cloth in her hand, and dried it.

"Drats! How dared Brother Hugo say she must do penance for killing the lout! The man would have killed her!" Catalin scowled. When the babe kicked hard and used his elbows to help him move around, she patted her heaving stomach. "Shh. Quiet, love. All is well."

"Men dinna like women to take a hand in their own protection." Elyne slid the dagger into the sheath before she tucked it under Muriele's pillow. She smiled up at Catalin. "She always places it there at night."

"Elyne," Catalin beckoned her close to whisper. "Did you know of Muriele's back before today? Someone has taken a lash to her. And not more than a year ago. The scars are bright pink, not faded like Ranald's." She chewed the corner of her lips as pity flooded through her.

"Nay, I did not. She shared the chamber with Aunt Joneta. Aunt hovered in front of her when Muriele changed clothing in the tent. I will wager it's the reason she always carries a blade." Her eyes narrowed in thought. "Whoever thrashed her is the one she fears."

Elyne's scowl was so much like her brother's that Catalin smiled. "So many cuts and bruises to add to her misery. She will be sore for a fortnight or more."

Catalin sighed and looked around the room. The good sisters had wanted Muriele to stay in the Infirmary, but Muriele herself had objected, insisting she room with her *friends*. The word had tugged at Catalin's heart.

A small table with two stools stood beside the door. The robed women had brought them a hearty vegetable soup for their evening meal, along with freshly baked bread, cheese, apples and cold milk.

The sisters had everything they needed to sustain them. A large vegetable garden, an herbal garden, orchards with fruit trees, a dovecote, pigsty, cows, goats, and sheep were within the outer walls. Chickens squawked and pecked their way across a grassy area. They provided a plentiful amount of eggs, and those that did not, added variety to the table.

"Oh," Catalin wailed and tears welled.

"What is it? Are ye in pain?" Elyne rushed over to her, putting a hand on Catalin's elbow to help her to the bed.

"Nay," Catalin blinked and swiped her hand over her eyes. "I just remembered the babe's clothing. I brought a small bundle sewed inside my cloak. It must have worked free."

Her shoulders slumped, thinking of the lovely little garments and blanket Elyne had helped her to sew.

Catalin hugged herself and shook her head.

"All of this is my fault. Ranald refused to send me to Letia's saying it was too near Rupert's lands. I near hated him for it. Never did I experience such danger as we were in today. He tried to spare me from that."

"Aye. But ye could not know Sir Giric didn't intend to take us to Letia's. Too late, I kenned he was planning to hold us for ransom." Elyne shuddered.

Catalin studied the drawn face on the other bed. How could she not have seen the blond was such a caring woman? She squeezed her eyes tight in shame. It was because of her sinful jealousy.

"I am so weary my back aches." Keeping the blanket wrapped tightly around her, she stretched out on the bed.

"Sleep, Catalin. All will be well on the morrow."

CHAPTER 31

"WHAT?" RANALD'S SHOUTS THAT next noon were loud enough to wake the dead sprawled in a sea of red before him. "Why did ye not tell me sooner?"

Anger contorted his face. Finn stepped back as if frightened Ranald meant to strike out at him.

"Ye were fighting Baron Hamon and I couldn't disturb ye. I carried news of yer victory to yer tent. The guard thought the lady slept later than usual and did not want to disturb her."

"Where has he searched?" Ranald tried to calm his rising fear. Catalin must be with his sister, grousing to Elyne of how he had refused her bid to go to Letia's.

"I checked with Lady Joneta." Finn backed up another step. "Lady Elyne is also missing," he gulped and near whispered, "and Lady Muriele."

"Lucifer's moldy arse!"

Hearing Ranald's shouted curses, Chief Broccin grinned and stepped around the carcass of a horse.

"What goes here?" His voice boomed above the din and turmoil normal after ending a battle. He waited, his lips turned grim at Ranald's answer. "Begone, for God's sake. Find her. If she isn't within the camp, send word before ye leave." He turned, and seeing Raik come through the doorway of the keep, whistled shrill and loud. "Take Raik and as many men as ye need." He looked over at Finn. "The pup can bring word back to us when ye find her."

Ranald knew he had no need to check the camp, for after questioning the guard, he knew that she... Huh! Not only she but Elyne and Lady Muriele had gone with Sir Giric and four men who were also missing.

Two foot soldiers had seen Sir Giric ride out into the woods, and pointed to the spot. By the fading light, Ranald studied the ground. Booted footprints, along with smaller ones from the women, showed in the damp earth. He and Raik started out, taking a dozen of Raptor's best warrior with them.

They rode hard and stopped only to study the ground and trees by torchlight. Ranald set a steady pace, confident their prey had kept to the road. At a fork leading south toward Seton Castle, they lost the trail and backtracked. Pain, sharp as a knife's blade, struck Ranald's heart. Every sign pointed east ... skirting Baron Rupert's land.

Ranald pushed harder, following the tracks left by Sir Giric's and six other horses. Soon after the sun of the new day reached the noon hour, Ranald saw what near made him howl with fear. The ground showed where horsemen left the woods to the left and followed them.

Before the sun started to dip, they came upon Sir Giric. And his men. From the looks of it, they had fought long and hard. They had taken many more with them than they themselves numbered. Ranald and his men searched the carnage, frantically grabbing fallen men and turning their faces upward, seeking Baron Rupert. His body was not amongst them. Sir Kerr, his face white, gently carried Sir Giric's body and laid it beside the Raptor bodies on a grassy clearing. Once Ranald found the women, he would send men to bury them.

"Ranald!" Raik called from the path on the other side of the dead men. "Mayhap Giric and his men doubled back to meet Rupert. Ahead are more tracks. Further on, they dinna lead back to Rupert's."

They threw themselves on their mounts and followed the road for at least a league, where they saw evidence of another stop. Not ten steps on the other side of it, Ranald spied a small bundle beside a tree. He recognized one of the bairn's blanket, for he had watched Catalin sew its seams one night not long past. Tied tightly within was baby clothing. His chest ached so much he could barely draw breath. He closed his eyes and crushed the bundle to his chest. It neither stilled the terrible pain there, nor quieted the rage that near boiled the blood in his veins.

He saw where two horses had followed close to the tree lines. One horse carried two, from the look of the prints. Heavier riders had kept to the path.

Someone had pursued the women.

He shoved the bairn's clothing beneath his hauberk. No need now to study the ground, for no bushes or trees appeared disturbed beside the road. Suddenly, something crashed and thrashed through the trees to their left. The resounding calls of a distressed horse spurred them toward it. There in a thickly wooden area, a massive brown warhorse fought to free itself. A body wedged between two trees held it tight.

How in heaven's name had it gotten there? Ranald could only guess the terrified horse had fought so mightily to rid itself of the body hanging by the stirrup that it had reared, tossing the corpse high. It had landed, wedged between the trees. The horse reared again then lunged forward. A pop and a sickening wet sound followed as the leg ripped away from the corpse. Raik grabbed the flying reins and fought the horse, until Dubne grabbed the bridle and pulled its head down.

"Follow us once ye have freed it," Ranald shouted as he led Satan's Spawn through the trees and back onto the road. He didn't envy Raik's squire having to remove the mangled leg from the stirrup. The corpse was not one of their own, for a quick scan of the area had shown fragments of Baron Rupert's colors.

They raced ahead until they burst out of the wood at the top of the hill. He brought Satan's Spawn to a halt and studied the valley below. In the distance stood the gleaming white walls of the Convent.

Milling the ground in front of it was Baron Rupert and his men. He quickly counted thirty men plus Rupert.

Hmm. One man for each of the squires. The seasoned warriors would take two or three. He would handle four.

Baron Rupert belonged to him.

He had a promise to fulfill.

His lips quivered and lifted at the corners, baring his teeth. A growl rumbled from his stomach, up through his chest and gained sound as it left his lips. He nodded. Pleased.

'Twould be a fair fight.

CHAPTER 32

CATALIN SPOONED BROTH PAST Muriele's scratched lips. She flinched seeing her in such pain. Not many places on the woman's body were clear of scrapes, cuts and bruises.

Hearing sounds of scurrying women and the bell atop the gate, Elyne had gone to see what was happening. She hurtled into the room, gasping for breath. Horror contorted her face, making Catalin's skin crawl with fear.

"Baron Rupert camps outside the gates. Mother Cecelia denied him entrance. Thank the good Lord the monks agreed. Lofty-nosed Brother Hugo is new to the area and is a returned Crusader. He brought an injured knight to Kelso and was on his way back to King Stephen. He offered to hear the good sisters' confessions. Brothers Norbert and Clement abide at Kelso."

Muriele held up a bruised hand. "Are you sure it is Baron Rupert, and not, some, uh, Highlander who crossed the borders?" She swallowed and her lovely blue eyes clouded over with terror.

"Nay, I have no doubt 'tis Rupert. A red 'R' is emblazoned on their tunics."

Why, Muriele's face lost some of its fear. How strange. Who could be more feared than Rupert? Catalin stared at the wall, for something about the last two days seemed familiar, like she should know of it. She turned on the stool, the better to see Elyne's face.

"How many men does the baron have with him?" She held her breath awaiting the answer.

"Thirty. I counted myself." Elyne's brows raised, her eyes

questioning. Slowly, their expressions changed. Catalin knew she, too, remembered her dream of not too long ago.

"That pox-riddled Lucifer! Why did my most fearsome dream have to come true?" Elyne shouted.

She fisted her hands and waved them in the air. Spying the other stool close-by, she kicked out at it. It crashed against the wall. Eyes blazing in anger, she looked around, searching. She snatched a pitcher of water and raised it high, then stopped and lowered it, shamefaced. Carefully, she set it back on the table.

"Uh, what dreams?" Interest wiped the fear from Muriele's eyes.

"Elyne sometimes has seeing dreams," Catalin murmured low.

"Stupid dreams is what I call them," Elyne spluttered and rolled her eyes in disgust at the ceiling. "They are cause for more mirth than anything else. But this one terrible dream is happening now."

"Mayhap it is only slightly alike?" Muriele looked hopeful.

"Nay. A knight and his men were taking us to King Stephen, but someone chased us."

"Well, now, that is different. I believe Sir Giric meant to take us elsewhere." Muriele nodded.

"Aye, but he brought us to a secluded place. Much like this convent. And thirty knights led by a scar-faced man threatened to besiege the convent." Elyne stopped to take a deep breath.

"Hm, would that not be Sir Ranald?" Muriele quirked her brows.

"Nay. He hovered overhead as an eagle big as a man ..." Elyne gulped and looked at Catalin. "Our only chance will be if that part of the dream stays the same."

"Baron Rupert's threats become more dreadful each time he opens his mouth."

Catalin stood on the narrow outer wall's walkway surrounding the convent and cautiously peeked around a merlon.

Unlike a castle's battlements, these merlons were set close together. They had built the battlements more for appearances sake, for a convent should have no need of such protection.

"After the way Brother Hugo lectured us, never did I think to admire him. He seems fearless. Brother Norbert looks uneasy handling a sword." Catalin said in a quiet voice.

"Brother Clement recently took his final vows. He says he learned to wield a sword under their last Protector." Elyne crooked her finger for Catalin to lean close. "He near sang Ranald's praises. I didna tell him the Protector was my brother and yer husband."

Catalin turned her head to smile at Elyne. Seeing something from the corner of her eye, she jerked her head back to peer through the opening.

"Look! Something black flashed atop the hill where we came down."

Elyne leaned close to gaze over Catalin's head. "Aye. Saints help us! I hope it's not more of Rupert's men."

They held their breath as they watched what looked like a column of ants, two abreast, coming down the hill. They were not the only ones interested.

Rupert's men shouted and pointed behind them, fear ringing out in their voices.

When the baron turned and spied the advancing horsemen, he stared, frozen. The riders galloped toward them, the chain mail on their hauberks glinting in the sun. Only the leader wore a black cloak. The wind played with the edges, lifting it in the air.

Baron Rupert cursed and drew his sword, laying it flat out against the backs of the unfortunate men who were close. They formed two half-circles, ten men each, between Rupert and the advancing warriors, and one half-circle behind him.

Catalin gasped. For truth, the feared predator galloping toward them, his black cape spread like wings gave life to the name Black Raptor. She held her breath watching Ranald charging forward as if he flew. His men behind him formed an ever-widening arrowhead as they charged on the wind. They looked like giant birds of prey flying behind their leader.

The three monks watched over the gate, no doubt waiting to see if Rupert greeted the advancing men as friend or foe.

They didn't have long to wait.

Before Catalin could brace herself not to flinch, the clash of a joined battle rang in her ears. Never had she witnessed fighting to the death so close to hand. The noise was deafening, steel striking steel, steel striking shields, men screaming and warhorses stomping and trumpeting.

All were sounds more ominous than the thudding of catapults or trebuchets, for it was men joined together.

She jammed her knuckles between her teeth to keep from crying out. Raptor's horsemen attacked the outer rings guarding Rupert, close enough now that she could make out the knights Kerr, the courtly Fergus, Dougald, the near-giant Dubne, Brodie, Duncan and Cormac.

Ranald's presence was unmistakable.

"Jesu! Look behind them." Elyne pointed at three specs gathering size as they raced toward the Raptor warrior's backs. "Raik and another! But why are they only now coming, and why do two horses with empty saddles follow Raik?"

"Is that not the lout's horse that pulled him and Muriele away? And Muriele's *borrowed* mount? How strange! They follow Raik like dogs after their master." Hearing a deep voice scream, Catalin hugged her belly and returned her gaze below.

Thank the blessed Saints! Ranald forged ahead, his aim easy to see. Only fools engaged him. Those that did soon fell. Two of Rupert's men bolted away. They might as well have stayed and fought, for they did not see Raik until too late.

Why had she not noticed the gates opening? Brother Hugo and the one called Clement rode out. The gate slammed tight behind them. There were no protective circles now. Every man had an opponent. Catalin could no longer tell friend from foe. When she thought she could stand no more, the fighting decreased until only Baron Rupert and Brother Clement faced each other.

Ranald and Raptor's men surrounded them and held back as they watched Brother Clement battle the baron. When Rupert's sword flew to land in the dirt in front of Satan's Spawn, all motion stopped.

"Rupert, do ye recognize yer opponent?" Ranald's voice rang out. "The monk who bested ye is a man ye once tortured. Brother Clement? I would have ye stand back now. Ye have taken vows at Kelso. Dinna stain yer soul with his death. I made a promise to this instrument of Satan's that I'm sure he remembers. I intend to fulfill it now."

Clement nodded and backed his horse to stand beside Satan's Spawn.

"Shite-eating coward! Ye would kill an unarmed man?"

Rupert's spittle flew with his shouted words.

Ranald ignored him. He thrust his sword into its scabbard, freeing his hands. He unfastened his cape and dropped it to the ground beside his horse. With slow, precise movements, Ranald removed his helmet and let it fall onto the cape. His blood splattered face was bare for all to see.

"Take off yer helm," he ordered Rupert. When he did not move, Ranald added, "Ye wish the tip of my sword to do it for ye?" He shrugged. "Ye will likely lose yer nose."

Ranald leisurely swung down from Satan's Spawn. In the deadly quiet, his sword shrieked as he again drew it from its resting place. He stared through hooded eyes at Rupert's helmet. As he stalked toward the mounted man, it appeared to shimmer with heat.

Rupert yelped and yanked it off. When he threw it from him, Ranald slowly squatted to pick up Rupert's sword.

"Now. Get off yer horse," Ranald ordered as he rose.

Rupert swung to the ground, cursing and keeping an eye on Ranald.

Ranald's lips twitched, baring gleaming white teeth.

"I found what remained of Sir Giric. If he had not held ye back, ye would have killed my wife. My son." A vicious growl rumbled from his throat. "It's time I carry out the promise I made ye."

He sliced through the air with Rupert's sword, testing it, then stilled, studying him.

"Catch!"

Ranald tossed the sword to him.

Catalin could not say who looked the more frightening. Baron Rupert's face wore near the same scars as Ranald's, only the baron's were still red and puckered. The two men looked like starving beasts snarling and stalking each other, waiting for the kill. All they lacked was spittle foaming from their lips.

Blades clashed together, the sounds ringing out on the cleared battleground as they fought. They circled and struck, each taking the other's measure. Sweat traced a crooked path down their scarred cheeks.

Catalin's glaze remained glued to the two figures — one side of each man's face very much like his opponent's. Ranald's contorted into a savage visage. But Rupert's? Evil clung like a haze around him. She swallowed back bile each time she looked at him. Rupert roared when Ranald drew first blood, though with all the cuts and blood staining their clothing, Catalin did not know where the new wounds had opened.

Bloodied steel slammed against bloodied steel, sending sparks flashing as the blades rasped down to their hilts. Catalin's stomach quaked as she watched the combatants jump back, then strike again. Step by step, Ranald forced Rupert backward around the circle. Blood stained their arms, their shoulders. They fought with such fury their weapons near locked.

Ranald heaved against his opponent, forcing distance between them. In a flash, he twirled to the right. His boots sent dust swirling around their knees. He caught Rupert with a backhanded strike. Rupert bellowed. Blood welled from his right shoulder, down his arm to his elbow, then across his chest. On and on they fought. Sweat dripped from their snarling faces, their shouts near beastly roars.

Tears streamed down Catalin's face. She held her hands over her ears. Elyne grasped her shoulders and tried to pull her away, but Catalin fought her like a wildcat. She couldn't tear her gaze from Ranald's wild face, his eyes as cruel as a maddened boar's.

In her horror, she near forgot this was the same man who had slept beside her for so many months.

The two men were locked together, the veins in their foreheads and necks swelling with strain. They heaved apart. Rupert crouched, leaving Ranald's blade to whistle inches over Rupert's head. Rupert's blade slashed out. Blood flowed down Ranald's leg, spreading down to darken his boots. For one quick breath of time, his leg buckled. Then straightened. Rupert roared with glee. With both hands, he raised the weapon high above his head, and started a great downward blow.

Ranald, hands tight around his own hilt and muscles bunching in his legs and shoulders, swiftly spun left, his sword singing through the air as he whirled and struck — sending Rupert's weapon spinning above their heads to land on the ground. Two bloodied, severed hands twitched. Finger by finger, they fell from the hilt.

Rupert's screams split the air, near drowning out Catalin's own. Blood jutted from his arms as he threw himself at Ranald, his mouth wide, striving to reach Ranald's neck. Ranald braced himself and anchored his sword. The force behind Rupert's leap drove the blade through his flesh, exiting at his back.

For one horrible moment, Catalin stared at Ranald standing below, holding the impaled man on his feet with the strength of his arms. Rupert convulsed against him then went still.

Catalin crumpled to the floor, unseeing, as Ranald fulfilled the rest of his vow to Baron Rupert.

The battle was over.

CHAPTER 33

"I CAN TELL FROM yer snarl that Catalin still refuses to leave." Raik gulped down a cup of cold water taken from the stream at his feet.

"Aye." Ranald stiffly swung his aching body from Satan's Spawn and handed the reins to Finn. "For three days, she has refused to speak with me. She sends Elyne to carry her words. Catalin swears she and the bairn will spend their life at the Convent afore she would let either me or my father near them." He wanted to stomp his feet in frustration. "I told her we will camp in these woods until Hell freezes and Lucifer wears furs!"

"Huh. That will be a goodly time." Raik grinned at him.

Ranald snorted. "It had to be. She may harbor thoughts of traveling to the de Burgh's. Knowing we watch from afar, she willna dare leave."

They had not long to wait after all. That very evening, Finn tumbled out of a tree in his hurry to tell Ranald what he had seen from his vantage point.

"My lord, a workman left the convent driving an empty cart pulled by a mule. I thought he was going for supplies and near stopped watching when he entered the trees. He disappeared for a while. Finally, there was movement further to the right. He had unhitched the cart and is making haste westward."

"Westward? Toward Kelso?'

"It looked so to me."

"Raik, keep watch here. Finn and I will follow to see what mischief he is upon."

Late that evening, they arrived at the gates of Kelso. The workman's face blanched when Finn joined him and called out for the gatekeeper to open in the name of Sir Ranald of Raptor Castle. Ranald trotted his horse to stop behind them and gestured for the man to precede him through the opening gate. On seeing Ranald, Brother Octavius sheathed his sword. His face split in a grin.

"Are you in a spot of trouble then, Ranald?" He looked at the quaking man and then back to Ranald.

"Aye. We would both seek words with Abbot Aymer." On seeing the man's eyes near pop from their sockets, he knew he had guessed aright.

The abbot listened patiently to a memorized plea from Lady Catalin seeking his aid. She knew of the friendships Ranald had formed at Kelso, and the respect he had for his fellow monks. She felt confident they could persuade Ranald to allow her and the babe to live at Hunter Castle under King Stephen's protection.

Abbot Aymer listened quietly until the man was through. He sent him to the kitchens to appease his hunger, before he heard Ranald's side of the story.

"Ranald, I cannot believe you *have* changed so dreadfully your wife would flee from you, terrified for her bairn."

Ranald's shoulders slumped. His face filled with shame.

"I have changed. Greatly. What I feared the most, I have become. I am as my brother was. As my father is ..."

Ranald went on to tell the abbot of all that had occurred since he last spoke with him after maiming Baron Rupert. Dusk had long since fallen when he had his answer from the abbot.

After sadly hearing his sins in the confessional, Abbot Aymer listed the penances Ranald must do to cleanse his soul. After he watched the man who was as a son to him kneeling at the altar, he returned to his office and called for the convent messenger.

"You will leave at first light. Brother Octavius and three

of our brethren most familiar with Sir Ranald will accompany you. Lady Catalin need have no further fear of him, for they will take her where she and her bairn will be protected and loved for the rest of their days."

"Look, Catalin! Four monks have arrived from Kelso." Muriele's arm was none to steady when she beckoned Catalin over to the window. "They brought a cart fitted with a pallet and blankets. For truth, ye have misjudged Sir Ranald. It is not too late to change yer mind."

Catalin shook her head, her lips pressed in determination.

"Oh, saints." Elyne peered over Catalin's shoulder and pointed towards the hills. "There at the edge of the forest! Ranald looks sorely upset to see them."

Elyne shook her head. Tears welled as she watched Satan's Spawn, her brother in the saddle, dart a short way down the hill then stop. As agitated as its rider, the horse pawed the air then thudded down on all four feet. Ranald's cloak caught the wind, his hood fell back freeing his dark hair and revealing the black mask covering his right cheek.

Catalin watched the dejected figure. His shoulders slumped as he turned and disappeared back into the woods. She felt no triumph. Only a strange sadness that he had given up without a struggle. She squared her shoulders and turned to Muriele.

"Speaking of changing minds, are you sure you wish to stay here, Muriele?"

Muriele looked around the room, then back at Catalin. "I will find peace here." She banished the sadness from her eyes, and grinned at her friends. "Think of me now and then, but if anyone ever asks, remember to say the last ye saw of me I was bouncing along the ground like an uneven ball until the horse dragged my body into the dark forest."

"Ladies?" a voice called from outside their curtained doorway. "Mother Cecelia would have words with you."

The sister escorted the women to a spacious, sunny room

near filled with the four black-robed monks. Except for one large man, they had their cowls lowered over their brows.

Mother Cecelia introduced the women to Brother Octavius first, then two smaller men as Brothers Cyril and Ambrose. Brother Octavius introduced the fourth monk, Brother Gregory, who was observing a week's vow of silence. His hands in his sleeves, the monk hesitated before he bobbed his head in acknowledgment.

"Lady Muriele, I know not how anyone learned of your plight, but Brother Gregory received a goodly amount of coins with the wish they be used for your upkeep." She frowned and pointed to a blue velvet pouch to her right. "It was written on an unsigned missive."

Muriele's eyes widened as she stared at the monk's bent head. Sir Ranald must have sent the dowry to Kelso and asked for them to deliver it to the convent. "Brother Gregory, I thank ye with all my heart for bringing it here." His head bobbed again, then stilled.

"You are prepared to leave?" Mother Cecelia asked. "They will take you to Kelso, for you can better be guarded there. I still fear you are foolish to travel at this time." She looked pointedly at Catalin's rounded body beneath the tunic.

Catalin knew she could not expect the monks to take her deeper into England. At least at Kelso, she might be able to persuade a visitor to carry a message to Letia at Seton.

"Well, now, if Ladies Catalin and Elyne are ready?" Brother Octavius picked up two black robes and waited while the women pulled them over their heads and shoulders. "They are much too big, but once you are in the cart, no one will see their length. Be careful you do not trip on the hems." He smiled solemnly at Catalin. "We must start while the day is clear. Do you have anything that needs carrying? No? Then let us go straightaway to the courtyard, my lady."

It did not take long for Catalin to tell Mother Cecelia how much she appreciated her kindnesses. As they made their way outside, they stopped to thank the kind sisters for their help.

When she hugged Muriele, she wondered if she would ever

see her again. When sadness welled, Catalin was surprised. Brother Ambrose lifted her into the cart, but Elyne needed no aid. She gathered the robe from where it swept the ground, sprang into the cart and sat against the side. They carefully hid their hair, for no monk would have curly tresses trailing down his back!

Brother Octavius rode in the lead. The cart came next, pulled by a handsome gray horse with Brother Gregory handling the reins. The last two monks trailed behind. Kelso was northwest of where Ranald and his men occupied the hill. She held her breath when they needed to pass near them. The Raptor men gave way, nodding in respect.

Ranald held back, still staring at the convent. Satan's Spawn felt his anger, for the beast huffed and stomped his hooves, fighting him. He sat stiff and unyielding in the saddle, his body telling of his anger as he watched. A lump formed in Catalin's throat, wanting to call out to him. She stole one last glance, but he was as before, stiff and unyielding. 'Twas strange, though, for his men were coming out of the woods onto the road, forming two lines behind them. From the looks of it, did they mean to follow them to Kelso?

Brother Cyril confirmed it when he spoke up. "As you know, Sir Ranald once dwelled at Kelso. He was our Protector before Brother Octavius had that post. I see he means to give his fellow monks added protection."

Her head lowered, she peeked beneath the hood at the dimness behind them now they were amongst the trees. Aye. Ranald rode last. He dropped back as if uncertain, twisted in his saddle and gave one last look behind him. When he faced forward again, his dark eyes studied the cart. Mayhap she had best turn her back before he caught sight of a woman's face instead of a young man's.

"Ye look pale and drawn, Catalin. Lay back and rest." Elyne grabbed a blanket and rolled it to make a pillow. She helped Catalin to stretch out on the pallet and slid it beneath her head. Satisfied, she moved back to lean against the corner of the wagon.

Catalin sighed and slept. She did not awake until she heard Elyne's voice say Kelso was ahead. She pushed herself up, blinking sleep from her eyes and looked around. Ranald's men had pulled so close while she slept that she feared they would see through her disguise. Kelso, for truth, could not be far. What goes here? They stopped at a fork in the road. A sign said Kelso was to the left.

"You will be safe now, my lady," Brother Ambrose said as he smiled down at her.

"But, but," Catalin sputtered, "We are not at Kelso. You cannot leave us here with Sir Ranald's men. She looked back as the men pulled closer, their faces solemn. She grasped Brother Gregory's shoulder, for he was turning the horses to the road on the right.

"Do not! You turn the wrong way. I must go to Kelso." She shook his shoulder so hard his cowl fell back.

Raptor's men murmured and surrounded the cart. She saw Ranald on Satan's Spawn picking his way around the edge of the men to come beside her. Oh Saints. She was going to be sick. Elyne put her arm around her, making shushing little sounds.

Oh, God. Ranald was in the deep shadows beside the cart. Fighting panic, her gaze probed the gloom as she stared at him. He reached up and pulled off his mask.

"Raik? What goes on here?" She scowled up at him. No wonder the horse was so restless! He liked no other than Ranald on his back.

"Did ye sleep well, Catalin? Brother Gregory was most cautious to avoid every hole and bump that he could." He leaned forward on the horse and tapped Brother Gregory on the shoulder with Ranald's mask.

A hand reached up to take hold of it — a hand that bore scars left by sharp blades. Some were still unhealed. He raised the mask. Hesitated. Then, shoulders squared, he swung around on the seat with it in his hand.

Seeing his face, a dreadful wave of sickness made Catalin gag.

Ranald's tortured gaze stared back at her.

Catalin near lost control. She was as furious as a child. She screamed every crude word she had ever heard spoken by men whilst in their cups.

She whipped out her knife and held it threateningly in front of her. When Raik reached to take it from her, Ranald motioned him away.

"It is a hateful trick you have played on me," she shouted. "I will not let you have this babe." She waved the knife in front of her like a banner. "Cast me off and let us be. Let me make my own way with the babe. I will *not* allow you to lock it away from people who will love it. I will kill to protect him from that!"

Ranald felt genuine terror that Catalin would do herself an injury if he did not calm her fears. His palms sweated thinking those same fears might cause harm to the bairn during the birthing. He had much for Catalin to forgive him for and so little time to plead with her.

"The bairn willna be locked away. It was to thwart my sire when I said what I did. Ever have I known he hated me from my first breath. He cast me away when I needed a father's love the most. Every hour of every day, I knew I was unloved. Unwanted. I was so much offal to him. Rubbish he wanted cleared away.

"When he made it clear he wanted this bairn because he believes it is Moridac's seed, it goaded my pain and jealousy beyond restraint. I wanted *him* to feel the agony of losing something he loved beyond measure. Though it took a while for me to work through all this, I knew I could never let ye or the child go. That is why I refused ye escort to the de Burgh's. I knew ye would make yer way to King Stephen. I would lose ye both. I near went mad with fear when ye disappeared.

"My love, it will be as I first told ye. I vow before God and man that I will be this bairn's sire. He will be my son; she will be my daughter. Ours."

"How can I trust you speak truth?" Catalin

"Ye were so easily swayed to think me a beast," he whispered. "Because my face sickens ye doesna mean my soul is the same."

"You fool! It does not sicken me." She gave a loud shriek of anger and grabbed the mask from his hand. She hit him on the shoulder with it before heaving it into the woods.

Before it had chance to land, shocked surprise crossed her face. Stiffening, she shifted her feet. She dropped her knife to grab her belly.

In horror, Catalin stared down at a darkening stain.

CHAPTER 34

CATALIN'S SCREAM SPLIT THE air as pain stabbed through her back as sharp as a knife's blade.

Ranald jumped over his seat and caught Catalin before her legs folded beneath her. His heart near beat itself to death against his ribs as he laid her down on the pallet. Thrusting the robe from her, he pulled her skirts aside to look at her creamy thighs, fearful he would see her life's blood staining them.

He heaved a sigh of thanksgiving.

"Raik. Take the reins and get us to Kelso. My son has decided on an early appearance." He looked around at Elyne. "Pull the pallet to the middle of the cart so I may lean upon it facing the horse." He picked Catalin up into his arms and stood while Elyne did as he said. Cradling Catalin to his chest, he carefully knelt on the pallet.

"Finn, get in and brace my back. Elyne, get afore me and help steady Catalin in my arms." He watched to see Raik had seated and taken up the reins. "Go, Raik." Part of his men thundered ahead of them while the rest rode behind.

"Shh, love, ye will be more comfortable once we get to Kelso." He rained kisses on her forehead and pressed his left cheek to hers. "Only once did a breeding woman stop to birth her bairn at Kelso, but I learned enough to help ye through this. And ye will have Elyne to help ye, too."

"Me? I know naught of birthing, brother."

"Ye are a woman, are ye not? That is all ye need to give comfort to another."

Catalin's whimpers near unnerved him. Had Finn not

braced his back, he feared he could not have held her thus. Being on his knees with her in his arms, he swayed and cushioned their ride so she near floated in his arms.

Sir Kerr rode ahead to have the monks open the gate before they reached it. As soon as the cart stopped, Ranald attempted to hand Catalin to Raik, but she held Ranald's neck tightly and wouldn't let go. He soothed her with soft sounds, sat on his arse and inched his way to the end of the cart so he could stand on the ground.

Robed men dashed around like they expected the king to visit. They drew water and put heavy kettles of it over the cookhouse fires, for some had been with wives and sisters before death and loneliness brought them to Kelso.

Her scream in his ear sent him running to the Infirmary. On the torturous ride here, the sounds of the many horses near drowned her voice out, but the peace and quiet of Kelso echoed with her shrieks.

Sweat broke out on his brow as he laid her on the white sheets of the bed closest to the fireplace. He sent all away but Elyne and the young monk he had been training before he left Kelso.

Ranald and Elyne soon stripped Catalin's clothes from her, while the monk kept his back turned and prepared potions according to Ranald's shouted commands. He pulled a clean sheet over his wife's naked body and pulled a stool close so he could hold her hand.

He counted, trying to judge if her pains were becoming closer or getting further apart.

"Love, can ye tell me what week of the month it twas when Moridac took ye as his lover?"

Catalin balled up her fist and slammed it into his face. He jerked back and grabbed his throbbing nose, surprised. Blood seeped between his fingers.

"I was never his lover. I only tried to be a submissive wife-to-be because he wished it."

"Submissive? Ye?" Ranald snorted.

She waved her fist again. Clutching his nose, he leaned

back out of reach.

"What week, love?"

"The last sennight in November. Hannah said the babe should be born a sennight or so into September."

"It is the end of August. Do ye think ye can get him to stay a bit longer?"

Ranald meant it as a jest. Catalin was in no mood for jesting. He swerved in time to avoid a backhanded splat across his cheek.

He ran his fingers through his hair, and felt a shock of surprise at his recently shaved tonsure. Near frantic for some way to soothe her pain, he placed his big hands on her belly and felt the changes in it until they became familiar. When her muscles relaxed, so did his wife. When he felt them starting to tighten, her face grimaced, her hands clenched. If they didn't last too long, she clamped her teeth, but more times than not, she shrieked loud as a mythical banshee.

"Ye are as loud with yer laboring as ye are with yer pleasures, wife."

Catalin was too busy yelling and crushing his hands to swat at him.

As soon as she quieted, he turned her on her side. He called out for the monk to give him a salve scented with lavender. When the man moved away, Ranald bared her back and spread it there. He rubbed and massaged her muscles, talking low and soothing, telling her what a beautiful bairn she would hold in her arms that night. When he felt her tighten, he gripped her hands and let her pull on him.

"Scrub a knife to cut the babe's cord. You will need a clean string or thin strip of cloth to tie around it first," Catalin told him between gasps.

He nodded toward Elyne, who hurried to ask the monk to prepare both. She rushed back, for Catalin's pains came more frequently now. Elyne kept busy wiping Catalin's face with cold cloths and peeking beneath the covers.

Ranald straddled the bed behind Catalin, holding her up against his chest in hopes it would ease the birthing.

"He is not there, Ranald. Should he not be out by now?" Elyne's muffled voice asked after ducking beneath the sheet.

Ranald groaned. "Elyne, have ye never been with a woman in labor?"

Her head popped back out into the open. "Once. Aunt Joneta tended a, uh, friend of father's. I but fetched and carried. They didn't want anyone to know she was in the keep."

"How could they hide the howls?" Ranald's brows rose. "My ears are ringing."

Catalin snorted.

"Aunt Joneta plied her with whiskey early on and kept a stick between her teeth to bite on."

"Well, Hell! That was barbaric. Look again and tell me if ye see the top of the bairn's head."

"Fool! Look for yourself," Catalin shouted. Her teeth snapped together as she strained to choke back a scream. Her head slammed back against his chest so hard he expected to hear his ribs crack.

As soon as the pain ebbed, he scrambled off the bed and had Elyne take his place. He threw back the sheets. And stared.

"Shite! It's there," Ranald yelled. "Catalin, pull on Elyne's hands and push yer belly muscles down." He reached up and cupped his big hands on the dome of her stomach. When it tightened, he gently pressed downward, aiding the struggling bairn.

"It comes!" He cupped the little head as it moved out into the world. "Little one, dinna be feared to greet us," he crooned. "Ah, there ye are, lovey. A little more and yer little shoulders will be free." He choked back his fear when the birthing seemed to halt. Then he realized he would have to guide the other shoulder out. Once he did, he was elated. Following each scream from Catalin's throat, the rest of the babe quickly came forth.

"It's our son!" He cupped the bairn's head and back in his big hand as he inched the little legs free of his mother. "Elyne, do ye have the knife and cord?" Hearing a gurgling noise beside him, he glanced up to see the young monk, his face pale, his eyes squeezed shut, holding them both on a clean cloth,.

"Tie it, Elyne," he ordered. She did. He cut the cord, then turned the bairn to lay, chest down on his big palm and forearm. The bairn squirmed, its little legs and arms waved as it gave its first weak squalls. Ranald stared, fascinated, at the wrinkled red body covered with a yellow and white substance.

He placed the bairn on a bathing cloth and cleared his little mouth before he laid him atop Catalin's chest. Her arms closed around him. Ranald looked at Elyne and shook his head.

From beneath his monk's robes, he pulled out the clothing he'd rescued from the path.

"Do ye not think he needs cleansing?" His nose wrinkled. "He smells."

Catalin awoke, and finding the babe was not in the crook of her arm sleeping, she screamed, "My babe, my babe." She tried to struggle out of bed. Elyne jumped from a stool and rushed over to her.

"The bairn is all right, Catalin." She was struggling to keep her on the bed when Ranald burst into the room, his eyes wide with fear.

Frightened by the noise, the babe in his arms squalled and beat tiny fists and feet in the air. Ranald had proudly been showing him off to Raik and the men who had gathered outside the Infirmary to croon and make over the little bundle.

Some had been fathers before; others had never seen a newborn. All marveled that one so tiny could have such a strong voice.

"Are ye in pain?" Ranald clutched the bairn to his chest, jiggling it gently up and down. White-faced, he stared at her swollen middle and gulped. "Dinna tell me another one is there!"

"Nay. She feared ye had taken the bairn from her," Elyne told him.

"Aye, but only to show Abbot Aymer and the men." He carefully placed the baby in Catalin's reaching arms. "Do ye still fear me so, even though I swore to ye the bairn is safe?"

Ranald stood back, his eyes stricken, as he watched his Catalin clutch the bairn to her breast. The tiny mouth latched onto her nipple and started suckling making soft, greedy sounds.

"I love ye, Catalin. I always have."

Her fearful gaze calmed as she watched his face.

"I love ye too much to have ye living in fear. But I would have ye safe. If ye canna bear to love a man as ugly as I, I will provide a safe place for ye and the bairn to live. I know ye still love Moridac. I canna take his place. I canna change being unsightly."

Catalin scowled and gave a very unladylike huff.

"I did not love Moridac. Nay, that is not true. I did love him. But in a different way. I knew it was expected that we wed from as far back as I can remember." She swallowed and smoothed her hand over her babe's head, then looked him in the eye.

"Did you never note that it was always you who made me angry? Always you, not Moridac or Raik whom I followed. Did you not know why I tried to rid you of all those slobbering women who sought you out?"

"Aye. I kenned ye disliked me even then."

"Huh! You had best be prepared for me to dislike you more every day for the rest of your life, then." Catalin rolled her eyes at Elyne, who was grinning from ear to ear.

"Ye are right block-headed, brother." Elyne slammed him on the back of his head with her open hand. "For me, it will take a rare man to earn a love as great as Catalin has for ye."

epilogue

Raptor Castle, Eighteen Months Later.

CATALIN HELD HER HAND over her mouth to hide her giggles as Chief Broccin, bent nearly double, took steps so small he near toppled over. Clutching his finger, Gregory, his black curls bouncing, stomped around. He chortled and turned his face upward to watch his grandsire with eyes so alike Moridac's that Ranald oft thought his brother's soul had returned with his son.

Ranald stood behind Catalin, his chin rested on her head, his hands splayed across her stomach caressing the bulge there.

"Do ye think 'tis twins ye carry? Or do ye grow a giant here?"

Catalin sighed. "Twins, for certes. You will have three to spoil now."

"Da?" Gregory wriggled his little fingers at Ranald, demanding he come to him.

"Aye, Little Man?" Ranald chuckled, swung Gregory up in his arms to the child's favorite spot — cheek to cheek — and hugged him close. Gregory liked nothing better than to kiss his father's cheek. His scarred cheek, for he would grab the braid at his temple and place drooling kisses over every scar. "Have ye told Granda all yer secrets? Hm?"

Ranald could not believe the change in his father since the siege of Hunter Castle. They spent most of the year at Hunter, but every third month they returned to Raptor for a fortnight. Though father and son still clashed wills, Chief Broccin held his temper in check when Gregory was about.

Hearing horses clattering over the cobblestones of Hunter Castle's barbican, they looked toward the castle entrance.

"Ah, mayhap the scouts have word of Raik." Ranald kissed Gregory's soft curls and handed him to Catalin.

Catalin watched Ranald and his sire hurry to the courtyard, while she and Gregory followed at a leisurely pace. Pray God they would hear good news about Raik, for no one had seen him for over a month. Why must men play such dangerous games? That is what it was when they crossed the borders and dared to raid each other's cattle.

This time, she feared the game had turned sour.

In his last foray, Ranald had received word his cousin was wounded. His three companions lost track of him in the dark, for they only did such foolishness during the darkest phase of the moon. They had not seen him ride away, but they could not find him after the raid. What puzzled her was Raik most often preferred to raid the de Burgh's. Yet when Catalin sent a message to Letia, she replied she'd not seen Raik.

Mayhap the men today knew. Hearing shouts, she held her hand up to shield her eyes, for the castle's entrance faced the sun. Her face spread in a wide smile. Though the man getting off his horse moved stiffly, there was no mistaking Raik.

Catalin hugged Gregory close and hurried across the courtyard, anxious to learn of Raik's adventures...

The End

COMING SOON
THE NEXT INTRIGUING
ROMANCE IN

Sophia Johnson's Raptor Castle Series

Each tale in the series has an unusual and exciting plot that will surprise you.

Book 2. *Seduced* – Find out what *sexy* adventures kept Raik behind locked doors!

Book 3. *Ruthless* – When a Highlander determined to honor his oath discovers Muriele, not even Ranald can protect her from Magnus. An *intense* cat and mouse game.

Book 4. *Surrender* – Elyne has to admit Ranald warned her that spying on naked warriors would some day be her undoing. Her downfall is Graemme, Magnus' younger brother! *Sensual and humorous.*

Visit me at www.sophiajohnson.net to read
more about each intriguing tale.

AUTHOR'S NOTE

Dear Readers,

I started Book 1 of the Raptor Castle Series with an unusual hero — a monk forced from his abbey to sire children. You can't get a story more original than that, can you?

Ack! Don't suck your teeth. It really did happen. I've always been fascinated with the clan Macpherson and its motto: Touch not the cat bot (without) a glove.

During the reign of David the First, Gillicattan, a significant figure, became captain of the clan Chattan. He sired two sons.

When he passed away, his eldest son took over but died without issue. Gillicattan's second son, Murdoch was the Abbot of Kingussie in Badenoch.

The duty of leading the clan devolved to Murdoch. After obtaining a dispensation from the Pope, the Abbot became head of his family and captain of the clan Chattan. He married a daughter of the thane of Cawdor and sired five sons.

The modern name Macpherson literally means son of the parson.

As in the Blackthorn Trilogy, please keep in mind that it is not always possible to use only words appropriate to the time. Also, Raptor Castle was quite close to the border. I kept the dialect down to few characters. Ranald and Broccin (Scottish) would not speak like Catalin and Letia (Northumbria), so you will find differences in speech patterns for them and for other characters.

Relax and let your imagination take you into this tale of love through the ages.

Sincerely,
Sophia

About the Author:

SOPHIA JOHNSON is well versed in the medieval period and supports her research with lengthy trips to Great Britain. As a child in Key West, she would sit beneath a coconut tree and daydream while she listened to the sound of the waves and enjoyed the briny smell of the ocean. She wondered what life would be like if she awoke one morn to find she had traveled back through the centuries?

Her parents were avid readers and passed on to their children their love of reading about far away places. Throughout her life, Sophia always had her nose in a book when she had free time. One day, her daughter and son-in-law came to visit and brought in a computer.

When she asked what they were doing, they told her, "We want you to stop reading and start writing your own stories."

So she did!

Her Tag Line is "Love Through the Ages," the theme of her novels.

www.sophiajohnson.net

MIDNIGHT'S BRIDE
ISBN: 0-8217-8049-2
Also available in Kindle Version

Finalist Colorado Award of Excellence.

"A heart-stopping love story wrapped in an enchanting mythic legend."
— Virginia Henley

"TOP PICK! Sophia Johnson writes the perfect book with just the right balance of all the elements that make a romance what it is. Sassy, smart, charming and overflowing with sexual tension and good old fashioned humor …"
— Romance Reader at Heart

"5 Stars! I can't resist Ms. Johnson because I know I'll not be reading another cookie cutter historical romance … (Her) ability to successfully distinguish each book in the Blackthorn trilogy but link the three together keeps the trilogy refreshing … *Midnight's Bride* is tenderly romantic, hysterically funny and deeply passionate. A delightful read in every way, the Blackthorn Trilogy is terrific!
— Joyfully Reviewed

"5 Stars! Ms. Johnson's witty dialog provides some very amusing reading, so much so that I lost myself in the tale … then there is the smoldering passion waiting to be unleashed in the ruggedly handsome Mereck; every woman's fantasy. Each of the Blackthorn books have a different temperament governed by its marvelous characters; which causes me to eagerly await more delightfully delicious stories … "
— Donna Zapf from Single Titles

RISK EVERYTHING
ISBN: 0-8217-7883-8
Also available in Kindle Version

Finalist Holt Medallion and the Maggie Awards

"Very Intense ... "
—New York Times Bestselling Author Susan Johnson

"4 Stars! *Risk Everything* has every element of a classis Johanna Lindsey: biting repartee, steamy sexual tension, a bold heroine and powerful hero and a rugged backdrop that suits the characters and their story. Johnson knows how to spin a tale that entertains and engages..
—Romantic Times

"TOP PICK! Sophia Johnson really knows how to tell a story. There is Depth and intrigue, a wonderful plot, and a beautiful love that took my breath away ... had me wishing that it would never end, and left me gladly awaiting for the release of Sophia Johnson's next book."
—Romance Readers at Heart

"5 Stars! One of the very best Historical Romances I have ever read. I cringe at the thought of anyone missing out on this book ... It has strong characters full of honor and dignity. Lots of action, adventure, romance, and betrayal ... (it) will grab your attention on the first page and never let go, reach for this title."
—Huntress Review